PRAISE FOR B
CALIFORNIA CHRONICLES

"*Far Hills* is a beautiful story of true love, loyalty, and betrayal. It gripped my emotions from the very beginning, and didn't let them go. Diane Noble is a master storyteller!"

—TERRI BLACKSTOCK

"*When the Far Hills Bloom* has everything I look for in a great novel— high drama, unexpected twists and turns, heart-tugging romance, and genuine, true-to-life conflicts. I not only fell in love with the characters, I fell in love with California in all her untamed glory. This is Diane Noble's best work yet!"

—LIZ CURTIS HIGGS

"Inside Tip of the Day: If you're looking for a great excuse to not do any housework, grocery shopping, or anything else for several days (if you can sleep), read *Far Hills*. This irresistible novel has an epic feel that made me think of romantic movies like *Far and Away*. I anxiously await the following two books in the series, as well as anything else that Diane Noble chooses to write."

—LISA TAWN BERGREN

"An engrossing historical novel, *Far Hills* has it all—love, suspense, heartache, and the triumph of the human spirit when coupled with abiding faith. I was irrevocably drawn into the drama of the Dearbourne and Byrne families, eagerly turning the pages to see what would happen to them next. I'll definitely be watching for future Diane Noble releases."

—ROBIN LEE HATCHER

"Diane Noble never fails to speak to the heart of the matter. With spiritual insight, wisdom, and joyous celebration, she leads us to a greater understanding of God—and of ourselves."

—ANGELA ELWELL HUNT

The Blossom and the NETTLE

The Blossom and the NETTLE

DIANE NOBLE

WATERBROOK
PRESS

THE BLOSSOM AND THE NETTLE
PUBLISHED BY WATERBROOK PRESS
5446 North Academy Boulevard, Suite 200
Colorado Springs, Colorado 80918
A division of Random House, Inc.

Scripture quotations are taken from the *King James Version*.

The characters and events in this book are fictional, and any resemblance to actual persons or events is coincidental.

ISBN 1-57856-090-X

Library of Congress Cataloging-in-Publication Data

Noble, Diane, 1945-
    The blossom and the nettle / Diane Noble.— 1st ed.
        p. cm.
    ISBN 1-57856-090-X
    1. Inheritance and succession—Fiction. 2. Wilderness areas—
Fiction. 3. California—Fiction. I. Title.

PS3563.A3179765 B57 2000
813'.54—dc21

                                                00-035931

Printed in the United States of America
2000—First Edition

10 9 8 7 6 5 4 3 2 1

To Maxine Hamner Dunham

Now let us do something beautiful for God.
—MOTHER TERESA

And you have. Your life reflects his beauty.

ACKNOWLEDGMENTS

Special thanks to my husband, Tom, for his unfailing support and belief in my writing and to my daughters, Melinda and Amy, who gave me extra measures of grace while I sequestered myself away to write.

To my writing buddy and cherished friend Liz Curtis Higgs, thank you for being there always, on-line and on the phone, to listen, encourage, and dispense huge measures of fabulous fiction advice.

To my wonderful editors, Lisa Tawn Bergren, Traci DePree, and Paul Hawley, my deepest gratitude for turning this manuscript into the best it can possibly be!

And to you, my readers, hugs of heartfelt thanks are yours for following me on my latest journey into the California of yesteryear! Bless you all!

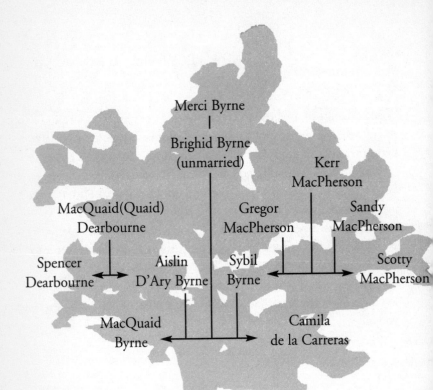

Merci Byrne
|
Brighid Byrne
(unmarried)

Kerr
MacPherson

MacQuaid(Quaid)
Dearbourne

Gregor
MacPherson

Sandy
MacPherson

Spencer
Dearbourne

Aislin
D'Ary Byrne

Sybil
Byrne

Scotty
MacPherson

MacQuaid
Byrne

Camila
de la Carreras

Rancho de la Paloma

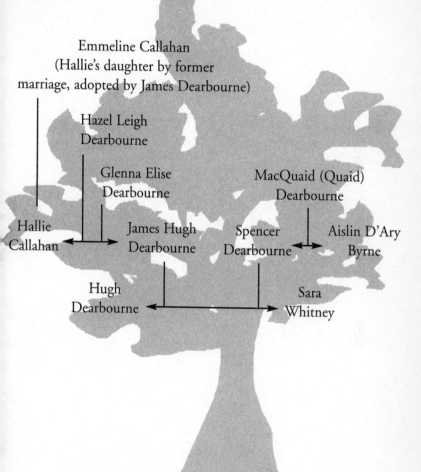

Emmeline Callahan
(Hallie's daughter by former
marriage, adopted by James Dearbourne)

Hazel Leigh
Dearbourne

Glenna Elise
Dearbourne

MacQuaid (Quaid)
Dearbourne

Hallie
Callahan

James Hugh
Dearbourne

Spencer
Dearbourne

Aislin D'Ary
Byrne

Hugh
Dearbourne

Sara
Whitney

*Rancho Dearbourne,
later Sunny Mountain Ranch*

PROLOGUE

Rancho de la Paloma
1864

B ad things happened when the wind blew hard.

Like the day that Jamie left Emma and her mama back in Kentucky. The wind kicked up something fierce that night. It rattled the shutters of their little house by the river. It sounded alive, it did, the way it moaned and whistled and broke the apple tree branches. Made them fall to the ground with a crack that caused Emma to jump.

Her mama cried for Jamie after she thought Emma was asleep. Her sorrow had frightened Emma more than the wind.

But Jamie had come back. He'd married them, and now he was her new papa.

That had been last year, when Emma was little. Now she was almost four and grown up. At least she would be soon. That was what Jamie told her. Then he laughed and said no matter how old she got to be, she would always be his little girl. Forever, he said. And forever was a long, long time. Her new papa had told her so.

She liked how his laugh sounded, rumbling inside him, and the way he and her mama looked at each other with gladness on their faces.

Sometimes he tossed Emma in the air, then caught her and held her fast near his heart. She liked the scratchy cloth of his shirt against her cheek. And the way his heart bumped beneath it. There she felt safe. With his big arms wrapped around her, she knew nothing bad could ever happen.

Except when the wind blew hard.

Just like now. It was blowin' hard as she'd ever heard. They were sitting in a chapel, her mama and papa and scads of kin she'd never met till now. And all of them looked worried.

The man with whiskers who made her giggle because he was always sayin' "eye" this and "eye" that. Papa Jamie told her to call him Grandpa MacQuaid, though he wasn't really her blood kin. And her new granny, the one called Grandma Camila, with her sweet smile and funny way of talkin' that someone said was because she came from a faraway place across the ocean.

And her Uncle Spence and Aunt Aislin. They kept lookin' out the window, then lookin' at each other, then out the window again, talkin' about the smoke they could see on yonder hills. Uncle Spence held a boy in his arms. He was much littler than Emma—he was just beginning to walk. They weren't blood kin neither.

She sighed. She'd been walkin' since as long as she could remember. That was because she was almost big. Well, at least she was bigger than the little boy. Though Papa Jamie said that someday, the way the little tyke was growin', he would pass her up.

The little boy's name was Quaid, which made her laugh. How such a puny little thing had the same name as a grandpa with whiskers, it was a puzzle, it was.

Another little girl was in the pew in front of her. Her hair looked like the curly squiggles of wood from the tool Papa Jamie used for shaving planks. Only orange. Bright, bright orangy red. And the curls stuck out everywhere on her head. When she turned to look back at Emma, she made a face, scrunching her nose and making Emma laugh out loud.

Then the little girl waggled her ears and stuck out her tongue. Emma giggled, then clasped her hand to her mouth. Emma's mother gave her a warning look. Emma scooted back against the wooden seat between her mama and her papa.

The girl's name was Merci. Like "mercy this" and "mercy that," only it was spelled different, Papa Jamie said. And her mother's name was something that Emma couldn't remember very well unless she thought hard. She sat thinking. Brighid. Sounded like Brigeed. That was it. She let the word roll over her tongue. Brigeed. Mercy.

Her Aunt Brighid turned around at the sound of her name and smiled. She was the prettiest lady in the chapel, Emma thought. Well, exceptin' her own mama. Merci turned around again, this time on her knees, resting her chin on the wooden pew back. She scrunched her nose, showing her teeth, before her mother reached over and drew her into her lap.

The wind howled again. Emma jumped, startled. Jamie circled his arm around her. She shivered and climbed onto his lap. She rested her cheek against his scratchy shirt.

Grandpa MacQuaid stood up and walked to the front of the chapel. Everyone quit talking. The room would have been quiet except for the wind. It growled and rattled things outside.

And the smell of smoke was stronger now. So were the looks of worry on her new aunts' and uncles' faces. Another aunt, one called Sybil, and an uncle called Scotty shifted in their pew a few rows forward. Aunt Sybil's face was puffy-round. She looked even more worried than the rest.

Maybe it was because they were getting a baby soon. Emma wondered how everyone knew that. Perhaps God told them. Or maybe an angel, like happened in the Bible.

"We have gathered here this day to bring a new generation to the Lord," said Grandpa MacQuaid, causing Emma to look from Aunt Sybil back to the front of the chapel. "'Tis a true blessing he has bestowed on us." He chuckled. "And though the wind rages and there's a firestorm starting in the hills, we will rejoice in our Lord. Aye, that we will."

There was that "eye" word again. Emma giggled and got another warning look from her mother. Merci turned around to stare. When Aunt Brighid tried to move her back to facin' forward, the little girl shrugged off her mother's hand with a yank of her shoulders.

Emma would never dare try such a shruggy thing with her own

mother—she knew how to act respectful. She lifted her chin, smoothed her skirt, and sat up straight.

"A few years ago," the grandpa with whiskers was saying, "sweet Brighid told me and her mama something I've never forgotten. She quoted these words from the prophet Habakkuk:

"Although the fig tree shall not blossom,
Neither shall fruit be in the vines;
The labour of the olive shall fail,
And the fields shall yield no meat;
The flock shall be cut off from the fold,
And there shall be no herd in the stalls:
Yet I will rejoice in the LORD,
I will joy in the God of my salvation.
The LORD God is my strength,
And he will make my feet like hinds' feet,
And he will make me to walk upon high places."

Grandpa MacQuaid smiled at everybody sitting before him.

"Through the years we've lived through tragedy and triumph," he said. "And this new generation of Dearbournes and Byrnes will be no different. Brighid told me long ago that God doesn't ask us to succeed at all we attempt; he only asks for us to follow him, to obey him." He smiled at the family and nodded his shaggy head. "We can't pray that life will be without bumps and brambles for these little ones, for surely those bumps and brambles will come. As sure as the wind that rattles the shutters of this chapel, adversity will strike us all."

He looked toward the window. Emma saw him fix his gaze on the far hills, where smoke rose like a cloud of thick goose feathers from a torn pillow. He nodded again, slowly. "Just as trees grow stronger in a harsh wind, so will our children prosper with whatever our Lord allows them to endure." His face drooped. "Suffering will cross their paths as surely as God's joy. But he will be with them. He will lead them—if they will turn to him. And turn to him they must."

Grandpa MacQuaid still looked sad, and Emma wondered why. And what was this suffering he talked about?

"We bring these, our children, before him today. As Hannah of ancient days brought her wee Samuel to the house of the Lord and said, 'For this child I prayed; and the Lord hath given me my petition which I asked of him: Therefore also I have lent him to the LORD; as long as he liveth he shall be lent to the LORD.' So it is that we give him our wee ones today."

He heaved a sigh and shook his head slowly, reminding Emma of a drawing of a lion she once saw in a storybook. "Aye, that we do, my beloved family. Each of these and those who will surely follow."

He smiled at the little boy. "Aye, 'tis with pride we bring Quaid Dearbourne and his parents, Spence and Aislin, before the Lord." He motioned for the three to come stand beside him.

When they were in place, Grandpa MacQuaid nodded to Merci and her mother and held out his hand to them. Emma noticed that her grandpa's eyes were especially shiny.

"And our wee Merci Byrne," he said with a rough voice. "Come, child, and let me hold you before our Lord."

Her own eyes widened, and she wondered if Grandpa MacQuaid's quaky voice might mean he was about to cry. Then Grandma Camila sniffled and blew her nose. Emma looked up at her mama's face, then to her new papa's, to see their eyes were filling with tears.

Frowning, she turned back to watch Merci who was now walking up the aisle toward her grandpa. He knelt and reached for her. More sniffling and nose blowing commenced. Emma wondered why everyone seemed ready to cry over this little girl and her mama.

Still kneeling and circling Merci in his right arm, Grandpa MacQuaid now looked at Emma.

"And the newest member of our brood." He gave her a smile that seemed to cover his ruddy face, every part that showed above his whiskers. "Perhaps not related by blood, but loved just as much. We welcome you, Emma, and your mama to our family."

She grinned and, without waiting for her mama or new papa, raced toward him. Once she'd snuggled into his free arm, she turned to see if she would receive the same sniffling sighs that everyone had given her cousin Merci.

The wind was howling again, this time clanging the bell in the tall rooftop tower. Not a pretty sound like on Sundays. But a noise like a fistful of piano keys all plinking at once.

Her new family wasn't paying a smidgen of attention to her. Even as their tears dried for Merci, they were now gazin' through the windows with worried faces. Emma shivered and looked up at Grandpa Mac-Quaid's face for reassurance. He was frowning, staring again at the smoke on the hills.

"Is a bad thing going to happen," she whispered, " 'cause the wind is blowin'?"

Papa Jamie was beside her now and knelt to gather Emma into his arms. "The wind sometimes blows hard in the Big Valley," he said, his voice a whispery rumble. "I've heard it blow like this since I was your age. It doesn't mean something bad will happen, Emma."

"But there's smoke."

He nodded. "Yes. Sometimes firestorms come on the wind. Most often they head into the hills. They move away from our land."

She wrapped one arm around his neck and nestled against his shoulder. Her mama took her other hand, and she was happy for the comforting reassurance of two parents. "But what if they don't, Papa? What happens then?"

Her new papa didn't seem to hear her. Instead he was watchin' her Aunt Brighid, holding Merci, and her Aunt Aislin and Uncle Spence, who held Quaid, move closer. Grandpa's attention was on the children again, which made Emma glad. It wasn't a bad wind if he didn't have to look through the window with worried lines on his face.

"Gather 'round, dear ones," he said. "Let's pray for our children."

Grandma Camila, Grandma Sara—Jamie's real mama—and Aunt Gertie, who once belonged to her Uncle Ransom—her mama's brother—and now belonged to them all, moved to the front of the altar.

Beside them stood Aunt Sybil and Uncle Scotty, the ones who were getting the baby soon.

The room was silent, except for Aunt Gertie who blew her nose louder than the gust of wind that rattled the windows. Emma covered her hand with her mouth and giggled again.

"Bow your head, child," Emma's mama whispered with a warning frown.

Emma nodded, squeezed her eyes closed, and folded her hands under her chin as Grandpa MacQuaid began to speak in a hushed voice. "Lord, we commit these your lambs into your arms, arms that are stronger than any of ours on earth. And we commit them to your heart."

Emma peeked around at the other children. Quaid, his back stick straight, was craning to look anywhere but at his grandpa, and Merci made another face at Emma. Aunt Brighid frowned and whispered something in her daughter's ear. But Merci shrugged and stuck out her tongue.

Meanwhile, Grandpa MacQuaid kept talking to God about them.

"Aye, we commit them to a heart that loves more fiercely, completely, and perfectly than any human heart could love. We commit them to your sovereign care, our heavenly Father, care that is filled with more grace and wisdom than we—their earthly family—can ever provide. We commit them to you for all their lives."

Outside the old bell clanged and clanked in the wind. Emma shivered and looked out the window at the smoke-covered hills.

Bad things happened when the wind blew hard.

Rancho de la Paloma
1865

In her pretty bedroom at the rancho, Merci Byrne stared at her mother. "Everyone else has a papa. Where's mine?"

Brighid, who sat in a rocker near her daughter, smiled easily. "Your papa went away, child. A long time ago. But you have a family who loves you. A mama. A grandma and grandpa. Aunts and uncles and cousins."

"I want a papa." She'd seen how papas acted with their babies. Aunt Sybil and Uncle Scotty had a new baby boy. Everyone giggled and cooed over the little red-faced child. His papa held him and rocked him, singing in a gruff voice. It made everyone laugh.

Merci wanted a papa just like Uncle Scotty. Or maybe like Emma's papa. She still remembered how Uncle Jamie trotted Emma on his knees like a pony, making her giggle. She'd watched and wished it were she who was riding the silly pony.

"Where did he go?" It occurred to her that if he left, perhaps he would return for her. Maybe he forgot he had a little girl. She pictured him giving her a pony ride or tossing her in the air, then holding her close to his heart.

"He's not ever coming back, baby," her mother said with a sad face. "Not ever."

"Why?"

Her mother reached for her and pulled her onto her lap. She held Merci close, wrapping her arms tight around Merci's shoulders. "Someday I'll tell you, but not now."

Merci craned her head to look up at Brighid's face. Surprised by the tears in her mother's eyes, she reached a hand up to pat her cheek. "Papa made you sad?"

For a long time her mama didn't speak. "Yes, baby," she finally whispered, "very sad."

"We don't need a papa, then," Merci said. "Not ever."

"I wish I could change what happened that day, baby," her mothered murmured. She laid her cheek on Merci's head. "But the past is done. God gave me the oil of gladness in exchange for ashes. That's all that matters."

Merci snuggled against her mama's shoulder and sighed. She wondered what ashes were. And how gladness could be oil. Then she popped her thumb into her mouth and noisily sucked while her mama rocked her gently.

Outside a wind kicked up and rattled the dry leaves on a sycamore near Merci's bedroom window.

Merci sat upright and grabbed her mother's hand. "It's the wind, Mama!" she said. "Let's go outside!"

Laughing, her mother swept Merci into her arms. Soon they were outdoors in the fading light of the day. The pepper tree's lacy leaves fluttered in the blowing wind. Merci giggled and danced and twirled beneath its branches. She liked the way the wind blew her curls and whistled sweet music in her ears.

A puzzled look on her face, Brighid stood back to watch Merci. "As wild as the wind itself, baby. I believe you're as wild as the wind."

The thought pleased Merci. She laughed again and ran to the edge of the yard.

"Don't go too far, baby," her mother called after her.

Merci turned. She made a face at her mama, then scampered just beyond her reach, still laughing.

"Merci, come back!"

Though it was growing dark and the river was forbidden to Merci, she headed toward it. The wind stung her face, and she squealed with delight.

"Merci!" her mother called again, now running after her.

But Merci merely laughed and raced away from the safety of her worried mama's arms.

Rancho de la Paloma
1867

Quaid grinned as Grandpa MacQuaid swept him into his arms then onto the saddle of the tall horse. He wrapped his fists around the saddle horn and watched his grandfather mount and settle behind him, sharing their seat.

They headed down the road leading from the rancho and into the open fields. The horse galloped like the wind, and Quaid laughed, leaning back against his grandfather's stomach.

They reached an overlook, and his grandfather slowed the horse to a halt, then lifted Quaid to the ground.

"Aye, but take a look at this, lad. Just feast your heart lookin' out at

God's creation." The old man shook his head slowly as though in awe.

The sun was just rising above the mountains, and bars of light slanted across the Big Valley. A mist covered the fields, and the damp smell from the sun hitting it made Quaid smile. He closed his eyes and breathed it in, just as he'd seen his grandfather do a hundred times.

"'Tis the land I love," Grandpa MacQuaid said. "Just as God made it. Without our roamin' cattle, without a house or Indian dwelling."

Quaid nodded. His grandfather nearly always said the same thing when they came here, but Quaid loved hearing every word. Already there was a seed of something growing in his heart, something akin to his grandfather's caring for the land.

"Just as our Lord created it in all its glory! Lift up your eyes to the hills, my lad." Grandpa MacQuaid looked to the San Jacintos, where the pointed mountains met the dawn sky. "King David once wrote that the rivers should clap their hands and the mountains sing for joy before the Lord. Aye, I believe there are times I can almost hear them rejoicing right along with me!"

His grandfather chuckled and turned to look down at Quaid. "Don't ever forget that this windswept land was created from our Lord's great heart for joy, son. And these lands are a reflection of his beauty."

Quaid nodded. "I won't forget."

"'Tis a great responsibility he's given us. Carin' for the land, son, is not an easy task. Nor should it be taken lightly."

"How can I care for it, Grandpa?"

His grandfather looked thoughtful as he squinted into the sunlight. "Already there are those who want to bring it harm. Cut down the forests to make houses, cover the land with roads, dam the rivers."

"Then the rivers can't clap their hands anymore." Quaid was serious, but his grandfather threw back his head and laughed out loud.

"Aye, but you've got my Irish imagination, lad! You do indeed." He wiped his eyes with a handkerchief, then went on. "You asked how you can care for the land? Someday this land will be yours. You may keep it or pass it along to others, perhaps your own children. But you must promise me this—you must promise me that you will never allow anyone to destroy its beauty."

"I promise, Grandpa."

"You must promise that every time you feel the wind on your face as you ride across the valley, you'll think of this day. Think of standing here with me, lookin' down at its wild, windswept glory, and rejoicing over the beauty of God's creation."

"I promise," he said again, solemnly.

"Good," his grandfather breathed, still looking at the distant hills. "Good, my lad."

A breeze rustled some nearby aspen leaves, almost like a whisper from God himself. Quaid's grandfather took his hand, and for a long time they stood watching the sunrise.

"Now if you listen with great care," his grandfather whispered, "you just might hear those old mountains singin' together for joy. You just might." He chuckled softly and squeezed Quaid's hand with his big, callused fingers.

Quaid frowned in concentration, listening hard. Behind him some birds sang. The wind whistled through the tall aspen branches. And from a clump of sunlit sage a grasshopper began to saw its legs.

"Yes, I hear them!" Quaid grinned. "I can hear those ol' mountains singing for joy."

Washington, D.C.
1867

A chilly wind blew from the Potomac, causing an icy rain to slice against the windows of the three-story Georgian manor.

A knock sounded on the door to Emma's suite of rooms. She jumped, as skittish as ever when the wind blew hard.

She had expected it to be her father and smiled at him as she opened the door.

"Your mama wants to see you now," he said.

"Is she all right?"

He looked weary but happy. "She's tired and needs to rest. But she wants to see you first."

Emma stepped into the long hallway, then followed her father to her parents' rooms.

He opened the door quietly and stepped through. Emma swallowed hard, trying to be happy for her mother and father. But it wasn't easy. First the move from her beloved Kentucky a year ago. Now this.

A new baby.

A baby that belonged to *both* her mother and father.

Her mother's voice was barely more than a whisper when she spoke. "You have a new sister, Em," she said, her eyes bright with joy. "Her name is Glenna Elise."

Jamie walked to the small wooden cradle he had made months before. He gestured for Emma to follow. "Meet your sister, Glenna Elise Dearbourne."

She followed, though she didn't want to.

"Look at her," he said in awe. "A perfect little face."

Emma nodded mutely. Even asleep, the baby looked too pretty to be real.

"Would you like to hold her?" Without waiting for Emma's answer, Jamie reached into the cradle and lifted the blanketed bundle into his arms. He gazed into the round, red face as though it was the most precious thing he'd ever seen. "Oh, what a love you are," he murmured to the baby. "You've come straight from heaven itself. Straight into our hearts to stay forever."

Then he turned to Emma, and she saw that his eyes were wet and the look on his face was one of love and joy. "Here, Emma," he whispered so he wouldn't wake the sleeping babe, "come closer and I'll place her in your arms. But you'll have to be very careful."

"No." Emma backed away. "I don't want to hold her." Her voice was high-pitched and angry, but she didn't care. "I don't ever want to hold this baby!"

Her loud outburst caused the baby to wake and cry. It made a strange, fussy sound.

Jamie started to reprimand Emma, but her mother held up her hand. "Jamie," she whispered, "Emma just needs time to get used to her new sister. That's all." She smiled weakly at Emma. "She'll soon love her as much as we do. Won't you, honey?" She gave Emma an imploring look.

But Emma was backing to the door, tears trailing down her face. She knew this baby had come to take her place in their hearts—her parents could never love her as much as they would love this one that was truly theirs. Both of theirs. She thought her heart might break.

Jamie started toward her, still holding the hated bundle.

"You didn't need another baby," she said, sobbing. "You already had me. Why wasn't I enough?" Then she turned and ran down the hall to her own rooms.

A moment later her beloved papa knelt beside her. "Emma, don't you know that you'll always be my little girl?"

She shook her head, still crying. "Not anymore."

He tried to pull her into a hug, but she pushed him away.

"You are my daughter—Miss Emmeline Amity Dearbourne. Nothing will ever change that."

"Not anymore," she said, her voice trembling. "I want to go by my *real* father's name. I'm Emmeline Amity Callahan."

Jamie looked as if she had struck him.

"I'm Emmeline Amity Callahan," she said louder.

Outside the wind howled and sleet cut against the windows. She lifted her chin and tried to look brave. What she really wanted was for Jamie to draw her into his arms and hold her close enough to feel the scratchy cloth of his shirt against her cheek.

Instead, Jamie looked at her for a long moment, then turned and left her alone, the sound of the storm growing stronger in his absence.

Bad things happened when the wind blew hard.

ONE

Washington, D.C.
December 1888

Emmeline Amity Callahan hesitated at the wide ballroom door. The Georgian mansion had been her home since leaving Kentucky more than two decades earlier. Yet the austere three-story house, with its straight, soldierly angles, had never felt like home. Her beautiful sisters thought it elegant; her mother and father thought it filled with love. Emmeline supposed all that was true. For them.

She stood for a moment in the foyer, under its soaring ceiling and blazing crystal chandelier. Letting out a nervous sigh, she prayed for courage and stepped into the ballroom.

Music filled the shell-shaped room, seeming to bounce from the top of the ornate dome ceiling. An ensemble—three violins, two violas, a cello, a trumpet, and timpani—was set up on a dais near a ceiling-tall Christmas tree aglow with candlelight.

Several couples whirled around the dance floor. In one corner, her sisters, surrounded by beaus, were giggling and blushing. Just to her right other eligible young lawmakers sat on settees or stood with crystal glasses in hand, looking arrogant and sophisticated. They laughed and nodded as they caught the demure glances of a gaggle of young women across the elegantly appointed room.

Emmeline patted her slicked-back hair, pushed up her eyeglasses, and then smoothed her skirt for the hundredth time. After another deep sigh, she set her chin at an upward tilt and sailed across the gleaming marble floor.

Around her rose honey-sweet music, snatches of conversation, and laughter. Emmeline loathed parties. And the forced gaiety of a holiday soiree was the culmination of her worst nightmare. Her beautiful half sisters would dance until dawn—should the Senator and his wife allow the party to continue that long. Which, thankfully, they wouldn't.

Emmeline planned to sit in a place where she wouldn't be forced into silly conversation with empty-headed young men. Much to her parents' dismay, she refused to smile and pretend to enjoy such social pursuits. And by now her reputation was so well known that most young men steered clear of the Senator's strange old-maid daughter.

She hesitated once more, pushed up her eyeglasses again, and peered around the room for a hiding place. A snow sculpture. The timpani. Anything would do.

There, in the corner, loomed the Christmas tree. Emma removed her eyeglasses for vanity's sake, tucked an errant strand of hair behind her left ear, and headed full-tilt toward the giant pine. It was ablaze with candles, quite nicely suiting her quest to blend into her surroundings. After all, who would notice her when their eyes would be drawn instead to the glory of the capital's finest tree outside the White House gates?

The ensemble reached a crescendo at the precise moment that Emmeline reached the center of the room. Circling around her, couples whirled and bowed and dipped into flourishing finales, a blur of brilliant holiday colors, a jeweled kaleidoscope in constant motion.

She smiled at the whimsical thought as she barreled along.

Until the unthinkable happened.

The most eligible bachelor in Washington society dipped his equally sought-after partner directly in front of Emmeline. A friend of her sister's, a porcelain-faced blonde named Aimée, looked up from her swoop in her partner's arm.

There was no time for Emmeline to correct her forward motion. She bumped square into the girl, her foot catching on Aimée's frothy ball gown. Emmeline's eyeglasses flew from her hands and clattered to the floor. At the same time, the young woman scrambled to regain her balance, but a terrible ripping sound carried across the now-hushed assemblage. Aimée let out a whimper of embarrassment and sank to the floor, covering her face with her hands. Emmeline felt her cheeks flame on the poor girl's behalf.

The good cheer that had filled the room when Emmeline entered seemed to have vaporized into the pine- and candle-scented air. Even the orchestra stopped its playing.

In a heartbeat Emmeline knelt beside the weeping girl. But before she could help her, Aimée's dance partner shoved Emmeline aside. His back to Emmeline, he gathered the humiliated Aimée into his arms and helped her to her feet.

Emmeline rocked back on her heels, her green velvet skirt spread around her like a wilted Christmas tree on Boxing Day. She sighed, knowing she had created yet another spectacle to vex her parents and sisters.

While she was deciding how to slip from the dance floor without creating a further stir, a figure moved closer. She blinked up at the decidedly masculine face, obvious even without her eyeglasses.

"May I help you?" The voice was the richest bass she'd ever heard. It sounded almost ethereal. *Ethereal.* A word she saved for only the most heavenly of moments.

Before she could answer, he placed her folded spectacles in her hand. She set them on the tip of her nose and pressed the curved wires around her ears, then blinked up at the most handsome face she'd ever seen. The color of leather, even in winter, as if he spent his days outdoors. He smiled, showing a perfect row of pearl-hued teeth, and a flush took over her face from her chin to her forehead.

He reached out his hands and gently drew her to standing. "May I escort you to someplace less…well, obtrusive, Miss Callahan?" He laughed in a low rumbling sound that caused her stomach to somersault. "It *is* Miss Callahan?"

She nodded, unable to utter a word in return, and allowed her hand to be placed in the crook of his arm. He led her as though she were the most beautiful woman in the world, and she fought the urge to prance along beside him like a filly on her first trip to the pasture.

They had passed a few of the gaping couples before she ventured a shy sideways glance toward him. He gave her a warm smile and patted her hand, the same that rested on the fine woolen jacket sleeve. His Italian cutaway spoke of cost and quality, in her opinion—though she normally didn't pay attention to such things. But it was the man who wore it that captured her attention. The jacket was merely the frosting on the Christmas cookie. She fought the urge to giggle.

Christmas cookie. Imagine! Her heart thudded in cadence with her rapid footsteps as she hurried to keep up with his long-legged stride. She was vaguely aware of the hushed whispers as they passed.

Standing a little taller, she moved alongside the prince who had come to her rescue. Not that she needed rescuing.

They passed more couples and whispering old maids, then the Christmas tree with its blaze of candles, and headed toward the verandah.

Merciful heavens!

The verandah! And on a night like this. It had been threatening to snow all day. She shivered as they stepped through the wide double French doors and onto the dimly lit porch lined with a row of seven Christmas trees, all ablaze with candles.

Emmeline and the handsome man were completely alone. It was no wonder—the weather was frigid beyond description. It was daring. And thrilling. She had never been asked to the verandah alone. She shivered again.

Her prince removed his soft woolen cutaway and dropped it in a most gentlemanly fashion onto her shoulders. No beau had feigned even the slightest act of gallantry toward her. She looked up at him in wonder.

"I'm being rude," he said, smiling into her eyes. "I've escorted you without so much as an introduction."

She stuck out her hand awkwardly. "My name is Em—"

"My name is—" he said at precisely the same time.

They both laughed, then he said, "Please, ladies first."

"I started to say, my name is Emmeline Amity Callahan, but then you already knew that. When I—well, when you helped me…" She swallowed hard to stop her teeth from chattering. "When you helped me just now, you called me by name." Then she realized that she was prattling and stopped abruptly.

He laughed again, putting her at ease. "Miss Emmeline Amity Callahan, my name is Derian Cadman."

Derian Cadman. *Musical.* She smiled up at him. He had a strong jaw and a face that was almost too handsome. Brows a bit too perfectly curved. It hurt her eyes to look at him.

He seemed amused, studying her as she admired him. His dark eyes flickered in the glow from the pale candlelight. "Tell me, Miss Callahan, why haven't I noticed you before?"

"Perhaps it was because I hadn't made such a spectacle of myself in front of you before now. It does happen from time to time."

"I thought you handled it with unusual grace."

"I did?" It was a pleasant lie, and she appreciated his effort to put her at ease.

"Everyone experiences embarrassing moments. But they always seem worse when they happen to us."

"Or in front of a hundred people." In the cold air little puffs of steam left her mouth with every word.

He chuckled. "Once I fell during a game of football at Choate. Flat on my face in the mud."

"You did?"

"Cost the team the game."

She couldn't fathom someone so self-possessed ever taking a misstep.

"In front of the entire school who had come to cheer on the team. My father was there—he wouldn't speak to me for days. Said I'd embarrassed him beyond measure." His expression was closed as if he guarded some secret pain.

Her heart went out to him. It never occurred to her that someone with his obvious physical gifts could embarrass his father, or himself for that matter.

Pushing up her eyeglasses—which always fogged at the most unsuitable times—she continued to gape speechlessly into his candlelight-flecked eyes. She was annoyed that her view was diffused by the foggy glass in her spectacles.

She swallowed hard. "Tell me, Mr. Cadman, have you lived in Washington long?"

"Actually, I'm visiting with friends from school."

"You're still in school?"

"Harvard Law."

"Ah, law school…" Her thoughts brightened. That made him older, perhaps closer to her age. "Which year?"

"My second term." He draped his arm around her shoulders and led her nearer the paned French doors. "But enough about me. Tell me, Miss Callahan, what you do in Washington. Have you lived here long?"

His undivided attention was giving her new confidence. This was the longest conversation she'd ever had with a gentleman of marriageable age, and the magic of it made her spinster's heart dance.

"I help my father with his correspondence," she said, "and I help my mother entertain. Sometimes I chaperone my sisters when their beaus come to visit."

"And do you have any beaus of your own, Miss Callahan?" He lifted her fingertips to his lips and kissed them.

She shivered with delight. From inside, strains of Mozart's *Sleighride Dance,* with its sleigh bells and violins and timpani, drifted toward them. Beyond the verandah, large, lazy snowflakes were falling on her stepfather's sculptured grounds. It was deliciously romantic.

"Does your father's correspondence keep you from entertaining beaus of your own, Emmeline?" His voice was husky and low. "And what it is that your father does that he should need someone to help with his letter writing?"

"He's a U.S. Senator."

The young man stepped back slightly, looking uncertain for the first time since they met. "Senator Callahan? I've never heard of him."

She laughed merrily. "He's my *step*father. Senator Dearbourne of Virginia. He married my mother when I was three. For some reason— perhaps because I was terribly precocious—I insisted on keeping my real father's name."

"*The* Senator James Dearbourne?" He glanced nervously over her shoulder toward the French doors and into the ballroom.

She nodded. "The same."

"And this is your home?" He fidgeted with his mustache and looked out at the expanse of lawn and gardens leading to the Potomac.

"Yes."

"Ah, then your sisters are the beautiful Glenna Elise and Hazel Leigh Dearbourne I've heard so much about."

"Yes," she laughed lightly, thinking of their surprise when they learned of her conversation with this handsome man. She stood a little taller, tilting her head back to get a better look at him. "They're the two I chaperone. They are beautiful, aren't they?"

He seemed to consider her face a moment. "Yes," he said, "they are."

Surely he was wondering how she had turned out the way she did. Her sisters were delicate and blond, with figures and faces like porcelain dolls.

And then there was Emmeline, she thought with a sigh. Taller, more robust than what was considered fashionable. Big boned, her mother called her. And she refused to cinch her midsection into the waspish eighteen-inch corset worn by Glenna and Hazel. Her only nod to fashion was her penchant for big hats. The bigger, the better. The more feathers and froth, the better. The more of her unruly stick-straight hair the hat covered, the better. Gave her sturdy figure better balance, she reasoned.

She disliked balls for many reasons, and at the top of the list was the fact that hats couldn't be worn. Tonight she'd attempted a simple French twist. She found the only way it would stay in place was to slick a three-fingered scoop of her stepfather's mustache wax onto the sides and neck-line. Even she had to admit the porcupine-stiff French twist wasn't quite what she'd hoped.

"I think you're beautiful," he said smoothly, as if reading her thoughts.

It was a lie. Still, it made her heart skip. Her sisters always said that it was a good idea for a young woman to avert her gaze at times such as these, but Emmeline wasn't like most women. She preferred to stare into Derian's eyes.

After another nervous glance through the windows into the ballroom, he bent toward her. She figured he was worried her stepfather might come out to the verandah and demand they come in from the cold.

But she soon forgot even that supposition because Derian Cadman was bending over her, moving his face nearer to hers. She'd never been this close to a man, and she prayed her glasses wouldn't fog so she could keep her gaze on his gold-flecked dark eyes.

He held her face in his hands, then, ever so gently, he stroked one cheek with his fingertips.

She took a quick breath and told herself to stop trembling as he smiled into her eyes, letting his fingertips trail to her chin.

"Merciful heavens," she whispered. "Perhaps we should go inside."

"Is that what you'd like?"

"No." The word came out as a sigh. Emmeline focused on his lips, now very near hers. She noticed his mustache was trimmed unevenly, reminding her of a hedge she'd once trimmed after she'd downed three mint juleps that her sisters promised contained no alcohol. She pressed her lips together in a straight line to choke back another nervous giggle.

She'd never been kissed before, and likely she would never be kissed again. So she closed her eyes, tried to think of anything but his uneven mustache. Then she caught her breath and leaned toward him, her lips pursed.

His lips had barely touched hers when an explosion of laughter brought Emmeline to her senses.

The laughter wasn't her own.

Emmeline's eyes widened in surprise. There, standing bunched in a group, were nine or ten of the young men she'd noticed when she first entered the ballroom. They grinned and winked and hooted at Derian Cadman. With a sinking heart, she knew they were his classmates.

She also knew she'd been the brunt of a very wicked prank.

The knowing hit her like a blow to the stomach. After staring at them for a moment and memorizing their faces, she turned and walked quickly through the snow to the dark, icy garden. She could hear every laughing word they spoke, every whoop, and every whistle.

"You said you'd do it, and sure enough, you did," one of the young men called to Cadman. "You said you'd kiss the ugliest girl at the ball before the hour was up."

"And it's been only forty-three minutes," one of the others hooted. "You could have stolen another few kisses for some extra points. This old maid was more than willing—I bet she's never been kissed before."

The laughter was raucous, causing Emmeline's face to flame even in the cold.

"You all owe me for this one," Cadman laughed. "Though the pickin' was easy."

"No problem," someone with a tenor voice said. "One of the homeliest yet."

"You placed your bets, and now it's time to pay up, my friends," said the man she had thought was her prince. "And I think that this time an extra reward is due me. She's the senator's daughter. Powerful man, Jamie Dearbourne."

Someone whistled appreciatively. "You kissed the senator's daughter?"

"I thought he had only two daughters," a deeper voice said.

"Only two that matter," chuckled the tenor.

After a few minutes, the laughter stopped as they all headed through the French doors to the dance floor.

Emmeline sat on a cold stone bench in her stepfather's garden, staring after them. The young men were again dancing with her sisters, with all the beautiful women of Washington society. The glittering gowns, the brilliant chandeliers, the candlelight from the Christmas tree melted together in a blur of tears, even as the silence of the snow swallowed the music and laughter.

She stared into the lovely ballroom for several minutes. The white flakes descended, covering her shoulders in crystal patterns that would normally delight her. Now they only served to make her shudder in the dropping temperature.

Shaking, she huddled in the warmth of Derian Cadman's jacket.

The jacket.

She stared down at the elegantly cut garment. Then a slow smile warmed her face. Standing, she shrugged off the coat, then walked toward the garden, letting the lovely woolen, custom-made jacket trail through the snow that covered the lawn, the muddy slush that graced the flowerbeds, the stones that made up the walkway. She enjoyed the little walk in the snow so much that she repeated it three more times, flipping the jacket this way and that to ensure it was thoroughly soaked and muddied.

"Oops," she whispered to herself as she stumbled across a sleeve. She grinned. "Oops," she repeated louder. She danced a little Spanish gypsy step on the wet lapels. She giggled and danced across the other sleeve, digging her heels into the cuff for good measure.

The orchestra was beginning a lively holiday tune when she returned to the ballroom, head held high, and spotted Derian Cadman standing near his new dance partner.

Emmeline waved gaily to him, stopped for a moment to rub the fog from her glasses, set them on her nose again in time to see him turning abruptly away from her.

"Derian, my dearest!" she called out in a honeyed drawl.

He turned around to face her as the second hush of the evening filled the room. The orchestra dropped from *forte* to *piano,* the string players stopped in midstroke, the timpanist halted with raised drumsticks, and the lone trumpet finally trailed to an awkward silence.

People turned to watch as she continued her march toward Derian. From the corner of her eye, Emmeline spotted her vexed-looking sisters, their friends with raised eyebrows, and Derian Cadman's surprised dance partner and his classmates stepping back to make way for her purposeful stride. A few throats cleared, a few whispers rustled, and from the back of the room rippled a lone giggle.

But Emmeline continued her march through the center of the group. They parted. Just like the Red Sea for Moses. She choked back another hysterical urge to laugh.

She marched closer, and Derian Cadman at least had the grace to look embarrassed.

Finally she stood in front of him and lifted the finely cut woolen jacket by her index finger. She tilted her face upward, adjusted her eyeglasses with her free hand and gave him a stunning smile.

He swallowed hard, and she widened her smile. And said nothing.

He reached for the coat. Teasingly, she pulled it away from him and giggled when his face flushed.

"My dear Derian," she said, her voice husky, "I believe we got so carried away that you forgot your jacket." Again she held it toward him. Its outer layer of snow and muddy slush was beginning to melt. And puddle on the polished marble.

Once more he reached to take the coat, and once more she pulled it back. His face was now crimson.

"You should be more careful about where you invite a girl." She giggled.

Behind the young man, one of his classmates snickered. One of the others let out a whistle, and they all laughed.

By now Derian Cadman's ears matched the vermilion of his face. "Give it to me," he growled between clenched teeth.

She stared into his gold-flecked eyes, took in his too-perfect brows and pretty chin, his uneven mustache, then she merely turned her crooked finger downward. The jacket fell at his feet.

He stooped to pick it up, then glared into her eyes as he stood upright.

She bent toward him, still smiling. "You, sir," she hissed, "are a rogue. If you and your friends do not leave the premises this minute, I shall tell a story that will chill this ball far more than the snow outside."

"What are you talking about?"

She giggled for the crowd's sake, fluttering her hand the way she'd seen her sisters do when talking with a beau. With a smile still in place, she turned her voice to sugar again. "Why, my dearest, I shall tell them how you took advantage of me on my father's verandah."

"But—but I didn't," he whispered. "It was a schoolboy's prank. That's all."

"Ah, but sir, you did. You took me for a fool. That gave you the advantage over me." She smiled at him sweetly. "I will count to ten. If you are not gone by nine, I shall tell the senator's very influential guests that you very definitely took advantage of me. And I shall cry. You have never seen me cry, sir, and I don't think you wish to."

He stared at her for one long moment.

"One," she breathed dramatically, "two…three…"

He spun toward his friends, walked toward them with the dripping jacket, and jerked his head toward the entry. They followed him sheepishly, obviously puzzled, as he marched, shoulders stiff, to the door.

Emmeline turned to the orchestra and gave the leader a decisive nod. A few of the violinists exchanged glances, then the viola began to play another of Wolfgang Mozart's dreary German dances. The timpani joined in, followed by the cello.

With her head tilted at a proud angle, Emmeline moved from the center of attention to the sidelines. Couples returned to the floor, and conversation resumed. She waited a moment, smiling and nodding to nearby guests. Soon she again faded into the wallpaper—for all anyone cared, she could have been the same oyster-gray hue.

She moved through the foyer, then slowly, shoulders sagging, she ascended the spiral staircase.

Once at the top, she slumped against the banister and covered her face with her shaking hands. Only then did she allow herself to weep.

Two

Emmeline gave herself only one minute to cry while leaning against the banister and staring across the foyer into the ballroom. That was all the time she ever allowed self-pity to darken her usually buoyant spirit. One minute. No more. No less.

Afterward she let out a sigh and smoothed her skirt, then blew her nose. As she watched the merry guests, it struck her that, though her parents had tried hard to give her the tools she needed to fit into Washington society, nothing had worked. No matter what they did or how hard they tried, she remained rough around the edges. So rough she could never fit into the polished Washington society that was so important to everyone else in her family.

First there had been the deportment lessons, followed by finishing school in Boston, and later, trips abroad with her beloved Aunt Gertie, who at ninety-something was still more of a rebel than she.

And music lessons! She giggled, remembering the maestro's angry face and penchant for throwing music books toward his least favorite students. Emmeline suspected he'd targeted her music stand just to watch her jump and drop her violin.

The dancing lessons were the worst. Even her father, normally a portrait of patience, grew weary of her treading on his feet. She supposed that her dislike of the elegant Mozart was a result of those lessons.

Nothing had made one fig of difference. Otherwise she would have been part of the merrymaking, coquettish and blushing right along with her sisters as they flirted with beaus.

Below her, the music continued. Mozart again, she noted with disdain. Something lively from Stephen Foster would certainly cause hearts to quicken. She stifled a chuckle. How she would enjoy taking over her parents' ball for just an hour! There would be none of this courtly dancing. Perhaps they would sing. And lively songs such as "Nelly Bly" or "Oh, Susanna!" Or something utterly romantic, such as "Jeannie with the Light Brown Hair."

And storytelling. Definitely storytelling. She smiled, considering it. Wild tales of the West. The stuff of dime novels. Dime novels. *Merciful heavens!* What a scandalous pastime that would be. She'd never read one, but she had heard whispers about their content. Delicious scalp-tingling tales. The sort of adventures that would utterly vex the proper young women of her social circle. She grinned.

And if she were in charge of her parents' balls, there would be no finger sandwiches and petits fours. Instead she would insist on a side of beef turning on a spit over an open fire, or a pig roasting in a hole dug just for the occasion in the middle of her father's manicured lawn.

An old-fashioned fandango would lift her spirits considerably.

Perhaps a bear and bullfight. Now, that would be a sight to see! Her father had often told her tales about the rip-roaring fights that took place at the rancho gatherings of his childhood.

She inched closer to the railing. The music reached a crescendo as the couples airily bowed and bobbed to Mozart's *Minuetto in D Major.* She might be unable to dance to Mozart, but she knew his allegros and adagios backward and forward, inside and out.

Propping her elbows on the banister and chin in hands, she imagined the sounds of Spanish guitars, the sights of brilliantly dressed gypsy dancers whirling and dipping around a campfire.

She sighed. *California.* The place of her secret dream. She'd visited only once, when she was a young girl. She remembered very little of her father's kin or the ranchos in the Big Valley, only that California seemed spread out in such open spaces a person could get lost.

Lost in a favorable way. Lost from the expectations of others, lost from the suffocating knowledge that she'd never fit in, and that no matter how hard she tried, she'd never be beautiful or desired by the beaus that buzzed around her sisters like yellow jackets around a pot of bacon grease.

Not that she'd ever wanted one. Oh yes, there had been those foolish girlhood dreams of one dashing man or another. But it wasn't a handsome face that caused her heart to drum beneath her ribs, it was the beauty of a man's soul. Something in his eyes that spoke of compassion, sincerity, and intelligence. That, in her book, comprised the heart of a dashing man.

Such men, those with golden souls, never glanced her direction, never looked past the plain exterior to see into her soul.

"Emma, child?" A soft, quavering voice behind her broke into her reverie.

She turned and smiled at the diminutive older woman. "Aunt Gertie, I thought you'd be in bed by now."

Gertrude Hill had been a friend of her father's for longer than Emmeline could remember. Gertie stepped closer and reached up to pat Emmeline's face tenderly.

"You look peaked, child." She frowned. "And you've left the doin's before supper. Are you ailing?"

Emmeline shrugged. "You know how I feel about these affairs."

"But usually you find a quiet corner to wait it out, to watch everyone else having a good time."

Emmeline laughed. Sometimes she thought that Gertie understood her spirit better than did all the people in her world rolled together—including her mother, father, and sisters. The frail old woman had no children of her own and willingly adopted nearly everyone God brought her way.

Spunky as a bobcat kit even now, Gertie reveled in her life's adventures, the least of which was the tale of how, aeons ago, she'd traveled with Jamie across the country by wagon on the Santa Fe Trail. And that had been only the first crossing; she'd made two more, side by side on the wagon bench with the man she married at age seventy-five. The groom was eighty-two and died four years later of consumption while they were visiting Venice. She'd never married again, but she didn't let widowhood get in the way of her adventures.

Emmeline's eyes filled as she beheld Gertie's wrinkled face, the small, round eyes that looked out at the world with bright curiosity.

"I don't belong here, Gertie. I realized it more than ever tonight."

Gertie placed her birdlike hand on Emmeline's forearm. "I can see on your face you've been hurt to the core by something, or someone, tonight."

"Actually, it's longing you see, not hurt. Sometimes I long to simply announce to my parents that I'm ready to strike out on my own. Head west as so many did in days of old. Head west and seek my fortune."

The women turned together to peer over the banister at the revelers. "Think of all I could do if only I had the gumption to leave. I wouldn't mind becoming a trapper—though their day is long gone. Or a cable car operator in San Francisco." She giggled. "Perhaps I could become a Harvey Girl." The notion of such independence pleased her.

"I have it in mind that you could do anything you set your cap to do, child. And as to your gumption, I believe you have that in full measure. It's the timing that isn't right yet. That's all."

Emmeline turned toward the little woman, gratitude flooding into her heart. "If I ever decide to go west, you will come along?" Gertie laughed, a low gravelly sound. To Emmeline it was more beautiful than a thousand Spanish guitars could ever hope to be. "Will you?" She couldn't imagine ever leaving her beloved friend behind.

Gertie grinned, looking younger than she had in months. "Tell me more, child. Tell me your dreams."

"It should be obvious to everyone now that I will never have the blessed company of a husband to care for me." She smiled. "Not that I want to find it necessary to depend on the good graces of a man."

Gertie laughed. "I should hope not."

Emmeline sighed, considering her options—as she had more times than she could count. "Perhaps I'll simply become a woman of independent means."

"I know you, child," Aunt Gertie said solemnly. "You've got a fire inside you that nothing can quell. A spirit fire."

Emmeline caught her hand. "I see such a quality in you, Aunt Gertie. I've often admired it and wished I had the same spirit and gumption."

"Don't sell yourself short, Emma. Perhaps you don't know it's there because you've never been tested."

They moved away from the balcony banister and strolled arm in arm back toward their bedrooms. Then quite suddenly the diminutive woman stopped and peered up at Emmeline. "I was standing by my window tonight, child. I couldn't hear the words that scoundrel said to you, but I saw him, the other boys laughing. I understand what they did."

Emmeline didn't speak for a moment. "I acted foolishly. I shouldn't have entertained such a dalliance in the first place. I should have known better."

"You were curious, that's all." A soft smile caused Gertie's wrinkles to deepen.

They started walking again, slowly for Gertie's sake, past the ornately framed formal oil paintings that flanked the wide hallway, portraits of her mother and father, her sisters, Glenna and Hazel, and finally to the large portrait of Emmeline.

Gertie stopped to look up at Emmeline's painting.

The artist had painted her image against a black background, causing her face to appear almost alabaster, her dark eyes to take on a wide, startled look, and her generous mouth to look much too prominent. And he'd painted her without her eyeglasses, which in her opinion gave her a blank, lifeless look. She'd sat for the artist for hours, leaning slightly forward as if impatient to be done with the painful process. Amazingly, he had captured her exact feelings. Her tense impatience. Her restlessness.

She'd always hated the painting.

"You are more handsome than you know, child."

"*Sturdy* isn't beautiful."

"Is that what you think you are?"

"That's what mother calls my big-boned frame."

Gertie turned and caught both Emmeline's hands in hers. "I once saw a statue in Venice. I don't know who the woman was, just some nameless goddess. But she was tall, just as you are, and powerfully built. Her arms looked like she could throw lightning bolts, and her face was strong. Showed strength in her high cheekbones—just like yours do. Yet the tilt of her head and the life in her eyes spoke of grace and beauty. For all her strength, there was no doubt that she had a tender soul. I could see it in her eyes."

Emmeline swallowed hard and nodded, afraid to trust her voice to speak.

"You often remind me of that statue, child."

"You never told me before."

Gertie grinned. "I didn't want it to go to your head." Then she laughed and slipped her arm around Emmeline's waist as they started walking again. "I see that glory in you when you're riding horseback or attempting that dance…that Spanish gypsy dance."

"You've seen me dance?"

Gertie's low, rumbling laugh erupted again. "Once you had a rose stem in your mouth, and you were beating your feet like this." She did a little trot to emphasize her point. "And you'd let your hair go wild. It flew out behind you as you whirled and stomped."

She laughed again, and Emmeline giggled with her. Without telling anyone, she'd practiced the steps from a book when she was ten. She still danced to the strange and haunting music in her heart, stealing away to the summerhouse or the gazebo when the family was away from home.

"Prettiest sight I ever did see, child," Gertie said as they walked slowly down the hallway. "And it comes the closest to showing me who God created you to be."

Gertie moved slower, weary from the exertion, and Emmeline adjusted her steps to meet the older woman's tiny ones. They reached Gertie's bedroom door, and she stepped aside so that Emmeline could open it for her.

"He created you to be joyful," Gertie said, "gave you a special soul-dancin' music that's yours alone."

The thought delighted Emmeline. "I always look at the social rules I'm forever breaking. The deportment I can't carry out, the titil-lating conversation my sisters seem to engage in so naturally, the pretty way they look…and I think that surely God made a mistake when he created me. I don't fit in."

"You're right about only one thing."

A slow smile overtook Emmeline's face. She pushed up her eyeglasses and sniffled softly. "That I don't fit in?"

"And about how glad I am that you don't." She stepped into her bedroom. "For now, child, will you turn down my bed? I'm weary."

The older woman rang for one of the house servants to help her into her nightclothes while Emmeline fluffed the feather-down pillows and arranged the comforters. Then Emmeline removed the copper bed-warmer from its hook over the fireplace and slid it back and forth under the covers.

"It stands to reason that if I don't fit in here, I should leave," Emmeline mused as she pulled Gertie's long flannel nightdress from the oak wardrobe. "You will promise to go with me—that is, if I decide to go?"

"Something tells me you've already decided," Gertie said wearily. Then she smiled gently. "Depends on how far you plan to travel as to whether I can make it."

Emmeline's heart sank as she thought of her dream to go west. Gertie was right. A journey of that length would be too difficult for the elderly woman. "We'll talk about it in the morning." Emmeline walked over and planted a kiss on Gertie's wrinkled cheek. When she stood, the maid entered the room and began helping Gertie from her dress.

She'd reached the door when she heard the rumbling cackle behind her. "By going far, I mean Cape Horn—or perhaps the moon—I've always had a hankering to go there."

Emmeline turned to see Gertie's grin.

"But there's another place I've always had a hankerin' to go again."

"Where's that?"

"California, child. I've always wanted to go back to that Big Valley. Haven't been there since that day back in sixty-four."

Emmeline threw back her head, and a laugh erupted in a most unladylike fashion. "California?"

Gertie nodded. "California. Think you're up to taking an old lady

clear across the country? Of course, we'd head there by train this time."
Her wrinkles softened as if with some unforgotten memory. "Though I
must say, I'm hankerin' to climb up on a wagon bench again."

Emmeline smiled. "I'd take you tomorrow if there was a way."

She closed Gertie's door and turned toward her own suite of rooms.
She had taken only a few steps when her mother and father rounded the
corner from the landing at the top of the stairs. The displeasure on her
father's face caused her heart to drop. He worked his jaw as they
approached, seeming too disturbed to speak.

"Emma, are you all right?" Hallie whispered once they stood in front
of her. "The rumors circulating downstairs…" Her voiced dropped, and
she looked into her daughter's eyes, her face lined with worry. "The talk
is that you were carrying on outdoors with a young gentleman."

"He was no gentleman, Mother."

"What did he do to you?" Jamie growled, stepping closer to her.
"Did he hurt you?" His white-knuckled hands clenched and unclenched. "If he did, so help me—"

Hallie placed a hand on Jamie's arm. "Listen to what Emmeline has
to say, Jamie. Maybe it's not as bad as we think."

Emmeline eased her face into a smile to reassure them that, indeed,
no real harm had befallen her. "First of all, I didn't 'carry on' with him.
When I handed him his coat, I was merely teaching the young
scoundrel a much-needed lesson."

"We heard about your exchange in the ballroom," Jamie said, looking grieved. "I should have been the one to order him from the house if
he disgraced you."

"He did disgrace me, but not in the way you think." It embarrassed
her to let on the extent of her humiliation, so she didn't tell them what
Cadman and his friends had done. "And he deserved to be ordered from
the house. It was a duty I needed to perform. You'll need to trust me for
acting as I did—and forgive me if I brought disgrace on our house
tonight."

Jamie placed his arm around her shoulders, and the three began to
walk down the carpeted hall to Emmeline's rooms.

"I probably could have handled it in a more acceptable manner," Emmeline mused as they walked. "But the young man is a thoughtless, dull-witted, smooth-talking rogue. I wanted to regain a small portion of my dignity." She halted and looked from Jamie's face to her mother's.

Jamie's was a mix of concern for her and anger toward Derian Cadman. His body was bent in an attitude of defense, arms half-bent, hands again clenched into fists. "What did he do to you, Emma?"

The childhood endearment brought hot tears to Emmeline's eyes. She swallowed the sting in her throat. "It doesn't matter now. Honestly." She slipped her hand into her father's. His fingers relaxed, and the strong warmth of them wrapped around hers brought her comfort, just as it had in her childhood. She smiled up at him. "The young man— Derian Cadman—was here on holiday from school. We'll likely never see him again."

Her parents exchanged a grieved look.

"We won't ever see him again," Emmeline repeated. "We won't, will we?"

"I'm afraid we haven't heard the end of this…incident," Jamie said. Her mother touched his arm as if warning him not to go on.

"Why?" Emmeline persisted.

"Derian Cadman is the president's nephew."

THREE

Long past midnight, when the last carriage finally rolled down the drive, Emmeline lay in her high-poster bed, unable to sleep. Soft moonlight, reflecting on the snow outside her window, filled her room with a silvery light.

She pulled back her thick comforter and padded barefoot to the window. Lifting the lace curtain to one side, she stared out at the fairyland of new-fallen snow. It covered the stands of maples and pines, fence rails, and hedges, with a blanket of white that glistened beneath the moon.

It seemed deceptively beautiful, covering knotholes and flaws she knew were on the fence, winter-dead branches that hung on the oaks, even the holes in the uneven hedges. Just like life in the social whirl of Washington, she decided. Beautiful on the surface, sometimes decayed at its core.

Some of the belles were like her sisters, pure and good, the best of intentions guiding their actions. Though if the truth were known, even their designs centered on finding the suitable husband of wealth, power, and a comely appearance.

She smiled as a cottontail rabbit hopped from under the hedge and headed across the smooth snow toward the road. She fought the urge to run downstairs and follow him. It struck her that her sole reason for wanting to go was to see her footprints. Hers alone. Unique and sturdy. Heading away from this house just as the rabbit's did. Heading anywhere but toward the tall entry door.

She laughed at the silly notion and, shivering, climbed back into the high bed, pulling the comforter under her chin. A gust of wind kicked up outdoors, and she shivered again. She'd never gotten over her childhood fear of the wind. For a few minutes, her teeth chattered as she snuggled deep into her covers. And she thought about the cottontail's trail, now being covered by the blowing snow. She wanted her footprints to last longer than the next snowstorm. She wanted to make a difference in the world.

Her father's work as a senator had substance. Her mother stood beside him, supporting him with all her heart and soul. She saw to the upbringing of her family and to the well-being of those less fortunate. She, too, had found substance in Washington. Together, Jamie and Hallie would leave a legacy to last far beyond their lifetime.

Emmeline wanted more than that. It wasn't simply because she didn't fit in with Washington society. No, the notion dug deeper into her heart than that. She wanted, with God's help, to create a life of eternal substance and meaning.

She pondered such a life for a few minutes, considering her possibilities.

She might try her hand at becoming a mail-order bride. She giggled, imagining such a thing. She wasn't marriage material, not even for a sight-unseen groom. *Merciful heavens!* That would be like trying to find meaning by buying a pig in a poke.

Or she might try her hand at employment. Perhaps becoming a Harvey Girl in Kansas or a cable-car operator in San Francisco wasn't such an outlandish idea afterall. She giggled again at the image such a notion conjured.

Letting out a deep sigh, she settled into the cocoon of blankets and let her eyes finally drift shut. The evening's disastrous events crowded into her mind, pushing aside her thoughtful reverie. Her eyes flew open, and she stared heavenward into the dark expanse beyond her window.

Lord, I certainly get myself into trouble when I don't abide in you and your words don't abide in me. You've said that if you do that…and I do the same…I can ask for whatever I wish and it will be done.

And when I get to wishing for something without abiding in you at the same time, what I wish for won't be from your heart.

Make my heart beat in time with yours.

And keep me from longing for those things I don't have…like beauty and wit and someone to love me.

Most of all, Father, remind me as often as I need reminding that your words need to abide in me and I need to abide in you.

She started to drift to sleep again, then her eyes opened with a start.

Oh, and Lord, tonight…when I thought I was going to be kissed, I'm sorry for how I was looking forward to it.

If it's all right, could you send me someone who might love me? Someone who might kiss me because he wants to, not because he's wagered someone that he can do it?

Oh, and one more thing, Lord. About my desire to find substance and independence…help me find what that means exactly. I mean, if it's not too late for me, being a spinster and all.

Merciful heavens! How I would enjoy such an adventure!

Emmeline finally fell asleep with a smile playing at the corners of her mouth.

<hr />

Thin morning sunlight slanted through the sitting room window, brightening patches on the rose-petal-hued carpet. Though the rest of the downstairs rooms were formal, decorated in gray and blue, this was a room in which Hallie had worked hard to create a sense of warmth.

It was a pale room, filled with soft rose, ivory, and peach, purposely chosen to match the garden just beyond the lace curtains, a garden now covered with snow. An oversized chair, an ottoman, and two small couches were covered with a fabric of faded floral chintz. Crocheted pillows, mostly made by Aunt Gertie, added more touches of warmth.

A small cherry secretary stood in one corner, with a silver vase of silk flowers atop a lace circle. Scattered around it was a grouping of hand-painted frames filled with family photographs: all three of the children; Jamie's mother, Sara Dearbourne; and his brother, Spence, his wife, Aislin, and their son, Quaid. Hallie's brother, Ransom, and his family. On the pale peach wall above the secretary was a delicately cut Venetian mirror, and just beneath it stood a silver oval frame with a wedding picture of Jamie and Hallie with little Emma standing in front of them.

To the right of the fireplace, where a fire crackled behind an iron grate, bookshelves were filled with Hallie's favorite books, the works of Jane Austin—*Lady Susan, Sense and Sensibility, Pride and Prejudice, Persuasion,* and *Emma*—the Brontë sisters, and Emily Dickinson among them.

Usually this room caused Hallie's heart to settle into the peaceful place no other room in the house could provide. Today, however, after a sleepless night, Hallie felt restless and concerned about Emmeline. She didn't worry about Jamie's reputation, and certainly she had no concern for her own.

But she knew her daughter's heart. She recognized that Emmeline felt awkward and unaccepted in Washington society. The events of the previous night would only deepen that feeling.

Washington was filled with those who loved nothing better than a tidbit of salacious gossip. The more scandalous the better. Emmeline probably was unaware that she had handed to those empty-minded and empty-hearted women the very thing they fed upon, a scandalous tidbit involving a senator's daughter and the president's nephew.

Her heart ached for Emmeline.

Hallie recognized the soft footfall of Jamie's approach from down the hall and turned to greet him.

He hurried across the room, took her hands in his, and kissed her cheek. He was as intriguing to her as he'd been the day he'd first arrived in Kentucky. She smiled now at the memory. It was during the war, and he'd been on the run from a federal prison camp. He was near starvation and had broken into her little cottage in the middle of the night, looking for food. She hadn't known that then—she thought he was a common thief. She had shot him while he stood looking down at Emma's doll cradle.

Even while she'd nursed him back to health and listened to his bitter tale, she'd found herself falling in love with him. She'd seen something beautiful deep inside him, despite his emaciated frame and pain-haunted eyes. Even then, she'd thought him handsome—the color of his eyes, the stubborn set of his stubbled chin. As Aunt Gertie was prone to say, he was a fine one, he was. She'd known it then. She knew it better now.

She gave her husband a soft smile. He looked worried, the lines around his eyes more pronounced than usual.

"You look troubled, Jamie. Does it have to do with Emmeline?"

He nodded and moved across the room to stand by the fire. He held out his hands to warm them, then turned, clasping them behind him. "I saw the president."

"Is he angry?"

"Surprisingly, no. He said the boy probably had it coming to him." He paused, looking out the window. "But I found out what Derian and his friends did to our daughter."

Hallie's heart dropped. The look on her husband's face twisted her stomach with icy fear. "What did they do?" Her voice was barely a whisper.

His gaze met hers again, and there was something about his expression that suddenly reminded her of the look in his eyes from that long-ago day when he told her about the little bugle boy who'd died in his arms in Elmira. A little boy who'd been without a champion except for Jamie. And when Jamie had defended the boy, it had nearly cost him his life.

"They made sport of her," he said, working his jaw in anger. "Cadman bet the others he could kiss the ugliest girl at the ball in less than an hour." His face was white, and his lips were a thin, pale line as he continued, "It seems they chose our Emma." He turned to look out the window again.

Hallie walked across the room to stand beside him and reached for his hand. "Our daughter is strong. This was hurtful to her, but don't even consider that it might destroy her spirit, her will. There is no truth in that. She is your daughter, and you've taught her an inner strength that I don't think even she is aware of."

But Jamie didn't seem to hear her. "I plan to call him out to a duel."

"No, Jamie!" Her voice dropped to a whisper, lest they be overheard by one of the children, or worse, one of the servants, who might spread yet more gossip. "Don't destroy everything you've worked for because of the idiocy of schoolboys."

"They're not schoolboys. Cadman is a grown man. Studying law so he can become a lawmaker. Wants to come to Washington." He shook his head slowly. "The president hinted that I could destroy his nephew's career by making too much of this. Didn't come right out and ask me, but I knew the promise he was hoping to exact from me."

"And you said…?"

"I said nothing."

Hallie walked to the small couch and sat down. She patted the seat to her left. Jamie joined her, leaning back, hands laced behind his head, staring at the ceiling.

He let out a long sigh. "I can't let this go. Simply do nothing."

"A challenge to a duel is illegal, Jamie. You of all people know that. Not only might you take the young man's life, you'll destroy your career. And Emma will gain nothing by your act." She didn't add that Jamie might be the one to lose his life. She couldn't bear to say the words.

"Except dignity," Jamie said. "She would know that I'm ready to die for her honor."

"It would take much more than what those boys did to rob her of dignity and honor." She smiled softly. "As I told you, she's her father's daughter. Tough. Resilient."

Jamie didn't speak for a moment. Then he turned to her. "I don't want her to be the object of ridicule."

She reached for his hand. "It hurts me to think of it too."

The only sounds in the room for a few minutes were the crackle of the fire and the ticking of the mantel clock. Then Jamie spoke again. "Emmeline has been patience itself while working for me. I've depended on her quick mind and astute observations to help me with my correspondence."

Hallie saw the thoughtfulness on his face, and she didn't hurry to fill the silence when he fell quiet.

"Perhaps I've not considered what she might like to do. She hasn't shown much interest in marriage…"

A smile played at Hallie's lips. "Perhaps because she's never been asked."

Jamie let out a snort. "Asked? Why, if she'd just given the slightest indication of interest, the beaus would have been lined up down Pennsylvania Avenue." Hallie chuckled as Jamie went on. "I think she figured she'd be better off alone than entertaining some vacuous boor."

"But you were saying, I mean, about her letter writing and all she's accomplished for you…?"

"It's occurred to me that Emma might like a change." Jamie frowned in deep thought as he spoke. "Has she ever said anything to you about California?"

"She's mentioned it, though the subject doesn't come up often."

"I remember when she was little how she would sit and listen for endless hours to my tales of my boyhood on the rancho." He laughed. "She actually memorized the stories until she could tell them better than I could, especially those of Spence and me riding across the Big Valley, the fort Aislin and I made when we pretended to be Gaelic warriors." He laughed, now relaxing. "She especially loved the story about Spence, Aislin, Sybil, and Scotty saving the ranchos by herding wild horses to New Mexico."

He turned to look at Hallie. "Even now, she'll ask me about California. About her shirttail relatives there, her cousins Quaid and Merci." He chuckled. "Though she's always quick to add that they're not real blood kin. She's often asked if the land might have changed since her one visit. And not too long ago she asked if I should go back to see my mother, perhaps take care of government business along the way."

"Maybe it's time for all of us to go. It's been some time since Sara visited us here."

Jamie shook his head. "Something tells me that Emma might want to strike out on her own. Maybe it's time to let her go."

Hallie caught her breath. Jamie was right—she knew it deep down. Emma was a grown woman. Still, it made her heart ache to consider that her daughter might choose to live a continent away. "I always thought she would settle near us."

"Are we being selfish by keeping her here?" he countered. His gaze drifted to the fireplace. "I must say I can't imagine what I'll do without her."

"Nor I."

He nodded. "Why don't we ask her what she would like to do?"

"We don't want her to think we're sending her away because of what happened with Mr. Cadman."

Jamie laughed. "As you've said several times already this morning, she's my daughter. And I can assure you, she's not one to look for hidden meanings beneath the words that are spoken to her. Somehow, I don't think she'll begin wearing her heart on her sleeve now."

A short time later there was a light knock on the door, and Emmeline poked her head into her parents' room. "Is this a private conversation?"

Her mother and father looked up, obviously surprised to see her. Jamie stood. "Come in, come in, we were just discussing you."

"Me?" She smiled, trying to look as though she couldn't imagine what they were talking about. Then she laughed as she sat down in the overstuffed chair across from them. Jamie settled beside her mother on the couch. "My sisters have just told me that already I'm being referred to as a strumpet. Can you imagine such a thing?" She laughed again. "This senator's old-maid daughter, a strumpet?"

"You really shouldn't take this so lightly, Emma," her mother said.

"If I don't laugh, I might cry," she answered. "I'd rather laugh."

"I saw the president this morning," Jamie said. "He wasn't concerned in the least about what you did—sending his nephew packing, I mean."

"Well, that's something…" Emmeline sighed. "I did worry that your campaign might suffer."

"Don't worry about me, child," Jamie said. "You are my primary concern. Your honor is utmost in my mind." There was a change in his demeanor as he spoke the words, and Emma felt an instinctive alarm.

"My honor is intact, Father." He had the same pale look of anger that she'd noticed the night before, when they spoke of the incident. "What else did the president tell you about Derian?"

"I'd rather not speak of Derian at all," Jamie said quickly. "Or of the events preceding your sending him from the house."

From his tone, Emmeline guessed that someone had told him the details about the humiliating prank.

"And if he dares show his face here again…"

Emmeline laughed. "Well, that is certainly not something any of us has to worry about."

But Jamie didn't smile. Her mother reached across the distance between herself and her husband to take his hand. As if to calm him. Emmeline noticed that the big hand wrapped in her mother's small one was trembling. As though his anger was too great to contain.

Honor. He'd spoken of it as though it was cherished. She wondered what her father might consider doing, other than blackballing the young man from Massachusetts. Mr. Cadman might be the president's nephew, but her father was a power to contend with in most political circles as well.

Hallie smiled and spoke almost too quickly. "In truth, Emma, we were just discussing what *you* might like to do."

Jamie let out a heavy sigh, and the lines of tension around his eyes relaxed. "We were speaking of California."

Emmeline's heart thudded beneath her ribs. "California?" she squeaked. "Out west?"

Jamie laughed. "Unless someone moved it. Yes, the California that's west of the Rockies."

"And just what were you saying about California?" She bit her tongue to keep from blurting out her plans, her fantasies about going west.

Jamie crossed his leg, resting his ankle on his knee. He leaned forward earnestly. "Your mother and I have selfishly used your talents, Emma. In my office. Here, with your sisters. We were just now speaking of how that could change. Should change. We're wondering if you might have something to say about that."

This was the moment Emmeline had been dreaming of, and now that it was here, she was almost speechless. She stared at her parents as the mantel clocked ticked and the fired crackled behind the grate.

"California," she finally managed. She licked her dry lips. "Well, my goodness. This is a sudden turn of events. Your asking about such a thing, I mean." She patted her hair absently.

Jamie and Hallie nodded, waiting expectantly.

Emmeline stood and moved to the fireplace. She stared at the licking flames, then turned. "It's been my dream," she sighed. "As long as I can remember. I don't recall much about our visit all those years ago. Only that it was a place with a big, noisy family. And love. The family seemed spilling over with love for each other." She twisted an errant strand of hair. "Even for me. A little girl who wasn't even blood kin."

Her eyes misted. "I remember the sky. It was bigger than I'd ever seen before. It stretched from one edge of the land to the other." She laughed self-consciously. "Of course, that's what skies do."

"And California is your heart's dream?" her mother pressed.

It was now snowing outside, and the room had darkened. Emmeline's mind was filled with a myriad of images. Sunlight, pure and bright. A sky so blue it hurt her eyes. Wind that made her shake inside.

"California," she whispered to herself, nodding her head. Then she turned to her parents and smiled. "Yes, going to California has always been my heart's desire. I just never thought it might be the thing to do. I mean, the proper thing to leave you both, leave my sisters, and strike out on my own."

Jamie rose to stand beside her. "If you were given the means to do such a thing—would you go?"

She didn't hesitate a moment. "Yes," she whispered. "Yes, of course I would." After all that had happened in less than twenty-four hours, she could scarcely believe what she was hearing. She cleared the lump from her throat. "And the means you speak of, can you tell me more…about that, I mean?"

"My mother is growing old. In her recent letters she's spoken of wanting to leave the rancho. I'm going to write her—that is, with your permission—and ask what she might suggest for a young woman who's ready for adventure and challenge. A woman who's got more spunk and grit than any ten Washington belles put together."

Emmeline bit her lip to keep from crying at his words. "Spunk?" she breathed. "Me?"

Hallie came to stand beside them. "It's your turn to live a life of your own, Emma," she said. "We both want that for you."

She looked into Jamie's face. "Your correspondence…who will take care of it for you?"

"I can never find anyone to replace you. But perhaps you can teach your sisters to handle it." He laughed. "Though, I daresay, it will take them both to do the job you've done by yourself."

His expression turned serious. "There is one thing I ask of you."

"Anything," she answered readily.

He studied her face for a moment, then spoke again. "The way people in this backbiting city are, the scandal is only going to grow. At least the mudslinging will, for a time. Especially if my political rivals feel they can somehow use what happened to you to attack my character. I can handle myself; I just want to protect you from gossipmongers. It hurts me to have your name sullied."

"I believe it hurts you more than it does me," she said.

"That happens with parents," her mother said. "It's something children can't know until they're parents themselves, even if they are grown women of twenty-seven."

"What is it you ask?" Emmeline looked at Jamie and was suddenly chilled by the cold anger she saw in his face.

"I don't want Derian Cadman to come near you."

She laughed. So that was all it was. Her father had a righteous temper, and though it gave her comfort to know that he wanted to protect her, she was relieved that Cadman was the sole reason for his anger now. Shrugging, she chuckled again. "As I told you both, the man will not be back. Why should he?" She didn't add that he had so thoroughly embarrassed and humiliated her that there was no need for him to damage her reputation, her honor, any further.

"He will not come near me," she said, reaching for her father's hands. "I promise."

Hallie spoke up, her concern showing in her soft voice. "I don't think you understand the seriousness of the request, Emma."

Emmeline stared at them both, trying to comprehend why they would think Derian Cadman would come near her. Finally, she nodded. "I'll accept your warning just as seriously as you've given it to me."

It was toward the end of a stormy January when the letter from Sara Dearbourne arrived. It lay unopened on Jamie's desk while he was away from Washington, visiting New York with two Congressmen. Emmeline thought she might die of curiosity during the week he was away.

According to her sisters, the scandal was still being whispered about throughout Washington. She seldom thought about Derian Cadman. It wasn't difficult to push him from her mind. Her sisters reported that he'd hightailed it back to Harvard and hadn't been invited back to the White House since disgracing himself…and her.

On the afternoon of the day Jamie was due home, Cordelia, the parlor maid, found Emmeline in the library, seated in front of the secretary near her stepfather's desk. She had been answering his correspondence since early morning, and at the sound of the maid's voice, Emmeline turned in her seat, removed her spectacles, and rubbed her eyes.

"You have a gentleman caller, Miss Emmeline," Cordelia said. "I've shown him into the sitting room."

Emmeline frowned. Who could be calling? She couldn't remember when such words had ever been spoken to her. "Did he give you his name?"

"Mister Cadman, Miss."

Emmeline gasped. "Cadman? Are you sure?"

Cordelia's dark face clouded. "I wouldn't make up such a thing, Miss Emmeline. No ma'am."

She considered her dilemma and decided that it was only right that she be the one to tell him that he wasn't welcome in their house. "All right, then," she said, standing. "Yes, yes. Of course, I'll see him." She followed Cordelia from the room, then made her way across the foyer to the sitting room.

When she entered, Cadman, who was standing by the fireplace, turned to greet her. He inclined his head slightly, looking sheepish.

"Mr. Cadman," Emmeline said evenly. "To what do I owe the honor?" She didn't attempt to keep the sarcasm from her voice.

He looked at her, a genuine remorse in his expression. "I came to apologize."

"Apologize for ruining my character?"

"That wouldn't have happened except for the unfortunate prank my friends and I played on you." There was none of the smooth, cocky tone she remembered.

For several moments she stood as still as a statue. She needed to tell him to leave without delay. She had promised her parents. Yet she stared into his face, searching for the words. He seemed so, well...contrite. Sorry. She couldn't find it in her heart to banish him again.

"Am I forgiven?" His uncertain smile seemed sincere, and, she noted, his mustache had been trimmed in a straighter line than before. But her words to her parents echoed in her mind—they didn't want him here, regardless of his apologies.

"You must leave," Emmeline said sternly. "I sent you away once before. Nothing has changed. You are not welcome here."

"I understand," he said, letting his gaze drift from hers as if embarrassed. "Let me say first, though, that what I did, what my friends said, was truly detestable. I've wanted to come to you before this and beg your forgiveness. Even if you set me out of your home on my ear again, I'll understand. But, please, first understand how sorry I am."

She hesitated. There was a manner about him that seemed desperate. And she noticed the same dark, guarded look he'd had that night on the verandah. She sensed it had nothing to do with the prank, with her, or even with his apology. "Why did you wait over a month, then?" she asked as he moved to the door. "And why have you come now?"

He stopped and glanced back at her. "My uncle sent me away from Washington."

"Your uncle—the president."

"The same. It seems you aren't the only one we humiliated that night."

"Did he send you here to apologize?"

"No. He doesn't know I've come."

She was intrigued by the transformation in the young man. When she'd met him before, he'd had an air of confidence that told the world he was sure of himself and his rightful place in the universe. Now he seemed about as sure of himself as a scolded puppy.

She laughed quite suddenly, and he looked at her in surprise as she spoke. "I accept your apology."

He gave her a quick, warm smile, showing his perfect teeth. Then he rushed toward her, lifted her hand, and brushed it with his lips.

"Now that I've forgiven you," she said, walking with him to the sitting room door, "you really must leave." The mantel clock told her that Jamie would be home soon, and she knew it was better for him not to find Derian in his house.

He stopped and looked down at her. "There's something else I wanted to ask—"

Emmeline cut him off. "I think we've made great progress in what's been said today. Let's leave it there."

He laughed out loud, an enchanting sound. She was surprised at how ready she was to laugh with him. Perhaps it was because no man had ever paid a smidgen of attention to her before. She couldn't deny that the feeling was pleasant. Very pleasant.

"And what if I don't leave, Emmeline?" He was still chuckling, and the light in his eyes told her his old confidence was returning. "Will you throw me out again?"

"I did that rather nicely the last time." Her tone was actually flirtatious, and she was probably more surprised than he was. "No doubt I can find a way to do it again."

"No one's ever done that before to me." He looked at her evenly. "Gotten the best of me, I mean."

One corner of her mouth quirked into a smile. "Then it was high time someone did."

He sighed, studying her face. "My uncle said the same thing."

Her heart softened somewhat toward him. "And the question you were about to ask?"

Flushing slightly, he cleared his throat. "I, well, I was wondering if I might call on you. I mean from time to time…that is, if the senator, if your father, that is, approves."

His difficulty getting the question out was almost too great for her to bear. "Why me? My sisters are the ones with the strings of beaus from here to the Potomac."

His eyes met hers. "That's precisely why I'd rather call on you."

"You don't like lines?"

"I don't like the belles who are at the end of those lines." His expression suggested he spoke the truth.

There was a moment of awkward silence while she searched his face, wondering if, truly, she could trust those gold-flecked eyes.

He leaned forward earnestly. "I was hoping you might accompany me on a ride tomorrow. There are some trails near the Potomac that are sheltered from the snow." He looked hopeful. "But excuse me, Emmeline, I didn't ask if you do indeed ride."

Gertie's description of how Emmeline looked on horseback came to mind, and Emmeline smiled. "Yes, I do ride," she said softly, then added, reminded of her father's concerns, "but I can't accompany you."

His gaze seemed to rest on her questioning eyes. "Your words speak of something quite different than what your eyes tell me. Perhaps I can convince you to change your mind."

Before she could answer, the door burst open. Jamie stood in the doorway, his face pale and his eyes dark with fury.

She swallowed hard. "Good afternoon, Father. Welcome home."

FOUR

Emmeline held her breath while Derian shook hands with Jamie, who was still glowering at them both without the slightest attempt to look pleasant. After visibly swallowing hard, the young man bade them good-bye and made a hasty retreat toward the door. A huffy-looking Cordelia was waiting for him just beyond the doorway in the hall. Emmeline watched him follow the stiff-spined woman into the foyer and out of sight.

Emmeline turned back to Jamie, wondering if allowing Derian Cadman to stay even those few minutes had been the height of stupidity. Never mind that Jamie had always told his three daughters to forgive with a ready heart, seventy times seven if necessary. And her mother had always added to the admonition some lines from Shelley, making her daughters recite the words back to her:

> To suffer woes which Hope thinks infinite;
> To forgive wrongs darker than death or night;
> This, like glory, is to be
> Good, great and joyous, beautiful and free.

Looking into her father's stormy face made Emmeline think her choice to forgive Mr. Cadman had been anything but beautiful and free. She sighed and attempted to soften his anger by smiling at him.

"It took every ounce of determination," he said, his words clipped, "to keep from challenging Mr. Cadman to a duel on this spot. Only the image of your mother's imploring face stopped me." He frowned, ignoring Emmeline's smile. "And I must say, if she'd been here..." He paused. "By the way, where *is* your mother?"

"She's volunteering at the hospital. Quilting, I believe," Emmeline reminded him. "It's Tuesday, her usual day."

Jamie rushed on as though he hadn't heard her. "As I was saying, surely she would have thrown the rogue from the house herself had she been here."

Never in her wildest dreams had Emmeline supposed she would have a conversation with Jamie about her mother throwing a rogue from their house. Worse, calling a man to a duel over her honor. It struck her as so preposterous that it was funny. Imagine! Emmeline Amity Callahan, plain as a church mouse, Washington's most talked about spinster. And now, her honor was at the center of talk of a duel. Biting her lip, she fought a sudden urge to giggle.

She blinked up at him. "A duel? You can't be serious, Father."

"I am completely serious." He drew in a deep breath as if praying for patience with her. "The man toyed with you. If I must call him to a duel to teach him a lesson, by dickens, I'll do it! President's nephew or not!"

She clamped her lips together even tighter to keep her giggles to herself. Her eyes teared with the effort.

Jamie's expression finally softened. "Please, Emma, tell me how I can make some sense of this rogue's visit."

"Father…" she began, then sighed. "He came to apologize. There was something about his manner that spoke the truth. It's hard to put my finger on, but…" She sighed again. "Well, you and Mother have often spoken of forgiveness. When I was a little girl you said a heart should drum forgiveness with every beat, that it should come to a person as easy as breathing, that—"

Jamie held up a hand for her to stop, a smile twitching the corner of his mouth. "Truly, all I wanted to know was what prompted you to allow Mr. Cadman to speak with you again." After studying her for a moment, he guided her to the chintz couch, and they sat. He removed his eyeglasses and rubbed his eyes. "Let's ring for tea. Something tells me this tale may take awhile."

Emmeline saw the wisdom in waiting, in letting her father's anger be doused by her cheerful countenance. So she guided the conversation to anything but Mr. Cadman while they awaited tea.

Cordelia wheeled in the teacart, sterling tea service on top, with plates of teacakes and finger sandwiches to either side of the pot. She pulled the bone china cups from the shelf beneath and poured a cup for Emmeline, then another for Jamie before leaving the room.

"Now, then," Jamie said after staring into his tea for a moment. "Tell me about Mr. Cadman's visit."

Emmeline began to speak but then stopped. She realized her feelings had little to do with Derian Cadman—they ran deeper than a little incident at a ball or a little flirting with a handsome Harvard man. They had to do with who Emmeline was in her deepest part. She set her cup down and walked to the window, pulled back a lace panel, and stared out at the snow for a few minutes. She began to speak without turning. "You can't know what it feels like to watch everyone else leave for social appointments. To watch my sisters dress for balls, then step into carriages and ride off laughing and chattering, an aura of gaiety following them like a cloud."

She turned from the window and walked across the room and settled beside Jamie again. "Most of the time I don't care a fig about beaus and soirees or gallivanting about Washington with a handsome escort in a carriage drawn by high-stepping grays." She fell silent a moment. "Then there are those other moments when I care a lot more than a single fig." She smiled. "Or several figs to be precise. I suppose today's surprise visit by Mr. Cadman brought one of those moments to mind."

Jamie reached for her hand. "I assumed you simply turned down offers from beaus. Turned them down because the young men weren't up to your standards."

It touched her that her father thought her old-maid status was her choice. Or he pretended it was. She swallowed the sting in her throat. "No one ever asked me, Father," she said, looking away from him.

"Until Mr. Cadman came waltzing into your life, full of lies and trickery."

She turned again to see Jamie's jaw working. She feared he might challenge Derian should he enter the doorway right then. "It's all right, Father. I sensed Mr. Cadman was sorry for the prank."

Jamie nodded without answering. After a moment he stood and walked to the fireplace, then turned to face her. He still held his teacup in his hand. "Sometimes I think you've got a purer heart, Emma, than anyone in the family." He gave her a gentle smile. "It takes more strength to forgive than it does to harbor bitterness and anger. And right now, that's the only emotion I can conjure up toward the man."

She rose to stand beside him. "You're right about Mr. Cadman behaving abysmally. But he also is genuinely distressed over what he did. I see no reason not to forgive him." She drew in a deep breath, watching Jamie's face. "I see no reason not to see him again."

Jamie's teacup rattled in the saucer as he set it down hard. "To do what?"

"See him again." She tilted her chin upward. "He's asked to come calling."

"Calling?" Jamie croaked.

"Calling."

"And you said yes?"

"I see no harm in spending time with him." She lifted her chin higher. "I would like to know what it feels like—just once—to have a young man come calling for me. For me, not my sisters. Just for me."

Jamie's jaw was working again, and his expression was as dark as the storm clouds outside. "You know how your mother and I feel about him. You have forgiven him, which is admirable, but that doesn't mean you should forget what he did."

"I'm not a child anymore, Father. I'm far beyond what's considered a marriageable age. Please, Father, I may never get another chance." She met his gaze with a pleading look of her own.

Jamie stared at her. Then quite suddenly the corners of his mouth began to twitch. "Ah, my little Emma. You're so like me." He threw back his head and laughed out loud. He led her back across the room, and they sat together on the couch again. Jamie crossed his leg, his ankle on his knee, and turned toward her. "Sometimes I think you're more like me than either Glenna or Hazel ever could be." He chuckled again.

"I am?" She felt a flush of pleasure spread over her face. Jamie had never been lavish with praise for any of his daughters. So when he did compliment her, she knew his words weren't spoken lightly.

"I've trusted your judgment from the moment you took over my correspondence. Through the years I've valued your opinions on everything from foreign policy to voting on bills that Congress is considering."

Her eyes widened. "You have?" He'd never said much one way or the other when she spouted off about this bill or that law. He always listened with a great deal of respect, but she'd assumed he was merely being polite.

"The point I'm making is, why should I disregard your opinion now? I may not agree with you in your assessment of Mr. Cadman's sincerity. But I can't disregard your opinion."

For a moment Emmeline simply stared at her father. He'd paid her the highest compliment ever, and she didn't know whether to laugh or cry or hug him or continue to sit there and blink at him.

Jamie seemed to sense her astonishment and laughed again, shaking his head. "As to why you're like me, Emma, I'll say this. You are as stubborn as the day is long. You see life and people a certain way, and no matter what anyone says, you follow your heart."

"Thank you." Emmeline swallowed hard. "I think."

He settled back against the chintz couch and studied her thoughtfully. Finally, he went on, "I stopped by my study before coming here. I found the letter from California. I read through it, and I think you'll be happy with its contents." He slipped it from the inside pocket of his jacket, unfolded it, and before Emmeline could say a word, he cleared his throat and began to read aloud.

Dear Ones,
I am very pleased to hear that your sweet Emmeline is interested in coming to California. Your letter arrived at an opportune time.

The hacienda is too much for one old woman to handle, even with the few servants who remain. Spence and Aislin visit as often as they can, but even with their watchful care, I find it too cumbersome a responsibility for me.

I have already spoken to your brother about my plan and have received his blessings. And my hope is this, son. I have a hankering to see my acreage covered with orange trees.

Orange trees? Emmeline grinned, but Jamie, obviously absorbed in the letter, read on.

Yes, and before you think me daft, let me explain. All of Riverview, it seems, is considering planting these beautiful, fragrant trees. Son, you would not recognize the land of your childhood. Already, evenly spaced rows of trees dot the landscape.

They are glorious! In spring the perfume of the blossoms hangs like a mist over the land, and from a distance, the froth of the flowers bears the appearance of the purest, whitest snow.

And not only that, the fruit is producing small fortunes for those willing to work hard and raise the trees with the love and care one might give her children.

Emmeline's grin widened. *Her* children? She suspected Grandmother Sara used the feminine pronoun with a purpose.

Jamie continued.

The orange varieties come from exotic places around the world. Even their names speak of romance. There are the Mediterranean Sweet and the Paperrind St. Michael, the dozens of other varieties from Australia, Hawaii, and even hothouses in England.

Emmeline sat forward, taking it all in, imagining such a variety of sweet and rare fruit, imagining the balmy climate in California that could support such exotic crops.

Recently, at a dinner party, a Mrs. Tibbets of Riverview told me about a new variety of orange from Brazil. It is named for the region from which it comes, the Bahia.

It is a large, winter orange, and seedless, of all things! It is a brilliant color, standing out from other varieties even at a distance.

I have done a lot of thinking about the Bahia and its suitability for the mild California climate. I believe it will be a perfect marriage of fruit and balmy weather!

Last year a crop of Paperrind St. Michael oranges from a small sixty-acre grove sold for $80,000. The seedless Bahias are expected to bring in twice that. Irrigation will dictate how many trees our land will support, but conservatively, we could farm three times that acreage. This means that once the trees are mature and bearing fruit, our crop yield could bring in as much as $240,000.

But this is not a plan without risk. The tree can propagate only through budding the trunks of mature trees. There are so few Bahias in California at this time that budding great numbers of them here is not feasible. The new seedlings would need to be brought from Washington, D.C., where they are being imported from Brazil. It could take months to gather enough to plant a successful first crop.

Jamie looked at Emmeline over the top of the page and smiled at her expectantly. She leaned forward almost afraid to breathe as he began to read again.

Son, my plan is this, and I hope you will agree. I've thought hard about which of my grandchildren to leave this land to. Spence's son will be receiving an inheritance of his own someday soon, and your Glenna and Hazel, from what you've written, are caught in a whirl of activities in Washington. The very fact that Emmeline has asked to come to California tells me I have chosen wisely.

Though she is not related by blood, she is as much my grandchild as any of the others. And there's something about her spirit that I recognize. I saw it even during her one childhood visit. I believe I'm not wrong in thinking I shall see it again.

Emmeline thought she might burst with glorious anticipation if Jamie didn't read faster.

But this gift comes with strings attached. I know nothing of Emmeline's business mind, and I do not want to see my land come to any kind of ruin. So I propose—and I hope she will accept—that she be given a trial period of three years to make a go of it. It will take that time for the first crop to mature and yield a small profit.

If her business sense is sound, she will be challenged by my proposal. I also feel she will be successful.

Emmeline swallowed her desire to shout with joy. Instead she impatiently nibbled her bottom lip and waited for him to continue.

Jamie read silently for a moment, his face becoming serious.

"What is it?" she finally managed. "Is there more?"

He nodded absently and turned the paper over to read the next page.

"Tell me. What else?"

He looked up at her. "My mother told you all the positive things about this venture first. Next she's detailing the problems you'll encounter."

She tilted her face upward, her hands moist, her heart thudding with excitement. "Problems are merely obstacles to overcome." She grinned at him and clasped her hands together to keep them from shaking.

"She says that you'll be given a stipend that you must live within while running the rancho. You will need to keep a strict accounting and send a full report to her once a month. She plans to live in a small house on Spence's property—that's a few days' ride by horseback."

"That's understandable. The stipend and accounting, I mean."

"There will be no household staff. You will run the household yourself. She also mentioned that you may need to hire a crew to help plant, weed, and pick once the crop is ready."

So far, Emmeline thought she could manage. She took a deep breath. "That doesn't sound too hard. Go on."

"There is one major difficulty." Jamie placed the letter on his desk and folded his hands over it.

"And that is…?"

"I know the land well, and this difficulty may be your single insurmountable obstacle."

She leaned forward, resting her elbows on the table. "Nothing is insurmountable."

He chuckled. "It's the water. California is known for its years of sudden drought. Sudden and long lasting. As long as there are no drought conditions, you'll have no water worries. However, if a drought should come—and you can be certain it will—water rights will become important."

"You're saying, then, the water rights might be my insurmountable problem?"

He studied her face. "There's long been a hint of dispute between my family and the Byrnes."

"Your brother married a Byrne. Surely there's no bad blood between the families now."

"Not now. But there were problems in the past."

"What do you mean?" Emmeline frowned.

He steepled his fingers. "Bad blood between my father and Mac-Quaid Byrne. I suspect that Spence knows the details, though he's kept them to himself. Out of respect for our father, I think. I doubt that even MacQuaid Byrne knows the full treachery of my father."

"And water rights are involved in this 'bad blood'?"

"Indirectly. When the new dam was built on the San Jacinto River, somehow the fork going to my mother's rancho was cut off. The only water flowing into the Big Valley is on the Byrne property. Flows right through Rancho de la Paloma."

"But the families joined forces when Spence and Aislin married." She leaned forward, fascinated by the change in her father's face at the mention of the two names.

For an instant, a wistfulness stole into his expression. "Yes, my brother, Spence, married my sweetheart, Aislin Byrne."

"Your sweetheart?" She nearly choked. That was the last thing she expected to hear.

"I must add quickly, before you get the wrong idea, that he married Aislin with my complete blessing." He laughed lightly. "Ah, yes, he did." Jamie turned to gaze out at the falling snow, a faraway look on his face. The clock ticked on the mantel for a full minute before he spoke again. "But I digress. Let's see, where were we?"

"About the water rights."

"Yes, the water rights." Surprisingly, he laughed again. "It seems that my mother and the Byrnes—MacQuaid and Camila—have had several months of discussion about turning over the ranchos to a new generation." The lines around his eyes crinkled. "I have a suspicion as to what's been decided for Rancho de la Paloma, but I will leave that to your discovery."

"Not a hint, Father?"

He seemed to be enjoying some private joke. "Not a hint, Emma." The lines around his eyes showed his amusement as he skimmed through the letter's closing lines. Then, folding the pages, he tucked them back into his pocket. "I will say this. It will take every bit of grit and passion you've got to overcome one final hurdle."

"What hurdle?" She was truly curious, though unafraid.

"You'll see, Emma. You'll soon see."

Emmeline stood to pour them each more tea. "Hurdle or not, I shall immediately set about learning where to order my seedlings." Her heart thrilled at the sound of it. "My seedlings," she repeated. "My hundreds and thousands of Bahia seedlings, those we shall import from Brazil." Though it made her impatient when she figured how many months it would take to gather her seedlings all the way from South America and take them to California.

"It's all up to you now, Emma. I shall write my mother and tell her you've accepted her challenge."

She sat a little taller, grinning. "I shall write her myself, Father."

"There is one more thing…" he began.

Emmeline frowned, wondering if it was more news from Sara about what to expect in California, perhaps this time having to do with floods, fires, or windstorms, she speculated. "What is it?" she sighed. Or perhaps he was about to indeed tell her about the hurdle he thought was so amusing.

Jamie was watching her with a mix of merriment and admiration. "Emma, I've never been prouder of you than I am this minute."

The following morning, there was a light tapping at the library door. Emmeline stood from where she had been sitting near the fireplace, poring over books on horticulture and California's Mediterranean climate, and went to the door.

Cordelia's eyes were wide with worry. "Miss Emmeline, child, that Mister Cadman is here again to see you. Should I tell him you're unavailable right now?"

Emmeline smiled. She'd wondered if Mr. Cadman might return. "No, you may show him in."

"But Senator Dearbourne, just yesterday he was a-huffin' and a-puffin' sayin' this man wasn't welcome here—"

"My father and I spoke about Mr. Cadman. He's leaving the decision to see him up to me."

Cordelia adopted the huffy, scowling look that had terrified Emmeline through her childhood years. It was only after she was grown that she understood the woman's gruff demeanor was directly related to her love for the senator's daughters. "But the senator said yesterday morning at breakfast," Cordelia said, "directly to your sweet mama, that if Mister Cadman sets one foot in this house—"

Emmeline broke in with a chuckle. "Tell Mr. Cadman, please, Cordelia, that I'll see him here in the library."

Cordelia shook her head slowly, showing her disapproval. "Yes, Miss Emmeline."

Emmeline smoothed her skirt and moved to stand by the fireplace. A fire crackled and popped, and she held out her hands to warm them. She turned when another knock sounded at the door.

"Here the man is," Cordelia said pointedly, then nodded toward him with a scowl.

Derian Cadman didn't seem to notice the maid's rude dismissal, but walked confidently into the room toward Emmeline. He was dressed in his riding clothes and boots. He carried a crop in his hand with casual grace.

His smile seemed genuine, and she returned it as he walked closer. He reached for her hands, and she let him hold them. "You look radiant this morning, Emmeline."

She had taken greater pains than usual with her hair when she dressed, pulling it back into a soft knot at the neck. Blushing at the compliment, she pushed up her spectacles and smoothed her skirt again.

"I know this is presumptuous of me after your response to my request yesterday, but might you be free to go riding?" He glanced toward the window. "The snow has stopped, and the skies appear to be clearing." Turning again, he smiled into her eyes. "I can't think of anything I would rather do. Or anyone I would rather do it with."

Emmeline considered the invitation for a moment, wondering still if he could be trusted. "All right," she finally said. "I'll meet you out by the stables." She looked down at her skirt. "I'll need to change, of course."

He grinned and tapped the riding crop lightly to his forehead in a salute. "Of course. I'll see you there."

A few minutes after Derian Cadman left the library, Cordelia returned. She had obviously been eavesdropping. "Missus Dearbourne and the senator have gone into town," she announced, her look of disapproval more pronounced than ever. "Didn't say when they'd be back. You won't be able to ask their permission to go riding with Mister Cadman."

"I don't need their permission, Cordelia." Emmeline turned to leave the parlor.

"That Mister Cadman took his horse around to the stables."

"Yes, I'm aware of that."

"You still planning to ride with him? I think you need to talk to your mama and papa about leaving this house with him unescorted."

No one in the family had ever been successful at keeping a secret from Cordelia. It was no use to try now. Emmeline let out a small sigh. "Yes, I'm planning to ride with him. And no, I don't plan to wait for permission from anybody."

Cordelia made a tsk-tsking sound and shrugged her big shoulders. Then, turning her back on Emmeline, she went back to dusting the tall porcelain figurines that graced the mantel, humming loudly to herself.

Emmeline turned toward the foyer and ascended the stairs, her heart light. She was going riding with a young man. *Merciful heavens!* She enjoyed the thought.

She hurried toward her suite of rooms at the end of the hall, passing Glenna's and Hazel's rooms along the way. When she heard both girls' voices, she stopped and tapped on Glenna's door. A musical voice called out for her to enter.

Her sisters were seated on the tapestry window seat, looking out toward the stables. Glenna looked up as Emmeline stepped closer. "Did you know that Derian Cadman just headed into our stables? He was leading his horse, of all things! Can you imagine such presumptuous gall?" There was awe in her voice. "I thought he wasn't allowed on our property. There are rumors flying around town that Papa spoke of challenging him to a duel for humiliating you."

Hazel's eyes were round with awe. "Duels are illegal, you know. I've heard that such a thing could land Papa in jail…" Her voice dropped to a whisper. "Or worse. He could be killed."

"Or kill Mister Cadman," Glenna added.

"First of all," Emmeline said, amused, "Father isn't about to challenge him to a duel. And second of all, I'm about to go riding with him. I've discussed it with Father, and he's trusting me to make the right decision."

Glenna and Hazel looked unconvinced. "Even if you're right about Papa, you would still be willing to accompany Mr. Cadman in public after all the rumors about you two?" Hazel asked, her golden curls bouncing with emphasis.

"Yes. Actually, I would. I don't care a fig about what people think of me." Emmeline tilted her head and shrugged as if it were the most natural thing in the world. "And if you think about it, if those rumors have done so much harm already, how can it be any more harmful to my reputation to ride with him now?"

"But you've always been the one with the level head," Hazel said. "This just, well, it just doesn't seem like you."

"Or proper," Glenna added solemnly. "It just doesn't seem proper."

Emmeline fought the urge to laugh at these beautiful social butterflies and their concern for their spinster sister. "Perhaps for once in my life, I'd like to try something that is completely unlike me."

Her sisters looked too stunned for words. Emmeline laughed, closing the door behind her, and headed to her room to change.

A few minutes later, Derian met her at the door to the stables, and her heart was warmed by his surprised look of admiration as she headed toward him in her black velvet and tweed riding habit. She smiled up at him, filled with a new confidence she hadn't experienced before.

"I've asked your stable boy to saddle your usual horse."

"That would be Dolly. Thank you." She strode past him into the stables.

Charlie had nearly finished buckling the tack, and he turned toward her with a smile. He stood back while she mounted. She flushed slightly as she looked down to meet another look of frank admiration from Derian.

He walked beside Dolly as they headed back out the door, then mounted his gelding and let the animal take the lead.

Derian had a proud set to his shoulders as he pressed his horse to a smart canter. As Emmeline tapped her heels into Dolly's sides, she wondered again if she'd been right to forgive this man who had laughed at her and caused her pain. She pondered the question as Dolly followed the gelding down the winding road toward the river trail.

Any ghost of apprehension that remained she merely attributed to an old maid's inexperience with courting. She brushed the worries away as easily as she flicked from her jacket the snow that had sifted from the branches overhead.

What could it hurt to know that just once in her life a handsome young man desired her company?

Derian craned in the saddle and grinned at her.

She waved, at the same time urging Dolly to move closer. What harm could come from a simple ride on a beautiful snow-covered trail?

FIVE

Leaning forward in the saddle, Emmeline followed Derian along the road leading to the river. New-fallen snow covered the rolling hills in the distance and lined the slender branches of the leafless maples that flanked the road, causing them to stand out in stark relief against a dark and threatening sky. The earlier promise of clearing had disappeared as the thin winter sun dipped behind the clouds, then out again. A sharp wind from the river kicked up, blowing the snow into shallow drifts.

Dolly, surefooted and sturdy, followed Derian's gelding to a brisk canter. Emmeline thrilled to the mare's pounding rhythm, the comfort of being one with her horse. She closed her eyes, letting the cold wind whip her hair and sting her cheeks.

After a few minutes, Dolly pulled up even with the other horse, then, moving still faster, soared by Derian to a full body-length ahead.

Derian caught up with her. She laughed out loud and dug her heels into the mare's flanks once more. The two horses thundered side by side, puffs of steam escaping their nostrils, clods of broken snow flying out behind.

By the time they reached the river, a light snow was falling. They slowed their mounts, then drew to a halt. Emmeline lifted her face and closed her eyes, letting the snowflakes dust her cheeks. When she opened her eyes, she realized that her spectacles were dotted with icy spots. Shrugging, she removed them and stuck them in her pocket. She was always surprised at how well she could see without them. But then, she mostly wore them because old Doctor McBean back in Kentucky told her parents that eyeglasses would help her headaches. The same headaches that began when Jamie announced that the family was moving away from the only home she'd known.

Derian, still in the saddle, was studying her, a look of amusement on his face. "Who could have predicted our day would turn out like this?" He held his gloved hands outward and shrugged.

She grinned. Indeed, who could have predicted *he* would turn out like this?

He let the gelding take the lead again, and Emmeline followed. The trail wound along the bank of the partially frozen river, barely visible through the snow-laden branches of a copse of evergreens.

The horses loped along, and now the wind kicked up, causing the snow to whirl against their faces. Derian halted and craned in the saddle.

Emmeline reined Dolly to a standstill beside the gelding.

"Let's ride to the river." He moved his horse a few steps closer and looked out toward the river. "I'd like to show you something—there, near the bridge."

She followed his gaze to a short stone bridge arching over a tributary to the Potomac, dull and gray in the frozen stillness.

"It's a place I found when I was a child. My parents didn't visit Washington often, but when they did, I was left to amuse myself. We stayed not far from here, and I rode along this river often."

Dolly danced sideways, and Emmeline patted the horse's neck. "All right, lead the way."

He reined his horse around and headed for the river. The snowfall was heavier, but Derian stayed within her range of vision as they left the trail. She looked back only once, realizing that as quickly as the two horses made their hoofprints in the snow, they were covered.

The bridge had nearly disappeared in the curtain of falling snow, so when it suddenly appeared, she felt relieved that they hadn't gotten lost. Derian halted the gelding and dismounted, then strode across the few feet that separated them to help Emmeline slide off Dolly's saddle.

"Over here," he said, circling his arm around her. He helped her along a hidden trail, leading to the crumbling bridge. Snow had caught on the stones, a stark outline against the dark granite. "This structure is at least a hundred years old. Some say it might have been built by Thomas Jefferson." He helped her climb up to stand on it. "Can't be proven though."

They reached the center of the bridge, and he turned her with his arm to look back toward the city. "On a clear day," he said, sounding disappointed, "you can see the Capitol building through the trees." He searched the skies. "I was hoping there might be the slightest clearing of this snow—just enough for you to see. For me to see it before I leave."

She assumed he meant that he was returning to Harvard. She followed his gaze, but a mix of snow-laden trees, white skies, and flurries blocked her view.

"Let's move farther back," he said, and laughed as they stepped backward a few feet. "Maybe here, just maybe…" his voice trailed as he studied the skies once again.

"I'm certain you've brought me here to see a spectacular sight." Emmeline laughed lightly to cover her growing nervousness. "But perhaps we should return when the skies are clear."

"Yes," he said without conviction, then nodded. "Perhaps."

He took her arm to head back to the horses. They walked in the dead silence of the falling snow for a few minutes, then he spoke again. "Not many women would have trailed along with me today in this blizzard, Emmeline."

She stopped and smiled up at him, enjoying the sound of her given name.

He held Dolly's reins so Emmeline could mount. She stepped into the stirrup and swung a leg over the saddle. Dolly danced a bit, and she patted the horse's neck while studying Derian's face. His demeanor had changed since they'd first left the stables. He seemed serious, almost somber. It was as if some kind of foreboding had overtaken him, though he was obviously trying to hide it from her. She shivered.

"I may not see you again," he said suddenly, regret in his eyes as he looked up at her.

"You are leaving soon for school?"

He looked thoughtful, and for a moment didn't answer. Finally he said, "Some of the things I told you that night in December were true."

She frowned, trying to remember all he'd said, to understand what he was leading to. And especially how it related to her not seeing him again.

"I told you how I'd disappointed my father at Choate." He mounted the gelding and moved the horse to stand beside hers.

"I remember." She nudged Dolly to a slow walk to keep pace.

"It wasn't the first *or* last time I've disappointed him. The latest in a long list is the realization that I'm not cut out for reading law."

She looked at him sharply. "Isn't it a bit late to discover that?"

The horses walked a few steps through the snow before he answered. "I've failed the last several exams. It's only a matter of time before my parents discover my shame." He laughed bitterly. "It's only because of their money that Harvard hasn't sent me packing."

She frowned, trying to understand what he was telling her. "You're leaving school, then?"

He stared into the snow flurries in front of them. "You have no idea the expectations," he finally said, shaking his head. "There really is no choice."

"Will you tell your family?"

"I'm not certain what I'll do. Only that I can't return to school." He sighed.

She halted Dolly. "Where will you go?"

He shrugged and kept riding, his back to her.

She nudged Dolly to move forward again until they were even with the gelding. She reached for Derian's reins and drew his horse to a halt beside hers. "Something tells me you could offer the world much more than this enormous case of self-pity."

He gave her a sharp look as if her words were the last he expected to hear. Then he laughed, shaking his head.

"All I hear you talking about is what you can't do…" She rushed on, "What about what you can do?"

"Ah, if only life could be that simple."

"Life is never simple, Derian," she countered. "But don't let the expectations of others bury you."

He laughed bitterly. "As if you would know."

She winced. "I may not be expected to graduate with honors from Harvard Law School, but there have been other expectations…" Her voice trailed off.

He reached for her hand. "I'm sorry. That was stupid of me. I didn't mean anything by it."

She pulled back her hand. "Don't you have a dream to follow? Something you've always thought might be deep in your soul, dying to get out?"

"Dying to get out," he mused, then laughed, his expression dark. "I've been too busy failing at everything to notice."

They rode on for a few minutes in silence. "I'm heading to California," she announced after a time, then waited to see his reaction. "A new start."

He looked at her, frowning. "When?"

"Not for some time, actually." She told him about the Big Valley and her chance to prove herself through Grandmother Sara's challenge, about the Bahias in Brazil and her immersion into horticulture. She chattered on, then suddenly stopped, realizing that she must surely be boring the young man beyond tears. "I'm so sorry," she said. "You should have stopped me."

He laughed, and his expression brightened. "I admire your gumption," he said. "I only wish I had the opportunity—no, more than that—I only wish I had the *courage* to begin again. On my own. Without anyone looking over my shoulder." The gelding snorted and danced a bit sideways, shaking his head. He reached across the space between them and took her gloved hand in his. "Thank you for showing me a bit of your courage, Emmeline."

He didn't release her hand. "I hope we meet again someday."

She nodded. "I hope so too."

She pulled back her hand, and a moment later they were again riding through the snow in silence. They rode onto the Dearbourne estate and around the house to the stables. At the doorway, Derian gave her a dazzling smile, touched his riding crop to his forehead, and wheeled the gelding around.

She watched him head down the road into the falling snow.

The following day at noon, she was still pondering the strange adventure with Derian Cadman, when Jamie sent word for her to join him in the library.

Even before she settled into the tapestry chair across from him, she could see the deep worry lines in his expression, the hunched angle of his shoulders. She leaned forward in alarm. "What is it?" He stared at her for several seconds in silence. "Father, what is it?" she repeated.

"Did you go riding with Derian Cadman yesterday?"

She looked heavenward, almost relieved. So that was it. The word had gotten back to Jamie, and he was offended that she hadn't mentioned it. She sighed deeply.

"Yes, I did."

Jamie continued to stare at her. "What time?"

"It was in the morning. You and mother were in town—"

He broke in before she could finish. "And you returned together?"

She hesitated. There was something more to Jamie's question than idle curiosity about her ride with a man he disliked. "I left him at the stables. We'd ridden to the river together, then parted here on our estate."

"Did anyone see him with you?"

"That's a strange question. I'm not sure. We rode to the old bridge. He wanted to show me something he'd discovered when he was a boy." She smoothed her skirt, then pushed up her eyeglasses and peered through them at Jamie's face.

"The police came by this morning. Apparently Mr. Cadman didn't return home last night, so a friend of his went looking for him. Found his horse down by the river."

Emmeline leaned forward. "He must have returned there after he left me at the stables." She paused. "While we were together he spoke of wanting to leave school, leave his home, parents—everything—behind. Perhaps that was what he decided to do."

Jamie's scowl deepened. "Near where they found Derian's horse, there were two sets of footprints in the snow. And on the bridge. Broken ice in the river where someone fell—or was pushed—from the bridge."

Emmeline gasped and put her hand to her mouth. "No!"

"That's why I need to know, Emma, if anyone saw you two leave the bridge after your ride."

"No," she whispered. "But it was snowing so hard after we left, there couldn't have been any footprints at all."

"But you can't prove it?"

She shook her head wordlessly.

"Honey, I have to tell you—Mr. Cadman's friend is already making blatant accusations."

"About me?" The thought was almost laughable, but her father's gray and haggard face told her he was taking this very seriously.

"He began by accusing me."

"You?"

"My careless words about a duel apparently have been overheard."

Tears filled her eyes, and she attempted to brush them away. "Oh, Father!"

Jamie pushed himself to standing and walked slowly to the window. He looked out at the whirling snow. He turned again to her. "I told him where I was during the time in question. There are witnesses to my whereabouts."

"Which leaves me."

Jamie nodded. "You have nothing to fear. I'm certain someone from the house must have seen Mr. Cadman escort you home from your ride."

"I don't care a fig about myself or my reputation, Father. I've done nothing wrong. The truth will come out. I care about the family, though. And I care about next year's election. You may find it a difficult win if I'm by your side, accused of murder."

Jamie gave her a sad smile. "You know I believe in you, and there's never been a time I haven't been proud for you to be there. I don't care what the gossipmongers conjure up this time. Even if I lose the election."

"There's no substance to the gossip because a body won't be found. And not because it's washed out to sea. I'm certain of it." She leaned forward. "I tell you, Father, Mr. Cadman couldn't bear the pressure a moment longer."

"Pressure about what?"

"I don't feel at liberty to say."

"You may be called on to say, Emma. If charges are brought against you."

"Do you really think they would arrest me? There isn't even proof that a crime was committed. For all we know someone threw a rock through the ice…"

"Well, it's obvious that we need to locate Mr. Cadman to quell these suspicions—especially after me shooting off my mouth about dueling. The first thing we need to do is hire a private detective to find him."

"And if we don't find him?" Emmeline's nerves seemed to calm with the formation of a plan. At least they were doing something, instead of waiting for the police to come take her away.

"Then the authorities are going to have to find evidence that a crime occurred and that you had some part in it—and that they won't find. In the meantime we need to live our lives as best we can."

She could see the worried concern in Jamie's eyes. She smiled dimly and said, "All will be well, Father. The truth is with us."

"I plan to sail to Brazil on the first ship sailing south."

Jamie looked up sharply. "Brazil?"

"Bahia, Brazil, to be exact. I've been sitting around here staring at the walls these past two weeks," Emmeline began to explain.

"You're right," Jamie put in. "The situation with Cadman has turned up nothing. You may as well get on with your life. Anyway, if something comes up, your mother and I will be in contact with you."

"But I am concerned about you...about what my leaving the country will do to you...the rumors about my guilt that will no doubt follow."

"Gossips will gossip." Jamie smiled at her. "I'm tired of trying to please everyone anyway. What matters is that we please God and speak the truth. If people want to believe lies, they'll believe them no matter what." He reached for her hand and gave it a squeeze, then smiled at her with approval. "Now let's talk about Brazil..."

He crossed to his desk and sat behind it. "But first, let's get your mother in here. I would love to know what she thinks about all this." He rang for Cordelia.

She settled back in her chair to await her mother's arrival. Hallie joined them within minutes, and the three began to plan the trip in earnest. By dusk, Jamie had sent for an aide to book passage out of Annapolis, found a government horticulturist who with his wife would accompany Emmeline, and sent a message to his banker to wire funds to Brazil when the time came to buy the Bahia orange seedlings.

⊰⊱

Three weeks later, Emmeline and Gertie stood on the Annapolis dock, their trunks and valises piled by them. Her mother and father embraced them both, then each of her sisters took their turn, curls bobbing, tears streaming down their faces.

Derian Cadman was still missing, but his parents had suddenly dropped the investigation into his disappearance. There was no legal reason Emmeline couldn't leave the country. But she and her father had been right about one thing. The gossipmongers had never had such entertainment to bandy about. The spinster daughter of Washington's favorite Senator was not leaving town—and the country—quietly. Nearly every tongue in Washington was still wagging about her scandalous behavior.

Emmeline laughed to consider it.

"Godspeed, my sweet Emma," her mother said, gathering her once more into her arms.

Tears filled Emmeline's eyes. "I'll soon be home." Even as she said the words, she knew it would be months before they would meet again.

Jamie took her hands in his. "My sweet little Emma, every breath we take will be a prayer for your safety."

Gertie stepped forward, drawing herself up to her full height, barely reaching Jamie's shoulder. "I'll take good care of her. Now don't you worry."

Jamie grinned. "If anyone can do it, you can, Gert!" He bent down to give her a kiss on the cheek. "You took care of me on that prairie schooner years ago!"

Aunt Gertie laughed and patted him on the cheek. "And you just watch. I'll be carin' for you and your family for years to come."

Touched, Emmeline slipped her arm around the frail old woman, wanting to hold her close so that she would never leave them. "Aunt Gertie always keeps her word," she said to her parents.

An hour later, the ship set sail and pulled away from port. Emmeline stood on the deck, a brisk winter wind in her face, and watched her family until they disappeared and only the vast gray ocean remained.

Six

Quaid Dearbourne rode to the top of the rise, halted the sorrel, and looked down at the Big Valley. Drenched in sunlight, it looked like liquid gold, pure and priceless. It was framed by a sweep of hills, some the color of wheat, others looking as though they had been painted in shades of purple and green. Dotted with his grandfather's cattle. There were at least a thousand head spread out in twos and threes, some wandering slowly in solitude, others dozing in the sun.

He pulled off his hat, wiped his brow with his sleeve, set it back on his head. Yanking it low, he squinted toward the horizon.

If he used his imagination, he could make out the Rancho de la Paloma hacienda, its adobe walls glinting copper in the sun. He was still grinning when he pressed his heels into the sorrel's flanks and headed down the pass that led into the wide valley below.

His valley. The place he felt more at home, more at peace, than anywhere on earth—even taking into consideration his ma and pa's horse ranch in the Tehachapis. No, this place, the Big Valley, was part of his soul. At least, that was how he had always fancied it. One with the land. Joined somewhere deep in his gut. One with the expanse, the windswept wilderness. One with the wind and the beat of the sun. Just as he'd felt the first time his grandfather pulled him onto his saddle and rode from one end of the valley to the other.

Quaid nudged the sorrel in the flanks, letting the big mare make her way around outcroppings of boulders and scrub pines. The steady thud of her hooves on the trail matched the rhythm in his soul.

When they reached the flat, dry grasslands of the valley, he halted the horse once more and pulled his hat brim low against the slant of the sun. He couldn't get his fill of it. He might as well have been a thirsty man longing for water, he thought with a chuckle. Instead he had been dry in spirit, longing for the wilderness of the Big Valley.

No doubt this place had been fashioned after heaven. What was the newfangled word he had heard describing such a thing? *Blueprint.* That was it—God's design for the finest wilderness that a man could find in all of creation.

Quaid grinned again, and with a bellow of pleasure, he yanked off his hat and waved it at arm's length as he kicked the sorrel to a gallop. The wind lifted his hair, and his shirttails whipped behind him. He bellowed again just for the pure satisfaction of it and rode as fast as the wind, eyes closed, his head facing heavenward.

After a few minutes, he felt sorry for the hard workout he had given the sorrel, so he slowed her and continued at an easy lope for a few more miles across the valley. He purposely skirted the settlements that had sprung to life along the way, especially Riverview with its well-ordered clutter and commotion.

He headed toward an outcropping of black lava stone, urging the sorrel to climb the trail to its peak, some two hundred feet or so from the valley floor. Once there, Quaid halted again, and this time he slid from the saddle and walked through a copse of cottonwood to the edge of the granite shelf.

Below him lay the San Jacinto River, a skinny ribbon of water flowing from a release in the new dam above the valley. It irked him that a man-made structure determined the river's flow. Another sign of developers encroaching on the Big Valley, feeding water for irrigation to farms popping up from Riverview to the ocean like fungi after a rain. Farms. Orange groves with perfectly spaced rows of trees. Ruining God's incredible artwork.

And then there was his latest gripe. Thanks to transplants from the east coast who'd become enamored with the climate, dozens of tuberculosis sanitariums had been built between Riverview and the ocean.

They were now beckoning sickly easterners by the thousands to mild, warm California.

Quaid's stomach twisted with annoyance. *Easterners must be mighty lily-livered to need such a thing as healing in the sunshine.*

He turned his attention to the river again, remembering how it was in his childhood. Before the dam was built, spring rains and melting snows caused the river to rush to the ocean with a roar so loud folks as far off as Riverview couldn't sleep at night. In summer and fall, it trickled then died, only to be reborn when the rains returned.

Now one had a hard time determining which season it was—the river stayed the same, spring, summer, fall, and winter. A tiresome ribbon of water. He let out an irritated sigh. Developers!

He sauntered over to a live oak, leaned against it, and looked out, thinking of the seasons that he had seen come and go in the valley. He fancied them all, he supposed, the clear purple skies of winter, the rain-shrouded springs, the balmy summers with wildflowers growing thicker than his grandmother's Chinese rugs. And fall days like today, when the wild winds and beat of the sun hit a man's face, making him feel more alive than ever before in his life.

A deer soared out of the thicket below him. It was a sight, with its small hooves and ripple of sinew. He worried about its freedom for a few minutes, considering how the farms and health hotels and orange groves had driven the creatures from their habitats. A couple of yearlings appeared and bounded after their mother.

He gloried in their freedom and, as he remounted, wondered if he might see a bear or two ambling along the foothills. This time of year they weren't as careful about hunting in the light of day. Too concerned with fattening up for winter, he supposed, to care about a lone horseman heading through the brush and cactus. Or it could be they were too used to seeing human beings to fear them as they should.

A dangerous thing for bears. Just as it had already been for wolves and cougars.

He pondered the wildlife in the Big Valley as he rode, feeling strangely fearful of its continuing decline in direct proportion to development.

Troubled him more with each visit to Rancho de la Paloma. A half-hour later, still lost in thought, he passed through the tall iron gates and reined the sorrel down the dirt road leading to the rancho.

His cousin Merci Byrne looked up as he rode closer. As usual she was wearing riding clothes—a split skirt that gave the appearance of cowboy chaps, a flannel shirt similar to his, and boots that threatened to swallow her slender legs. Her face wore a rosy glow from the sun. And when she smiled, her nose wrinkled in a way that hid most of her freckles. Seeing that smile was like seeing the sun had risen after a long winter.

She was smiling now, and there was a teasing glint in her eye. That could be dangerous when it came to dealing with Merci Byrne.

"G' morning," he said with a grin as he dismounted.

Of all his cousins, she was his favorite, but also the one who usually brought him the greatest consternation. Always challenging him, making him think, making him so aggravated at times that he'd ride off in a huff without saying good-bye to avoid another spat with her.

"So, what brings you to the ranch?" she asked. Without waiting for him to answer, Merci sauntered to the fence and, crossing one leg across the other at the knee, kicked her boot against the post to rid her sole of packed dirt. "You were here just last week," she said, still looking at her boot.

"You think you own this place?" he called to her backside, then with a sigh, he followed her to the fence. It was no secret they each hoped to inherit the family land.

She gave him a smirk. "Not a laughing matter, Quaid."

He gave her a nod in half-apology and shrugged. "What are you doing here? I thought you were going to help your mother at the school this week."

"I asked you first." The sunlight hit her eyes as she looked up at him, making her irises seem colorless, her red lashes blond.

He shrugged, figuring he would get more out of her if he walked away.

"If you must know," Merci called after him, "I decided I have better things to do with my life than teach Indians how to read."

"Such as?" He didn't turn.

"Such as…" she called, halting in midsentence.

He turned and waited her for her to continue.

Merci's hands were on her hips, thumbs hooked through the belt loops of her skirt, elbows akimbo. Her thicket of fire-hued curls caught the sun.

He shook his head slowly. "So? I'm waiting. What is it that's so all-fired important that you couldn't help out at the school? Which, I might add, I think is a fine occupation for your time. Something you always seem to have too much of."

She glared at him as she sauntered toward him in that way she had, her boot heels making a soft thud on the hard soil with each step.

"Gramps is heading into Riverview to see his lawyer today. Thought I'd ride into town with him."

He looked her up and down. "You've still got cow manure on your boots. I'm sure the folks in Riverview will be impressed."

She shrugged. "So I'll change boots."

"I hope so." He turned again toward the house.

"Wait."

He halted, knowing what she was going to ask.

"Is that why you're here? Did Gramps ask you to go?" Her boots crunched on the packed dirt behind him, and a moment later she was facing him. "Is it?"

"Grandfather summoned me, but he didn't say why. Just wanted me to be here today. He didn't say a word about a trip into Riverview. Did he ask you to go?"

Merci didn't answer, but she turned to look out across the fields of grazing cattle. Her silence gave him the answer he was looking for—their grandfather hadn't asked her either. A breeze lifted some of her wild curls. Merci had more fire in her belly, more spunk than anyone he knew. She also loved the rancho. Since birth, she had lived here with her mother. Rancho de la Paloma was the only home she had ever known.

Too independent for her own good, and if truth be known, too ornery for beaus to put up with longer than a few nights looking at the stars on the porch swing. He supposed it was her beauty that drew them, but her temperament made courting her a challenge.

Merci was walking back to the fence now, and as Quaid looked after her, she hooked one boot heel over the bottom rung and stared toward the mountains in the east. After a moment she placed her forearms on the top rung and let her chin rest on her hands. The slope of her shoulders saddened him—she looked so downhearted.

He headed toward her again, then leaned his back against the fence rail, crossing one boot over the other at the ankle. "Would it make you feel better if I said I didn't know anything about this mysterious summons—or the trip into town, either? And moreover, I really don't care."

She laughed, turned, and leaned against the fence, hooking her elbows over the top rail. "I don't believe you about the 'I don't care' part, but let's talk about the possibilities anyway."

He knew precisely what she was leading to. Only he was too polite to mention them out loud. There wasn't a polite bone in Merci's body, so he let her talk.

She stuck a length of dried grass in her mouth and worked the end of it awhile, her brow knit in thought. "Now, the way I see it, Gregor, Kerr, and Sandy won't ever want to leave Monterey. To come here, I mean, to inherit the rancho lands, should Gramps split it among us all."

"I'm sure Aunt Sybil would prefer they stay in Monterey. Scotty too, though he doesn't say much about it. Maybe because it's expected."

Merci's look was intent. "They must remain there. They're needed."

She was right. Their three cousins were already entrenched in the family sardine business. Gregor captained one of the three fishing boats; Kerr helped in the factory; and Sandy, who had more schooling that his brothers, helped his father with the shipping and accounting. It was doubtful that any of the boys would want anything to do with Rancho de la Paloma.

"That leaves the two of us." She was looking him square in the eye. "Who do you think Gramps will choose?"

He laughed at her intensity. "Probably neither of us, Merci."

She lifted a pale brow. "Or both."

Quaid rolled his eyes. "Now that's a thought! But not a very good one."

She narrowed her eyes in concentration. "But you've got a strike against you."

"What do you mean?"

"You'll inherit your parents' horse ranch in the Tehachapis someday."

"Someday…perhaps."

"But think about it, Quaid. I have nothing." Her words fell out in a rush. "My father was killed before I was born, leaving my mother with nowhere to go—except here." She looked back at the hacienda. "This is my home."

"Our grandparents no doubt will be here for another hundred years. We need to keep in mind that this place is theirs, not yours *or* mine."

She sighed. "I'm not talking about them dying, for heaven's sake. But they keep talking about going north—to live near Scotty and Sybil. They say the rancho is too much to run by themselves."

He stood up taller and frowned at Merci. "When did they say this?"

She tossed her head. "It's no secret. Gramps often brings it up. Says he can't see us through another drought, spring flood, or firestorm. Just doesn't have the strength anymore."

Suddenly his grandfather's summons was making sense. "Maybe he wanted me here so he could talk to me about helping him run the place. It probably has nothing to do with the Riverview lawyer. Or Gramps's will." He turned again toward the house.

"There's something else," Merci persisted.

He couldn't stop an exasperated sigh that fell from between his lips when he glanced back. "There's more?"

She nodded. "Your Grandmother Dearbourne has been here hours on end every day. This started months ago."

"Why didn't you tell me?"

Merci shrugged. "Didn't think much about it till lately."

"They've always enjoyed each other's company. What's different about their spending time together lately?"

"I overheard them talking about giving their grandchildren a challenge—some sort of test of our mettle."

"Test of our what?"

"Mettle, dear cousin. As in guts, grit, fortitude."

"Okay, okay. I get the picture."

"See what we're made of."

He laughed. "That's all?"

"No. More often than not, it's your name and Emmeline Callahan's that I hear bandied about."

Quaid let out a guffaw. "Emmeline Callahan?" He knew she'd been west for one visit back when they were babies. He had no memory of her, but he'd heard plenty, especially that—at least according to his cousins who were as likely as not to embellish whatever they told—she was a plain and snooty spinster. At least that was their judgment after seeing Emma's photograph one Christmas.

Glenna and Hazel were beautiful, and the tilt of their heads said they knew it. Emmeline, on the other hand, with her wire-rimmed eyeglasses, big hat, and high-necked, ruffled blouse, had stared into the camera as though she were facing a firing squad.

"You're sure it was Emmeline being discussed? Why ever would they be talking about her? I mean, where the ranchos are concerned?"

Merci still stood leaning against the fence. There was a smirk on her face as though proud as punch she had finally captured his attention. "From what I've heard, she was involved in some scandal in Washington. Something so hush-hush no one will tell me what it was."

"Maybe it's none of our business."

She ignored his comment. "I overheard Sara telling Gram. But just as they got to the heart of whatever it was, their voices dropped. I couldn't hear the details."

"It's unbecoming to eavesdrop."

Merci stuck her nose in the air. "Not that you're Mister Perfect."

He gave her a brotherly poke of his elbow in the ribs. She stepped daintily out of the way.

"You're just as curious about her as I am."

"I don't know what you're talking about." He let out an exasperated sigh. Again. "I came to see our grandparents, not listen to you prattle about Emmeline's scandalous life in Washington."

"And I didn't say her *life* was scandalous, only that she was rumored to be involved in some Washington scandal."

"If we haven't heard it firsthand, it's only rumor."

Merci shrugged. "If you were guessing, do you think Sara's planning to test someone's mettle with her spread? Maybe give it to Emmeline or one of Emmeline's half sisters?"

A slow grin spread over his face. "Glenna Elise?" He laughed. "I can see it all now—I've heard the girl doesn't have a connecting idea in her brain unless it has to do with soirees, balls, and beaus. No. Definitely not. Sara couldn't possibly give the rancho to Glenna."

"What about Hazel Leigh?"

He laughed again and shook his head. "The last I heard about Hazel, she was flightier than a robin in a birdbath. No. Hazel wouldn't want anything to do with Rancho Dearbourne."

"Then we're back to Emmeline…"

He laughed, picturing again the plain young woman with a demeanor that said she might be shy and difficult at the same time. A rancher? He laughed again at the thought.

She hooked her arm through his as they began to stroll toward the house. "There's something else you haven't considered, my dear cousin," he said.

She glanced up at him.

"My pa and Jamie are loved equally by their mother. Maybe both properties will go to me."

Merci stopped cold and glared into his face.

He enjoyed teasing her. The dangerous glint in her eye never failed to make him laugh. It was a stretch, he admitted, but nonetheless, a wonderful ploy to get her ire up. "Don't tell me you hadn't thought of it?"

But instead of the ire he was expecting, Merci's face turned pale. "I—I hadn't really…" Her voice faltered, and she stared at him for a moment in silence. She swallowed hard and cocked her head. "Not even the cruelest relative in the world would leave a fatherless child homeless."

He saw deep pain in her expression and wanted to reassure her. "No, they wouldn't. I wouldn't."

Together, they walked into the hacienda to look for their grand-parents.

SEVEN

The following morning, Merci was up at dawn. She slipped out of the house and headed to the stables, planning to be on her way before anyone knew she was gone. After she opened Knight's stall, she gently touched the stallion's neck, stroking and rubbing as she whispered to him. Everyone in the family considered the horse a dangerous menace. Even her grandfather, an expert horseman, refused to ride Knight unless he had no other choice.

She rested her face in his mane, breathing in the strangely sweet perfume of hay, stall, and animal. The stallion was as stubborn as she was and half as ornery, she supposed. That was probably why she loved this stunning beauty. Black as velvet, with a gleam on his hide that reminded her of lightning in a midnight sky.

After saddling him, she led him out of the barn. She mounted, and once she was settled on the big horse's back, she nudged his flanks with her heels.

"Come on, Knight. Let's go." Knight took his lead, first walking, then gracefully moving into a lope, finally to a canter. Merci settled into the rhythm of his movement and bent forward, her cheek resting on Knight's mane, her arms wrapped around his neck. She closed her eyes against the sun.

The wind lifted her hair, and she breathed in the morning air, willing away the strange sense of terror that plagued her lately. Terror that her life was about to change in ways she didn't understand.

She stroked Knight's mane absently and squinted into the rising sun as he continued to run. The shadows were still long, and from the shade of a nearby cottonwood, a quail sentinel called out a warning to his covey, which clucked and scattered in a dozen directions as Knight thundered past.

The sun soon struck the dew-damp earth, and the scent of soil and grass filled her senses with the beauty of the morning. She pushed the dark fears from her mind and looked instead to the rise in the distance—the place she headed every morning.

As they drew closer, she reined Knight toward a small hidden trail she had found a few years ago. It pleased her to use an Indian trace that none of her cousins knew about. Perhaps even the few remaining Sobobas had forgotten it existed. The incline was steep, and she slid from Knight's back, leaving the horse to graze beneath a live oak at the foot of the hill.

Merci continued on, gingerly picking her way among the stones, being careful of nettles and burs as she walked to the summit of the small rock-strewn mountain. It was only after she reached the final few feet of trail at the top that she heard voices and realized she was not alone.

She paused, confused.

It was her mother. With a man. She was sitting on a low stone wall, the man standing near her. A Soboba Indian, judging from the awkward way he wore his clothes. And Brighid was staring at him with such loving intensity that Merci suspected that if she had thundered up the trail on Knight, her mother wouldn't have noticed. Their horses grazed in a thicket just beyond.

Frowning, Merci slipped behind the trunk of an oak, almost afraid to breathe. She waited a moment, then crept closer, carefully picking her way around a pile of stones and over a beavertail cactus.

Merci could now make out a few words and phrases. They weren't particularly intimate, but the very idea of her mother meeting a man alone made a pulsing begin in Merci's temple. She was of a mind to march right over and tell her mother about her embarrassment and disapproval.

But before she could take a single step, the man reached for Brighid's hands and drew her to standing. He spoke earnestly, staring into her eyes. Merci glared at the two as he continued speaking in low, earnest tones.

Her mother shook her head in answer to something he said and gently moved away from him. Their voices grew louder.

"I can't," her mother said, shaking her head. "I can't tell her."

Merci frowned. *Tell whom...what?*

"The lie is too entrenched," her mother continued. "It's too late. I can't change the past. I can't undo what's been done. For her sake. Also for mine." Brighid sounded ready to cry.

Merci crept closer. What past was her mother talking about? Losing her father? That had to be it. What other past did her mother have? As long as Merci could remember, her mother had taught the Indian children. She had no other life. Not then. Not now.

Even from this distance Merci could sense that Brighid's eyes had filled with tears. Brighid flicked them away with her fingertips as she sank to the small rock wall again and covered her face with her hands. "You don't know what I went through..."

The Soboba knelt in front of her, then reached for her mother's fingers. He kissed them! Tenderly.

With that, Merci almost leapt from her hiding place. Her knuckles were white where she clutched the small fort wall, holding herself back.

Her mother gazed into his eyes. There was a glow about her that made Merci ill. She clamped her lips together in anger and leaned forward again, listening intently.

"It would break her heart, Songan," her mother was saying. "She is my child. I've always protected her from the truth. I haven't meant to lie. I just wanted to shield her from unnecessary hurt."

The fine hairs on the back of Merci's neck raised. They were talking about *her*. "Go on, Mama," she breathed. "Go on..."

The Indian spoke next. "Her anguish will cut far deeper if she hears the truth from anyone else. You must be the one to tell her." He paused. "Besides, Brighid, she is no longer a child. She is a woman and deserves to know the truth from you. No one else."

"There aren't many who know the truth," her mother said. "I'm certain no one would purposely hurt Merci—by telling her, I mean."

Merci told herself to stay where she was. It took every ounce of determination not to run to her mother and demand an explanation. To her annoyance, the Indian, the intruder, stood next to her. Merci willed him to leave so she could speak to her mother alone.

The rocky ground crunched beneath the man's boots as he stepped toward Brighid. "My darling," he said as he touched Brighid's face with his fingertips.

Merci almost choked. *My darling? My darling?* She considered her mother, Songan, the endearment for a half-minute. *My darling?*

She let out a deep sigh of relief. Brighid and the Indian were in love—perhaps planning to be married—and they didn't want her to know. A mixed marriage was something of an embarrassment. But Merci didn't care what the neighbors thought. All she cared about was her mother—and not wanting to lose her to anyone, especially to a Soboba.

It wasn't as though her mother's heart *hadn't* been with the heathens for years. She had devoted her life to them, teaching at their school, tending them when they were sick, spending days at a time on the reservation—instead of on the rancho with her own daughter.

With that thought, long-held resentment in her heart turned to white-hot anger. She peered around the side of the wall. Her mother was stepping into Songan's arms.

Perfect timing to reveal herself. They deserved it. She waited until Brighid lifted her face to the Indian's, and without a sound, she stepped from her hiding place.

By now the couple was lost in an embrace.

Merci cleared her throat.

Her mother pulled back, dropping her arms to her sides. The Indian, whose back was to Merci, stood as still as a statue. She could see the muscles in his neck tense.

She laughed. It was a short, bitter sound. Then she strode forward, head high, an angry look fixed on her face.

Her mother's pretty face paled, and the hand she brought to her mouth was trembling. "Mer—Merci," she finally managed. "How—how long—have you been here?"

"Long enough to hear—and to understand—the secret you were plotting to keep from me." Merci laughed again.

Songan turned to look straight into her face. There was kindness, understanding, in his eyes. Rage twisted Merci's heart—how dare he presume to gaze at her with such...such pity? She took three more confident steps closer to her mother, and turning her stiff-spined back to the Indian, she planted herself between them.

Brighid seemed to have regained some of her composure and stared at her daughter. "What exactly did you hear?"

Merci lifted her chin. "Enough to realize that the two of you"—she shot a glance at Songan—"have met for a romantic liaison. It didn't take me long to understand you have other plans as well. Plans you're ashamed to tell me and everyone else." She gave her mother a condescending smile.

Her mother's shoulders drooped, and a deep sorrow seemed to settle on her like a cloak. A look was exchanged between Brighid and Songan, who had moved from behind Merci and now stood beside Brighid.

"You are wrong, Merci." Her mother's voice was low, and the words were as soft as a sigh...or a prayer.

"Would you like for me to leave you alone?" Songan asked Brighid.

She inclined her head only slightly, and as if in response to an unspoken language between them, he went to his horse, mounted, and headed away. Silence fell between mother and daughter as they watched him leave.

Her mother's face was dark with uneasiness. Or was it sorrow? For a moment she didn't speak but looked deep into Merci's gaze.

Finally she began, though her words were little more than a whisper. "For a long time, I've tried to imagine this day...imagine the words I would say."

"About that Indian, you mean?"

"His name is Songan, not 'that Indian.'"

Merci stared at her mother, narrowing her eyes. "You always did have a soft spot for the Sobobas, Mother. You left me alone at home while you busied yourself serving them." She flung the words, knowing they were unfair. But she didn't care; she was hurt to the core that she had been replaced in her mother's heart. Again.

"What I have to say to you is harder than anything I might have to say about Song and me."

Merci shrugged. "Nothing could be harder than knowing I'm about to lose you to an Indian."

A bird sang from a nearby branch, its cheerful note incongruous against the tension between them. Merci glanced at her mother to see why she hadn't answered. Brighid's eyes were closed and her lips formed silent words as if in prayer.

"It will rock your life, my little one," she finally said.

There was something in her mother's face that made the morning sun suddenly too bright, the breeze too harsh. Both stung Merci's face and made her eyes water. "I'm not your little one anymore, Mama."

"True." Brighid considered her a moment, seeming unfazed by Merci's bitterness. "But right now I would give anything to gather you into my arms and hold you close. To try to take away the pain you will feel when you hear me out."

"What are you trying to tell me?"

"A long time ago, when I was little more than a child, I had grand ideas about making the world a better place. All I knew was the love of my family, the security of the hacienda, the beauty of the far hills that surrounded this world I thought I knew so well."

She turned again to face Merci. "Even then I felt a burning desire in my heart to help the Soboba children. I began teaching a few of the youngest children how to read and write." She smiled faintly. "I was eventually able to obtain the reluctant blessing of the chief, Songan's father."

"What does this have to do with me?"

"Please wait, Merci," she sighed, "and I will tell you everything." She shook her head, and the smile that crossed her face was tender. "You've always been so impatient." Then she stood and moved away from her daughter and lifted her gaze to the rugged peaks of the San Jacinto Mountains. Her hair was pulled into a severe twist at the back of her neck, but a few loose strands fell across her forehead. The wind blew them away from her face; she reached up unconsciously and hooked a tendril behind her ear.

She walked back to stand in front of Merci. There was something deep and sorrowful in her expression, maybe the death of the youthful dreams, a pain in her eyes too difficult for expression. Merci wondered why she hadn't noticed all that before. "Sit down, Mama. And tell me what you have to say."

Her mother eased herself to the stone bench. "Every day I rode from the rancho along the dry riverbed to the Soboba village. Your grandfather was in a dispute with the government over the boundaries of our lands. When he bought the rancho, property lines were described in the vaguest terms—trees and boulders, old barns, or maybe an Indian burial ground. After a few decades, trees die, boulders get carted off for buildings, barns burn, sacred sites are obliterated by the Europeans. Your grandfather and Hugh Dearbourne—all the rancheros of California— were required to come up with proof of land ownership. The process nearly caused us to lose the rancho. It took every penny Papa had.

Merci nodded. "Grandmother and Grandfather told me about all that."

"While Papa was working to settle the dispute, squatters were allowed by the government to move in. It wasn't right, but there was nothing Papa could do." She looked away from Merci's eyes, off in the distance, somewhere over Merci's shoulder. She seemed to be struggling with something too horrible for words.

"What is it, Mama?"

Her mother didn't turn to her when she continued, this time in a barely audible monotone. "I headed to the Soboba village as usual, alone, on horseback. I remember the birds were singing, the breeze whispering, and the afternoon that stretched ahead lifting my spirits. I loved teaching even then. My little ones were just beginning to respond. The day seemed so…so full of…promise—" Her voice broke, and she put her hands to her face and began to weep.

"Mama…? What happened?"

"The squatters…came. There were five, maybe six or seven. They blocked the trail. I couldn't get around them." She stopped, her face covered by her hands. Her shoulders shook with silent sobs. "I tried to get away…" Again her voice choked with weeping. "But they shot my horse. He fell on me. I couldn't even get up and run…"

Merci's heart was pounding with fear for her mother—even now, twenty-some years later. "Mama, they didn't…hurt you, did they?"

Her mother didn't look at her. She nodded, still sobbing. Now she'd begun rocking slowly, and Merci slipped her arm around her mother's shoulders. "Mama…" she choked. "Oh, Mama…You kept this secret all these years. You should have told me."

Merci suddenly thought of her father, and he became a greater hero in her heart than ever. He must have loved Brighid so much that he helped her heal, made her feel loved…Then she stopped to consider that if her mother had kept the secret from her own daughter all these years, perhaps she had never told Merci's father before he died. "Papa knew, didn't he?"

Her mother stopped crying and drew in a deep breath. Still, she refused to look at her daughter. Or answer the question.

The harsh wind gusted again, and somewhere in the distance the call of a mockingbird carried toward them. Overhead a red-tailed hawk circled.

"When did this happen, Mama?" Merci's voice was a whisper. There was suddenly a fear in her heart that threatened to overtake her entire being, a blackness that threatened to extinguish the light of her spirit. "When—what year?"

Her mother swallowed hard, visibly fighting to recapture her composure. "It was the year before your birth."

Merci let out a shaky sigh. "A full year?"

"Seven months and a few days. You were born prematurely."

Merci struggled to keep the desperate hope out of her voice. "You were pregnant then, before the men…" *Raped you.* She couldn't utter the hideous words.

"No."

The darkness turned black and whirled inside her, as if liquid, as if pulling her under, as if to drown her in its vile truth. "You're trying to tell me that you've lied to me all these years…that your disgrace was not from a pregnancy with a man you loved, a man who died before your wedding day."

"I lied to protect you." Her mother was crying softly again.

"My *father*"—she practically spat the word—"my *father* doesn't exist, or should I say, *never* existed anyplace except in my childish heart?"

Her mother nodded and turned to her, finally. "Please forgive me."

"Forgive you?" Somewhere in her darkness, she searched for the words to say that she understood, that her mother was forgiven for the lie meant to spare Merci the horror of the truth. But the words weren't there. She stared at her mother unable to utter a sound. Not a sound of sadness, sorrow, or forgiveness. Nothing.

Brighid reached for her daughter, tried to pull her into her arms. Merci shoved her away with a violence she didn't know she possessed. She didn't want to be touched. She stood and walked to the edge of the overlook, gulping huge breaths of air.

She was the daughter of a rapist.

As the horrible thought took root, she laughed aloud, a sound that brought with it an image of madness. Though it came from someplace deep in her own soul, it frightened her.

Her mother was instantly beside her. "My darling, please let me bear some of this burden, this terrible thing, with you…for you," she murmured, again drawing Merci into her arms. Her mother's face was wet with tears.

Merci pushed her away again, almost violently. "You don't understand, do you?"

"I understand that you are my daughter. Do you hear that, Merci? *My* daughter. Nothing can change that fact." Brighid held Merci by the shoulders, and she shook her. "My daughter, child. My beloved daughter!" She was shouting and crying at the same time.

Merci reached up and flung her mother's hands from her shoulders.

"Don't ever touch me again." Her voice was a low growl. She took a few steps away from Brighid, then looked back. "Perhaps you don't understand. I am the daughter of—"

Her mother interrupted. "You are God's gift to me, a symbol of his mercy—"

Merci laughed again. "I am merely a symbol of his indifference." She gave her mother a hard look. "You've always told me that his angels watch over us no matter where we go. And now you tell me this? How can you believe such lies after what happened?" She turned on her boot heel to leave her mother.

Brighid called after her. "Merci, I long ago made my peace with what happened. I have so much more to tell you. Please hear me out."

"There's nothing more I want to hear from you," Merci tossed over her shoulder. "Your indifference all these years is merely a confirmation of God's indifference. It's obvious to me now. The reasons you left me to go to the Indian village, I mean." She turned to face her mother again. "You simply gave me over to my grandparents to raise while you gallivanted off to the Sobobas each morning, probably hoping against all hope I would disappear while you were gone."

Her mother's face was deathly white, and her lips were trembling.

"It's true, isn't it?" Merci hissed. "Dare to tell me it isn't!"

Brighid's eyes again filled with tears. She seemed unable to speak.

Merci narrowed her gaze and spat her words. "I am the daughter of evil. Nothing you can say will change that truth." She paused to glare at Brighid and let her lip curl in anger. "And if I am the daughter of evil, what does that make you, Mother?"

She let the beat of silence that followed drive her point home. Then she laughed in the face of the one who had betrayed her. Turning once again, she headed toward the stand of trees where she'd left Knight grazing.

EIGHT

Quaid leaned back in the plush leather chair, his gaze fixed on the balding Grady Ledbetter, the man who had been his grandfather's attorney for more than a decade. His grandparents sat to the right of the lawyer's desk.

Something important was about to be disclosed. He'd noticed the looks exchanged between MacQuaid and Camila, the secret smiles, the crackling tension in the room. He stifled a grin and drew in a shaky breath, wondering if Merci had been right about his grandparents proposing a test of his mettle. If so, he was more than ready to rise to the challenge. He'd leap right over Ledbetter's desk if they wanted him to.

Thinking of his cousin, though, brought to mind how she'd looked yesterday when he teased her about his inheritance. Her expression had held some deep and desperate hope. It was a look that wouldn't leave his mind and brought him a mild sense of discomfort that he was sitting here without her right now.

Ledbetter cleared his throat and removed his eyeglasses. Cleaning them with his handkerchief, he replaced them on his bulbous nose. "Have you told young Quaid here why you've brought him along?"

Another glance was exchanged between his grandparents. They were fairly beaming with some unspoken news. "No," his grandfather said. "We haven't said a word to him."

"Do you want to tell him, or shall I?" Ledbetter settled back in his big chair, hands behind his head, elbows akimbo, as if he already knew the answer.

"He is your namesake, my husband," Camila said. "You must be the one to tell him."

"Aye, then that I will." MacQuaid leaned forward, his eyes bright with anticipation.

"What is it?" Quaid said, willing his heart to slow its mad drumming.

"Now then, my boy. 'Tis a long time your grandma'am and I have been considerin' this change. For a while we thought we were daft to consider givin' up the land we love. Then we decided we were daft not to." He chuckled, shaking his head. "We're getting older, and it's time for youth to bring new notions and spirit to the Big Valley. It's time for the winds of change to blow across our land."

"Winds of change?" Quaid was afraid to breathe.

Camila smiled at her husband, then looked back to her grandson. "Sometimes your grandfather fancies himself a poet."

MacQuaid went on as if no one had spoken. "We canna stay at the ranch much longer. You wouldn't know it by lookin', now, would you, but I'm getting too old for the everyday running of things." Quaid started to protest, but his grandfather lifted his hand to quiet him. "Your grandma'am and I no longer can see to the details, oversee the workers, the cattle." He paused, his gaze taking on a faraway look. "One time I couldn't think of anything else, but now…?" He shrugged.

"Go on now, husband," Camila said. "You are taking too long. Tell him the rest."

Ledbetter chuckled. "Judging from the look of the man, his heart's about to explode from wonder. You'd better spit it out, my friend."

MacQuaid laughed and reached over to give his grandson a good-natured slap on the back. "Son, your grandma'am and I have a proposition to discuss with you about Rancho de la Paloma."

Even as his grandfather spoke, Merci's words about the rancho being the only home she'd ever known came to mind. The memory was disquieting, and Quaid tried to put it from his mind but couldn't.

MacQuaid leaned closer. "Son, you have a love for the land unlike anyone else in the family."

Merci loved the land; he should speak up and remind them. He should protest that she wasn't included in the conversation. He should suggest they wait until Merci could join them. But Quaid kept silent.

"If you agree to it, someday Rancho de la Paloma will be yours."

Quaid nodded, then said, "At this point, I'm ready to agree to anything."

"La Paloma hasn't made a profit for several years. Hide prices have dropped. Shipping costs have risen, even with the completion of the Santa Fe. But the ranch can be turned around. More than that—it can be made to turn a tidy profit—with the right man leadin' the charge. A man who's not afraid of a challenge."

"You think I'm the right man?"

His grandmother leaned forward. "We *know* you are, Quaid."

"And we've had papers drawn up with Ledbetter here," MacQuaid said, "stating that the rancho and all its acreage will be yours at the end of 1891—if indeed you can show a profit has been made."

He smiled at Quaid. "It won't be easy, son, though it might appear so from where you're sitting. I mentioned the drop in the price of hides. There's also a slack market for tallow. Something we've always counted on selling in abundance. With the coming of electrification, it's no longer needed in such quantities. People would rather have a dim light bulb hanging in the middle of their ceiling than dirty lamps in their corners." He chuckled. "And there are the droughts, floods, earthquakes, and fires California's known for." He was still laughing. "You'll have to learn to live with them, work them into your plan—and still make a profit."

Quaid nodded, understanding. He'd lived in California all his life and had experienced most of the quirks of nature that his grandfather described. Even as a child he'd felt the violent rocking of a quake, diving under his covers to pray, sure he was about to die. He'd seen firsthand the devastation of floods and droughts, and he'd watched the raging firestorms take everything in their paths—homes, wildlife, ancient trees. Dreams could turn to ashes in a heartbeat. He didn't take his grandfather's challenge lightly.

Quaid turned to the elderly man, surprised that MacQuaid seemed to be studying him. "You haven't said whether you'll accept the challenge, lad," MacQuaid said. "Or even if you're pleased with the offer."

"What about Merci? And the others? Kerr, Gregor…Sandy?"

"First of all, I don't want the land parceled up, which would happen if we gave it to be shared equally among all the cousins. You have always had a passion for the land, the wild acreage, raising cattle. I see myself in you. Always have." He gave Quaid a gentle smile. "You need not worry about their inheritance. There are other family holdings. When all is said and done, they will be pleased." His grandfather paused, studying him. "Is something else troubling you about this transaction, son?"

Yes, something was troubling him. *Merci.* How could he rejoice in this astounding gift, when he knew his cousin's heart would break when she found out? She wouldn't care about any inheritance other than the only home she'd ever known. He stared for a moment at his grandparents' beloved faces, wondering how much he should say, if anything, about all that Merci had told him about her desires for the land.

"It's Merci, isn't it?" his grandmother said, astonishing him. Since his childhood, she always seemed to know what he was thinking.

He nodded. "She loves this land as much as I do."

His grandfather laughed. "A woman can't be expected to run a ranch of this size—to take land running at a loss and turn it into a profitable venture. I dare say, she would not want to."

Camila broke in with a scolding tone, "You know better than that, husband! She could run it as well as any man—even as well as Quaid."

"Grandmother is right," Quaid added. "Merci loves this land."

"Love and ability don't necessarily go hand in hand," his grandfather said.

Quaid started to protest again, but his grandfather held up a hand to quiet him. "I have considered this for months now—"

Ledbetter broke in, his tone earnest. "Believe me, Quaid. Your grandparents have weighed their decision with great care. It's by no small whim that you were chosen."

Camila leaned toward Quaid, her gaze seeming to search his heart. "We ask one very important consideration from you."

"Anything."

"We ask that you provide Merci a home at La Paloma for as long as she needs it."

"Of course. You didn't even have to ask."

"Merci is a young woman with many gifts," MacQuaid said. "She has had the best education money can buy. She has had young men by the dozen attempting to court her. She enjoys light flirtations but has taken none of them seriously. And she has not even put the education we provided to good use."

His grandmother looked uncertain. "Merci is still trying to find her way." She paused, seeming to consider her granddaughter. "And if anything happens to you or your future descendants, son, the land—all of it—will go to Merci. We have added that stipulation in our will."

He knew it would be small consolation to his fiery, independent cousin, but he nodded. "It is as it should be." His heart was heavy as he thought of Merci and her disappointment. "When will you tell the family?"

MacQuaid reached for Camila's hand. "We have already asked that the family join us tonight for supper." He pulled out his pocket watch. "They are on their way. The house will be full to overflowing once again with the Byrnes and Dearbournes. Aye, my lad, 'tis a day to rejoice! We plan to announce to all, at least to all who have not guessed it already, that we intend to move to Monterey." He sighed, giving Camila a soft smile. "Much as I love this land, I've missed the sea."

He looked back to Quaid. "You will be given all the help you need with your venture. The foreman and cattle hands have already agreed to stay on as long as you need them. Most of them you know; they've been at the rancho for years. As you expand—in any way you deem necessary—you'll need to hire on more hands. That will, of course, be up to you."

After the documents had been signed, Ledbetter stood and shook hands all around. "Congratulations," he said to Quaid enthusiastically, as he pumped the younger man's hand. "I'm here if you need me."

It was indeed as Merci had guessed, Quaid thought sadly as they left the building. And tonight she would hear it when the others did—in front of her mother, in front of Sybil and Scotty and their sons, in front of his parents.

A few hours later, Quaid drove the buggy down the long driveway leading to the rancho. He drew the two-horse team to a halt near the verandah, then stepped down from the driver's seat to help his grandparents out of the buggy. When they were indoors, he drove to the carriage house and unhitched the horses, turning them out to pasture.

And he practiced what he would say to Merci when he saw her. He figured that if he told her ahead of time, at least she wouldn't have to bear her disappointment in front of the entire family.

He checked the house first, but none of the servants had seen her. Next he strode to the barn, thinking she might have returned from her ride. But Knight wasn't in his stall, so he headed out to have a look in the pastures behind the stables, but there was no sign of her there either. He asked some of the ranch hands, but no one had seen her all day.

Meanwhile, the first of the family carriages could be seen approaching the rancho. He grinned and waved when he recognized his carrot-topped cousins riding behind the vehicle.

How his elegant Aunt Sybil could have borne such loud-mouthed hulks was more than he could understand. The carriage pulled behind the house. He opened the door and took his aunt's hand as she stepped to the ground. Sybil stood on tiptoes to draw her nephew into a ferocious bear hug, and Scotty shook his hand. By now his cousins had dismounted and took turns socking him on the arm.

"How's the train robbery business?" Gregor asked, looking Quaid up and down with a quirked brow. All three cousins, who considered themselves thoroughly citified, needled Quaid each time they saw him, complaining about everything he wore, from his boots to his leather duster. Said he looked more like an outlaw than Jesse James himself.

"Train robbery?" Kerr jumped in with a guffaw. "I thought it was bank jobs you were wanted for."

"We saw your poster on the wall in the Riverview station," Sandy added with a snort. "Good likeness. One that should cause the women to fall all over themselves to find you."

Quaid rolled his eyes. "You three desperados have told so many tall tales—someday there'll be a posse after me just because of your big mouths."

"Take your cousin's words as a warning, sons," Sybil added. "Your good-natured lies may well turn on you."

Gregor shrugged off his mother's words with another laugh. "Personally I'd like to see a posse head after my slick-as-a-newly-hewn-arrow cousin. Couldn't happen to a better man." He punctuated his words with another punch to Quaid's arm. "You only look as mean as a griz' disturbed during hibernation. In reality, you're as gentle as a—"

"Peeled rattler," Kerr interrupted.

"A coyote eatin' a yellow jacket," snorted Gregor. "You may be a soft-spoken, gentle-appearin' cowpoke, but in reality you're—"

"Okay, okay," Quaid held up his hands in surrender. "I get the picture. You lily-livered city folks are more gurgle than guts." He grinned and playfully socked his nearest cousin in the arm. "And you bellyache more than bulls in green corn time."

Sybil rolled her eyes heavenward. "Mark my words, someday someone will overhear you and think you're making serious accusations about Quaid." Shaking her head, she took Scotty's arm and the couple headed for the hacienda. Scotty looked back with a grin that said he was enjoying the jesting as much as his sons were.

Quaid considered his three cousins for a moment, thinking about what he needed to tell them. They might want to string him up from the nearest oak once they heard the news about his inheriting the rancho. He figured he ought to be the one to tell them. So he did.

To his surprise, they were delighted. More effusive pounds on the back followed as each extracted a promise that Quaid would bunk them down whenever they took a notion to visit.

"What about Merci?" Sandy was the first to recognize the pain it might cause their cousin.

"She'll be welcome here as long as she likes."

"You know she won't like having you as her landlord," Gregor said.

Kerr snorted. "Not that anyone would."

The others ignored their brother, and Quaid went on. "I know how she'll take this, and I'd like to warn her about what's coming. I wanted her to hear it from me first—before the rest of the family knows. She left for a ride at dawn, and now she's nowhere to be found."

"Do you know where she might have headed?" Sandy said, now completely serious.

Quaid shook his head. "She takes off every morning on Knight. Doesn't ever tell anyone where she goes."

"We'll find her," Kerr said, looking at Quaid. "You could track a wood tick across solid rock."

Quaid couldn't help laughing. "I can track most anything or anyone, but our Merci may be harder to find than even that tick."

"You think she's hard to find now," added Sandy. "Just wait till she hears about your inheritance."

The others let out soft whistles of agreement.

"She'll be mad enough to swallow a horned toad backwards," Gregor said.

"This is serious," Sandy reprimanded with a frown.

"I am serious," Gregor said. "She's one gutsy, determined, hardheaded woman."

There were more murmurs of agreement from the others.

"Let's go find her," Quaid said. "I've got to get this over with."

But before they reached the barn, the thud of hoofbeats carried toward them. Judging from the speed and power of the sound, it had to be Knight. All four men turned as the rider approached.

It was Merci, flame hair whipping behind her, her face red from the afternoon sun and the obvious exertion of the ride. Shoulders proud and chin lifted high, she rode past them without acknowledgment.

Sandy let out another whistle. "Whooeee, I think she may've already discovered your news, Cousin."

"Could be she's just stirring one of her usual stews," Kerr observed with a shrug. "Personally, I think it's the better part of valor to let Quaid here give her the news. Besides, I need to go kiss Grandmother hello."

He turned away from Quaid and sauntered across the yard toward the house, his brothers following.

"I always knew you were lily-livered, but now I'm thinking you're lily-livered chickens," Quaid muttered as they left. Then he added, "Thanks for backing me up here, dear cousins."

"Anytime," Gregor called over his shoulder. He chuckled, and his brothers laughed with him as they stepped onto the small verandah sheltering the back door to the hacienda.

When Quaid reached the barn, Merci was there, unbuckling the saddle, her back to the wide door as he approached.

"Merci?" He strode closer. But she remained silent, her shoulders rigid. He wondered if she already knew about the property. "Merci," he said again.

When she turned to face him, her face held such a tragic expression it took his breath away. He stopped several feet from her. "Merci...what is it?"

"I can't talk to you, to anyone, right now. Please leave me."

His heart caught in his chest. "Merci, you know, then?"

She studied him for a moment, then she started to laugh, a low, sorrowful sound. "It seems I am the last to find out the very thing that will forever change my life." Her eyes filled with tears, and she swiped at them angrily. "How could they...my own mother, the others...?" she cried, her voice hoarse. "How could such a thing have been kept from me?"

"I'm terribly sorry," Quaid didn't know what else to say.

It surprised him that she looked grateful. "What's done is done." She laughed bitterly and shrugged.

"You're part of this place, Merci. Don't ever doubt that."

She rolled her wet eyes, still chuckling with that awful, brittle sound. "Yes, my place."

"As long as I live you'll have a home here."

Suddenly she seemed to focus on his face. "What do you mean, 'as long as I live'? What does that have to do with..." Her voice faltered, then dropped to a whisper when she continued, "Something tells me we're not talking about the same thing."

He realized it at the same moment she did.

"You went to the lawyer today, didn't you? While I was gone?"

He nodded.

"And it's yours." She gestured wildly. "All this is yours."

His heart twisted at the look on her face. He nodded again. "It's not that way…it's not what you think. It has to do with the test you told me about."

"It's your spirit they're testing. Not mine."

"Merci, please—"

"You didn't wait for me. You promised."

Her face had turned so white that every freckle showed as if in relief, even in the dimly lit stable.

"Leave me now, Quaid," she said quietly. "Please."

He thought he might be sick from the burden of knowing she spoke the truth. He could find no words.

"It's all right," she said, not looking at him. "I need air." As an afterthought, she muttered to herself, "The air in here is suddenly putrid." She cinched the buckle into place, then stepped into a stirrup and swung her leg over the saddle.

"It's getting late, Merci," he said, looking up at her. "When will you be back?"

"You can boss everyone else around on your new land, Quaid. But not me."

"I'm not trying to boss you. I'm concerned for you." He reached for her reins, wanting desperately to keep her from riding off.

She grabbed them back. "I said I'm taking Knight out for a ride, and that's exactly what I intend to do."

"Merci—"

She wheeled the horse and rode off before he could utter another word.

Quaid stared after her until she disappeared down the rancho road, her shoulders sloped, her head down. A feeling of disquiet settled over him like a heavy cloak, and throughout the evening as his parents and aunts, uncles and cousins congratulated him, he thought about the set of Merci's shoulders as she rode away from the rancho.

Several times he noticed his Aunt Brighid's unusual silence, the purple circles beneath her eyes, her forced gaiety on his behalf, and especially the way she watched the door as if for her daughter's entrance.

Long after the household had settled to bed, Quaid listened for Merci to come riding down the road.

But no hoofbeats broke the midnight silence.

NINE

Quaid tossed in his bed, listening for Knight's hoofbeats on the road leading to the rancho. When the clock struck one, with a full moon to light his way, he rose and headed out to the barn. After saddling the sorrel, he rode toward the old adobe where Merci had been born. He had a hunch that she might have returned to the place where she'd spent her first months of life, the place where they had played as children.

He followed the thin strip of river until he came to a rise overlooking the autumn-shallow Mystic Lake. And there stood the adobe, crumbling and strangely beautiful in the moonlight.

A lone horse grazed in a patch of grass near a cottonwood. For a moment his spirits lifted, and he rode closer. But it wasn't the magnificent Knight. And now he recognized the mount that his Aunt Brighid often rode. He halted the sorrel beside the horse, dismounted, and called out.

She answered immediately from the rickety porch, and he turned to see her standing in the doorway. In the soft light cast by the moon, her face glinted with tears.

"I rode out to see if Merci might be here," he said as he walked toward the adobe.

"I did the same," she said, and blew her nose. "When she didn't come home tonight, I knew something was wrong."

"I didn't know that anyone else was aware that she'd ridden off."

Brighid studied his face but didn't comment.

"I wish I could turn back the clock," he said, climbing the stairs to the porch. Leaning against the rickety rail across from her, he explained how he'd so awkwardly told Merci about the inheritance. He let out a deep and ragged breath, feeling miserable. "I should have been more careful of Merci's feelings."

Brighid shook her head. "Her leaving had little to do with what you told her, Quaid. Don't blame yourself."

"She would still be here if I hadn't spoken about it."

His aunt's voice was little more than a sad whisper as she continued, "Merci would have left anyway. She left sooner than planned. That's all." She lifted her handkerchief to her nose again. "We'd had…words, just before you saw her."

An owl flew by, swiftly, silently. For a moment neither of them spoke.

"I was finally honest with my daughter today," she said. "I feared she would hear the truth from someone else. I wanted to be the one to tell her."

Quaid let his gaze drift away from the pain in his aunt's eyes, unable to bear what he saw there. He wondered what truth she spoke of and frowned, turning back to her. Brighid didn't seem to notice his quizzical look. Or if she did, she was choosing to ignore it. But he didn't press her to reveal what she had told Merci.

"I don't know what she'll do, Quaid," she said. "I've never felt such sorrow. I've never felt so helpless. I know God is with her—I gave her to him a long time ago. But Merci must find him herself to belong to him completely. He's given her the will to choose her own way." Brighid was blinking up at the moon again, her face still shiny with tears. "I am so desperately afraid for her, afraid of the direction she'll choose."

Quaid reached for her hand. "God knows the beginning and the end. Merci is in his care—no matter what the truth was she learned today."

Even as he spoke the words, even as he knew them to be true, his heart was fearful for his cousin. One look into his aunt's troubled gaze told him that whatever she'd told Merci had been something so tragic, so devastating, that Merci would never be the same for hearing it.

He suspected that his own news about the rancho paled in comparison. He looked back to his aunt's tear-stained face. "Tell me what I can do."

She was weeping again, and she shook her head slowly. "This is one of those times when I have to trust God to take care of her. I don't want to. Everything in my heart tells me to run to Merci—to search the ends of the earth for her. And that I may well do if she doesn't come home soon." She gazed out toward Mystic Lake and the moonlit sky beyond, dabbing absently at her eyes.

"I'll lead the search for Merci at first light," he promised. "Think of the posse we can get together with the family still here. We'll find her in no time." Still, he knew that if Merci didn't want to be found, she would leave no trace of her whereabouts. She was better at covering her trail than he was.

Brighid nodded, her expression grateful. "Thank you."

"Can I escort you back to the rancho?" he asked after a few minutes.

His aunt touched his arm. "You go back, Quaid. I need to stay here a while longer."

"This is the place where you bore Merci, isn't it?"

"Yes. And the place where God healed me." Then she gave him a rare smile. "Merci doesn't understand that her life was a gift. God's sign of mercy and grace." She paused, then said to him as he headed down the porch steps, "Sometimes, I come here to pray because it is here I learned to trust him again. Merci's very life is a reminder of his faithfulness."

Quaid nodded, wondering at the transformation he saw in Brighid's face. She no longer seemed troubled. Only filled with peace.

"I'll see you in the morning," she said and gave him a wave as he mounted. "First light."

After leaving the adobe, Quaid reined the sorrel to the east, climbing the trail leading into the high country of the San Jacinto Mountains. He didn't have a destination in mind but figured it wouldn't hurt to ride to a lookout, a place high enough to see campfires in the valley that spread below. It was a long shot, but maybe he might see one that would lead to Merci.

On clear nights, he'd often seen the campfires of the cattle hands across the rancho lands, sometimes even the glow of lamplight from the hacienda. If he did spot a campfire, he told himself, he'd not wait an extra minute for the search party to form at daybreak; he'd ride right out to Merci and tell her a thing or two about how worried and grieved they'd all been. And he'd bring her back; even if she kicked and screamed, he'd bring his cousin and that glorious stallion back home where they belonged.

He'd turn over the rancho to Merci this minute—and get his grandparents to see the wisdom in it—if it would bring her home to stay.

He urged the horse through the pass that led to a rocky overlook, surrounded by pines and centuries-old oaks, at an elevation of some five thousand feet above the valley floor. The sorrel was surefooted, and as usual, Quaid let the horse take her lead as they moved up the trail. The breeze blew through the pines, causing them to murmur in song, their fragrance spilling over him like a freshwater stream, quieting his troubled soul.

Finally, he halted at the top of the incline and slid from his saddle. Leaving the sorrel to graze, he walked out to the end of the outcropping. From below, the herd's faint lowing carried toward him on the wind. The pale moonlit valley stretched before him, here and there a few dark clumps of live oaks and brush, some stands of pines, and giant boulders.

There was no telltale pinpoint of fire. Not even the faintest glow. Though he'd known it wasn't likely she'd be so careless. He was disappointed. It seemed she truly wanted to cover her trail, and if so, the odds of finding her were slim indeed.

He settled onto a slab of granite and leaned his back against a boulder. He let his thoughts drift away from his cousin's whereabouts and back to the land itself. Though he'd scrawled his name on every piece of paper required by Ledbetter, he wasn't certain if the land was truly his. Legally it was, or would be, should he pass the challenge his grandfather had laid out. In other ways, though, it didn't feel right. And wouldn't, until he found Merci.

He stared across at the Big Valley, stretching away in its wild, natural state. It struck him suddenly how proud he was of his grandfather for keeping the land from the moneygrubbing developers. Many of the rancheros had sold without a twinge of guilt.

If the land truly became his, lock, stock, and barrel, he would leave it as wild as it was this moment. He'd let the animals, native to the desert wilderness, roam free. Birds, dependent on the flourishing plant life, would soar on the wind.

He leaned back, clasping his hands behind his head, and considered it. Yes. Under his care, native plants and animals would flourish. He would keep the cattle, of course, but most of the year the herd would be limited to the land near the river where the grass grew tallest.

And he would find better ways to see his cattle to market. He had promised his grandparents a profit, so he would see they got one.

But profit held little meaning for him. If it were his choice, he would run only enough cattle to keep the rancho operable. Nothing more.

He would plant a kitchen garden for the family, staff, and hands. He would see to enough barley, hay, and alfalfa for the herd. Nothing more. The rest of his acreage would be turned into a wilderness for use as a wildlife refuge.

He smiled for the first time since Merci rode off.

A friend of his father's, John Muir, had stopped by the Tehachapi ranch twice in recent years. And on the third visit, the three men hiked into the back country of the Sierra. It was a trip that Quaid would never forget. In fact, by the journey's end, he felt he'd been on a pilgrimage.

Muir pointed out the diminishing wildlife as civilization encroached on natural habitats, the sad disappearance of the magnificent animals such as the grizzly bear, once the proud symbol of California statehood and now a distant memory. Thousands had been slaughtered, Muir had told them, for mere meanness or for the mistaken notion that they killed livestock. In reality, few cattle had been taken down by either the griz or the mountain lion, another magnificent beast mostly unseen except in the mountains—and then at a healthy distance from civilization.

He had seen his first wolf on that back-country trip. A big timber wolf with eyes the color of moonlight. One look into its powerful gaze and Quaid silently vowed he would never kill one, that he would do what he could to preserve the beast's wild sanctuary.

He sat forward, following the landscape to the western horizon, where it became one with the moonlit sky. He would protect it for the sake of his grandmother and grandfather, for the coming generations, for himself.

Muir's words came back to him. "When I was a boy in Scotland, I was fond of everything that was wild, and all my life I've been growing fonder and fonder of wild places and wild creatures."

Everything that was wild…the places and the creatures. Muir's words fit inside him as if they'd come from Quaid's own heart.

He grinned and settled his back against the boulder.

A lone sparrow sang from the branch of an oak just as dawn's approach painted the sky a pearl gray above the black silhouette of the mountains.

A doe bounded from a thicket, and Quaid laughed aloud, startling the graceful creature. The deer gave him a curious look as she soared across the trail. Quaid stood and dusted himself off, then headed for the sorrel. Within minutes he and the mare were moving back down the trail toward the Big Valley.

And he prayed for Merci as he went, entreating God to impress on her that she needed to come to her senses and return home.

He brightened at the thought. Maybe she had come home while he was gone.

He pressed the sorrel in the flanks, urging the horse to move faster. And he considered the words he'd say to Merci as he scolded her for worrying them beyond imagination—right after he gave her the biggest bear hug she'd ever had.

Aislin watched her son ride in, and she left the verandah to meet him as he dismounted. The worry lines in his face touched her. Quaid reminded her more of her husband, Spence, every day, a handsome bear of a man—quiet and sometimes gruff without meaning to be, but with a heart both tender and strong.

He brightened when he saw her. "Mother, what brings you out here so early?"

She smiled and reached up to receive his embrace. "I've just spoken with Brighid. She told me you'd talked last night." Her sister had also told her what a comfort Quaid had been to her, willing to listen as she cried, providing her strength by simply being there with her.

He nodded, and she fell into step with him as he led the horse to the barn. "I was looking for Merci."

"She told me."

"She's not home, is she?"

Aislin shook her head. "No, son. She didn't come home at all last night."

His lips were in a straight, white line, and he worked his jaw just the way his father did when perturbed. "Are the menfolk up yet?"

She nodded. "They're ready to ride. Just waiting for daylight—and for you."

He smiled down at her. "You came out here just to tell me that?"

Aislin chuckled. "You know me well."

"I know you don't do anything without a purpose. Never have. Never will." He laughed lightly.

She touched his arm to stop him. "Brighid asked me to speak to you."

"About Merci?" He frowned, his concern even greater. "Has something happened?"

"She wants you to know the truth about Merci's birth…about the circumstances leading up to it. She thought it would help you understand why Merci's run off now." She paused, seeing the alarm in his face. "Take your horse to the stableboy, then meet me in the courtyard. I'll tell you everything."

He stared at her for a moment quizzically, then did as she bade. A few minutes later, he strode into the courtyard, barely light with the rising sun. He sat beside her on the old stone bench beneath the century oak. She glanced around the beloved ranch house, with its second-floor balustrade and cascading bougainvillea, the fountain in the center where, when she was a child, she'd planted pots of ferns and palms.

It was in this place that she'd learned of Brighid's rape years ago. She and Sybil had just returned from the trail ride to New Mexico Territory, rejoicing to be home once again—until their parents told them about the tragedy that had befallen their little sister. The same tragedy that Aislin now needed to explain to her son.

Brighid had asked her to tell him the truth about Merci. Her sister said that Quaid needed to understand that he wasn't to blame for his cousin's disappearance, that he needed to be glad for his inheritance, and not to let his troubled spirit about Merci keep him from accepting his grandparents' gift of love.

Aislin drew in a deep breath. "Son, I have something to tell you. It is something that you can never tell another person, unless Merci or Brighid gives you her blessing to do so."

He turned toward her, leaning forward slightly. "What is it?" His blue-gray eyes darkened, his expression reminding her again of Spence's.

"You are your father's son," she said, patting his big, callused hand. Then she wrapped her fingers around his and held them tight.

As she spoke, she watched his beloved face turn from revulsion to anger, then to overwhelming grief on behalf of Brighid, on behalf of Merci. She felt her own eyes fill with tears.

She hadn't seen her son cry since he was a little boy. Now he wept unashamedly, staring up into the branches of the oak overhead. "Oh, God," he whispered, his voice ragged. "Oh, God, be with them both!"

Merci Byrne had spent the night in a deserted barn at the southernmost corner of her grandfather's property. *Her cousin Quaid's property,* she corrected herself with a bitter laugh. And now she was stiff with cold and hungry enough to eat a possum, or any other critter that might cross her path.

She chided herself for leaving the rancho without so much as a change of clothes—no money, nothing to her name but the riding clothes. Shaking out her hair again, she combed it with her fingers, picking out pieces of hay and flicking them to the ground.

The sun was just slipping above the distant mountains when she reached the westernmost boundary of Rancho de la Paloma. She headed to a cottonwood near a stream that was more dust than water, slid from the saddle, and let Knight drink.

The horizontal sunlight struck her in the face, and she shielded her eyes while gazing back toward the rancho. Just beyond the low range of golden mountains, the household would be rising. The fragrance of fresh-brewed coffee and baking bread wafting from the kitchen, the clinking sounds of china as her mother and grandmother helped the aging Josefina set the table. No doubt the entire family would be gathering, just as they had last night, Aislin and Spence, Sybil and Scotty, their sons, and of course, Quaid, sitting to the right of their grandfather. The house would ring with laughter and chatter against the early morning birdsong outdoors.

Morning. Her favorite time of day, when everything was fresh, bathed by dew, fragrant with the ocean breezes that came inland during the night. In the breakfast room, sunlight would pool on the tile floor as the sun rose and flooded the room with a warmth that was much more than light.

It was strange that she hadn't realized until this minute how much she would miss mornings on the rancho.

She wondered if anyone had noticed she was gone. Or cared.

More than likely, it was a relief.

She considered the years she had lived there. Each time her mother, grandparents, or aunts or uncles—each time *anyone*—looked at her, they had to remember what had happened to her mother. Remember the vilest act one human being could do to another.

And she was a constant reminder of that vile act.

She looked down at her hands, turning them over in the sunlight. She had always considered them pretty, delicate yet strong. Often she had wondered at the God who created every inch of her being—what was it her mother used to read to her from the family Bible?—even knit her together in her mother's womb. God made these hands, hands that now looked grotesque to her.

She turned from the sunlit hills and plains, signaled to Knight, then swung a leg over his back to continue her ride to Los Angeles. It was the only place she could think to go.

What she would do when she arrived there, she didn't know. Without a coin in her pocket, and having only the clothes on her back, she would need to find employment immediately. She had a certificate from Massachusetts Teacher's College, so maybe she could find employment as a teacher, perhaps a governess.

Then she laughed, more bitterly than before. Of course the certificate wasn't with her. And even if she could find employment without the document, it didn't change who she was. She could always keep the truth of her parentage to herself. No one would have to know she was the child of evil.

But she would never forget.

Child of evil? She laughed until sobs wracked her body. She halted Knight and hung her head over the trail to lose what little was left in her stomach.

Perhaps that made her the daughter of the devil himself. The madness, the laughter, shook her until she ached.

TEN

One week after she left the rancho, Merci looked for a Los Angeles mercantile where she could sell Knight's hand-tooled Spanish saddle. It made her sad to think of parting with it, but she had no choice. For seven days, she'd slept in deserted barns and eaten what she could steal or beg along the way. She needed food and clean clothing. Without it, she would never find decent employment. The saddle was all she had of value. And Knight. But he didn't count. He was as much a part of her as an arm or leg. She would never part with him.

She urged the big stallion to head down Spring Street, surprised at how much the city had changed since her last visit with her grandparents. Los Angeles, once a dusty pueblo, was becoming a real city with tall buildings and an electrified trolley system. It teemed with newly arrived easterners, Indians from a variety of local tribes, Spanish *californios*, Chinese railroad workers, developers looking for land, and businessmen looking to make a quick fortune.

Cowboys, in town for a bit of excitement, sauntered along the boardwalks on Spring Street, dodging the bright yellow trolleys that rumbled up and down the center of the town. Shameful ladies of the night, leaning against streetlamps and smiling at the cowboys, tried to look inculpable in the bright light of day.

The thuds of horse hooves, snatches of conversations, jangles of bicycle bells, and creaks of buggy wheels blended together like some strange music. Merci halted Knight in the middle of the street, trying to remember the location of the mercantile.

Two boys rode by on bicycles, ringing their little handlebar bells. A dog nosed along the gutter, sniffing and nosing some more. The city was filled with constant motion, sometimes a cowboy on horseback, but most of the traffic was made up of wagons and buggies, and people crisscrossing on foot. In the center of it all, the bright yellow trolleys with their red trim lurched along, bells jangling.

Knight's ears were back in irritation with the clamor and crowds, and Merci rubbed his neck to calm him. They were shoved along with traffic, but Merci didn't care since she had not the vaguest idea where to look for the mercantile.

Near the corner of Third and Broadway, she spotted the small sign and headed Knight for the hitching post in front. She'd visited the place a few times with her grandfather, but was surprised when the shopkeeper, a middle-aged bespectacled man, recognized her as she stepped through the door.

"I'm looking to sell a saddle," she said, adopting an air of indifference. "An expensive handmade Spanish saddle."

The man smiled. "Miss Byrne, I'll be happy to help you. Known your grandpappy for many years. You leave it here, and I'll contact you as soon as I sell it. We'll do a fifty-fifty split."

"Fifty-fifty?" She was outraged. "That's highway robbery," she scoffed and turned to leave.

"Sixty-forty, then?" he called after her.

She turned again and shook her head. "You're not even close."

"Where's the saddle? I'll have a look. See what I can do—as a favor for an old friend."

"On my horse."

He frowned. "What?"

"You said you want to see the saddle. It's on my horse."

He gave her a patronizing smile. "All right, young lady. I'll have a look. See if we can strike a deal." He followed her out the door to the hitching post where Knight was tied. He circled the horse, commenting on the wear of the leather and age of the saddle, then shook his head. "Sorry, Miss Byrne. I don't think you'll fetch much more than a few dollars for this. It may seem to be in superb condition to you, but in reality—"

He was interrupted by a dark and sinewy-looking cowboy who

happened to be within earshot. "Few dollars?" He stepped closer to have a look. "What'd you say it's worth?"

The proprietor quoted a price. An appalling price.

"No deal," Merci said between clenched teeth and unhitched Knight's reins. "I know saddles, and this one is worth far more. It was custom-made in Spain. I know how much my grandfather paid for it. A small fortune, you can be sure." She put her foot in the stirrup and started to swing onto the saddle.

The cowboy moved closer and whispered, "Meet me at the stable, and we'll make a deal. It'll be worth your time."

The proprietor overheard and glared at Merci. "Your grandfather would be ashamed of you, missy. You cut me out of the transaction, and you might as well be consorting with the devil himself."

Merci stared at him, her heart twisting at his words. *The devil himself.* How fitting. "My grandfather would be ashamed to do business with you," she growled. "He'd call you a thief and a liar. And he'd be calling it right!" She reined Knight away from the mercantile and, without another word, headed for the livery stables.

The offer the cowboy made was more than she would have received by working with the proprietor at the mercantile, but it was still pitifully low. At first she refused, then she glanced down at her worn riding skirt, scuffed boots, and soiled shirt, and reconsidered. In silent anger, she agreed to the price and accepted payment.

As the cowboy sauntered off, Knight's beautiful saddle balanced on his shoulder, she placed the coins and folded bills the man gave her in a leather pouch and tried not to cry. Setting her mind on anything but the treasured saddle, she swung onto Knight's back and headed to a clothing goods store on the west side of the city.

It took less than a half-hour to make her purchases. First she chose a sensible gray dress with a high white collar and lace cuffs that covered her wrists. Next she pulled a pair of high-top button shoes from a box in the corner of the room. She sat down between a pickle barrel and a tall stack of gingham pieces, slipped the right shoe on her foot, then tried three more before realizing the shoes came in one size only, a full size too large for her small feet. She took them anyway. The proprietor handed her two small bags of sawdust to stuff into the toes, and an old flour bag in which to carry her old dress and boots after she had changed clothes and laced up her new shoes.

Next she asked him where she might find a boardinghouse. The nearest was a mile away, he told her, and it had no stables. She left Knight in the livery where she'd sold his saddle, then headed to the boardinghouse by foot.

Blisters the size of liberty-head half-dollars sprouted on both heels ten minutes after she left the livery. By the time she had limped a half-mile farther, the blisters had turned to angry sores. She considered changing to her boots but figured the sores would only be aggravated. With a shrug of indifference, she walked barefoot the remaining distance.

Minutes later she stood in front of the tall plain house, hands on hips, considering the place. The picket fence that framed the yard was in serious need of whitewashing, and the broken-down gate, partially open, hung by a single hinge. She suspected it had been in such a state for years.

Lifting her gaze to the house itself, she attempted to repress a shudder. Surely it was older than Methuselah, with its sagging roof, crooked turret, and cockeyed wraparound porch.

A loose shutter banged against a squat window to the right of the front door. She stared at it for a moment, then swallowed hard. Tears of self-pity filled her eyes. She was, after all, somehow deserving of such a place. She might attempt to cover her background—which she fully intended to do—but she would never forget the vile inception of the blood that coursed through her veins, the obscene creation of life that caused her heart to beat.

With a heavy sigh she opened the gate. It squawked against rusty hinges, then hung pitifully askew, unlatched, as she moved away from it and up the dusty path to the house.

It took several minutes for someone to come to the door after she knocked. Finally, an older woman pulled it open.

"I'm looking for a room for the night," Merci said.

The woman looked her up and down, seeming to focus first on Merci's disheveled mass of curls then on her dirty and bleeding bare feet.

Merci bit her tongue to keep from giving the woman a piece of her mind. "I've been traveling, and I need a place to bathe and rest." She'd never had to plead for anything in her life. She lifted her chin defiantly, staring the woman in the face. "I have money. Plenty of it." Her tone was purposely haughty.

Finally the woman spoke, and her voice was surprisingly gentle. "You are welcome to stay here as long as you like."

"I'm not looking for charity." *Not even in a place like this.* She met the woman's clear gaze. "I simply need a room." To emphasize her point, Merci reached for the pouch at her waist and drew out several coins. She hoped the woman couldn't see how few remained. No matter; after a bath and once she had again donned her new dress, she was certain employment would be hers. She counted out more money than was necessary in what she knew was an irresponsible, cavalier act, even as she dropped the coins into the woman's hand.

"You can call me Mrs. Johnson." The proprietress put the money in her apron pocket. "And you are…?"

"Merci Byrne. *Miss* Merci Byrne."

"Miss Byrne, you can follow me." Mrs. Johnson stepped back and pulled open the door so that Merci could enter.

The house smelled of lemons and pine, and the wooden floor was polished to perfection. Merci was suddenly ashamed of her filthy and bleeding feet and wished she'd left her shoes on, no matter the pain. Frowning, she followed the woman to the bottom of narrow stairs leading to the next floor. As she ascended, the woman moved slowly, favoring one leg. The worn wood creaked with each tread of their feet.

They reached the landing, turned, and continued the ascent. Finally, she led Merci to the end of a dimly lit hall, then stopped to swing open the door to a small, bare room.

Merci stepped inside, again surprised at the sweet clean smell and scrubbed appearance. An iron bedstead stood near a small window, a scarred bureau was crowded into one corner, and in the other a spool-legged sewing table with a lamp and a couple of books. A faded floral paper, yellowed with age, covered the walls. Worn and mended lace curtains hung from the window, and dust particles floated in the beams of sunlight that poured through to the floor.

For an instant that seemed to last forever, Merci stared at a pool of sunlight on the shining floor and her thoughts went back to the rancho's breakfast room. A longing washed over her, an ache so deep it made her lightheaded. She touched the wall to keep herself from swaying.

Mrs. Johnson cleared her throat, and Merci looked up to see the older woman studying her. Perhaps pity. Perhaps simple kindness. She hadn't seen such a look since her mother had begged Merci to listen to her, to let her love her. A lump formed in Merci's throat, and it surprised her. She gave Mrs. Johnson a curt nod of dismissal.

The woman walked to the door, then turned to look at Merci who stood, suddenly feeling lost, in the center of the room.

"The privy is out behind the house. Behind the rose garden."

Merci nodded.

"If you like I will ask Mr. Johnson to bring a bathtub to your room. You'll have to carry the water up the stairs yourself, though. His back's been ailing him, or he would do it for you. And as you probably noticed, I have a hard enough time carrying my own self, let alone a bucket of water." She laughed, surprising Merci with the musical sound.

"Thank you. I—I could use a bath." She hated herself for feeling so beholden to someone's kindness.

"I'll put the kettle on to heat, then." Mrs. Johnson hesitated as if to say something more, then merely nodded and stepped to the door.

"Thank you."

"You let me know if there's anything else I can do for you."

The charity in her voice brought another quick sting to the back of Merci's throat. It made her angry that such tenderness threatened the wall she was trying to build between herself and the world. "That will be all," Merci said gruffly. "Please leave me."

Mrs. Johnson closed the door behind her, and Merci settled onto the edge of the sagging bed. The iron springs squawked their complaint. She ran her hand over the worn quilt. The wedding ring pattern. Her grandmother had used the identical design to make five such comforters—one for each grandchild, Sandy, Gregor, Kerr, Quaid, and herself.

Her gaze moved again to the pool of sunlight on the floor, and she remembered a Spanish rhyme Camila once taught her as she pieced together Merci's quilt.

There is beauty in the sunlight,
In the soft beams from above.
Blessed child, the world is full of beauty
When the heart is full of love.

Merci curled onto the bed, her eyes hidden in the crook of her elbow. *A world full of beauty?* She clenched her hands into fists so hard her nails dug into her palms. There was a time she thought it true, but not now. Until a week ago, her life had been perfect for as long as she could remember. Her world had been perfectly ordered. Her home, her schools, her friends, even her beaus. All her world had been beautiful. Even she had felt beautiful.

But now? She might be beautiful on the outside, but only ugliness existed inside her.

A heart full of love?

And what about love? Her grandparents had given their home and all their vast holdings to Quaid. That was proof enough of their lack of love, their disgust for her. It was all the proof she needed of her own worth. To them, she was nothing more than a constant reminder of her mother's rape.

How could her grandmother have taught her such a song? Grandmother Camila had known even then the vile blood that pumped through Merci's heart.

She rolled onto her stomach, her face still covered, her shoulders shaking with silent agony. She was still lying on the bed when a knock sounded at the door.

"Miss Byrne?" called a soft, gravelly voice.

Sitting up quickly, she drew in a deep breath to compose herself. "Yes?"

"Miss Byrne, I've brought your bathtub."

She gulped in another calming breath and closed her eyes, fighting to regain control of her emotions. Finally she headed to the door and pulled it open. A stooped-shouldered man looked at her sheepishly.

"I'm sorry to disturb you, child. But the missus said to bring this up to you." A stout tin bathtub rested by his side.

Merci took a single step through the door and stooped to pick it up. He blocked her way, holding up a trembling hand. "I wouldn't think of allowing it, child. A lady shouldn't be hefting such a weight."

She gave him a curt nod and stepped aside as he wrestled the bulky bathtub into her room and placed it on the floor at the foot of her bed.

When it was in place, he started to the door, then turned to look back at her. "When we have guests, we like to set out flowers in a pot— over there." He pointed to the small sewing table. "But I haven't been myself this year. Too tired to tend the roses." He shrugged. "If I could've, I'd have seen to it that you had flowers."

Merci set her lips in a line, refusing to let his kindness touch her.

He reached for the worn brass handle, halted again, and turned. "There—over by the sewing basket in the corner—you'll find books, if you have a notion to read while you're with us."

"Thank you." She gave him a curt nod, hoping he would hurry and leave.

"The *Holy Bible* is there on top." He looked pleased with the selections he offered.

A brittle laugh erupted from her lips. "That's the last book I'd pick up to read," she said between clenched teeth.

He didn't seem surprised, but fixed a bright, blue-eyed stare on her face. He didn't say a word, only nodded slowly as if musing about something, before turning again to shuffle through the open doorway.

Merci closed the door a bit too hard behind him, then turned back to the small, spare room. She stared at the empty metal tub, then to the

Bible at the top of the stack of books, wondering why it disturbed her so. After all, it was the same as the others. It was made of paper and cloth, nothing more.

Mrs. Johnson called to her from the bottom of the stairs. "Your bathwater is boiling, child. You can come down now to fetch it."

Merci made three trips from the kitchen with the steaming kettle of hot water, then three more with cold water in pails. After the last trip she closed the door, slipped off her clothes, and stepped into the tub of water. Mrs. Johnson had thoughtfully given her a bar of handmade soap on her final trip down the stairs with the empty kettle. It smelled of rose petals and glycerin.

She leaned against the backrest, then realized too late that she hadn't meant to face the sewing table with its lamp and small pile of books.

There it was at the top of the stack. *The Holy Bible.*

Everything she had ever believed about God had turned to ashes a week ago. What kind of God would play such a cruel trick on his creation? The filth coursing through her veins was part of that joke.

Staring at the Bible beneath the lamp, she picked up the bar of soap and a brush. With all her energy, she began to scrub herself. The coarse bristles stung and scratched, but still she pressed them into her skin and moved the brush back and forth on her limbs, her torso, her back, her neck.

Her skin turned crimson. Scratch marks covered her arms and legs. Her tears flowed unhampered, spilling into the water and mixing with the lye and fat that made up the cleansing bar.

And directly in her line of vision was the vile book that she'd been told was God's Word. The book that her mother and grandmother had read to her. The evidence they used to fill her with lies about a God who loved her.

She scrubbed harder.

I HAVE CALLED YOU BY NAME; YOU ARE MINE.

Ha! She pressed the brush into her skin and scrubbed her left forearm until tiny lines of blood droplets formed and coursed from her elbow into the water.

I HAVE LOVED YOU WITH AN EVERLASTING LOVE.

She washed her legs, digging into the flesh with the stiff bristles. Lies. Obscene lies. As vile as she was inside. Tears streamed down her face, dripping from her chin onto her scratched knees.

YOU ARE PRECIOUS IN MY SIGHT, BELOVED. YOU ARE MINE.

Precious? No such word could be uttered in the same breath as her name! None!

She let the brush float from her hand, and she considered sliding downward into the water until it covered her face, letting it fill her nostrils, her throat, her lungs.

She stared at the water, her thoughts bitter and cold. There would be no tomorrow, if she allowed herself such an act. No more pain. No more darkness.

YOU ARE PRECIOUS IN MY SIGHT, BELOVED...

If she took her life, darkness would win. The thought intrigued her.

LOOK TO ME, I AM YOUR LIGHT...

She sat up straight and brushed the tears from her cheeks. Suicide would be a cowardly act. And though her nature might be a myriad of base traits, cowardice wasn't one of them.

She lifted her chin. She was self-reliant. She might be rotting from the inside, but somewhere in the decay, a defiance existed that would see her through.

If she did decide to end her life—and she wasn't ruling out the possibility—it would not be in a bathtub in the middle of some godforsaken boardinghouse. And it would only be after she had exhausted all of her resources.

She stared at the marks that covered her limbs. If she took her life, no one would know, or care, what happened to Merci Byrne. Fitting, somehow. She laughed, letting the bath's tepid water trail through her fingers.

No one would care.

Her mother's face appeared in her mind, but it only made her more determined. Her mother had lied to her all these years. How could love and lies exist together?

They couldn't. Therefore love didn't exist. She would exorcise all remnants of it from her heart, just as she would scrub her vile self clean until the day she died.

The following morning when the boarders had seated themselves around a large circular oak table, Mr. Johnson bowed his head for the blessing. All followed his lead, except Merci, who glared at him as he prayed.

"Father," he said quietly. "We ask your blessing on your children gathered here today. Go with them on their journeys. Let them be aware of your presence, your guidance and grace."

Merci's cheeks heated with anger. It was a mockery to speak such lies.

"May they be aware of your deep love…"

She clamped her lips together. *Love? Ha!*

"Draw each one nearer to you with every step they take…"

She continued glaring at the top of his head as Mr. Johnson closed his prayer. The boarders joined in the "amen" at the end.

He seemed to sense her bitter scrutiny and met her gaze with those unnerving clear eyes. She didn't look away. The other boarders were chatting amiably about the beautiful, late October day.

Mrs. Johnson handed Merci a basket of warm-from-the-oven biscuits. "Will you be staying with us again tonight, Merci?"

"It depends on whether I find employment nearby." She took a biscuit and passed the basket to the boarder on her left, a stoop-shouldered older woman who wore her hair in a prim knot.

"What kind of employment are you looking for?" The woman to her left turned toward Merci as she split her biscuit in two and buttered one side.

"I am trained as a schoolteacher."

Mrs. Johnson beamed and nodded. "Now that is a fine profession, Merci. You must enjoy children?"

She shrugged one shoulder. "I suppose so."

There was an uncomfortable silence at the table, then another boarder cleared his throat. "You might try looking for a position west of here. I hear some of the new settlements might be looking for a schoolmarm."

Merci looked up in surprise. "Thank you. I'll do that."

The man gave her a friendly nod. "I heard about a position in Santa Isabela a few weeks ago. It's a pleasant little fishing village. An hour's ride from here. I hear tell they're on the lookout for young, educated women."

Merci looked at him with greater interest, trying to ignore his red-rimmed, rheumy eyes. "Who told you they might have need of a teacher? Can you give me a name?"

"I certainly can." He beamed at her. "There's a well-known horse ranch near the cliffs. Man who owns it wants to be mayor of the new city when it incorporates. Says he thinks starting a schoolhouse for the new families moving in might be a way to get elected."

"And his name?" Her heart was thudding in anticipation. Perhaps this was just the change in fortune she needed.

The man chuckled. "Just about everyone around these parts has heard of him. Richest horseman this side of Kentucky. Raises Arabian horses."

"His name?" she prompted again.

"Adam Cole. When you arrive in Santa Isabela, just ask the first person you come to. They'll tell you how to find his ranch."

"Thank you." Merci gave him a brilliant smile, and the man reacted just as she knew he would. He knocked over his coffee mug. She was learning that her physical charms could be used to her advantage. She glanced at him again from beneath her thick fringe of reddish eyelashes, just to see the result.

He fumbled with the overturned mug, grabbed for his napkin, and yanked the tablecloth instead. She almost laughed. There was a clatter of knives and forks and plates, then finally Mrs. Johnson stood to help him.

The poor man's face was vermilion as he ventured another glance at Merci. This time she gave him an aloof stare, which seemed to put him in his place. After a few more moments of embarrassing silence, the conversation continued.

Later that morning, Merci hiked to the two schoolhouses within walking distance. She didn't bother with Knight, wanting to look more dignified upon her arrival at the school. Without riding clothes, she would have to hike up her skirt or ride sidesaddle, neither of which was appealing.

The first school, a mile and a half to the east, was Hunter Street Grammar School. She knocked boldly on the door while school was in session, only to be greeted by a disgruntled schoolmarm who let her know in no uncertain terms that her chances for employment at Hunter Street were nonexistent.

Merci trudged back the opposite direction three and a half miles to Bluebell Grammar School. There, the headmaster told her that his school was closing in two months. He explained sadly that Hunter Street's better building plus the declining numbers of students enrolled at Bluebell were the cause. But he suggested she try the Merriam Stonehall Agency for Exceptional Young Women, a service placing teachers in homes to teach sickly housebound children.

Sickly children? The thought appalled her, but off she trudged again. Her feet were tired and the blister-sores were bleeding through her stockings. She spotted a trolley stop, weighed the use of her last coins for such frivolity. Foolish but necessary, she decided as she limped to the bench and sank down onto it.

She glanced around and, relieved to see she was at the trolley stop alone, pulled off her right shoe and rubbed her toes with a deep sigh. She'd just replaced the right shoe and removed the other when the trolley pulled to a stop in front of her. She grabbed her shoe and headed for the trolley door, before it might leave again. People appeared, seemingly from out of nowhere, hurrying toward the vehicle.

A man laughed behind her. Her cheeks flamed, and she looked back, even as she continued her awkward one-shoed hop to the trolley.

She grimaced. It was the rheumy-eyed man from the boardinghouse. He hurried to help her to the trolley door and gave the driver two coins to pay their fares as she dropped to a seat and finished lacing up her shoe. He settled onto the bench beside her, sweeping his bowler from his round head.

She pulled out her money pouch and attempted to reimburse him for her fare. But he laughed and said, "Keep your money. It's nothing. Really."

She had been taught never to accept such favors from a man, not even something as small as a coin for trolley fare. But so many of the proper niceties that had been drilled into her had nothing to do with the life she lived. "Thank you," she said simply.

"Where are you headed?" He leaned a bit too close, and she backed away from him toward the window.

"I've learned of an agency that hires young women to teach children in their homes."

"You're seeking employment as a governess now?"

"Well, yes. I suppose it's the same thing. The headmaster didn't say." She fell silent as the trolley jerked forward. "I'm still hoping to find a job as a schoolmarm, if possible. But I might as well explore other careers." She shrugged, uncomfortable giving him more information than necessary.

He was crowding her again, and she glared at him until he moved back. He stared past her through the window for a short time, then moved his gaze directly to her face.

"Merci Byrne, your name is almost as pretty as you are," he said, his voice low and a bit too friendly.

Merci looked straight ahead, wishing the man would get off at the next trolley stop. The agency was still three stops away.

"I've decided to head back to Santa Isabela," the man said, obviously attempting another ploy to engage her in conversation. "Day after tomorrow."

She didn't answer.

"I'll put in a good word for you with Adam Cole."

With a sigh, she turned to him again. She didn't like the man, but he could be useful. "I could use a well-placed recommendation."

"When you get to Santa Isabela, if you'll call on me, I'll let you know what Adam Cole thinks of my recommendation. I'll be staying near the oceanfront, a small place called the Ice House."

She nodded. "And your name is?"

He looked pleased that she asked. "Harley Pink."

She swallowed her smile. The name couldn't have been more fitting for a man with a face the color of a bowl full of strawberries. "All right, then, Mr. Pink, I will contact you at the Ice House."

"Splendid, splendid!" He glanced out the window as the trolley slowed. "Ah, now. Here is my stop. Will I see you at supper tonight?" He rose, took her hand, and kissed her fingertips gallantly.

She resisted the urge to withdraw her hand and instead gave him another of her brilliant smiles so he wouldn't forget her—or, more appropriately, wouldn't forget to recommend her to Adam Cole. "I will be there, Mr. Pink."

"Please, my friends call me Harley." Behind him, the trolley car operator jangled the bell.

"I will call you Mr. Pink," she said firmly. "And you may call me Miss Byrne."

"All right, then, Miss Byrne." As the vehicle pulled away, he waved his bowler vigorously until a buggy passed between them.

She settled back and let out an irritated sigh. She could put up with his attentions, she supposed, if in the end he helped her get a job with this Adam Cole's assistance. At least he gave her a glimmer of hope.

Her thoughts were still on the employment possibilities in Santa Isabela, when the trolley jerked to a stop once more. She stepped down to the street and scanned the crowds. It occurred to her that she was in a section of town frequented by her grandparents and mother. She turned in a small circle, looking for the elegant Byrne brougham and the team of spirited grays.

Relieved, she moved her gaze to the brightly colored building facades above the board sidewalks. The elderly and young, some with children, others with babies in prams, jostled her as she moved down the boardwalk.

Not a single face was familiar. No one turned toward her with the remotest sense of caring. No one knew her.

Suddenly a longing for her family twisted her heart, squeezing it until she thought she might die. She'd never before felt so alone.

Distracted, she stepped into the street.

"Ho, there, girlie!" a horseman yelled as he rode toward her. "You better git yerself outta the way!" The horse's hooves almost struck her as he rode by.

She scampered toward the sidewalk, only to be narrowly missed again by a buggy heading the other direction. Its driver cursed at her as he popped his whip above the old nag pulling the rig.

Then she spotted the sign on the facade directly across the cobbled brick street. In bold, dignified-looking letters, it stated, *The Merriam Stonehall Agency for Exceptional Young Women.*

Merci fixed a smile on her face and drew herself up tall. Then squaring her shoulders, she strode purposefully toward the door.

She reached for the handle. Her hand was moist, so she paused to dry her palm on her skirt.

At the precise moment she lifted a small pleat from her dress to dab at her hand, she glanced inside through the glass.

She frowned, hesitating, her hand once more on the door handle. Through the window she could see an older woman sitting behind a small desk, intently discussing something with another woman who sat directly across from her. Beside the second woman stood a man.

A man she recognized. The Indian Songan. The one her mother called Song.

Though her back was to the door, the woman seated in front of the desk was easily recognizable. Merci would have known her mother anywhere.

Merci leaned her forehead against the door and closed her eyes for a beat of her heart. She longed to run into her mother's arms, to feel encircled in her love and protection.

Instead she turned and walked away, her spine stiff. She had gone only a few steps when the agency door flew open with a bang.

"Merci!" her mother cried.

Merci heard the soft thud of Brighid's footsteps on the boardwalk. But she didn't wait, or turn. She ran into the street, attempting to lose herself among the trolleys and carriages and milling crowds.

Tears trailed down her face at the sound of her mother calling her name.

ELEVEN

Merci ran into the crowd in the street, then slumped low to hide her bright red curls. Two buggies and a wagon creaked along the street just as her mother and Songan attempted to cross. They stepped back, giving Merci time to dart into a mercantile.

Heart thumping wildly, she knelt between an apple barrel and a stack of flour sacks. When she could breathe again, she wiped a spot on the dusty window with her sleeve, then peered through. Her mother and Songan were heading down the street opposite the trolley stop.

She waited until they were out of sight, then hurried to the counter where the elderly proprietor was measuring out a length of calico for a talkative customer.

"Please, sir," Merci panted, "do you have a back entrance I could use?"

He looked at her over his wire spectacles. "Well, now. I might, young lady. May I ask what's your hurry?"

"It's faster to get to the trolley that way. And I need to get there fast. I absolutely cannot miss that trolley."

"Well, then, I suppose so. You can come around here behind the counter and…"

Merci didn't wait for him to finish. She hurried around the counter and raced to the back of the shop. Moments later she was again on the street. After a quick glance both directions, she headed to the stop, hoping she wouldn't have to wait long for the next car west.

She stepped backward into a cobbler's shop near the trolley bench, gave the man a quick and friendly smile, as though she was awaiting her ride in the most ordinary way. With a puzzled look, he went back to hammering the sole on a tooled boot.

Merci nibbled at her lip until she saw the yellow car moving slowly up the street. When it jerked to a stop in front of her, she raced to the doorway, drew out a coin, and dropped it in the driver's hand.

She fell into her seat, breathing hard as she scanned the crowds for her mother and Songan. Barely two minutes later, the trolley eased forward at precisely the same instant her mother rounded the corner, obviously searching frantically.

As if Merci's face were a magnet, Brighid lifted her gaze to her daughter's eyes just as the trolley moved away. As the vehicle picked up speed, Brighid ran behind it. Merci craned in her seat and watched as her mother stumbled, slowed, and finally gave up altogether.

Merci lowered her head, fighting to keep the tears from coming again. As the trolley rattled along the road and the center of the city disappeared, she reached the conclusion that she could no longer stay in Los Angeles. Her mother now knew her general whereabouts. The risk of being seen again was too great.

That night at supper she told the Johnsons she planned to leave at daylight. A few minutes before nine o'clock, Mrs. Johnson knocked on Merci's door. The older woman's lined face spoke of her concern.

"Mr. Johnson told me you like to read," Mrs. Johnson said, looking inside Merci's room as if she wanted to enter and talk.

Merci didn't invite the woman in, neither did she bother to correct her about the assumption.

"You can take along any of our books, if you'd like…when you leave. Maybe someday if you're back in this neck of the woods, you can return them for another traveler to use."

"I don't need books," Merci finally managed. "I have nothing to carry them in, so it's really no use."

Mrs. Johnson limped through the door and headed to the small lamp table. She gently touched her fingertips to the worn leather cover of the Bible. She seemed to be hesitating, or perhaps praying, then she turned back to Merci, the volume in her hands.

"This one is especially helpful for life's journeys, child."

"I don't need any help on my journey."

"We all need help." The shadows around the older woman's clear eyes were accentuated by the lamplight, but there was kindness in them. The lines at the corners spoke of someone who had laughed a lot, but who had also known much pain.

Merci shrugged. "Maybe so. But I've heard all about this God, how he can provide guidance and wisdom and mercy and love—I no longer believe any of it. So you might as well keep it here for another traveler, someone who will find it more useful."

Mrs. Johnson stood still, the leather book in her hands. She studied Merci's face for a moment. Uncomfortable, Merci let her gaze drift somewhere beyond Mrs. Johnson's shoulder.

She replaced the Bible, then turned again. "It's up to you, of course. If you ever need help, help of any kind, will you come back here?"

"I don't need help—not from you, not from God, not from anyone."

Mrs. Johnson nodded as if understanding the bitterness in Merci's heart. Her expression said she didn't judge, that she didn't even need to know the details of Merci's pain. She simply understood it.

"All right, then," she said softly. She moved slowly to the open door, stepped through, and turned again to Merci. "When you get to thinking there is no God, or when you get to considering that if there is a God, he wants nothing to do with you…" She paused. "What I'm trying to say is that even if you think he wants nothing to do with you, that doesn't make it so."

"He is a cruel God."

"You can think that, too, but your thinking it doesn't make it so."

Merci had no argument for the woman's logic, but she let out a bitter laugh anyway. "No better than fairy tales," she said, letting her gaze fall on the leather volume. "At least in fairy tales, the princess finds she is loved after all."

Again Mrs. Johnson's bright eyes scrutinized Merci's face. "Don't you know, child, that you're the daughter of the King? That he loves you as if you're the only one in the world to love?"

Merci laughed again, a short, sputtering sound. "There's nothing you can tell me that I haven't heard before, Mrs. Johnson."

"Nonetheless," she said quietly, "any of the books are yours to take if you change your mind."

Merci's annoyance increased at Mrs. Johnson's persistence. She shook her head irritably and shut the door in the old woman's face.

She leaned against the door for a moment, her jaw clenched so tight it ached. Finally, she turned and studied the pile of books. Hers to take, the woman had said. Any of them. A new thought occurred to her. She could sell the Bible. It might not be worth much, but at least it could provide her with a meal or two.

She moved to the table and touched its leather binding. It was soft and worn, and judging from the ornate lettering and snap closure, it had probably belonged to a woman of some means. It was small enough to be tucked into her money pouch until she had the opportunity to sell it.

Smiling at her wise decision, she dropped it into the drawstring bag that hung at her waist. Its weight added to her feeling of well-being. If only the heavy bulk came from coins and bills instead of the pack of lies that filled its pages.

She slept fitfully that night and woke well before dawn. With haste, she pulled on her riding skirt, tattered blouse, and boots, then headed to the dining room sideboard where she stole two hard rolls and three apples. She bit into the largest of the apples as she headed to the livery to fetch Knight.

The stableboy hadn't come around yet, which was as she'd planned. It wasn't her true intent to be dishonest with her business dealings, but she needed her few remaining coins for lodging while she traveled. To assuage her conscience, she promised herself she would someday return with the money she owed.

She'd earlier packed the gray schoolmarm dress in the flour sack, and now, holding an apple between her teeth, she strapped the sack around her waist, tucking it in the belt that held her money pouch. She pressed the apples and rolls into her lace-up shoes, then tied the shoelaces to her belt loops. After she mounted Knight, she nudged him gently to a trot, taking care to remain as quiet as possible as they headed down the dirt road. She finished her apple and tossed the core to one side at the edge of town.

The magnificent beast responded to her urging, almost anticipating the direction she had planned. By sunup the city was behind them, lost in a filmy mist that had moved in from the ocean during the night.

The air was brisk, and soon she could smell the sea air. As she rode, she planned where she would head first, settling on the stretch of ocean-front hotels that Mr. Pink had mentioned. She didn't want to stay in the same establishment as Mr. Pink, but surely there was another similar place of lodging, maybe a boardinghouse, nearby.

If she could pay for another night's lodging, perhaps two, then likely she would have employment by the time her money was spent.

Bolstered with new confidence, she pressed Knight to move faster toward the sea. By noon they'd entered a sparsely populated valley, headed over a ridge, then into another valley, this one narrower and longer. A small mountain range blocked her view of the water, but the smell of sand and fish and ocean spray filled the air.

Finally she reined Knight to the top of a small rise and drew him to a halt.

He danced sideways a few steps, and she reached down to rub his neck. There, stretching before her, was the Pacific. She'd seen it only once before in her life, and its magnificent power struck her now, just as it had then.

Wave after wave of rolling swells pounded the sand. They crashed, rippling onto the smooth beach, foaming and splashing, then ebbing as a new wave billowed. She slid from Knight's back and, holding the reins, led him closer to the water. The beach was deserted. Knight whinnied slightly, his ears flicked forward in interest. He tossed his head a few times, then sidled away as another wave crested and rippled up toward them.

"How about it, boy?" she whispered. "Are you ready for your first ride on the beach?" She rubbed the velvet between his eyes, stroking him and whispering close to his ear, just as her Uncle Spence had taught her.

Another wave crashed, and this time Knight danced sideways again, but without the same nervousness. She laughed and rubbed his neck, pressing her face into his mane. "There's just you and me now. No one else. We're family. We've got to stick together. If one of us wants to ride on the beach, the other has to want the same thing. Now, that makes sense, doesn't it, baby?"

Her cheek still pressed against the stallion's neck, she looked out over the waters. The late morning sun slanted against the waves, casting millions of dancing jewels of light to explode across the breaking waves.

"I think it's time to ride, big boy," she murmured, still stroking his neck. "What do you think?"

She swung a leg over the stallion's back, then leaning low against his mane, she urged him forward. At first he sidled away from the water again, keeping well to the drier sand. She let him take his lead, allowing him to walk and trusting him to know when to head nearer the ebb and flow of waves and when to quicken his gait.

The breeze caressed her face and lifted her hair, and she drew in deep gulps of the fresh, salt-laden air, delighting in the strange rotten-sweet aroma of seaweed that had washed up on the shore.

Knight seemed to sense the abandon that Merci felt. He moved from a trot to a gallop, and the rhythmic thud of his hooves on the sand matched the beat of her heart. Her arms were circled around his neck, her eyes closed. She bent low, so close his mane became one with her hair in the wind. She cared for the beast so deeply her heart ached. He'd been hers, a gift from Uncle Spence, when he was a colt. She'd learned from Spence how to gentle him, how to calm him with a touch, with communication that went deeper than words.

And now he was all that remained of her old life, all that was left for her to love. It made her attachment to the horse even stronger.

She didn't know how long they rode into the wind. She only knew that when Knight tired and slowed his gait, she looked up surprised to find her face wet with tears.

A small brook flowing into the ocean had stopped him, and she let him walk to it. She slid from his back and sat on the sand while he drank, then grazed on the slender stream's bank.

Watching him browse in the tufts of dried winter grass, she was aware—perhaps for the first time—how dear was her responsibility to him. He was a magnificent beast and deserved better than the treatment she'd given him since leaving the ranch. She studied him, knowing it wouldn't be long until his gleaming coat dulled from lack of attention, his bulk and muscle diminished from lack of food. He would suffer if she didn't bring in some money soon.

She got up and walked over to him, then stood quiet and still, stroking his neck, combing his mane with her fingers, murmuring softly, her forehead pressed against his warm coat. The waves beat gently against the sand, and above them gulls cried as they circled. Knight seemed to sense her dark thoughts and lifted his head, shook it slightly, one ear forward, one back.

"All right, big baby," she laughed. "You're asking me, why, if I'm so concerned, don't we get on our way, find that job for me, some decent oats for you." She hoisted herself onto his back, then reined him back to the north as she gently pressed her heels into his sides. Again she let him find his own gait, knowing he was still skittish about the water. But soon they were galloping along the spit of sand, and Merci threw back her head for the sheer joy of it. For a moment she almost forgot her heartache.

They kept to the smooth strip of beach until they reached Santa Isabela. It was midafternoon when they rode up a sloping cliff to the houses and shops at the top. She'd let Knight stop to drink and graze along the way, but she was hungry, so they stopped to rest beneath an arbor heavy with the gnarled branches of a dying wisteria vine. She pulled out another apple and crunched into it while surveying the small village comprising fewer than a half-dozen businesses and a scattering of houses along the cliffs in both directions.

An abandoned mercantile, its shutters banging in the chill breeze, its windows layered with dust, caught her attention first. Then her gaze traveled up the road to the blacksmith's, to the livery adjoining the smithy, finally resting on the saloon at the far end of the road. Even from this distance, she heard raucous laughter and tinny piano music coming from inside.

A fog was rolling quickly inland from the ocean, and Merci shivered as she looked up and down the empty street.

The town appeared to be abandoned except for the saloon. She frowned and began walking, still munching on her apple. It occurred to her that perhaps she'd gotten the directions wrong. Maybe this wasn't Santa Isabela after all. Then her breath caught as she read the name on the decaying facade of the saloon: The Ice House, Santa Isabela, California.

Even more disturbing was the lack of a schoolhouse or anything that appeared to be used as one. Surely it was on the opposite side of town.

With a sigh, she examined her options. She could ride back to the Johnsons', but judging the time it took coming west, it would be impossible to reach the boardinghouse by nightfall.

She frowned as she surveyed the few houses stacked against the cliffs. Ramshackle at best, she thought with a shudder, imagining those who lived inside. Probably the same folks frequenting the saloon at the end of the street. Better not to knock on their doors and put herself in danger.

The fog was lying thick against the ground now. Swallowing hard, she decided that she would head to the far end of the small town, perhaps ride a few miles north to see if there were any other settlements.

She mounted Knight and headed slowly down the center of this strange, empty village. Just as she reached the saloon, the double doors swung open, and two men stumbled to the boardwalk.

She kept Knight moving as a sudden shudder of alarm caused the fine hairs on the back of her neck to stand on end.

"Well now," said one of the men, moving awkwardly toward her. "What have we here?"

The other let out a whistle and, swaying slightly, joined his companion. Merci kicked Knight in the flanks, and he reeled at her sudden motion, front hooves in the air. Her first thought was to calm him rather than save herself. She reached down to pat his neck, and murmured softly to him, at the same moment the first man grabbed her wrist.

Twisting it painfully, he took advantage of her distraction and snatched the reins away from her clutches. He yanked them hard to stop Knight from rearing.

The horse brought down his powerful front legs and stopped still, quivering.

"Let go," Merci growled.

"A lively miss, eh?" The man laughed, keeping her wrist clenched in his iron grip. "Now, where would a pretty girl like you be off to all by your lonesome?"

"I—I'm not alone," she said. "My—my husband is back a ways. You'd be wise to let loose of me. He'll not take kindly to you bothering me."

The second man grinned up at her, his tobacco-browned teeth hideously visible between the split of his mouth. "If I had a wife as purty as you, I wouldn't let her out of my sight. No sir, I wouldn't. Would you, Jed?"

The first man chuckled. "Maybe we ought to watch over her till he gits here. What do you say, shall we?" He gave her arm a playful tug, nearly pulling her from the horse. "Keep her safe."

Both men laughed.

"Give me the reins." Her temper was quickly taking over her fear. "Now!" She made a reach for Knight's reins, but without a saddle to give her support, she might as well have been reaching for the moon.

The man let her almost touch it, then pulled it back, grinning at the sport. "Here, missy. Try it again," he taunted in a singsong voice.

"This is gonna be fun, Jed," the second man said. "Try it again. Bet you can make her fall off."

Merci waited until they laughed again and stumbled backward to make her move. With all her strength, she dug her heels into Knight. The big horse seemed to be awaiting her command. He reared with a scream, front legs kicking. The reins dropped, and Merci, pressing close to Knight's neck, made a grab for them.

By now a crowd was gathering outside the saloon, and there were whistles and catcalls. Merci let Knight rear again. Then, pressing her heels into his flanks, she gave him the signal to run like lightning.

The horse's response was quick, and he thundered forward, hooves pounding. Merci wrapped her arms around his neck in a death grip, clinging to his mane, willing herself to become one with him as he soared along the fog-shrouded road.

She held her head to one side and saw how his nostrils flared and how his breath let out small clouds of moisture. She ventured a quick look back and saw no one approaching, so she slowed Knight to a walk and finally halted him. She craned, staring into the twilight gloom, but she could hear only the sounds of waves crashing a hundred yards down the sea cliff.

She slid from Knight's back and landed beside him with a thud. Still holding the reins, she walked the horse slowly along the road. The heavy ocean mists laced in and out of the coastal forest, nearly enshrouding the stunted pines and century oaks, the peeling trunks of the eucalyptus.

From time to time she stopped and listened for someone trailing behind. But all she could hear was the dripping of moisture from the trees joining the low roar of the surf. She peered into the darkness on both sides of the road, but the glow of lights from nearby houses—if there were any—eluded her in the gathering gloom.

They had walked at least three miles when they came to a small bridge. Merci led Knight down the bank to one side and, in the waning, gray light, made out a pond just east of the structure. It was obvious by now that they would have to spend the night without shelter. She drew in a deep breath, trying to find some spark of courage inside, but she felt lonelier and more discouraged than ever.

The night was the longest she had ever endured. The damp chill sliced through clothes and flesh to her bones, and though she pulled her gray dress over her and piled some rotting leaves on top of that, still she shook with the cold.

She rose before the first hint of morning and sat with her arms wrapped around her knees, her forehead down, considering what she should do next. When the ashen dawn lit the eastern sky, she looked down in dismay at the gray schoolmarm's dress. The layer of leaves she'd used as a blanket had smudged it black and brown.

Holding it up, she considered it for a few minutes. She remembered hearing that the Soboba's rubbed their clothing in sand instead of soap, so she headed to the pond and plunged the dress beneath the icy-cold water.

Today was the day she'd planned to find Adam Cole. She scrubbed harder. She couldn't hold out much longer. There were so many things she needed. Money and shelter. A place where she was known. Food for herself. For Knight. She held out the dress with stick-straight arms and, staring at the stains with dismay, plunged it into the frigid water again.

Angry tears flowed as she scrubbed the cloth against the sand. She couldn't stop repeating the action. Scrubbing. Staring at the stains. Scrubbing harder. Staring at the holes, the flaws, that had begun to show. Scrubbing again until her knuckles were raw.

Finally she let go of the dress, and it floated toward the center of the pond. It remained there, and for a moment she wondered if the current might carry it back to her. It didn't. Still kneeling, she watched it float west toward the bridge. She didn't wait to see whether it was carried out to sea or if it hit a bramble or snag along the way. She was beyond caring.

She stayed two more nights at the place near the pond. Her days passed slowly. The first day, she finished the hard rolls and the single remaining apple, while Knight grazed in the clumps of yellowed grasses. They both drank from the mountain stream that fed the pond. By the second night her stomach cramped so that she couldn't stand upright because of the pain. She didn't know whether it was from the brackish water or the lack of food.

As the sun threatened to burn off the fog the next day, she decided it was time to act. She gathered her strength, and with Knight walking slowly behind her, she headed back to Santa Isabela.

She was weak with hunger and fatigue when they finally rounded the last curve leading into town. The Ice House was her destination, and when its ugly edifice loomed through the fog, she strode purposefully toward it.

Two men stood on the boardwalk in front of the swinging double doors. Both turned with interest when they heard her approach. She recognized one of them as Harley Pink.

He grinned when he saw her, and even on the gray day, his face turned a bright vermilion. "We've been expecting you." He exchanged a knowing look with the second man, then turned again to Merci. "This here is Adam Cole."

There was a hard, brittle look in the man's eyes that made Merci want to flee. But too much was as stake, so she drew in a deep breath, put on her most dazzling smile, and stuck out her hand amiably. "It's truly a pleasure, Mr. Cole."

"Please, call me Adam," he said.

She looked up at him shyly through her fringe of lashes, a calculating look that had never failed her. "All right, Adam," she drawled. "I believe I'm doubly happy to make your acquaintance."

He chuckled and put his arm around her waist to guide her into the saloon. "Take care of the lady's horse." He spoke to Harley, though he didn't move his gaze from Merci's face.

Then to Merci he said, "You look hungry."

"I am." She laughed. "You wouldn't believe the trouble I've had these past few days." She looked around the saloon. Maybe it wasn't such a bad place after all. Several women sat with men at tables. They were laughing and carrying on. Some were pretty and wore beautiful clothes. None of them looked hungry.

"Tell me about your troubles." Adam slid back a chair and helped her into it, then seated himself across from her at the small round table. "Maybe I can help."

She fluttered her fingertips. "We'll talk about me later. First, Adam, I want to hear about you. About your plans to run for mayor of Santa Isabela." She gave him another of her devastating smiles. "And I hear you're planning to build a schoolhouse here for the children."

He chuckled as if at a joke, rolling his eyes skyward. "Oh, that!" He laughed again, and called out to the men scattered along the bar. "Here we go again with those wild rumors, pardners."

"What do you mean, rumors?" Her mouth felt like cotton.

He reached for her hand and rubbed the backs of her knuckles with his thumb. "Did you see any children when you rode in?"

She shook her head. "No." The word came out in a small croak. She pulled back her hand.

"Actually, I have no need to run for mayor. I already run this town." Then he looked to the men at the bar again. "Fact is, you might say I own it. Ain't that right, pardners?"

There were a few grunts of assent.

"I really…must be going, then," Merci said and pushed back her chair. "I came here to speak to you about becoming the town's school-marm. There's obviously been some mistake."

"There hasn't been a mistake, Merci. I've heard you need help, that you're on the run from someone or from something." His voice had turned warm, and his eyes didn't strike her as so brittle and cold anymore.

Besides, the food he ordered for her arrived. A steak the size of Rhode Island and a tin cup full of cowboy beans. Adam pulled her chair back to the table and moved his hand over the tempting food like a magician with a trick hat. Without waiting for his order to arrive, she picked up her fork and knife and cut into the juicy slab of beef.

He laughed as she hurried through her plateful of food. "It's good to see a woman with an appetite."

He snapped his fingers to the saloonkeeper and called for two shot glasses of whiskey.

"I don't drink," she said, wiping her mouth with her napkin.

"You might want to make this one exception," he said with a laugh. "My powers of observation tell me you've been awhile without food—am I right?"

She nodded.

"I thought so. The whiskey will help the food settle. If you are indeed bordering on starvation, your stomach will react. Just give it a few minutes. Believe me."

She hadn't noticed a bit of queasiness, but what he said made sense. "All right, then. Just one."

The saloonkeeper headed to their table and placed the two shot glasses between them. "Leave the bottle," Adam said.

And the man did, though not before giving Merci a look of admiration. She didn't know if it was for finishing the entire steak dinner, for being brave enough to down a shot of whiskey, or simply for the turn of her cheek or the color of her hair. He blushed when she smiled at him.

"You do that with great finesse." Adam poured her whiskey and handed her the glass.

She held it while he poured himself one. "Do what?"

"You know very well what I mean." He lifted the glass to his lips and smiled at her over the rim.

Watching him, she lifted her own glass and drained it. It stung her throat, and she blinked back the hot tears that formed, then coughed.

"Now that's what I call gumption." Adam laughed and filled her glass again.

After a few more sips, a gray haze settled into her mind. Adam didn't seem to notice and began to tell her about his business, that which made the town such a success.

She frowned, trying to follow his words.

"The way I see it," he was saying. "You have two opportunities. It's obvious that you have no money—or at least very little. Is that true?"

She couldn't stop herself from nodding. "Not much left." Her tongue was too thick to form the words. She laughed and tried again. "A few coins," was all she could get out.

"As I was saying, you have two opportunities here."

"I do?"

He reached for her hand again. This time she didn't pull it away.

"Oh yes," he said with a slow smile. "I say, you can sell your horse. He should bring a handsome sum. A handsome sun indeed."

"No. Oh…no. I could…never do that…" She tried to focus on Adam's face, imploring him to understand. "Knight is…my family. I will never sell him."

"I understand." Adam poured her another drink.

She lifted it to her lips, nodded, and drained the glass again. Her lips were starting to feel numb, and some of the amber liquid sloshed down her chin. She giggled and dabbed at her face with her napkin. "Now, as I was saying…" She pointed at him, but her elbow slipped off the table. She giggled again, still wagging her finger. "I could…never, ever…sell my horse. I don't care…what the offer is."

"Then that sets aside that opportunity."

"Opportunity?"

"I raise thoroughbreds. And I know a good piece of horseflesh when I see it." He chuckled. "I can judge a horse nearly as well as I can judge a woman."

She waggled her finger at him again. "If you're such a successful horse breeder…what are you doing in this, this…privy of a town?" The word privy struck her as funny, and she let out a loud guffaw. "Privy of a town," she repeated loud enough for everyone in the room to hear.

"I have another business on the side, Merci. That was the next opportunity I was going to mention. Let me tell you about it."

He poured her another drink, and even in her dark haze, she noticed that his calculating look had returned. He spoke of his business, the women who worked for him, and how they pleased their clients.

"Clients?" She frowned, attempting to make sense of what he'd told her. "What do you mean, clients?"

He laughed softly, and leaning closer to her, whispered exactly what his women did for the men who came to their door. He also told her about the money she would earn—and that she would never be hungry again.

She pushed him away, understanding him clearly, even in her drunken state. She scooted back her chair. "I don't want to do that…what you said…" She pushed herself up from the chair, but she couldn't stand. She stared at him helplessly and, when he made no move to help her, settled back down.

"You need money, Merci. And I have just offered you two ways to get it, and get it fast. Then you can be on your way, never to look back. Go wherever it is you're headed."

She slumped forward. "That would be nice."

"I've arranged for a room for you tonight. You need to rest and bathe." He took her hand and squeezed it. "You need time to think this offer through."

Merci nodded, though she could sense something wasn't quite right about the arrangements. What was it her mother always said? Never take even a hatpin from a man; he might want the whole hat in return.

But where would she go if she left this saloon right now? What would she do? She stared at him, trying to formulate a plan. She could think of nothing except her horse. "Where's Knight?"

He waved his hand, dismissing her worries. "Don't you fret your pretty little head about your horse. He's being taken care of very well. Believe me."

"No, no!" she cried. "I want to see him. I have to see him now."

"All right, little dove," Adam Cole said, grinning. "If you insist. We'll go see him."

She nodded and tried again to stand. Her knees gave way, and she slumped to the chair, feeling sick.

Cole quickly stepped behind her and lifted her by placing his hands under both her arms. With a grunt, he twisted her around and hoisted her like a sack of flour over his shoulder. Shrill whistles and catcalls filled the room, mixing with raucous laughter and piano music.

She pounded his back, which made the laughter grow louder. "Put me down," she cried.

Without a word, he carried her in that most undignified manner, behind the bar and up the stairs at the back of the room.

"This isn't the way to the stables," she cried, still pounding his back with her fists. "Put me down!"

He threw back his head and laughed.

"Put me down," she howled.

"I'll take good care of you," Cole said to her in a soothing voice. "Haven't you figured it out? You're mine now." His laughter was now low, seductive. "Or should I say, tonight you're mine? Tomorrow will be another story. That's when you'll start to earn your keep."

They entered a long hallway. He carried her to the very end and set her down in front of a small, dirty door. He fumbled with the locked handle until it swung open. Sweeping her into his arms again unceremoniously, he carried her to the bed and dumped her onto the rumpled bedclothes. She bounced awkwardly a few times while he stood grinning down at her confusion.

Merci turned her gaze away from his bright and expectant eyes, letting it drift across the room. The walls were covered with flocked red and gold wallpaper. A lone lamp stood in the corner, its fringed crimson shade covering a dim light. An ornate mirror hung opposite the bed, and small twin tables flanked the headboard. Various powders and vials were scattered on one, and a whiskey bottle and two dirty shot glasses were atop the other. The room smelled of cheap perfume, so sweet and overpowering she thought she might retch.

Cole stood at the foot of the bed, his gaze flicking over her. He leaned low, one hand on either side of her shoulders, so close she could feel the heat from his breath.

"Ah, my pretty one," he said, "from this moment on, you work for me. Eighty percent of every dollar you make will come to me." He trailed his fingertips along her jaw. "With your remaining twenty percent you will buy yourself clothing, scents, and baubles to please your clients. Your food and lodging will be free—as long as you please me. If you disobey, those luxuries will be withheld until you repent."

His mouth now twisting into a cruel smile, he considered her for a moment. "Should you try to run away, certain, shall we say, *penalties* will result, each reprimand more painful than the last." He paused, a brittle mirth lighting his eyes. "Trust me, you don't want to know what methods we use to keep our little birds in the nest. Suffice it to say, no one ever tries to run away after the first time."

Merci stared at him in terror. She was too numb to move, to walk, to run. She shoved against his chest and tried to roll away from him. Standing with surprising agility, he grabbed her ankle and yanked her back to the middle of the bed.

He glared at her. "I told you earlier that I own everything in this town," he said. "That wasn't the whole truth. I do own everything in this privy of a town." He studied her with a hungry expression that made her blush. "I also own everyone in it."

He twisted her ankle until tears formed in her eyes and trailed down her cheeks, dripping from her ears to the bed. "Let me remind you, my pet, lest you forget. You now belong to me. You will do exactly as I say." He sat down beside her and lifted her limp hand to his lips. "After tonight," he murmured, "you'll be known as Little Dove."

Merci turned her face to the wall, her shame bringing a new flood of tears.

A night bird called from somewhere in the distant hills, reminding her of the rancho. But the memory was short-lived. Cole turned her face with his big rough hand, forcing her gaze to meet his. "By morning," he murmured, "you'll know everything you need to know. Everything."

He was right. By morning Merci knew the meaning of evil. She had looked it in the face. His cruel face. And she knew that everything she'd thought about herself was true.

TWELVE

Glorieta Pass, New Mexico Territory
November 1889

The train whistle blew, causing Emmeline to awake with a start. Gertie snored lightly beside her, undisturbed by the jostling and whistling and loud clacking of rods and cylinders, the screech of metal wheels on the rail with every curve they rounded. Other than traveling in a luxurious car with steam heat and fine plush seats, it mattered not that she and Gertie were traveling first class. They might enjoy linen tablecloths and fine food, butlers at their beck and call, seats that converted into berths at night, but they choked on the same soot as those riding in day coaches.

Emmeline glanced down at the older woman's beloved face and lifted a prayer of thanksgiving that she had survived the voyage and rigorous journey to Bahia, Brazil, without any ill effects. If anything, she seemed to thrive in the warmer climate and the excitement of traveling again after decades of staying in the same city.

Two first-class tickets in the elegant hotel car had been her father's gift when they left the East Coast, mostly because of the aging Gertie. Emmeline laughed to herself. Truth be known, Gertie would have been happier in the day coaches, sitting next to gamblers, cowpokes, and squirming babies.

As they wound through the steep switchbacks in Glorieta Pass, the small woman's head bobbed with the swaying rhythm of the train. A dime novel lay faceup on her lap where it fell as she drifted to sleep.

Emmeline removed her glasses and rubbed her eyes before peering out the open window. On either side of the train, piñon pines and junipers grew as thick and tall as some medieval forest. She drew in a deep breath. For once, the wind was blowing soot to the opposite side of the train. She set her glasses on her nose and squinted again. Small log cabins dotted the hillsides; ribbons of smoke drifted from adobe chimneys, the scent of wood smoke mixing with the fragrance of fresh pines.

She settled against the soft velvet seat, watching the blur of dark forest pass by the window. After nearly a week on the train, she and Gertie would cross the California state line in a matter of hours, leave the mountains, and head across the great desert.

She closed her eyes and let images of the past months flood her mind, the enchanting journey by ship to Rio de Janeiro, the trek inland to the land of the beautiful Bahia. Even now the fragrances from the lush flowering plants and the taste of the luscious fruit of the Bahia orange filled her senses. Thousands of groves had colored the landscape, and when she bit into her first piece of fruit, she knew that Sara Dearbourne was right. This was a magical fruit that would do well in California's climate.

While she awaited propagation of her young trees in Brazil, she had studied horticulture with some of the best-known growers in South America. She had learned about the different varieties grown throughout the world, hundreds more than Sara had mentioned in her first letter.

Emmeline had arrived home with three steamer trunks full of books and a head full of knowledge about the soil and water her trees would need, the pests she would fight, and the frosts that could kill her entire grove overnight. More than anything, she had arrived home with a determination to be successful for her own sake and for that of Sara Dearbourne. She opened her eyes and watched the forests pass by her window. It had been nearly a year since she left Washington. She had advised her parents by letter that she and Gertie needed to board a train west immediately upon disembarking in Charleston. Time was of the essence. Her young trees couldn't survive long in the harsh eastern climate.

Jamie and Hallie met the ship in Charleston, with Glenna and Hazel in tow. The family had only three days together before Emmeline and Gertie boarded the train for California. Her sisters divulged that Mr. Cadman's body had never been found and that the authorities, upon finding no solid evidence of chicanery, had quietly dropped the investigation. No one in Washington society spoke of her indiscretion, Glenna told her, sounding disappointed. Or even linked the word murderess with her name, Hazel added breathlessly, also sounding sorry.

So it had been a tempest in a teapot after all, Emmeline thought with a smile, leaning back in the plush seat. The train rounded a wide switchback, and she glanced back at the freight cars, twenty of them all together, stacked high with trunks and parcels. She smiled, correcting herself. Actually, sixteen boxcars full of baggage plus four cars full of orange trees. Her beautiful Bahias.

Eyes still closed, she listened to the rhythmic clack of the pistons as the wheels moved along the tracks. Then she stretched, yawned, and sat up, first letting her gaze drift to the forests outside the window, then to the valise propped open on the seat beside her. At the top were her volumes on insects, fertilizer, and smelting pots. She had read and reread them, nearly committing them to memory. She was reaching for the book on insects when the bright cover of Gertie's dime novel caught her eye.

Glenna had slipped Gertie several Greenlief Hildebrand westerns while the family visited in Charleston. So far, Emmeline had resisted them. That was, until lately, when Gertie decided to read certain sections aloud. Her book of choice was *The Grizzly Bear and Zeke MacNab*, and the scenes she read were heart-stopping renditions about train robberies, gunfights, and outlaws.

The train hit rough track, and the car shook slightly. *Zeke MacNab* slid from Gertie's lap, and Emmeline reached to catch it. Before setting it aside, she thumbed through, thinking she might read the first page or two.

At the very least, it was an amusing pastime, to laugh at the writing and characters of the touted-to-be-true stories from the Wild West. She skimmed the next few pages. *Merciful heavens!* It was better than she imagined. She turned a few more pages, then with her foot moved the valise filled with horticulture books under her seat.

Greenlief Hildebrand was an accomplished storyteller. So engrossed was she in the story that she didn't notice Gertie was awake until she heard the older woman chuckle.

"Child, I never thought I'd see the day that you would choose readin' about an outlaw over a smudge pot." The small woman sat up and stretched her birdlike limbs before smoothing her hair and adjusting her hat. Then she gazed out the window. "Where are we?"

Since first leaving Charleston, she asked the same question after each of her several naps a day. Her eyes were no longer as sharp as they used to be, and even with her thick spectacles, she could barely see across the room. She could still read words on a page, though, by holding the book close to her nose. "Those trees out there? And mountains?" She squinted toward the window.

"We're heading through Glorieta Pass."

"Mean's we'll be to Lamy soon. Maybe by nightfall."

"I think we're scheduled to stop at the station. There's not much there, but we can get out and stretch our legs."

"Mercy me," Gertie said with a sigh. "I never thought I'd live to see the place again." She turned from the window to peer up at Emmeline. "The time I crossed by wagon with your father we came through Lamy. The tracks must be laid nearly on the same road we followed—the Santa Fe Trail. Jamie was somethin' in those days. He was still recovering from his imprisonment. And was worried sick he might be caught by the Federals any minute." She shook her head, admiring him still, even all these years later.

"He'd just met your mama and you back in Kentucky. You two were warming his heart even then. He told me often enough every detail he could remember of his stay with you, how your mama nursed him back to health, how you cried and clung to him when he told you good-bye."

"I remember."

Gertie watched the landscape slide by for a few more minutes, her lined face thoughtful. "I remember so well how I knew God had sent him to me." She peered up at Emmeline. "He does that, you know."

"Does what?"

"Sends folks various places."

Emmeline laughed. "I'm certain he does. He sent Jamie to you, and you to the rest of our family."

Gertie adjusted her hat and again seemed to be considering something important.

"I know you well, Gert. What are you pondering so hard?"

The older woman lifted a white brow. "I was just wondering who he's sending us to now. Or who he's sending to us. He's taken us from nearly one end of the earth to the other. He's surely got a plan in mind."

"He says abide in him and he'll give us the desires of our hearts. I figure that's what we're doing. As long as we're abiding, he'll show us the way—his way."

"That wasn't exactly what I was pondering," Gertie said with a grin. "But it'll do for now, child. It'll do." She chuckled, then nodded toward the book Emmeline held. "So you've finally given in to a small frivolity?"

Emmeline laughed. "It's your doing. The passages you've read to me piqued my curiosity."

"I declare I'm half smitten with that outlaw myself." She chuckled, low and gravelly. "He's a fine work, that one."

"You prefer Zeke MacNab to the lawman...what was his name?" She frowned.

"Honey, there's no comparison." Gertie sighed and rolled her eyes. "I can just see Zeke's snapping black eyes, the way he pulls his hat low on his forehead." She sighed again. "Sheriff Tucker Penn seems as dull as dirt compared to our hero, Zeke."

Emmeline giggled. Before Gertie awoke, she'd been picturing Zeke MacNab. Tall, dark, and handsome, the author called him. A hint of danger in his voice and manner, yet he walked with the grace of a deer. She sighed in chorus with Gertie, then giggled again. Quite out of character for herself, she thought, and blushed.

"Why, young lady, I don't think I've ever before heard you sigh with such abandon—at least not since you were knee-high to a katydid." Then she reached for Emmeline's hand. "You need more than a book hero in your life, child. You've never known real love."

Emmeline nodded. "I've concluded that real love isn't for me. It would have happened by now if God had intended it for me." She held her chin high, trying to convince herself. "Perhaps that's why Zeke Mac-Nab appeals to me. No danger other than the scrapes he gets himself into, and they're on paper, not written in the heart."

An hour later, when the train squealed and screeched into the Lamy station to pick up passengers and supplies, the two were still discussing the lawman versus the outlaw in *The Grizzly Bear and Zeke MacNab*.

"Maybe we'll see a real-life outlaw in one of these stations," Gertie whispered as Emmeline helped her down the stairs and onto the platform. "My, my, wouldn't that be something?"

As they strolled among the other passengers, Emmeline's breath rose in puffs of steam and fogged her eyeglasses, and Gertie's teeth chattered with cold. The promise of warmth drew the women into the station house. They hesitated only briefly at the door, taking in the room. A few travelers milled around. A squat potbellied stove sat in the center of the room, with chairs circled around it. Two empty seats beckoned them.

Emmeline helped Gertie into one and settled herself into the other. She pulled off her gloves and held her hands toward the warmth of the stove, rubbing them together.

Gertie was still clutching *The Grizzly Bear and Zeke MacNab*. When she pulled off her gloves and held her hands toward the fire, the book slid from her lap and dropped to the floor.

A tall red-haired man, sitting nearby, reached to help. He glanced at the book before handing it back to Gertie. "Ma'am, that's not a book for the fainthearted," he drawled, his voice full of admiration.

Gertie's eyes were merry. "No sir, it's not. And I've never been accused of being fainthearted."

He leaned forward, and his voice dropped. "You did know that MacNab lives around these parts, didn't you?"

"Noooh." The word came out in a sigh of delight. "He doesn't… does he?"

A shock of red hair bounced when the man nodded. "I hear tell, it's not far." He nodded knowledgeably. "Yes ma'am. Not far at all."

"Noooh," Gertie breathed again.

The man looked honest, wide-eyed and fresh-scrubbed. But it was the freckled face that gave him a rather boyish look. A trustworthy look.

Emmeline pushed up her eyeglasses and leaned forward to peer at him. "My aunt has been reading the works of this dime novelist since we left the East Coast. They've been entertaining but, I must say, a tad unbelievable."

"From the East, you say?"

"Yessir," Gertie put in. "Been on this train for nearly a week now. Heading to California." She gave him a quick nod. "Where're you headed, young man?"

"I'm heading to St. Louis. My train's not due till morning, though. I'll be bunkin' here in the station house overnight."

While Gertie *tsk-tsked*, Emmeline stuck out her hand. "My name is Emmeline Amity Callahan. And this is my traveling companion, Miss Gertie Hill."

A flicker of something lit his eyes, though his expression didn't change. Surely it was her imagination. Most anything might color her thoughts after reading the unbelievable tales in *Zeke MacNab*.

"Which part you headed for? Southern or northern?" He leaned back to study the two.

"Southern."

"Emmeline will be taking over a rancho. Plans to plant orange trees," Gertie said and tilted her chin upward with pride. "Not many women can boast of that these days."

The red-haired man narrowed his eyes, studying Emmeline with an amused look. "And is this a large rancho?"

"Yessir," Gertie said. "Thousands of acres near a town called Riverview."

"I've been there," he said, looking more amused than ever. "Know it well."

"Do you?" Emmeline sat up straighter. This was good news. "Tell me about the place—the people in the Big Valley. That's where the acreage is, a place called the Big Valley. Do you know the people there?"

He seemed to be considering something a thousand miles away. "I do," he finally answered. "I do indeed. There are some good people there. The Byrnes have lived there for decades. Also the Dearbournes."

"That a fact?" Gertie said, still peering at him with interest.

"Good people," he said, "except for the grandson."

"The grandson?" Gertie and Emmeline said in unison.

"Which one?" Emmeline added quickly.

"From what I hear the grandsons who live in the north—there are a passel of them—are fine, upstanding citizens."

"We've heard that too," Emmeline added.

"Handsome boys, all," the red-haired man said solemnly. "But that other young man, the other grandson of the Byrne family—what shame he's brought upon their heads."

Emmeline heard herself gasp. "Shame?" Her words came out in a whisper.

The young man shook his head slowly, back and forth, then sighed heavily. "He's an outlaw."

"Quaid Dearbourne? He—he's an outlaw?" Emmeline croaked. "I hadn't heard." She let the news sink in as she and Gertie exchanged a bewildered look. "An outlaw?" she repeated. The news was hitting too close to home.

The young man nodded. "Yes ma'am. One of the worst. Wanted all over the Wild West for his crimes." He glanced at the dime novel clutched in Gertie's hands. "Far worse than even your Zeke MacNab. Far, far worse. And meaner than MacNab ever thought of bein'. Far meaner indeed."

Just then the conductor called for passengers to board, and Emmeline helped Gertie to her feet. They had taken a few steps when she turned around.

"Sir," she called, "we didn't get your name."

But the young red-haired man was engrossed in conversation with another man who looked enough like him to be his brother.

The conductor called for boarding again, so Emmeline shrugged and took Gertie's elbow, and they moved along the platform to the train.

That night in their berth, Gertie exclaimed again and again her delight in having a real outlaw in the family! The only time she let the notion go was during the few minutes they knelt for their prayers. And as soon as they stood to dress for bed, she brought it up again.

"We're not even blood relatives," Emmeline reminded her. "So we can't claim him as family. Even if we wanted to."

Gertie laughed. "I can. It's never stopped me in the past." Then she thought about it a minute. "I've adopted plenty of strays but never an outlaw. And I like the idea just fine."

Emmeline rolled her eyes as she buttoned her high-necked flannel sleeping gown. "Heaven help us. Taking over the land was going to be hard enough—but now I've got an outlaw to contend with?" She slipped into her small bed and reached for the light to turn it down. She was lost in thought for a few minutes before she added, "I just hope he doesn't come to visit his grandparents often."

Gertie laughed again. "The man must be more devious than we thought. We should have read between the lines in Sara Dearbourne's letters. Poor dear. He's her grandson too. She didn't want us to know about his life of crime. Whenever she mentioned him, she just said he was stubborn and disagreeable."

Emmeline stared at the ceiling. "I wonder if outlaws even visit their grandparents."

Gertie *tsk-tsked.* "You're hoping to see him come riding across their land."

Neither woman spoke for several minutes. The train clacked along the rails in a pleasing rhythm. Organ music from the parlor car carried toward their berth. Emmeline smiled as she recognized *Jeanie with the Light Brown Hair.*

"As for me," Gertie mused, "if I see that outlaw riding across the Big Valley, even from a distance, I'll be happier than a bear making his home in a hollowed-out honey tree" She yawned noisily. "Think of it, a shirt-tail relative meaner than Zeke MacNab. And an outlaw to boot." She fell quiet as the train gently swayed. Soon she was snoring louder than the clacking of rods and pistons.

Emmeline lay awake, staring into the darkness. Zeke MacNab sauntered into her mind from the pages of Gertie's book, big-shouldered and graceful, hat pulled low. She grinned to herself. Maybe Quaid's being an outlaw wasn't so unpleasant after all.

She tried to keep a smile from playing at the corner of her mouth as she drifted to sleep.

THIRTEEN

Merci stared into the shot glass on the scarred plank table, hoping the amber liquid it contained might dull her pain. Snatches of coarse conversation drifted toward her, and in the corner of the saloon near the piano, a john sang out a ribald ditty. Others soon joined in, laughing and making lewd remarks between verses.

A few weeks ago she wouldn't have known the meaning of the words. Today she did. Carnal knowledge. Wasn't that what it was called? Laughing to herself, she again focused on the glass before her, lifting it to her lips.

She hated her life. No, hate wasn't the word. Hate required emotion, and she was too soul-weary to feel any emotion at all. She was indifferent—cynical and indifferent—though she hid it well. Already, her reputation had spread, and men fought for Little Dove's favors each night. She gave them what they wanted, and relentless in their appetites, they took a piece of her soul with each repulsive act.

The men, young and old, spoke of her flawless beauty, her fiery hair and creamy skin, even as they used her, sometimes with violence. She'd stopped scrubbing her skin bloody after Adam Cole's brutal thug, a gorilla of a man, meted out her first punishment for the self-inflicted act. She fetched more money without flaws, Cole had explained later as he gently spread liniment on the places where the gorilla had hurt her. Hurt her without leaving a mark.

Nightly she received drunken proposals of marriage, and she'd learned how to refuse without offending. She held her head high, laughing with her johns as if they were the most charming of men. She sat on their laps in the saloon and winked and flirted and batted her lashes.

Her clothes, personally chosen by Cole, were made of fluff and frills, corseted at the waist, immodest at the neckline. The other harlots had taught her how to apply paint to her face, down to the heart-shaped mole above the corner of her mouth. She gave each man her body with feigned enthusiasm, and her heart turned harder with each act. She wondered if it would ever be anything other than a mass of granite in her chest.

She'd considered killing herself at least once each night since her arrival at the Ice House, but the temptation to leave was greater than the temptation to give up. If only she could find Knight, she might have a chance of escape.

Even as she entertained the endless line of men, she thought about, and planned in great detail, how and when she would leave. She imagined where Cole might have taken the stallion, supposing it was to his ranch, which she'd heard was on hidden acreage several miles outside town.

It wasn't likely she could find it, even if she were lucky enough to escape Cole's clutches. Still, the thought of being reunited with her horse kept the faintest hope alive within her. Kept her from taking her life. Kept her thoughts from the vile acts she performed, numbing her consciousness with dreams of escape.

Silently she cursed the thought of the stallion in the care of the most despicable of men. Her lower lip trembled, and she lifted the glass toward her mouth, again praying the liquid would give her the courage to get through another night.

The strong whiskey burned her throat on its path to her stomach. She took another sip, swirled the amber fluid around her mouth, and let it slowly make its way down her throat. Finally the lazy warmth she needed spread through her senses. She lifted the glass and emptied it in one swallow.

She was learning to do that well, and it was the one thing Cole allowed her to have without restraint. She figured she was luckier than other girls who worked for him. He'd filled them so full of laudanum that they couldn't get along without it. They would do anything for its promise. Sometimes she worried that he might slip it into her food or drink. She wouldn't know she was an addict until it was too late.

She placed the glass on the table and stared at it for a good half-minute.

An older man's raspy voice drew her attention away from the empty whiskey glass. "Can I buy you another?"

"Cole sent you?" She didn't need to ask. Of course he had.

She looked up as he swung a chair from another table and sat heavily across from her. Two teeth were missing in the split between his lips, and a red face swollen from too much drink leered at her.

"Another for the lady," the man called out to the saloonkeeper, then flicked his gaze to Merci. "Orwell Crosby at your service." He inclined his head. "And yes, your Adam Cole sent me. I ran into him in the stables. He said I wouldn't be disappointed. Didn't even bother with your name. Just said to look for the prettiest woman here, the one with hair like a flame and skin the color of ivory."

She gave him a dazzling smile and reached for his hand. "Mr. Cole was correct. You've come to the right place for a good time." She kept her smile in place while the liquid splashed from the saloonkeeper's bottle into her glass.

"Your voice is gay," Orwell Crosby said, "but your eyes tell me you are sad. Tell me how I can help your distress." He squeezed her fingers. Cole had said she was to never pull away from a john's advances. She didn't. Releasing her fingers from his, she played with the back of his hand seductively, just as she'd been taught.

His dark eyes studied her over the rim of the glass as he lifted it to his lips and swallowed heartily. He signaled for another whiskey. There was cruelty in his face, and it frightened her.

She took another long swallow, hoping it would dull her fears. Crosby leaned forward, staring intently into her eyes. "How I can help you, sad lady? Tell me."

Something told her that this man was different than the rest. Her heart pounded as he reached across the table and stroked her cheek with the backs of his fingers. "So pretty," he whispered and drew his hand away slowly. "But does this pretty lady have a name? Or shall she forever remain nameless in my dreams?"

"Little Dove."

"Fitting," he said, looking into her eyes again, "for a pretty lady—innocent and pure." He laughed. "But such ladies should never look sad. Tell me now, my precious dove, how I can help you be happy." His expression didn't match his lighthearted words, and he studied her as though she were something to scrape off his boot.

She swallowed hard and fluttered her lashes. "Tell me about the livery," she said easily. "You said you saw Cole there?"

He nodded. "He rode in just as I did."

"They say he has a new addition to his stables. A handsome black stallion."

"I don't know if the stallion he was riding is the one you speak of, but it was a superb piece of horseflesh. Black as coal. A powerfully built beast."

Knight. She knew it. Her heart beat faster as she tried to formulate a plan of escape. First she had to get to the livery.

He kissed her fingers again, holding his lips on her knuckles. He lifted a brow, his meaning clear—he was waiting for her to invite him to her room. She ignored the cue, her mind racing with the possibility of escape.

She waited too long. He suddenly grabbed her wrist, pulling her arm tight across the table. "Aren't you forgetting your manners?" She yelped as her elbow knocked over his whiskey glass. The amber liquid pooled then dripped off the edge of the table onto his pant leg. She stared at his face now turning dark with anger. She wondered what Cole's punishment for such clumsiness would be, and a chill ran up her spine.

The man surprised her by laughing. "You need to come with me now, Little Dove," he said, mouthing her name with a precision that frightened her. "You've been a bad girl, spilling whiskey on my clothes. I can punish you. Or I can call Adam Cole and the big man I saw him with to do it for me."

He leered at her, his red face now beading with sweat. The strange glint in his eyes made her shiver with fear. If there was ever a time she needed to escape, it was now.

She thought of Knight in the livery and drew in a deep breath, forcing herself to speak lightly. "Of course, my dear man, I prefer you to Cole. However, I need some air first." She smiled into his eyes. "Would you mind accompanying me on a stroll."

"That's not the punishment I had in mind," he growled.

"Oh, sir. I didn't expect it would be." She met his gaze without blinking.

"I will accompany you on your walk, and we shall find a place perhaps more suitable than your little room." He moved swiftly to her side and wrapped his arm around her waist. His eyes shone with ugly passion.

Merci lifted a painted brow in a coquettish manner, as if considering his words for a moment. "You mentioned the stables earlier. Do you suppose it's quite deserted?" She gave him an enticing smile.

He stared at her in surprise, then laughed. "Yes. Of course, the livery, but only if you promise to make it worth my while."

"Oh, my dear Mr. Crosby, I will indeed." She pursed her lips as if blowing him a kiss. "I think you'll find that no punishment is necessary."

Crosby kept his lust-filled gaze on her face as he reached for her hand. She swallowed her irritation as he roughly pulled her to standing and again slipped his arm around her waist. "Let's head to the livery, then," he whispered in her ear. Then holding her close, he steered her toward the swinging saloon doors. Once outside, he looked her up and down, the corners of his mouth curling upward.

A cold rain was falling. She shivered as he pulled her along, his arm gripping her with iron strength. A few minutes later they reached the end of the boardwalk, and he led her down the three plank steps and into the muddy street.

By the time the livery loomed in the pale and rain-misted twilight, Merci's clothes were soaked through, the hem of her frilly dress caked with mud. She was trembling now, her teeth chattering, her knees shaking with fear.

Crosby became more aggressive as they walked, alternately shoving and pulling her toward the livery. Merci emptied her mind of everything save the task ahead.

He opened the door and pulled her inside. A familiar fragrance of damp hay filled her nostrils, reminding her of her grandfather's stables. A lantern hung to one side, and Crosby quickly struck a match to light it.

He let his gaze travel down the double row of stalls that lined the length of the barnlike building. In the center were buggies and wagons, to one end the tack room. He seemed to be choosing the place where he would take her.

The livery was strangely quiet, and she worried that Cole might have taken Knight from the place already. She closed her eyes, wishing she knew how to pray.

"Let's take the stall at the end," he said, staring at her with lust in his eyes. "A fitting place for a dirty trollop like you." His face was twisted, and there was a fire in his eyes now that spoke of the violence to come.

Shivering, she let her gaze drift from him to the far end of the stable, searching for a sign of Knight, hoping above all hope she could reach him in time—if he was even there.

Crosby grabbed her arm with one hand, pulling her the length of the livery. With the other, he fumbled with the ties at her bodice. It was more than she could bear.

"No!" She shoved at him with all her might.

With a yelp of surprise, he let go and stumbled backward. A moment of utter silence followed. He stared at her, his expression filled with rage. "Just who do you think you are?" She trembled at the mix of disgust and wild passion in his eyes. "Some highfalutin' society woman? You may sound like some educated, landed gentry's daughter, but you're no different from any other harlot on the streets. You don't fool me for a minute."

Head down, he lunged like a bull, catching her off-guard. She tumbled backward and landed on the ground, her arm pinned behind her. She tried to coil away from him, but he held her fast. Breathing hard, he knelt over her, his back to the far end of the livery. She smelled the foul stench of his breath and felt his rough hands pulling at her clothes.

A hard knot formed in her stomach. She screamed.

He covered her mouth. She bit his hand. Tasting blood, she screamed again.

At the sound of her cry, Knight exploded from his stall. Fury propelled his massive body toward where she lay.

She rolled from beneath the stunned man just as the stallion shrieked and thundered toward them. In one great surge of energy, Knight reared above Crosby, his muscled haunches supporting his massive body, his front hooves churning.

Crosby curled into a ball to protect his head. Knight screamed in fury and pounded his front hooves down on the man, then backed away for another charge.

At that instant—in a single swift movement—Merci leapt onto the stallion's back and dug her heels into his flanks. Head low to his neck, she clung to the horse's mane as he burst through the double wood doors of the livery.

Her yells had caught the attention of the townsfolk, and at least a half-dozen men carrying weapons ran through the rain toward the commotion. Knight reared again.

She spoke low to him, still clinging to his neck. Calming him. "It's all right, boy. We're going to be all right."

His nostrils flared. Merci rubbed his neck with trembling fingers.

"Just go, boy. Just go! Now."

The big stallion reared once more, sidled to the left, and headed down the street toward the saloon.

He had carried her only a few yards when Adam Cole appeared out of the darkness. He yelled, and two of his men ran into the street. She glanced back to see them take aim as they lifted their rifles.

She pressed her heels into Knight's flanks, and he thundered away, hooves beating the dirt road.

Merci didn't look back, not even when the shots rang out.

FOURTEEN

Emmeline stared through the train window at the curious California landscape. It was bleaker than she remembered, with its sagebrush, dried grass, and barn-sized boulders blended together on a flat, colorless terrain. The only geographical points of interest were a few sharp mountain peaks to the east.

She nudged her spectacles slightly higher and squinted, trying to imagine how the flat land would look with a cover of lush, green orange groves. Then she smiled. It would be very nice indeed.

The train headed around a switchback, then another, before climbing a gently rising incline. At the summit, Emmeline leaned forward for a better view, a small sigh escaping her lips.

The city of Riverview seemed to spring out of the desert. Her gaze was drawn first to the palm trees that seemed to lift their fronds upward like hands praising God in his heavens and then to the elms and eucalyptus whose graceful branches hung like angel wings. And just as Grandmother Sara had said in her letter, rows of citrus trees seemed to embrace the small city from all sides.

The train wound along the river until it was directly across from Riverview. Then it crossed and slowed as it approached the station. Within minutes the locomotive clattered and blasted, belching steam as its metal wheels screeched to a halt.

Gertie pressed the stickpin into her hat and adjusted it on her head, and Emmeline brushed her hair into its usual tight topknot. Then with both hands she took up her own hat from the seat beside her. It was the only hat she'd brought along, but it never failed to lift her spirits. She placed it on her head, the crown covering the topknot of hair, then tied the moiré ribbons into a large bow.

She peered into a hand mirror and sighed while considering her too-plain face, framed by stick-straight strands of muddy, coffee-hued hair that had already sprung loose from the twist under the hat.

She replaced the hand mirror in her satchel, smoothed her skirt, and fluffed the enormous pouf of her sleeves. Drawing in a deep breath, she summoned a porter to fetch their trunks. The women followed him to the door at the end of the car, Gertie hobbling in tiny steps, Emmeline with her head high and her heart pounding.

After Emmeline had shot a prayer heavenward, she sailed down the metal stairs and onto the plank platform, ostrich feathers bouncing.

She felt like dancing as she stepped into the California sun and breathed in the balmy air. Grinning, she turned to help Gertie down the stairs.

Quaid watched the passengers emerge from the cars and mill around him on the platform. He leaned against a post with his ankles crossed and scanned the crowd. Families bustled by, a few stopping to greet one another. Beautiful young women with wasp-waists and bustles. Round grandmothers, portly grandfathers, skinny cowboys, and bright-faced children, squealing and laughing and carrying on.

Certainly no Emmeline Amity Callahan among them. Not that he'd know what she looked like.

The steam from the locomotive still hovered near the train, lacing in and out of piles of trunks and carpetbags and porters hurrying along the platform. Quaid frowned, pushed himself to standing, then slowly sauntered down the tracks toward the end of the train.

Then he spotted a young woman standing near a boxcar, a tall figure in a hat as wide as her shoulders. A hat covered with what surely had to be an entire flock of exotic birds.

Emmeline Amity Callahan.

Beside her stood a traveling companion, a wiry older woman, keenly interested in all that was going on around her. Gertie Hill.

Emmeline—if he'd guessed right—was animated, hands flying this way and that as she gestured toward the boxcar door, back to herself, then to the open door again.

He drew closer and saw that the boxcar was filled with a forest of trees.

Trees as dry as dust. Spindly branches, most without leaves. Those leaves that remained were twisted, brittle, and brown.

Now he could hear the woman quite plainly. She didn't turn when he approached, but there was a distinct wail in her voice as she continued speaking. "I gave the conductor precise instructions yesterday. He was to water my trees while we waited at the water tower this morning in Box Springs. They cannot be without water for more than a day. He promised he would see to their watering."

The conductor held up his hand. "I'm sorry, ma'am—"

"Miss."

He frowned. "All right then, miss. I'm sorry, miss, but this is not my responsibility. There is nothing I can do. It was up to the conductor on this particular route to see to your trees' needs." He shrugged. "I really can't do anything for you."

"You could get water for me immediately. M-my trees…" She pulled out a white handkerchief and blew her nose.

Quaid braced himself and cleared his throat. "Excuse me, ma'am, but—"

She turned and fixed her teary-eyed gaze on his face. "Miss."

"Er, excuse me, Miss—" Quaid stopped midword, and for an instant he couldn't speak. This woman had the most glorious eyes he had ever seen. They were almost lost under that…hat. And behind the ridiculous set of wire eyeglasses perched on the end of her nose.

But those eyes. A person could get lost in the warm, soulful depths. Chestnut. Or maybe the color of buckeye pods, the most comely hue in the world.

Her cheeks flushed slightly, the color of a rose from his mother's garden. She almost looked distressed, as if admiring glances weren't something she often received.

Emmeline Amity Callahan wasn't anything like what he'd expected. And it threw him for an instant.

"You were saying?" She peered at him with a frown.

He turned up his duster collar another notch, adjusted his scowl, and rolled his shoulders forward. "You seem to be having some difficulty with your trees," he growled as he sauntered toward the boxcar and looked in. He glanced back to where she was still staring after him. "These *are* your trees?"

"Yes," she said without hesitation. The doe-eyed look was gone. "I need to get them to water immediately. This man—" She wagged her finger toward the conductor. Her hat feathers bounced with each wag. This woman was making it awfully hard not to smile. "This man refuses to admit there's been an error. He is refusing to help me. As you can see."

"Now wait a minute, ma'am," the conductor broke in.

"Miss," Emmeline corrected.

"Missy, you just wait a minute. I never said there's not been an error."

"You do, then," she persisted.

"Do what?"

"Admit there's been an error."

The man pulled off his cap, wiped his forehead with his sleeve, and sighed. "Perhaps the conductor on your train should have seen to the watering. I just took a close look at your trees there. They still got life in them. Plenty of it. The root balls aren't as dry as the rest."

With that, Emmeline hiked up her skirts and climbed into the boxcar.

After he tore his gaze away from her perfectly formed ankles, Quaid stood rooted to the platform, gawking up at her as she stooped over the small, sick trees. Her shoulders were shaking—with silent weeping, he was sure. Beside him on the platform, the old woman was wagging her index finger at the conductor, giving him a piece of her mind.

Quaid shuddered. They were both as mad as banshees. He let out a grunting sigh and hefted himself into the boxcar beside her. Emmeline was still crying.

"M-my trees…" she wailed. "Th-they are j-just about d-dead!" She shook out the wet wad of a handkerchief and blew her nose again. Noisily. Still kneeling before one of her pitiful twiglike specimens of an orange tree, she looked like a frightened deer. He tried to rid his face of the scowl and started over. "Miss, I'll give you a hand. I'll help you get your trees to water. You got enough money to hire a fleet of wagons?" He looked at the small grove. "You must have a hundred trees here."

"Y-you'd do that for me?"

"I said I would, didn't I?"

Her cheeks flushed the pretty rose pink again. "Actually, there are more than a hundred here. And there are more on the way. In a separate train."

He pictured his wild rancho lands with the glory of God's natural handiwork disappearing as they spoke, replaced by row upon row of evenly spaced trees.

"How many?" he growled.

She laughed and tilted her chin upward. A prideful woman, he could see that plainly now, or she could be in certain instances. His scowl intensified.

"Besides these, I have three more boxcars full. Nearly needed an extra locomotive just for my little forest of trees! The others are coming straight from the *Queen Victoria,* currently harbored in Charleston." She gave him a watery smile.

"How many boxcars are coming?"

"Nine."

He stifled another growl and worked out a quick reckoning in his head. "A thousand trees then, all together."

She laughed again. "Oh no! The rest are younger. Some only fingerlings."

"Fingerlings?"

She held up a slender, perfectly beautiful index finger. "This size. They're just babies." She smiled, and those glorious eyes threatened to melt him in their liquid depths.

He intensified his scowl. "So how many would you guess?"

"Four thousand."

"Four thousand trees?" He couldn't muster more than a whisper, and even then his voice broke like a twelve-year-old boy's.

She nodded, looking proud as punch again. "Four thousand."

A brief and wicked thought crossed his mind: If they wilted and died, his pristine wilderness would remain unspoiled. "Four thousand, assuming they've been watered properly," he muttered.

Her eyes filled again, and she reached for a dry and twisted leaf that clung to a skinny branch. He watched in helpless silence as she stroked the dead thing, as if trying to coax life back into it. He thought the look on her face might break his heart. The leaf broke loose from the branch and floated to the floor of the boxcar.

His voice was gruffer than he expected. "Like I said. I'll help you get these to the river. You wait here, and I'll head to the livery to hire a few wagons."

"Just a few?" She looked disappointed.

He cringed. "It'll take the biggest freight wagons in town. And teams to match." He imagined the hoots he'd get riding through the streets of Riverview with Conestogas overflowing with half-dead hothouse exotics.

He checked his pocket watch. "Should be back by four o'clock. Still plenty of time to get these trees to water before sundown."

Still kneeling by a spindly dead tree, she sniffled and nodded. "Thank you."

Quaid shrugged and got himself off the boxcar and onto the platform. He strode a few yards toward the brougham.

"Sir?" Emmeline called out.

He turned. "Me?"

She nodded and rose to stand in the boxcar doorway. "I completely forgot my manners. We haven't introduced ourselves."

He stepped forward a few feet, close enough to look into the dark eyes beneath her hat.

"I am Emmeline Amity Callahan. And this is my traveling companion, Gertie Hill." Beside Emmeline, Gertie nodded vigorously.

He pulled off his hat and raked his fingers through his hair. "Emmeline Amity, we've been expecting you."

She looked pleased. "Merciful heavens! You have?"

He nodded. "Yes ma'am, we have."

"Miss."

"Like I said, miss, we've been expecting you."

The roses were back in her cheeks. "And who is 'we,' pray tell?"

"My kin. Grandparents, MacQuaid and Camila Byrne. And my grandmother, Sara Dearborne, who's awaiting your arrival before she heads off to live with my parents in the Valley of the Horses."

Her face had gone white, and now she was twisting the handkerchief. "And what is your—I mean, who are you?"

He gave her one of his rare smiles. Poor thing deserved it after what she'd been through. Then he nodded, just like a gentleman should. His mother would have been proud. "Well, Miss Emmeline Amity, my name is Quaid Dearbourne." He gave her a small bow.

When he looked up, he could have sworn she was ready to faint. She grabbed hold of the boxcar side, clinging to it with white knuckles. "Quaid Dearbourne…?" she gasped.

Then she looked heavenward, and for the life of him, he thought he heard her talking to God about the uncivilized outlaw standing on the station platform. *Uncivilized outlaw?*

The hair on the back of Quaid's neck stood on end. He glanced back toward the station to see what outlaw was there. He looked to the right and to the left. But the platform had cleared.

He glanced back to the two women, pointed to his own chest. "Uncivilized outlaw?"

Still white-faced with fear, Emmeline Amity Callahan nodded. "Merciful heavens!" she whispered.

He shot a look at Gertie Hill, expecting to see her face as unexpectedly pale as Emmeline's. Strangely, the old woman was grinning from one wrinkled earlobe to the other.

Fifteen

Emmeline was waiting on the platform, arms folded, foot tapping, when Quaid rounded the corner driving the first of a long line of Conestogas. He leaned against the wood-slat back of the bench, his hat low, and flicked the whip above the mule team.

The man's duster was open, flapping against the wind, showing a plaid shirt underneath. The sun glinted off the golden chest hairs at the neck opening. If she hadn't been so vexed over the discovery that her Good Samaritan was in truth the outlaw Quaid Dearbourne, Emmeline might have enjoyed the sight.

She narrowed her eyes, pushed up her eyeglasses, and squinted again. Beside her, Gertie exclaimed about his handsome looks as Quaid drew his wagon close to the platform. The remaining big freight wagons rumbled and rattled along behind.

He tipped his hat toward the women, boldly returning Emmeline's gaze. This time the flush crept from her chin to the roots of her mousy-brown hair. *Merciful heavens!* She wished her heart wouldn't skip the way it was doing today. She fanned her face. Surely it was glowing as bright as a California sunset.

"Emmeline, Gert," her outlaw stepcousin said, touching three tapered fingers to his hat. He hefted himself from the bench with one fluid movement.

"Miss Callahan and Miss Hill," Emmeline corrected. And though this outlaw was her stepcousin, she wasn't about to get on friendly, familiar terms with him.

"*Miss* Callahan, *Miss* Hill, then." He set his lips in a thin line, then looked beyond the women to the open boxcar as he sauntered toward them.

Aunt Gertie gave Emmeline a scowl, then peered up into his face. "You can call me Gert any time you want to, son. All my children do." She patted his arm affectionately.

He gave her a crooked smile and swept his hat from his head. "Thank you, Gertie."

The second wagon had now halted behind the first. The driver, a red-haired man with legs so long and skinny they reminded Emmeline of a grasshopper's, sauntered toward the stairs, taking them three at a time. He looked vaguely familiar, though she couldn't place him, and he smiled at her. For the first time since arriving in Riverview, she felt like smiling in return.

"Pardon my uncouth cousin," the redhead said, shouting to be heard above the din of still more wagons rattling to a stop. "Though I don't know why anyone should or would." He shook his head, though the grin was still in place. "The man's an outlaw."

"So I heard."

The redhead raised a brow. "You did?"

"Yes." She lifted a brow knowingly. "Ran into a man in Lamy who said he had quite a reputation."

He chuckled. "Well, I'll be. Word does get around."

"Sandy, my man," Quaid growled from where he was spreading a layer of canvas in the third wagon. "You're making a nuisance of yourself, giving away family secrets."

"So you're Sandy MacPherson." Emmeline couldn't help smiling into his friendly face.

"And you're our long-lost cousin Emmeline," he said, sweeping his hat from his head and giving her a mock bow.

"I'm Emmeline Callahan," she said with a nod. She didn't point out that they weren't blood kin.

His eyes were merry as he kissed her hand. "Let me guess," he said when he again stood erect, "about the man who told you about this irascible son of a possum, Quaid Dearbourne, and his outlaw ways."

She narrowed her eyes and felt Quaid's gaze on her.

Gertie stepped up and held her hand out to be kissed. "Looked just like you, young man. Spittin' image, if you ask me."

Sandy chuckled. "In Lamy, you say."

"Lamy. Just a few days ago."

"Well, I'll be," he said, his grin widening. He glanced over at Quaid, who was still spreading out canvas in the wagon beds. "My brothers were heading east through Lamy. Could be you ran into one of them—or both."

Even as Gertie began to laugh in that throaty chuckle of hers, Emmeline felt her cheeks redden.

"You mean Quaid Dearbourne's not really an outlaw?" Her cheeks were hot with embarrassment. How could she have been so gullible? Again. Her stomach twisted as dark, unsettling memories of Derian Cadman's deceptions filled her mind. The hurt was still raw, even after a year.

"Well, it depends on your definition of outlaw." Sandy threw back his head and laughed out loud.

She nodded, the ostrich feathers above the rim of her hat shaking. She felt Quaid's gaze and turned slightly to meet his look of amusement. Her stomach was now a knot, and she turned back to Sandy. "I hope we can get started for the river without delay," she said. "The sooner, the better. My trees are in desperate need of water."

"Point me to them." Sandy followed her gaze to the open boxcar. Then he yelled at Quaid, who had finished placing the canvas in the remaining wagon, "Better get moving before the law gets here."

Quaid shrugged, shaking his head. Sandy guffawed to the beat of Gertie's gravelly chuckle.

"I see no humor in the prank," Emmeline said.

By late afternoon, drivers and their helpers had loaded only half the trees. Emmeline oversaw every step of the process, trailing along behind them, directing the placement of each delicate tree trunk. Begrudgingly she realized that Quaid had estimated her grove size down to the last root ball. When the trees were finally loaded, the small train of freight wagons held them with little room to spare.

Before they left for the river Emmeline insisted they take Gertie to the Riverview Hotel. Tomorrow they would return for her after unloading the trees at the rancho. For now the older woman needed rest.

An hour later, as the shadows were almost horizontal across the landscape, Quaid helped Emmeline onto the bench of the lead wagon and popped the whip above the backs of the two-mule team. Sandy MacPherson drove his wagon behind them. The remaining fleet of wagons lurched noisily into motion.

"I misjudged you," she began, once they were on their way. She sensed that he had glanced at her, but she kept her eyes on the road ahead. "I'm sorry."

For a moment he didn't answer, then he said, "If you were duped by my incorrigible cousins, I can only imagine how you'll do running a rancho."

She turned, a swift anger rising inside her. "You don't think I can do it."

"I *know* you can't. You're a woman. Inexperienced. Gullible." He chuckled and flicked the reins. The wagon rumbled along the dirt road, dust rising in a cloud behind them.

"A *woman?* You don't think a woman can have her mettle tested and succeed?" Her voice was shrill. She didn't care. "It occurs to me you'd prefer to be in my shoes and that alone, dear sir, is the reason for your condescension."

He threw back his head and laughed out loud. "I'd prefer to be in your shoes?" He guffawed. "Growing orange trees all in a pretty row?"

"You're envious because you weren't the one asked to take over your grandmother's rancho."

A smiled seemed to play at the corner of his mouth. "You think I want or need your land?"

She tilted her face and squared her shoulders. "Why not?"

He kept his eyes on the backs of the mules. He didn't answer.

They had left Riverview behind as they headed east. From behind them the sun cast a golden light on the mountains ahead. It would have been a glorious sight if Emmeline hadn't been so irritated with Quaid.

They rode without speaking for a few minutes, surrounded by the creak and jangle of wagons and the brays and hoofbeats of mules.

"You made a point of telling me you're not interested in my land."

He shrugged, keeping his eyes straight ahead.

"Why?"

"Aren't you ever quiet?"

Quiet, indeed! She'd show him quiet. She clamped her lips into a thin line and glared at him.

He turned toward her and smiled. A wicked and devious smile. She thought of Zeke MacNab and enjoyed the look.

"Perhaps," he drawled, "I don't need yours because I have land of my own." He grinned at her. "Bordering yours."

She gasped and fell back against the buckboard seat. "You what?"

"I'm running the rancho for my grandparents. Someday it will be mine, if I pass the challenge they've laid out."

"Challenge?" she whispered.

"A test of my mettle."

"And grit."

"Yes, grit." Grinning, he nodded in agreement. "I thought you knew."

"No!"

"No what? No, you don't like the idea? Or no, you didn't know?"

"Both."

He chuckled. "We'll be neighbors," he said, completely ignoring her point, "but you'll be on your own. Don't expect me to coddle you."

"Coddle me?" She sputtered, choking on the words. "That is the furthest thing from my mind!" She stood up, holding on to her hat while the feathers bobbed and waved. "Stop this…this vehicle…these mules, this very minute!"

"Sit down, Emma." He flicked the whip above the team's backs.

"My name's not Emma, and I'll thank you to remember it. And I will not sit down." She was swaying with the wagon's movement and was feeling more foolish by the second for standing. "I order you to stop these beasts right now."

"Order me?"

She lifted her chin two inches and nodded. The hat brim flapped and the feathers were now streaming out behind her.

Quaid shook his head slowly, held up a hand to stop the train, then with a heavy sigh, drew the mules to a halt.

Attempting the utmost dignity, Emmeline drew up her skirts and exited the wagon. The effort was clumsy, and Quaid didn't offer to help. Her petticoat caught on a rough board, and she heard it tear as her feet hit the ground with a thud. Shoulders back and head straight, she reached for the torn ruffle and ripped it from the side of the wagon. When she let it go, it hung limply in the dirt. She kicked it aside.

He had the gall to laugh. "And what shall I do with your trees, pray tell? Shall I unload them here beside you?"

"I assume you're gentleman enough to bring them along behind me."

"Behind you?"

She nodded. "You may follow me."

"Follow you?"

Behind them, Sandy was laughing. One of the mules brayed impatiently, and another pawed the ground.

"Okay, okay," Quaid grumbled after a minute. "I apologize for my rude behavior. Please return to the wagon so we can get your trees to water."

She stared into his face. He might have said the right words to hurry her back into the wagon, but it was evident he didn't mean them. She shook her head. "You may follow me to the river."

She turned, head held high, and started to walk.

After a moment of stunned silence—or perhaps just plain consternation—she heard Quaid call to the mules. A jangle of chains, the creak of wagon wheels, and Sandy's merry laughter carried on the evening breeze as she trudged along in the ankle-deep dust.

Quaid tried his best to hold his irritation in check as the mules plodded behind Emmeline.

She held her head as if she were Queen Victoria herself—back straight, shoulders square, the laughable hat bobbing with each step.

She looked as if she were heading to a women's temperance gathering.

He expected Emmeline to give up after a few yards, but her determination seemed to grow with each long stride. Quaid glanced back at Sandy, who was still grinning. With an irritated grunt, Quaid turned again to face forward and clucked to the mules to follow the stiff-necked woman in front of them.

His grandparents had said his running of the ranch would be a test of his mettle. As the mules moved behind the stubborn woman, he considered how wrong they were.

It wasn't the land that would test him; it was this woman, Emmeline Amity Callahan.

Arms swinging, Emmeline lengthened her stride as she moved along the rutted road. She swallowed a smile. In reality she was enjoying the brisk walk after the long days confined to the train.

The landscape was bathed in the golden light of the setting sun. She drew in a deep breath, relishing the fragrance of dust and sage. She belonged on this land, and with each step, she was more sure.

Never again would she have to endure the restrictive atmosphere that stifled her to the point of snuffing out the light in her soul.

A covey of quail skittered across the road, heads bobbing as they clucked and scratched and half flew a few inches above the ground. Their sweet music was joined by a scrub jay somewhere in a squat live oak.

Her heart was light enough to dance, click her heels, maybe spin around in circles, her arms straight out. She almost giggled as she thought about picking a manzanita branch, clinching it in her teeth, and launching into a Spanish gypsy dance.

She was home. She could feel it in her bones. At last she had come home!

They reached the entrance to the riverbank a half-hour later, and Quaid nodded to a spit of land that caught a shallow pool of the thin river. Emmeline looked at it with satisfaction; it would do quite nicely.

It was growing dark by the time the trees were unloaded and placed in the eddy to soak.

"We'll need to camp here with the men," Sandy said.

"I'll stay here and keep watch," Quaid said when they had finished. He nodded to his cousin. "Why don't you drive Emmeline back to Riverview?"

It annoyed her that Quaid spoke as if she weren't present. She stepped between the two men, hands on hips. "I will stay with my trees. Only I can determine when their roots have had enough of a soak."

The men exchanged a glance, which aggravated her further. But she didn't budge; she stood looking first to Sandy, who grinned back, then to Quaid who scowled.

Sandy said, "I'll go with the men to make camp upriver a ways."

"Make sure it's far enough to leave me my privacy," Emmeline said.

Quaid shot her a dark look.

"Go," she said and fluttered her fingers at them.

"I can't leave you out here alone," Quaid said. Then he turned back to Sandy. "Perhaps we should set up camp nearby."

"I'm paying the wages of these men. They must do as I insist." She set her hands on her hips and her mouth in a straight line.

Sandy was chuckling as he clucked to the mules. "See you in the mornin', sweet cousin Emmeline," he called as he turned the mules back down the road, leading the other wagons away.

"There are still some bears that roam these hills," Quaid said. "They come down to drink at night."

"I thought they hibernated this time of year."

"In most of the country they do. Our winters are late."

"I know how to take care of myself."

"It'll get down to freezing by morning. You don't have a coat."

"I saw a blanket in the wagon. You can leave that for me, if you will."

He let out another exasperated sigh and stepped closer. "Look, you might as well figure that I'm not going to let you stay so far from camp alone."

"You're not going to *let* me do anything," she said. "Ever. If I think it's necessary to stay here alone to watch over my trees, then that's exactly what I will do."

It was nearly dark now, but she could see that he'd lifted his hands almost as if in supplication. He started to speak, then thought better of it and shrugged.

"Give me the rifle I saw in the wagon," she said, "if you're truly concerned about my safety."

He considered her quizzically for a moment, then sauntered to the wagon, pulled out the blanket and the rifle, and walked back over to her. He dropped the blanket near her feet and propped the rifle against the trunk of the cottonwood. She'd never fired a rifle or gun of any kind in her life, but she didn't want Quaid to know.

She walked over to the firearm, looked it up and down like an expert. "Nice," she murmured knowledgeably.

He grinned, his eyes filled with a curious amusement. "Do you want me to light a fire for you? It'll help keep away the mountain lions."

"Mountain lions?"

"Yes. They don't hibernate."

She swallowed hard. "All right, then. Yes, please set a fire for me."

He gathered some dry branches and set them tipi fashion into a circular clearing. He ringed the circumference with fist-sized stones. "And bobcats," he mused while lighting the fire. "You might see one or two by morning."

"They don't bother people, do they?"

"Not the way cougars do."

"Cougars?" An owl hooted in the distance, and she shivered. It was a lonely sound.

"Same thing as mountain lion. Just a different name."

"Oh." Her voice sounded small, even to herself. She stepped closer to the fire, which was now crackling nicely, and held her palms toward its warmth. "This region doesn't have snakes this time of year, does it?"

Squatting on the opposite side of the fire, he tossed on a few more branches and gave her another grin. "Nope. 'Fraid not. That's one critter that does hibernate." Then he stood, brushing off his hands. "You'll need to gather more firewood. You should find plenty under the cottonwood."

She nodded. "I'll be fine. Really." She hesitated. "You can go now."

She glanced at her little orange trees swaying a bit in the rippling eddy, wondering if she'd made the right decision. A decision based solely on the desire to prove to Quaid that she had grit.

He was watching her carefully. She gave him a smile of dismissal, reached up to remove her hatpin, and lifted her hat with both hands. Finally, she yawned and patted her mouth with her fingertips. "Oh, me, it's been a long day." It was meant as a sign for him to leave.

Instead of leaving, he headed back to the wagon, rummaged around noisily, then returned with a worn saddle blanket and a lantern. When he tossed the saddle blanket to her, he gave her a curt nod and said, "You'll need a pillow."

It smelled of old horsehair and manure, but she didn't let on. She nodded her thanks and clutched it close as he set the lantern down under the cottonwood and lit it with a twig from the fire. A dim yellow glow illuminated the ground in a soft circle.

Now she could see the half-grin on his face as he headed to his wagon, chirked to the mules, and was on his way. After a time the creak of the wheels faded into the darkness, and she was alone, though she thought she heard Quaid laughing out loud from a ways down the road.

She sat on a small boulder near the fire and shivered. An owl hooted from the top of some nearby sycamores and was answered by another on the far side of the river. A strange rustling sound in a thicket caused the hairs on the back of her neck to stand on end. Then a mouse scampered out from a clump of sage and back again. Emmeline laughed nervously.

"Merciful heavens, Lord, what have I gotten myself into?" She leaned back, smiling, and beheld the canopy of stars overhead. A million tiny points of light twinkled against the black-velvet firmament. Never had she seen such a sight or been in such a quiet place. A place where she could almost feel God's heartbeat, almost hear him breathe.

"Father, you are here. You are with me…" she whispered in wonder. "Oh, how you have blessed me. In spite of my doubts and fears, in spite of my headstrong ways, you have brought me to this promised land." She laughed softly. "Though it will be some time before it's flowing with milk and honey."

She wrapped her arms around her knees, blanketing her ankles with her skirt, and stared into the orange and gold flames as they licked skyward.

The spirited sound of a harmonica carried toward her on the evening breeze. She figured it was Quaid, who'd likely camped nearer than she had earlier insisted, keeping himself within earshot. It was the most pleasant sound she could imagine hearing right now, in this place.

With a contented sigh, she settled back, sometimes watching the blaze of starlight overhead, sometimes staring at the images in the firelight. Through all her musings the harmonica played, and the two owls hooted across the river at each other. After a while a coyote yipped, then several others joined in. The music of the California night.

When an hour or so had passed, she walked to the eddy, holding the lantern in one hand, and checked the roots of her orange trees. Pleased with the damp, spongy feel of the root balls, she gently patted a few of them, splashed some water on a few others, then turned back to the fire.

After another satisfied sigh, she extinguished the lantern, wrapped herself in the blanket, and curled near the fire, saddle blanket under her head. She'd just closed her eyes when doubts about her safety invaded her imagination.

It would be prudent to have the rifle by her side, she decided. So she rose, grabbed the firearm from where it still leaned against the trunk of the cottonwood, and lay down again by the fire. She placed the rifle by her side and adjusted the saddle blanket as best she could for her pillow.

In the distance the harmonica played on into the night. She smiled as the songs filled her heart. Stephen Foster, of course, she thought as she drifted to sleep. Just as it should be on her first night under the stars in the Wild West.

A sliver of a moon was high in the western sky when Quaid slipped back to Emmeline's camp. The fire had died to embers, and the young woman was so still he was certain she slept.

Creeping closer, he hoped to find some dry branches to rekindle the fire. He stopped just short of the small circle of embers and glanced down at Emmeline, her face just visible in the pale glow.

Something in her expression tugged at his heart. A childlike innocence, perhaps, mixed with a determined set to her chin. Or was it an almost angelic beauty that she'd hidden all day behind her silly eyeglasses and beneath her enormous hat? Maybe it was the soft curve to her cheek where her long eyelashes touched and curved upward. Or perhaps it was the way she seemed to be no nonsense about who she was, from her stick-straight hair to the tip of her practical lace-up boots. He fought the urge to brush aside a strand of hair that had fallen across one of her closed eyes and onto her cheek.

After studying her lovely face for a moment, he headed for the sycamore where he'd earlier picked up some twigs. He stooped, his back to Emmeline, figuring he would gather enough to last the night. He'd just loaded his arms full when she spoke.

"Get up, mister, and point your hands to the sky," she growled.

He heard the unmistakable clack of the rifle being cocked. He let the dried branches roll from his arms, and slowly he turned.

Sixteen

Emmeline trembled, holding the rifle pointed at the intruder as he slowly turned. In her haste to catch the man off guard, she'd left her eyeglasses on the ground beside the saddle blanket. Not that it mattered. The fire had died to a few glowing coals, and it was nearly impossible to make out any details about the prowler.

"Emmeline," a gruff voice sighed patiently. "It's me. Quaid."

"What are you doing here?"

"Please drop the rifle."

She wouldn't know the first thing about shooting anyway. It was only by pure luck that she'd figured out how to cock the thing. To actually aim and pull the trigger would have taken a miracle. "What are you doing here?" she repeated, letting the firearm drop from her shoulder, barrel-down to the ground.

"I was planning to stoke the fire for you. Thought you might get cold."

More than likely he'd come to point out how inept she was at seeing herself through the night, then report back to his cousins. Or worse, to the entire regiment of workers he'd hired on her behalf. Then they would all have a good laugh. "I don't need to be coddled," she said. "I'm perfectly capable of gathering firewood myself."

When he didn't comment, she added, "I can take care of myself."

Quaid stared at her a moment, then walked back to the cottonwood, stooped, and gathered the firewood he'd dropped a few minutes before.

"It will be daylight soon," he said, stacking it log-cabin-like on the coals. He tossed some dried leaves and twigs into the center, and, with a crackle and spit the flames shot skyward. "I told Sandy to have the wagons hitched and ready to head back here at daybreak. We'll reload the trees and get you delivered to the rancho in nothing flat. There are many who await your arrival."

"I'm eager to see your grandparents…Sara, all of them." She frowned thoughtfully. "And Merci. I've been remiss in asking about her," she said, remembering the little red-haired cousin from all those years ago. "Will I see her today?"

He carefully laid another branch on the fire, then turned, still squatting. The slope of his shoulders told her something was wrong even before he spoke. "Merci left some time ago."

"Left to go where?"

Quaid stood and dusted off his hands, let out a deep breath, and shrugged. "Anyone's guess."

"She didn't say?"

"No."

"Grandmother Sara wrote that the two of you are close, more like brother and sister than cousins. I'm surprised that Merci didn't tell you."

He looked at the ground, seeming uncomfortable. "It was right after my grandparents turned the rancho over to me that she rode off and never returned."

"It was her home. Maybe she felt cheated."

"The only home Merci had ever known," he agreed, surprising her.

Emmeline pulled the blanket around her shoulders and settled near him to warm her hands over the fire.

He rocked back on his heels and stared at the licking flames. "I'm not certain why my grandparents didn't include Merci in their plans. I only know she felt betrayed."

"By you?"

He didn't look at her. "Perhaps," he said. The fire popped and sizzled, and he rubbed his hands together in front of it. "I suspect she thinks she's been betrayed by everyone she loves. No matter what else happened in her life, she counted on my friendship. This was the one time I wasn't there for her." He tossed a pebble into the fire, still staring at the flames. "She doesn't know it, and perhaps never will, but I would willingly give her the ranch should she come back."

His words of unselfish sacrifice stirred Emmeline. And that stirring made her uncomfortable; she didn't want his tenderness to touch her. She didn't want any man's words of kindness to reach her. She'd trusted a man before and had been hurt. Her tone was harsher than she intended when she spoke. "That's easy to say, knowing she may never return."

Quaid stood abruptly, towering over her, and glared down at her upturned face. "You have no right to judge me, Emma. Not me. Not my motives." He narrowed his eyes at her. "You know nothing of the heartaches Merci has endured."

His eyes, reflecting the firelight, burned with anger. "Our family is filled with secret pain," he said slowly, his voice dropping. "Merci has borne the brunt of it. No one can understand her sorrow."

"I won't ask you what happened to the family or to Merci," Emmeline said quietly. "I'm sorry I misjudged you." She paused, staring into the fire. "I understand heartaches, at least the mild ones. My prayers are with Merci."

He stared at Emmeline for a moment, then turned to walk away from her, heading toward the road without so much as a break in his stride. He walked on, and she wondered if he would return.

A moment later, he turned to look at her, walking backward. She thought he might be grinning. "Keep the fire stoked, sweetheart," he called to her.

Sweetheart? She fumed, certain that he would later laugh with his cousins that he'd called her such an endearment. She didn't grace the outrage with an answer.

"Don't forget!" he called gaily, then turned and trotted down the road.

Emmeline sat down again on the rock by the fire, pulling the blanket closer. She considered this man, Quaid Dearbourne, his gruff arrogance, his certainty about his place in the Big Valley. His certainty that she had no place here.

She swallowed a small laugh. She would show him what kind of grit a woman was made of. Oh yes, she would show him. This man with his crooked grin and sun-bronzed face and eyes that crinkled when he smiled, this rugged man whose yip was worse than his bared-teeth snarl.

In the east a thin sliver of dawn backlit the jagged San Jacintos, and the color of the pale gray skies reminded her of Quaid's eyes. Light against the dark hue of his skin.

He did indeed look like an outlaw when he wore his hat low on his forehead and let his duster flap in the wind. But she wondered if any outlaw could pull off his hat with the grace of Quaid Dearbourne. Or rake his fingers through his buckskin-colored hair just the way he did.

"The fire still going strong?" Quaid called out, interrupting her thoughts.

She was glad he couldn't see the flame in her cheeks as he hopped down from the wagon bench. He held an iron skillet in one hand, a net full of fish in the other, and a blue speckled coffeepot under his arm.

Wordlessly she nodded, then bent to toss another branch or two on the coals.

He'd obviously forgiven her earlier barb and grinned as he headed to the fire, holding out several silver foot-long trout. "Rainbow!" he announced triumphantly. "Hope you're hungry. I've got a mess of 'em to fix." He sat down beside her. "Figured I ought to give you a real California welcome. Best breakfast you'll have this side of the Rockies."

First he fetched a pot full of water from the river, added a handful of coffee and a pinch of salt, then set it in the coals to boil. Then he greased the skillet, and after letting it heat in the coals for a minute, tossed in a couple of the trout. She noted with appreciation that the fish had been cleaned and scaled, though the heads were still attached.

He laughed, seeming to read her thoughts. "Only way to tell if they're done. Eyes turn white."

He flipped the fish into the air, then caught them again with the skillet. "Want to see me catch 'em behind my back?" He lifted a brow in her direction as if waiting for her praise of the feat.

The sun now cast a honeyed light across the landscape, and the soft lapping of water carried toward them on a gentle breeze, mixing with the sweet voices of quail feeding and scratching beneath a stand of manzanita.

The beauty was too severe to take in, too much to bear. But she knew it wouldn't last, the joy of being with Quaid in this wild place. Her thoughts went back to the night Derian Cadman and his friends tricked her. They'd called her the ugliest woman at the ball, and when she had heard it, she'd known they spoke the truth.

A man like Quaid would never look at her twice. Why was she allowing herself to admire the color of his eyes, the warmth of his voice?

She was homely. Plain. Unattractive. She could go on, but the list would only serve to make her feel worse.

"I'm not hungry," she said stiffly. She set her lips in a straight line and, attempting to ignore her grumbling stomach, stood and moved to gather the supplies he'd given her the night before. She felt awkward and unlovely, and worst of all, embarrassed at the tears that threatened.

She felt his gaze bore through the center of her shoulders as she folded the saddle blanket. When she finished, she bent to lift the lantern, aware that he was still staring at her in silence.

The fragrance of the sizzling trout made her faint with hunger. She realized suddenly that her last meal had been on the train the day before. But she ignored her stomach's complaining. Clutching the blanket with one hand and the lantern with the other, she headed to the wagon.

With the rising of the sun came an awareness of her wrinkled skirt, the torn petticoat that still dragged behind, the straight sticks of hair that sprung from their clasps. She could only imagine herself through Quaid's eyes.

Fresh embarrassment caused her to lengthen her strides. She dropped the lantern and saddle blanket into the wagon bed. As quickly as she could, she hurried down the road, almost running toward a bend in the river, a place hidden from view by a stand of willows and aspen.

She bent over the water and splashed the clear, cold liquid on her face. Her humiliation about her appearance stung her heart as surely as the icy water stung her skin.

"Emma."

She held her face in her hands, not bearing to look up. She didn't want to see the pity in his eyes.

"Emma, did I say something wrong? I'm always sticking my big boot in my mouth. My mother is constantly after me for my rude behavior."

His mother? She swallowed a giggle. This rough-riding, gruff-talking man listened to his mother? She didn't dare look up, but felt him kneel beside her.

"Please don't cry," he said, his voice hoarse. "I hate it when women cry."

"Please, leave me alone," she mumbled into her hands. "It's me. Not you. You…you didn't say anything. You weren't rude."

"Can you tell me what's wrong…what's happened?"

Obviously, Quaid wasn't about to leave her. His mother had taught him to be a gentleman, and he wasn't about to go back on her teaching. That meant he likely wouldn't leave her alone to finish her cry.

Emma sniffled and gave her face one last splash, realizing as she did that she had nothing to dry with. So, with a sigh, she used the hem of her dusty skirt.

Finally she ventured a sidelong glance at Quaid through watery eyes.

He was still kneeling very close to her, a worried expression in his eyes. As she looked up, he reached for her hands to help her to stand. She nodded her thanks and looked down again to smooth her wrinkled and soiled skirt.

"Maybe this wasn't such a good idea after all," she said. "I can only imagine what I look like." Her head slanted downward, she looked up at him, managing a small smile.

His eyes, filled with amusement, still reflected his concern. "You can't spend the night in the woods and expect to awaken to pressed frocks and clean shoes."

She smiled a bit wider. "True."

"Did the thought of trout make you ill?" he ventured. "If so, I apologize. I just assumed…I mean…I thought you might enjoy a camp breakfast. Some people find fish disagreeable, and I should have realized—"

She placed her hand on his arm. "Perhaps it was the long journey, the excitement of the arrival, that brought this on. But I'm quite well now, thank you."

Quaid still wore a worried frown. "Or maybe it was the night in the chilly air. My grandmother would skin me alive if she knew I allowed you to do it." His eyes widened as he considered yet another reason for her discomfort. "You must be hungry beyond words. I just realized you probably haven't eaten since you got off the train."

His grandmother? This man also paid attention to his grandmother? This time Emmeline bit her lip to keep from giggling. "We were too busy with the trees, remember?" she managed. "And truly, the night was lovely. I enjoyed sleeping under the stars."

He looked relieved. "There aren't many women who would've done what you did. Stay out in the wild without a man around to protect them."

She started to retort something about not needing a man for any-thing, then noticed the admiration in his eyes. She swallowed her words.

"You showed gumption," he said.

His praise made her feel immensely better. "I'm ready for that breakfast now."

Grinning, he took her hand and placed it in the crook of his arm as if escorting her was a privilege. As he led her back to the campfire, she thought how strange it would be to trust a man to be what he said he was, trust him to be true in his heart to the actions he showed on the outside.

Quaid slid a trout from the skillet onto a blue speckled plate, then poured coffee into a matching, chipped mug. He handed them to her as if to a queen, then watched expectantly as she took her first bite.

He awaited her approval; she could see it in his eyes. She wanted to weep again, it touched her so. She nodded slowly. "Delicious," she mur-mured and took another bite.

He filled the iron pan with two more fish, set it in the fire, then chuckled as he settled against an old stump, his plate in his lap. Lifting his steaming coffee to his lips, he watched her above the rim of the mug. Surprisingly, his expression told her he liked what he saw.

But she trusted few looks cast her way, no matter how flattering they were meant to be. Taking another bite of trout, she let her gaze drift to the road where the fleet of wagons approached, filling the morning with noise and clouds of dust.

A few minutes later, Sandy halted his team behind Quaid's wagon. The other teams pulled in behind. At Emmeline's insistence, the men hurried to help her carefully load the trees into the wagon beds, and by midmorning the wagon train again headed east to Rancho Dearbourne. This time Emmeline chose to ride with Sandy in the second wagon.

It should have provided her some relief from the strain of sitting next to Quaid, but instead her consternation resulted from him remaining in her line of vision. The graceful flick of his wrist as he popped the whip above the team, the indifferent slouch he adopted as he rode along, the laughing rumble of his voice as he and Sandy bantered back and forth, only served to draw her attention to him.

An hour later they reached the entrance to Rancho de la Paloma, a dirt road that led off to the north. Two sculpted iron doves in flight graced the center of the arch, with intertwined grapes and ivy cascading down either side of the ornate gate that blocked the road.

Quaid halted the train and headed back to Sandy's wagon. He propped his foot on the bottom step and looked at Emmeline. The slant of the sun caught the side of his stubbled jaw, and it struck her that for all his gruff mannerisms, something in his face—in his eyes—spoke of a light in his soul. She pushed the thought aside. It might be what she wanted to see; but it might also be the furthest thing from the truth.

"This is the entrance to La Paloma," he said. "If you weren't so all-fired set to get your trees in the ground today, I'd invite you over to have a look."

"I'm surprised you allow anything other than sagebrush or buckeye to dignify the entrance to your spread."

Beside her, Sandy let out a guffaw. "She's got you pegged, cousin."

"Besides," she went on, "the moist roots of my orange trees will last only so long in this dry climate. You're not a planter—I'm not surprised that you'd not be aware of it."

"I plant oats and alfalfa," he said, grinning up at her. "And I used to help Grandmother with her wild roses. Doesn't that count?"

She told herself not to smile. Instead she gave him a curt nod. "We'd better be on our way."

With another of his graceful, indifferent shrugs, Quaid strode back to his wagon, climbed onto the seat, and chirked to the team. The fleet was on its way once again. Sandy kept his rig far enough behind Quaid to let the dust settle and drift to one side in the breeze.

The sun was well above the horizon now, in a cloudless, purple-blue sky. A touch of autumn remained, seen in the golden leaves of the aspen and cottonwoods near the riverbank and the oaks on the slopes of the distant mountains.

Emmeline held her hat on her lap and tipped her face toward the sun, letting the beat of it warm her forehead and cheeks. Eyes closed, she breathed in the scent of the sun-warmed soil and sage, the late-blooming wildflowers. *Merciful heavens, it was altogether lovely!*

"Ho, there!" Quaid called out after a while.

Sandy halted his team, and Emmeline's eyes flew open as the wagon pitched and jerked to a stop at the apex of a small incline. The other wagons rattled to a stop behind them, to a loud chorus of braying mules and grumbling, cussing teamsters.

The terrain dropped to a bone-dry riverbed, then stretched across a small valley framed by some boulder- and cactus-covered foothills. Not a single wildflower such as she'd enjoyed just a few miles back was to be found on the rock-strewn soil.

"This is it!" Quaid craned in the wagon seat. "Right out there in all its wild glory."

He jumped down from the buckboard and headed a few steps through the sandy soil to a lookout. He propped one boot on a large rock and leaned his elbow on his knee, looking as proud of the land as if he'd given it to her himself.

She gave Sandy a quizzical frown.

He hopped down from the wagon bench and turned toward her with a mock bow, his hand out. "Your spread, sweet cousin Emmeline," he said, his eyes alight, his red hair gleaming in the sun. "This will give you an idea of how much land you've got to cover with those fancy fruit trees. Best view in the county."

Emmeline took his hand and stepped from the bench. She walked over to join Quaid on the side of the road, trying not to notice how arid the soil was. Sandy trailed a few steps behind. She frowned. "Which part of it is mine?"

"All of it."

Her spirits dropped as she took in the panorama. "It's so…so brown. And dry. And all those rocks. And boulders."

They stood for a while in silence, then she looked up at him. "I thought we shared a water supply. Sara said something about water rights, about some sort of an arrangement she had with the Byrnes through all the years they were neighbors."

"She didn't tell you?" Quaid met her gaze, looking perfectly virtuous.

"Tell me what?"

"About what happened when the dam was built?"

She sighed, remembering the letter Sara sent her father. "The dam cut off my fork to the river. I remember now." She paused, lost in thought. "I figured it wouldn't be a problem because everyone knows dams are built for irrigation purposes."

Behind them, Sandy cleared his throat. "That's a correct assumption. Anyplace else in the world but here. The dam's new. And there hasn't been enough rain and snow in the back country to fill the reservoir behind it—not with the years of skinny rainfall since it was completed."

You're trying to tell me there's no water…" She swallowed the lump in her throat. "No water behind the dam…for irrigation?"

Sandy's face was sober. He shook his head. "Not much, I'm afraid."

She looked to Quaid, who confirmed his cousin's words with a nod.

Emmeline stared at the barren land, speechless, then noticed a crumbling adobe off to the south, tucked in the far end of the V-shaped valley. Surely it was that of the overseer, or the cattle hands. Perhaps where the vaqueros of old had bunked.

"Is that the Dearbourne adobe?" she asked, praying that it wasn't.

"It looks a little run-down from here, all right," Quaid said, "but it's actually quite lovely on the inside. Tile floors from Spain."

"It needs work," Sandy added. "It was never repaired after the earthquake."

Earthquake! She couldn't utter the word. It was as if her breath had been cut off.

Quaid was watching her intently. "Don't tell me Sara didn't mention that either."

"No." She tried to ignore the squeezing around her heart. "She didn't."

"It wasn't one of our worst," Sandy said, "but it was strong enough to shake loose some of the adobe bricks. Lost quite a bit of the roof."

"At least there hasn't been much rain lately." Emmeline's voice was a whisper.

"My father and I did what we could. We boarded up some of the holes, then spread a canvas tarp over the rest to keep out the varmints."

"Varmints?" This time her voice was little more than a squeak.

At least Quaid had the grace not to laugh.

Emmeline couldn't tear her eyes away from the distant, ramshackle house. "Why didn't Sara tell me what to expect? Her letters painted quite a different picture. They were filled with hope—hope at what could be accomplished here."

Quaid seemed to measure her for a moment before answering. "I suspect she didn't know the kind of grit you've got. Perhaps she was afraid you wouldn't take on her challenge."

Emmeline barely heard his words. Already she was figuring how to run irrigation to her land, make the necessary repairs before the year's rains hit. And plant her trees before the roots shriveled.

The eastern wind gusted, kicking up the dry, sandy soil in its path. The plantings would have to be deep in this hostile land, and the taproots would have to seek their water source by plunging far into the earth. The winds would be harsh, but that would be good.

She smiled, remembering an experiment related to her by a Brazilian horticulturist. He had withheld water, beat the tender young trunks until they were scarred, and shook the branches until few leaves remained. In three years, those trees were the strongest, heaviest-producing ones in the grove. Their thick, gnarled trunks resisted disease, their leaves clung to the branches in the harshest winds, their roots were so deep they could withstand any drought. And their fruit was the sweetest in the Western Hemisphere.

"Sara should have told me," she said, looking out at the wild beauty of her land.

"You would have changed your mind?" Quaid asked.

Shaking her head, she kept her gaze on the rancho lands. "No," she whispered in awe. "I would have moved heaven and earth to get here sooner."

SEVENTEEN

Spring 1890

For weeks Merci wandered along the California coast, sometimes drifting inland, most of the time staying near the sea.

By day she kept to trails and back roads and spent her nights away from populated areas, always on the lookout for Cole. Nights were the worst. Dark and desperate nightmares plagued her, so real they caused her to cry out. The dreams were always the same. Cole had come for her, only this time there would be no escape. His gaze flicked over her, mocked her, and told her who she was. What she was. Heedless of her protests, he dragged her back to Santa Isabela. She would wake sobbing, terrified he was in the room with her. Hiding. Waiting.

At first she hadn't wanted to sell herself again. After weeks of desperate hunger, however, she changed her mind, conducting her business in dark alleys or behind saloons. She told herself it would be only until she made enough money to eat, or enough to feed Knight. Later she knew she was made for nothing else, nothing better. As always, during the few minutes she was with a man, she retreated into that black place inside herself, a place where numbness reigned, where the john's base hungers couldn't touch her.

The days turned into weeks, and she moved from town to town. With a quirk of a brow, a knowing look, a bat of her fringed lashes, a coy glance mixed with a dazzling smile, she could coax the most reluctant man right out of his wife's loving arms. She never forgot the power of her beauty. Or the detestable, ugly interior it covered.

Once in a small, prosperous-looking village north of Los Angeles, she attempted for the last time to find decent employment as a governess.

The woman of the house slammed the door in her face. Sauntering back to the street, Merci took a good look at herself, sat down, and laughed until she cried. Until that moment she hadn't realized that she'd actually become the person Cole taught her to be. She'd become a prostitute. That day she picked herself up, vowing never again to cry about what she was or what she couldn't be.

She would accept her fate and make the best of it. Her heart was so hardened now that it made no difference. She scoffed at the days she'd once spent longing for home. Home was a distant memory now, her childhood almost seeming to have happened to someone else.

She didn't allow herself to dwell on the circumstances that led her to this life. She never thought of the future. One day melted into another, each as bleak and colorless as the one before. She was numb. Emotion came to the surface only if a customer tried to cheat her or if she couldn't buy feed for Knight.

One day in March she came upon Mission Buena Ventura. The crumbling Spanish adobe was no longer a working mission, but she found a church caretaker—a balding, round-faced man, his hair tonsured like a monk's—who invited her to stay in the drafty sanctuary.

That night the caretaker, whose name was Neal O'Brian, brought her a pot of stew fixed by his wife Molly and some castoff clothing, a worn gingham dress sizes too big and a woolen cape that appeared to have been a child's. Then he produced a clean blanket and a straw-filled pillow.

"Don't you know what I am?" she asked.

"You are God's child" was his simple reply. "It's enough for me."

Mr. O'Brian returned the following morning with a loaf of bread still warm from the oven and a map he had drawn pointing the way to all the missions. "Most of them are abandoned," he explained. "But at the least they might provide you with shelter."

He pointed to the trail he'd drawn. "It's known as the Camino Real, the Royal Highway leading to God's kingdom. Some call it the King's Highway. It was named by the early padres who built the missions a day's walk apart."

The King's Highway. Merci's stomach twisted. Other memories might have dimmed, but her anger toward God had increased with each mile she traveled. She chuckled bitterly at the caretaker's words, deciding the dusty road named to signify a journey to God would be the perfect place to conduct her business.

Mr. O'Brian gave her a gentle smile as he pressed the map into her hands. "God bless you on your journey, my child. Don't ever forget you're on his road."

Her smile fading, Merci turned away with a shrug. That night she slipped into a neighboring town and, after numbing her mind with whiskey at the local tavern, made enough money to buy food for two weeks. She flaunted her pocketful of coins in front of the caretaker and his wife the next morning, handing them a dollar for board and room.

The man returned it, which didn't surprise Merci.

"What's the matter? My money's not good enough for you?" She laughed in their faces before gathering her things to move on. She piled the old clothing they'd brought her, like so much rubbish, in a corner.

She turned to leave the small, crumbling adobe room, then with a stab of conscience, pulled out the small leather-tooled Bible given to her months ago. She shoved it between two stones. Perhaps when the O'Brians found it, they could sell it and use the money for something they needed.

It had been with her, tucked in her drawstring purse, which was tied to her money belt, even while she was working for Adam Cole. She didn't know why she'd kept it this long, and once she'd released it from her hands, it was a relief. The small volume had nagged at her since the day she took it from the Johnsons' boardinghouse.

She meandered along the King's Highway, finding great irony in plying her trade near the missions. One time after another, her pattern was always the same. She went to the nearest saloon, filled herself with just enough whiskey to dull her pain, earned her money, then returned to the shelter of the mission well after midnight.

On a mist-clouded day in early spring, Merci headed through Santa Barbara to a small mission just north of the city. She gave Knight a nudge toward the side of the trail, and when he halted, she slid off his back. Below her in a small green valley lay Santa Inez. Even from this distance, she could make out some pepper trees and eucalyptus sheltering the tile-roofed adobe. A row of rosebushes flanked the path leading to a gate.

Farther back and to one side, a live oak provided a canopy of shade, and a stone bench—surely placed there for the purpose of providing rest for travelers—sat beneath the gnarled branches of the tree.

A squat bell tower with a crude wooden cross rose above the entrance to the sanctuary. A pleasant enough place to stay, she supposed, and perhaps one that would bring her luck. If the town of Santa Inez was half as prosperous as its mission appeared, business would be good tonight.

She mounted Knight again and nudged him down the winding trail, lacing between live oaks and tangles of cascading bougainvillea. Soon they came to a clearing, and the small valley stretched before them, framed by the oak forest.

At the end of the stretch of tall grass loomed the mission, now appearing larger than it had from the buttress of stones at the lookout point. She halted the horse to let him graze, then slid from his back once more. While Knight browsed, neck outstretched, in the tender spring shoots, she walked the short distance to the adobe structure.

The door was open and she stepped inside. It was cold and dimly lit. She stood for a moment to let her eyes adjust to the darkness, then walked into the sanctuary. A single aisle led to an ancient altar. She walked slowly toward it, looking for signs of life, signs that this might be a working church.

It certainly had the look of use on the outside, with its beautiful gardens, but here in the dark sanctuary, years of dust choked her. She sneezed and looked around more thoroughly, thinking that perhaps there was something she could steal and sell in town.

She stepped to the altar table and lifted her eyes to the faded and crumbling altarpiece that seemed to soar heavenward, even in its state of ruin. In the center was a sculpture of Christ's body hanging from a cross. It was chipped and peeling, but her gaze was strangely drawn to the figure's face.

Christ's bleeding head was in a position of repose, his eyes open as if looking into the hearts of all of mankind.

His expression was one of utter compassion.

Merci turned away, unable to bear the likeness, walked a few steps back down the aisle, then turned again and looked up.

It was just a statue. It held no importance to her. She turned again to leave the building, but there was something peaceful in the dusty, dimly lit place that drew her.

She slipped into a century-old pew and sat to look up once more at the figure. She laughed out loud at the sight she must have presented.

"So here I am, God, a product of your making." Her voice was shrill with sarcasm. "Aren't you proud of me, your child?" She laughed again. "Proud of who I've become. I was knit together in my mother's womb—don't you remember? You were there on that fateful day. Oh yes, the all-knowing God was there all right. And you watched while my mother was defiled."

Tears were filling her eyes. "You, the loving God of the universe did nothing to help her." The words came out in a low growl.

"And here I am, another of your mistakes. The blood of sinful man pumping through my heart. Filthy. Unredeemable. Am I your loving daughter now?"

She stared up at the silent face. "Answer me!" She shook her fist. "Answer me, God!" The tears coursed down her cheeks, and she angrily swept them away with her fingertips.

Her voice dropped as she narrowed her eyes at the Christ figure. "Lies," she growled again. "All lies."

She buried her head in her hands and wept. "You're as silent and dead as that statue on the altar. Dead to me. Dead to my poor mother."

YOU ARE THE DAUGHTER OF THE KING, a voice spoke in her heart.

She continued to weep.

I HAVE LOVED YOU WITH AN EVERLASTING LOVE.

YOU ARE MINE...I HAVE CALLED YOU BY NAME.

"Lies!" she cried. "Everything I was ever told about you, all of it—lies!"

YOU ARE MY LAMB, BELOVED.

EVEN NOW I CARRY YOU CLOSE TO MY HEART.

Merci wept harder. "No! I am the vilest of sinners. My very blood is tainted."

THE GRAVE CANNOT KEEP YOU...AS IT COULD NOT KEEP ME.

"I am as dead to you as you are to me!"

COME TO ME, BELOVED. TEST ME, AND SEE THAT I LIVE.

She looked up at the plaster statue and gave it one last pronouncement. "You are dead to me forever." Then with another swipe at her wet cheeks, she rose.

A figure stood at the back of the church, and Merci stopped dead still, her heart racing.

"I'm sorry," a woman said from the shadows. "I didn't mean to startle you."

Merci walked toward her. "How long have you been here?"

The woman didn't answer, but Merci was close enough now to see from her expression that she had indeed heard Merci's one-sided conversation. She shrugged at the woman, attempting to sweep past her on her way to the door.

"You are looking for shelter?" the woman asked.

Merci stared at her for a moment. "Do you work here?"

"I take care of the grounds, the garden, the vineyard."

A caretaker. The last one she encountered had fed her, clothed her. She softened her voice. "So you work for the church...or the mission." She glanced around. "I was under the impression that the place had been abandoned."

"It isn't a working church, if that's your meaning. Caring for the grounds is just something I do. I'm not given wages to care for them."

Merci frowned, attempting to follow the woman's thinking. "Are you a sister…or something?" The woman wasn't dressed as though she had come from a convent.

She laughed. "No, nothing like that."

Merci shook her head, shrugged one shoulder, and started to turn.

"It's a gift."

Merci stopped and looked back into her face. "What's a gift?"

"What I do—it's a gift."

"Do you mean you give your time, your work, as a gift to someone else?"

"Yes."

Merci stared at her, then chuckled and shook her head. She was so intent on earning enough money to survive, the very idea of laboring as a gift was laughable. The woman was probably the wife of a wealthy banker and labored in the garden and vineyard as a pastime. It annoyed Merci that someone could have time for such a leisurely activity. A gift? She laughed again. Let the woman enjoy her little amusement.

"I asked you earlier if you need a refuge."

"Why would I need a refuge?" Merci asked.

The woman didn't answer, and Merci started for the door again. "I can offer you a bed…and food. That is, if you need them."

Something about the woman disturbed Merci. She seemed too sure of herself—too sure of Merci's needs. But Merci knew her kind. She was naive and wealthy, likely using her money to change the world one beggar at a time.

Well, this lady of the night didn't need changing. With a toss of her head, Merci brushed past the woman and headed from the sanctuary.

She followed a few steps behind. "My name is Sadie," she called to Merci. "I live just beyond the church. Around in back, just off the courtyard. If you need me, you can find me there."

Merci spun around. "You live off the courtyard…you mean, here in the mission?"

Sadie walked over to a statue of St. Francis of Assisi and stood by it. The sun slanted against her face. She was younger than Merci had originally thought, though she could have as easily been thirty as fifty. Her eyes held a clarity and depth that unnerved Merci. Her silver-streaked hair gleamed in the sun and hung straight around her face.

It was then, there in the sunlight, that Merci got her first good look at Sadie's clothes. They were clean but threadbare and a few sizes too large for her bony frame.

Puzzled, she walked back to the statue. "You live here at the mission?"

Sadie nodded.

"But you told me you're not part of the mission, that your work here is a gift."

She smiled and caught Merci's hand in hers. "Come, I'll show you." She led Merci around the corner of the church to a wooden gate that opened into the mission courtyard. When she swung it open, Merci let out a small gasp of surprise.

Sadie looked proud. "This is the first year it's looked so grand."

Merci was too stunned to speak. The courtyard was a riot of color—reds, purples, yellows, and blues. It was sectioned off into quarters, each much like a room, stone bordered and terraced. A lovely fountain splashed in the center, and around it in clay pots grew cascades of rosemary, covered with pale lavender blossoms, and basil and thyme. In two sections, opposite each other, carrots, squash, and lettuces grew squat to the ground. Farther back the taller vegetables stood as if at attention—corn, tomato vines, and China peas on poles.

In the two remaining quarters, a profusion of roses, lilacs, and irises lifted their blossoms joyfully to the sun. Small olive trees were sprinkled among the flowers with ferns thriving in the shade they provided.

"You did all this?" Merci glanced at Sadie with admiration.

Sadie nodded. "It didn't happen overnight."

"It looks…well, sacred, somehow," Merci whispered, walking deeper into the courtyard. "How long did it take you?"

"I count seasons instead of years." She quickened her pace to stroll beside Merci, then laughed again. "Sometimes I feel more at home in my garden than anywhere else on earth." She glanced at Merci as they walked. "This is my fourth season of celebrating new life."

Around them sparrows sang, and from the tile roof of the square building that framed the courtyard, two mockingbirds trilled and warbled, flipped their tails, and warbled again. Hummingbirds busily attacked a stand of hollyhocks at the far end of the garden.

"My room is over here," Sadie said after they had circled the courtyard.

She stepped onto the stone walkway, and Merci followed. Most of the rooms were abandoned. They passed the candlemaker's shop, the blacksmith's, the kitchen with its massive brick ovens. Next they passed a row of rooms that had once housed the resident priests. Some rooms were slightly larger, perhaps for visitors.

Smiling, Sadie stopped, then stepped aside for Merci to enter. A small bed graced one corner of the tiny room. Its heavy wooden frame looked at least a century old, and the mattress, though lumpy with what appeared to be cornhusks, was clean.

In fact the entire room looked scrubbed from stone floor to ceiling, and a fresh coat of whitewash made the walls gleam. Colors nearly rivaling those of the garden seemed to explode in the room—the oval rag rug in the center, the patchwork quilt on the bed, the vase of roses by the lamp that graced the small bedside table.

On the wall opposite the bed was a steamer trunk covered with a lace cloth. On it were several books, writing implements, and three sticks of sealing wax. Another panel of lace hung at the room's single window, adding a touch of charm and beauty. An ancient-looking chair sat beside the window, facing the courtyard. And another multicolored comforter lay across its back.

They walked back outside. "You've turned this into a beautiful place. Earlier you said you do it as a gift…?" She pictured some benevolent overseer requiring it of her in exchange for room and board.

"It is a gift."

"To whom?" They walked over and sat on the wide base of the fountain.

"To my Lord."

Merci narrowed her eyes at the woman. Her irritation flared, then she realized that Sadie must have been tetched in the head. "That's lovely," she said with a disappointed sigh.

But Sadie looked amused. "That's it? I was certain you would question me about such an act."

"If that's how you want to delude yourself, it's not for me to question." She got up and turned to go to Knight.

Sadie fell into step with her. "And you think I'm a wee bit fey for thinking such thoughts."

Merci laughed, shaking her head. "To each her own." She turned again to the gate.

Sadie caught Merci's hand to stop her from leaving. "If it's a place of shelter you're looking for—you're welcome to stay here." She gestured to the garden. "I have plenty to eat for both of us."

Merci considered the offer. "I don't think my kind would be welcome in this place. It's, well, too holy. You don't know who I am or what I do." She threw out the words as a challenge.

Sadie met her gaze with an even one of her own. "I do know."

There was deep compassion in Sadie's eyes, and unable to bear what seemed like pity, Merci turned away and shrugged.

"You are welcome here no matter what you've done in your past."

Merci looked back at Sadie and practically spat the words, "It's not in the past—it's my present."

"I only ask that while you are here, you do not ply your trade in town."

Merci stood, staring at Sadie's kind face, and she could sense a kind of understanding that she hadn't felt for a long time. It was as if this stranger actually cared about her, actually knew her and didn't hold who she was against her. Merci looked around at the beautiful grounds and thought of how restful it would be to live in such a place. If her food and shelter were taken care of, and there was plenty of spring grass for Knight, there was no reason to work the saloons, she reasoned, at least temporarily.

She nodded. "All right, then. Yes, I will stay."

"I also ask that you help me in the garden," Sadie put in.

"If you don't preach to me."

Sadie surprised her by throwing back her head and laughing. "So, that is your reluctance? Your anger at God includes those who serve him? You are afraid that you might see him in a different light, be forced to give up your anger?"

Merci clamped her lips together. Staying here might be harder than she thought. "I just don't want to be reminded daily what a sinner I am."

Sadie's expression softened. "I will honor that request—but not because you asked it of me. I will honor it because I am not without sin. I won't judge you." She fell quiet a moment. "I only ask that you abide by my rules. If you don't, I will ask you to leave."

Merci let out a sigh, wondering of what use it would be not to ply her trade—a chippy was a chippy. It didn't matter how much time passed between tricks. It made no difference to her whether she abstained for a few hours or a few weeks. She was Little Dove. A few days of chaste behavior wouldn't replace the blood in her veins.

"I'll stay just long enough to rest my horse, perhaps buy some clothes in town, then be on my way."

"We'll need to prepare you a place, then," Sadie said with a gentle look. "Follow me."

Through the rest of the afternoon, the two women scrubbed the walls and floor of another cell across the courtyard from Sadie's. As soon as it was dry, Sadie lugged a bucket of whitewash from a storeroom near the kitchen, and the two set about painting the adobe walls. Then they found a wooden cot, cleaned off the cobwebs and polished it till it gleamed, then dragged it into the small room. Sadie pulled out another dried cornhusk mattress—stitched together for another traveler, Merci assumed—beat the dust from it, and hung it in the courtyard to freshen.

By nightfall, Merci's quarters had taken on a welcoming look, completed by Sadie's spare patchwork comforter and a small lamp table. It smelled of fresh paint and damp plaster, a sweet fragrance that mixed with the blossoming courtyard outside the open window. It seemed to Merci that the room had been prepared for someone to stay a good while. It also struck her as a pleasant prospect.

"I'll teach you how to make a rug tomorrow." Sadie placed a tin cup full of lilacs on a table in front of the window.

"You plan to keep me busy."

Sadie fussed with the lilacs, then turned to Merci and smiled. "I've found that there's nothing like hard work to feed body and soul. My days are long, but I think you'll find rest in them even so."

True to her word, at sunup the following morning, Sadie knocked on Merci's door. "Time for breakfast," she called. "It will be ready in ten minutes." The sound of a crowing rooster mixed with the songs of birds feeding in the courtyard and drifted through her window.

Merci stretched and looked around the small room. Drawing in a deep breath, she realized that for the first time she felt safe. The knowledge brought a stinging to her throat, and she swallowed hard. She rose and dressed in the clean garments Sadie had given her the night before, then headed to the privy before finding her hostess.

It didn't take her long. She merely followed her nose to the open kitchen where Sadie was pulling a loaf of bread from the oven. Slicing off a large hunk, Sadie dropped a spoonful of butter on the piece and handed it to Merci.

Merci took one bite, then closed her eyes, relishing the flavor. "Butter…" she murmured after she swallowed. "Where did you get it?"

"There's a cow out back. And I've got a henhouse and plenty of eggs. Even enough to sell in town." She poured Merci a cup of the coffee boiling in an iron pot above the coals at the side of the oven.

The women walked into the courtyard and sat near the fountain. The sun was just rising, and Merci blinked at the feel of its bright, clear warmth on her face.

"We need to put in some ferns I found yesterday." Sadie looked at Merci over the rim of her tin cup. "I'll need your help to dig them up, bring them here to transplant."

"I'm willing." Merci bit off another piece of the warm, buttered bread. It was dark with grain and contained flecks of dried fruit. "Is the place nearby?"

"It's on a ridge just beyond Santa Inez—not far from where you rode in yesterday. I can fashion a saddlebag for your horse so the plants will be protected. While you're gone, I'll prepare the soil."

While Sadie made the saddlebags from some flour sacks, Merci groomed Knight with a brush she found in the stables. It had been much too long, and it grieved her that this magnificent beast hadn't had the proper care. It took her an hour to comb out the tangles in his mane and tail, then she spent another hour brushing him until her arms ached and his coat gleamed in the sun.

By noon Merci had mounted Knight and headed into town, saddlebags lying across the horse's back, a spade handle protruding from one. She had skirted Santa Inez the day before, and now looked forward to riding through town to have a better look. She figured that, true, she would mind Sadie's rules while she was at the mission, but perhaps as early as her departure day, she might try to earn some cash for the road.

Knight took his lead, moving to a brisk trot. They passed through some meadowlands, then across a rocky ridge, and finally threaded through a sparse forest of live oaks. When they reached a clearing, Merci could see the town below them, a mix of white adobe and red tile and aging wood, all of it looking dusty and neglected. On the far side was the small mountain range Sadie had described.

She pressed her heels into Knight's sides, and the stallion moved at a faster clip.

The sun was high now, and his hours of rest and grazing in the lush grasses of the mission had already served him well. She smoothed his neck with her hand, smiling at the look of his newly brushed coat.

He was the only thing left in her world to love. Slowing him, she bent low over his neck, wrapping her arms around it. More than once, the simple duty of caring for him had pulled her from a despair deep enough to tempt her to take her own life.

She let her eyelids close, breathing in the musky smell of his sun-warmed hide, and ran her fingers through his mane. She felt the sting of unshed tears. He was her last connection to her past, and on a perfect sunlit afternoon like this, she realized he was the one slim thread of hope that life might someday be different.

Knight seemed to sense her pleasure and flicked his tail. She sat upright as he carried them down the main street of town at a brisk trot.

She thought he had never looked more majestic, this horse. She couldn't keep the smile of pride from her face as people turned to watch.

Tilting her cheeks upward, she put on a coquettish expression and squared her shoulders. With a jangle of the reins, she let Knight prance from one end of town to the other. Then she threw back her head and laughed out loud at the awestruck faces.

You would prefer Lady Godiva, perhaps? I could easily comply if you would make it worth my while!

Laughing again, she dug her heels into his flanks, and Knight took off like lightning, hooves thundering, his silky mane flying. They soared to the outer edges of town.

For the next few miles, Merci had a good chuckle about her little amusement, then put her mind to the task ahead—finding the clumps of bleeding heart fern for Sadie.

Suddenly she had the eerie suspicion that she was being followed. She slowed Knight and craned, her gaze taking in the sleepy town in the distance. Nothing seemed out of the ordinary. Surely the sense of disquiet was her imagination.

She turned again and urged the big stallion to move on. He did, though with one ear cocked back, he snorted uneasily. Again Merci slowed the beast, then headed him to a small hill and halted beneath a sycamore tree. She was afforded a panoramic view of the Santa Inez Valley, and now she could see the mission just beyond the town.

She thought of Sadie, considering what the young woman was doing that minute—likely one of her ordinary tasks, such as gardening or baking. Maybe quilting. For the first time Merci wondered what it would be like to settle into such a life. Or even if it was possible.

Knight seemed calmer now. So she nudged her heels into his sides, reining him back onto the trail. By the time she reached the small clearing Sadie had told her about, she'd nearly forgotten her earlier apprehension.

She had just dismounted when the sounds of approaching riders caught her attention. Frowning, she turned to see three men on horseback.

They circled her, their horses breathing hard, and cornered her at a tree. She screamed, and Knight, who had backed away at their arrival, reared, his front hooves churning the air.

"Grab him!" one of the men ordered.

The other two hesitated, their fear of the beast evident.

"Get him now!" the same man shouted.

"No!" Merci cried. "Don't touch him!" She attempted to get around the horsemen who still had her pinned close to the tree trunk. When she saw the futility of escape, she yelled again. "Go, Knight. Go! Now, boy. Go!"

The stallion reared again, a sound of equine rage erupting. He beat the ground with his forelegs, then thundered toward where Merci was held fast.

The leader of the group shot out his hand, capturing Knight's reins. "Down, boy," he said calmly. "Down. Settle down."

Knight's nostrils flared, and the sounds of his heavy spurts of breath broke Merci's heart. "Don't hurt him," she said. "Do anything you'd like to me, but don't hurt him." She attempted a trembling smile, a flirtatious wink and a lift of her brow.

One of the men laughed, looking her up and down. "My ma told me never to consort with the likes of you."

The man holding Knight's reins snorted. He rode closer to her, the black stallion in tow. "My ma said I'd likely catch somethin' if I even looked at a cheap trollop like you, honey. You ain't got anything we'd want. There's high-class ladies of the night, and then there's trash. I'd say you look more like the second category."

Merci slid to her knees and covered her face with her hands, too soul-weary even to cry, too certain of the truth of their words to care anymore.

When they left with Knight, she didn't even look up…or whisper good-bye.

EIGHTEEN

Brighid clutched the buggy seat to keep herself upright, and she glanced at the beloved man beside her. Songan met her gaze with a tender smile, then looked back to the road, flicking the whip above the back of the dappled mare pulling the buggy. The horse rounded a curve leading into Santa Isabela, and the vehicle swayed.

They had known each other for nearly three decades and had worked together for the last few years at the Soboba school—Song as headmaster, she as one of the too-few teachers. One year she came to him with a plan to take some of the more promising students to a higher level of scholarship, hoping to give them the skills needed for university or college entrance.

Song had caught hold of her dream and joined her work with the students, two the first year, three the next, and a dozen by the end of the first five years of the program. Seven of their students had graduated from California universities and three had attended college for at least two years.

They worked together, searching for books to enlighten the Indian students and methods to light a fire of curiosity under them. Somewhere between the third and fourth term of their program, Song and Brighid had been surprised to find their friendship had grown to deep caring. It wasn't an easy love. Racial bigotry was alive and well in the Big Valley.

Song had been Brighid's rock during the tragic first months of Merci's disappearance, and now, during a weeklong holiday between terms, he was setting out with her for another search.

Song reached for her hand. His expression was tender, and Brighid knew he understood her deep heartache better than anyone. Song and his father, the Soboba chief, had come to her after she was violated, had stood beside her in comforting silence when she retreated into the dark shadows of unreality. Song had been there with the other Indian children that day—he had watched her draw pictures, she remembered, of a story about horses.

It was the same story that unlocked the fortress of fear that had held her captive. Songan, standing silently by his father, had seen her transformation. Though he never spoke of it, she saw in his eyes now, the deepest understanding and compassion one person could give another.

She met his gaze, feeling comforted by the warm strength of his big hand wrapped around hers.

They had followed every lead about Merci since the day they saw her in Los Angeles. One of the ranch hands reported that he'd heard she was headed east on the Santa Fe, but checking all the local ticket agencies revealed that report to be false. A woman in Riverview said that she'd heard Merci found employment as a governess to a wealthy family raising their children on a schooner, and that they'd all set sail from Los Angeles Harbor. A check of the shipping activities in and out of the harbor proved that statement was also in error.

Last week a drummer selling tonics appeared on the rancho with an old swayback mule and a faded snake-oil wagon. He set up shop just under the entrance gate, but before Quaid ran him off, the grizzled man boasted about a woman called Little Dove he'd met in a brothel. Later, the man said, he'd heard rumors from other men who bought her favors that she was from Rancho de la Paloma and that she had changed her name from Mercy-something when she became a fancy lady.

He'd pointed to the doves on the gate and laughed, saying he knew nothing more, only that this woman plied her trade at a place called the Ice House in Santa Isabela.

After Merci ran away, Brighid didn't think her heart could twist any tighter in her chest. On the day the drummer came to town, she discovered she'd been wrong. That day, it nearly twisted in two.

As if reading her thoughts, Songan squeezed her fingers.

"I don't know what I'll say when I see her." Brighid's throat ached with unshed tears as the dapple trotted into Santa Isabela.

"You will know." Songan slowed the horse to a walk as they approached the first of the businesses on Main Street. "Just trust your heart to tell you."

The place appeared nearly deserted, some of the businesses were boarded up, and those that seemed open had faded, peeling facades and broken windows. A scattering of men stood on the boardwalks, watching sullenly as the buggy passed.

Brighid shivered.

At the end of the street stood the Ice House, a few yards ahead of where the road curved, then disappeared as it wound out of town. Brighid gripped Songan's hand tighter, inclining her head toward the place.

The big man worked his jaw as he parked the buggy at the hitching post. "A woman shouldn't step through the door of such a place. I'll make the inquiries." She could feel his already seething anger.

Brighid shook her head. "If my daughter is inside, nothing can stop me from seeing her. I don't care what kind of vermin frequent the place. I must go."

His face was solemn as he stepped from the buggy and helped her down. He tucked her hand in the crook of his arm and escorted her through the saloon doors.

Inside, a few men sat at tables, a few more at the bar. A tinny piano played in the background, punctuated by the laughter of men and women from a room in the back. The place reeked of brimstone. Brighid's stomach clenched tight.

The barkeep looked up from where he was polishing glasses with a rag. "What can I get for you folks?"

Brighid stepped toward him. "We're looking for a woman named Merci Byrne."

The man glanced around the room, then gave her an insolent shrug. "Do you see her here?" He laughed, and some of the other men joined in.

Songan drew himself up to his full height and lowered his voice to a low growl. "We have a report from a reliable source that she is here in…this establishment." His eyes bored into the man.

The barkeep stared at Songan for a moment, seeming to weigh his words. "Merci Byrne left quite some time ago. She lived around these parts for a while, then decided to move on to greener pastures…" He winked at Songan. "If you know what I mean."

Brighid glanced down and watched as Songan's fist clenched, unclenched, then clenched again. She could feel the tension in his arm.

She forced herself to remain calm. "Where did she go?"

The man laughed. "She left in rather a hurry. I heard she was afraid the law was comin' after her."

"The law?" Songan stepped forward, and for an instant Brighid worried he might go for the man's throat.

"Merci Byrne's a horse thief."

"That's impossible," Brighid breathed.

"Seems she'd made a deal to sell her stallion—a big black—in exchange for, well, how shall I say it in mixed company?" He glanced at Brighid. "Well, being taken care of—or kept, you might say." He laughed nervously.

Songan's anger was palpable. "Go on," he growled.

"She turned out to be somewhat of an Indian giver—no offense." He glanced at Songan before continuing. "Wanted the horse back and stole him right out from under Cole's nose."

"Cole?"

"Adam Cole. Owns this place."

"And he threatened to turn Merci over to the authorities?"

The barkeep laughed heartily. "He *is* the authority. At least that's what he'd like everyone around here to think."

Brighid pictured the terror her child must have felt. The shame. She closed her eyes for a moment, thinking she might be ill. Merci, who had been the joy of her life since the day she was born. Images of Merci's babyhood flooded her mind: the tiny fist that grasped her finger, the sweet baby fragrance of rose petals and talcum powder, the first smile and chortling squeal.

That was yesterday.

Brighid widened her eyes to keep her tears from spilling. Folding her arms across her chest, she turned away from the barkeep, struggling for composure.

Behind her, Songan asked, "Do you know which direction she fled?"

"The whole town watched her ride that stallion out of here that night. The horse screamed with the kind of fury you only read about. Looked wild. Shots were fired, but as far as we know, Merci Byrne and her horse weren't hit. Leastwise, the following day when folks went searching, they didn't find any signs of blood. Some say she headed north."

Brighid shivered, and Songan wrapped his arm around her shoulders and led her to the exit. He hesitated slightly at the swinging doors. Finally, with his left hand on one of the doors, Songan turned around. "Prostitution is illegal in California, you know."

The barkeep was polishing a glass, held it to the window light, and then gave it another swipe with his rag. "Who said anything about prostitution?"

"One mention to the proper authorities, and you'll be shut down."

The man gave him a knowing smile. "As I told you, the only authority we care about runs our town. Your 'mention' will get you nowhere, my friend. You can prove nothing."

Songan pushed open the door and escorted Brighid through.

"I'd be careful on that road north, my friends," the barkeep called out. "Many a buggy wreck is strewn on the cliffs below."

Brighid and Songan traveled three more days, staying at inns along the way. Always they asked about Merci and the big stallion, thinking the horse might help identify her, but the answer was always the same. No one had seen the beautiful young woman with the flaming red curls.

They reached Buena Ventura and, disheartened, turned back toward the Big Valley.

Brighid looked over at Songan, an idea occurring to her. "We have been asking for Merci at inns and taverns , but where else might she go for shelter?"

"A church?"

"That would be the last place she would go for help." The road was rough, and the buggy bumped along, wheels creaking.

"Where, then?" He flicked the reins, and the dapple mare trotted along, easily moving along the ruts and ridges even as the buggy swayed.

A breeze caught Brighid's hair, and she leaned back to enjoy the feel of the wind in her face, closing her eyes against the sun. "Merci has never been afraid of sleeping outdoors," she continued.

"You think she's been camping along the way?"

Brighid nodded thoughtfully. "Perhaps in abandoned barns, stables… the like."

"Maybe that's why no one has seen her." He stretched his arm across the seat behind Brighid.

"If she's afraid of capture, that's an even greater reason for her to remain unseen."

The buggy wheels rolled along, and a small cloud of dust lifted behind them. The only sound was the horse's hooves thudding on the dirt road.

"The old mission we passed a ways back…" Brighid mused, more to herself than to Songan. "I'm wondering if we should stop and have a look around."

"The Buena Ventura."

"Yes."

Songan nodded and slowed the horse to a halt. He turned in his seat. "Are you certain? It's been little more than a pile of rubble for years."

"I know. That's why she may be there—or perhaps she stopped there."

Songan studied her face for a moment. "Brighid," he said gently, "you can't continue like this."

Fresh sadness knotted inside her. They'd had this conversation before. After Merci rode off, they'd searched for days. Then the days turned into weeks. They followed every rumor, traveling north, south, east, and west.

"I know, Song." Her voice was little more than a whisper. "But I can't stop looking. I love her so. I don't care what she's done...or even how she's living. No, that's not true. I *do* care." She paused, looking past the soft green hills with their dappled splash of poppies to their dark shadows. "I feel responsible, I suppose, for keeping the truth from her. Her shock at finding out..." Her voice dropped, and she couldn't go on.

He circled his arm around her and pulled her close enough for her to feel the warmth of his broad chest, the steady drum of his heartbeat.

"You aren't responsible for what Merci does, Brighid. Only she can decide which way to turn—where to turn—and when. She's in God's sheltering arms, even now. We need to trust him to keep her there. To do whatever it will take to bring her back to him."

His words mirrored her heart's prayer. How she loved this man whose character was so close to God's! His words did bring her comfort. But letting go was the hardest thing she'd ever had to do as Merci's mother. She drew in a shuddering breath. "I can't, Song. I try to let go, but then I think how much Merci needs me right now, and I just can't let her go."

He pressed her close and rested his cheek on the top of her head. Outside the buggy, the mare snorted impatiently, and a soft breeze carried with it the scents of spring. From the branch of a live oak a scrub jay squawked, and a mockingbird warbled from someplace in the distance. Nearer, a couple of grasshoppers sawed their legs, adding to the music of spring.

New life. Brighid remembered when Merci was born after the tragedy that had befallen her—God had given her the oil of gladness instead of the ashes of mourning.

Every day of her life, Merci reminded Brighid of God's faithfulness. His mercy. He had brought triumph from the ruins of unspeakable tragedy.

With each new spring, Brighid was reminded of God's creation power. And each time she had looked in her daughter's face, Brighid saw the miracle of his grace. Her quest, as much as anything, was to find

Merci and make her understand that she was cherished. Her life held more value to Brighid than did her own.

She'd told Merci about the tragedy of her birth, but she never had a chance to tell her the rest. That she would have endured even worse to be given the wondrous miracle of Merci's life. That it was the life of the child in her womb that brought her back to reality, that made her want to live again.

"Let's go to the mission," she said finally. "We'll ask one last time if someone has seen Merci. Then we'll turn back to the Big Valley."

Minutes later, Songan reined the dapple mare to the grassy hillside next to the mission, and drew her to a halt.

The mission's adobe walls were cracked, and though it appeared that work was being done to restore it, the church and grounds around it were in a state of disrepair. The bell was missing from its tower, and the whole place was overgrown with weeds and brambles.

Songan came around to Brighid's side of the buggy and reached up to help her step down. When they turned, a short, balding man was hurrying toward them.

"Greetings!" he called out. "How can I help you weary travelers?"

"We'd like to ask you about a young woman who may have passed your way," Brighid said.

"We get many travelers coming to our door," he said. "This is the King's Highway, you know. *El Camino Real.*"

Brighid smiled at the man's exuberance. "Yes," she said. "We've heard it called that."

"The highway of the early church fathers," Songan added.

"Come in and sit a spell," the man said, "and you can tell me about the young woman." He stopped abruptly, and smiled. "Forgive my manners. My name is Neal O'Brian, and my wife, Molly, is inside. We would be delighted to have you sup with us."

Brighid and Songan followed him through the yard's rubble, around the church, and across the courtyard to a small bungalow behind the stables. Molly was as bustling and friendly as Neal was. She beamed as she vigorously shook their hands.

When they were seated around the couple's modest wooden table, and Molly had poured them each a cup of robust tea, Neal spoke again, "Tell me, now, about the young woman you're searching for."

"It's my daughter," Brighid said. "Her name is Merci. Merci Byrne."

Molly and Neal exchanged a glance, and Brighid knew in that instant that they'd seen Merci.

"Tell me," she said, leaning across the table. "Tell me everything you know."

"Your daughter did stay here," the caretaker said. "She seemed sad and alone. My Molly fixed the little slip of a thing food and clothing for her journey, though she left the clothes behind. And we haven't missed a day of praying for her since she left us."

Brighid reached for his hand. "Thank you." Just knowing her daughter had sought shelter at such a place warmed her soul. This couple had provided Merci with some measure of comfort. Brighid swallowed the sting in her throat. God was with her child. This was the first tangible proof, and her heart warmed at even this small hope.

"She seemed to be holding so much pain inside it was threatening to spill over," Neal said. "It troubled us that she wouldn't stay longer."

Songan leaned forward. "Did she say where she was going?"

Molly shook her head. "No, but my husband did provide her with a map, showing her the way north."

Brighid caught her breath. "A map?"

"To the missions—all of them are on the King's Highway," Neal said as Molly stood and poured them more tea.

"They're all a day's journey apart," Neal added.

Brighid met Songan's gaze then looked back to Molly and Neal. "You mean, my daughter left here with a map to all the missions?" She felt like laughing with joy.

Suddenly they were all talking at once, Molly and Neal explaining which missions were in disrepair, which had been partially restored, and explaining about the map and promising that he would draw a new one for them to trace Merci's steps.

"Think of it," Brighid said after a few minutes, "in a few weeks we may have found my daughter. We might be on our way home with her as early as tomorrow." She looked heavenward for a moment, her heart overflowing with emotion, then back to the others. "Perhaps we'll even stop by here on our way home and let you know we've found her. We'll rejoice together that our prodigal is returning home."

Her pronouncement was met by silence.

"Ah, but the prodigal son returned home on his own," Neal said. "His father didn't go after him."

Brighid turned away from their scrutiny as the thin thread of hope died. Hot tears threatened to choke her. How could they have come this far only to let Merci go? She was Merci's mother. No one in the world loved the girl as much as she did. Wasn't it her responsibility to rescue her daughter—to help her through this time of trial and fear?

Brighid dropped her head into her hands. "I don't know if I can release her. Everything inside me tells me to go to her." She thought of those things left to be said and looked back to the three faces around the small table. "I'm her mother. I want to take away her pain."

"You can't take it away," Neal said gently. "No one can but God himself. And Merci must be the one to decide if she wants him to."

"Don't forget," Molly said, "there is One who loves her even more than you do. Merci isn't alone. Don't follow after her because you think you can do God's work better than he can himself."

"She's been hurt, so desperately hurt." Brighid searched Molly's eyes for understanding. "I'm the only one who understands what she's going through."

"Are you, child?" Neal asked kindly. "Are you certain?" His face was filled with compassion.

Songan took Brighid's hand. "I am willing to go with you to the ends of the earth, if necessary, to help you search. If you want to continue on the Camino Real, I'm ready to go—if you want me. If you would prefer going alone, I'll honor that as well."

"If you would like some time alone…to think, to consider what you should do," Neal said, "I can show you to the room where your daughter stayed while she was with us."

Brighid let out a deep breath. "Thank you. I would like that."

"It's in a state of decay, but you can't miss it," Neal explained. "There's a small room to the left of the courtyard. It's there she spent the night."

"I can find my way alone," Brighid said with a sad smile.

Songan pressed her fingers as she stood, a questioning look in his eyes as he looked up at her. He understood her need to go by herself to where her daughter had been.

Minutes later, she picked her way through the rubble—red roof tiles, bricks, and an odd assortment of rusting farm implements once used by the mission fathers. It didn't take long to make her way to the room Neal had described.

It was little more than a three-sided cell filled with clutter. There was no bed or mat on the floor. No doubt it was a haven for rats.

Brighid shuddered and moved farther into the dimly lit shelter. There in the center of the cell, she settled onto a couple of stacked adobe bricks. She took in the dirty walls, the dark cobwebbed corners, the musty sweet smell of decaying wood, knowing that her daughter would have done the same. She wondered if Merci had compared the place to her pretty rooms at the rancho.

Would she have remembered the lace curtains, the four-poster bed with its delicate canopy, the wardrobe filled with gowns, as tangible evidence that she had been loved from birth onward? Or would she think those things merely instruments of some kind of misplaced guilt on Brighid's part, perhaps to make up for not loving her daughter?

Brighid remembered the rocking horse her father had made for Merci when she was a baby. Long after she was grown, her daughter had refused to let it be taken from her room. It sat there now, teething imprints across its wooden head and varnish rubbed off the handles from her tiny hands.

Would Merci ever remember those loving times, those loving gestures, and consider that she was cherished?

"Oh, Father," she breathed, "bring to her mind every moment that she was loved! Don't let her tragedy bury the good. Please, Father, I implore you..." Tears were sliding down her cheeks.

SHE IS MINE, BELOVED. LET HER GO.

"I can't! I love her so," she whispered.

IS YOUR LOVE GREATER THAN MINE? I KNIT HER IN YOUR WOMB. I
HAVE LOVED HER WITH AN EVERLASTING LOVE.

"How will she hear of your love? How will she hear your voice
through the bitter wall she has erected?" Brighid shook her head. "I
must go to her. I must make her understand." Brighid wept into her
hands. "I can't let her go."

I LENT HER TO YOU, AND NOW IT IS TIME TO GIVE HER BACK TO ME.

"Oh, my Merci, my child," Brighid wept, "how I love you! How I
wish I could take your sorrow and bear it myself."

Wasn't that what Christ had done? He had borne the sins, the sor-
rows, of all the world. He had suffered for his children. He had died so
that they might be free from the bindings of the Evil One. So that Merci
might be free.

Merci couldn't free herself from the chains that bound her.

Even Brighid, who loved her daughter with the deepest mother-love
possible, couldn't free her.

Only God could do it. Only the blood of his beloved Son could
break Merci's chains of sin and sorrow.

Brighid stopped weeping and looked up, considering the notion. A
small piece of leather caught her attention. It appeared to be a book
cover, tucked between two stones in the pile of rubble. She stood and
walked across the room. A moment later, she pulled a small leather-
tooled volume from its hiding place.

Turning it in her hands, she unsnapped the cover and opened it. It
hadn't belonged to Merci, at least she had never seen it in her daughter's
possession. But it wasn't weathered or worn, and somehow she knew it
hadn't been in its hiding place long.

Holding it tenderly, she headed back into the caretaker's house.

"I found this in the little cell where you said my daughter stayed."

Molly nodded and smiled. "Yes, we found it right after Merci left.
We figured she might come back for it."

Brighid felt waves of peace overtake her. She clutched the Bible to her chest and smiled at the small group. "Do you see?" she whispered. "Meeting you…finding this…tells me that God is leading Merci even now.

"He led her here, and you gave her food and clothing in his name. You were his arms of love reaching out to her.

"We may never know who gave her this Bible or how she came to receive it, but we do know that someone else became his arms of love before you."

She drew in a deep breath and silently prayed for strength. Hugging the soft leather volume close, she rubbed her fingertips across the tooling.

"I can let her go now," she said, looking up again. "My daughter must learn things about herself, her place in the world, and about her Lord that only he can teach her."

Songan circled his arm around her.

"It won't be easy," she whispered. "But I can let go."

Nineteen

May 1890

Quaid rode onto Emmeline's property and swung off his hat a half-second before sliding off the saddle.

Emmeline was sitting next to Gertie, snapping beans from their kitchen garden. Gertie wore a poke bonnet, but Emmeline had lately taken to pulling her hair back and tying it with a ribbon at the nape of her neck. It suited her and showed off her eyes, which, he had decided the first moment he'd seen them, were eyes a man could get lost in if he wasn't careful.

She waved as he approached.

In the six months since Emmeline arrived, he had watched her blossom in the California sun. Last March she lost the eyeglasses while weeding the groves and didn't bother to buy another pair. She seemed to relish the feel of the sun in her face. Lately a spray of freckles had begun to grace her nose, and her high cheekbones were rosy with health. When she'd worn the ridiculous little spectacles, he had never noticed the elegant slope of her nose, how it turned up the daintiest bit at the end. Now he couldn't keep his gaze from it.

For that matter, lately he'd noticed how Emmeline's smile seemed to light her whole face. She was always laughing at this detail or that, taking fresh delight at a sprig of cauliflower in her garden or an orange blossom on a tree every time he turned around.

The woman had the stamina of granite, he'd decided. She seemed undaunted by each setback on her property.

And there had been many. The rains had been too few during the winter and spring, and her spindly orange trees were barely hanging on to life. She was attempting to lead the other grove owners in a fight against the county, trying to get more of the water that had been dammed released for irrigation. But most of the other horticulturists, as the highfalutin growers called themselves, had well water or access to the new canal that had just come through the highlands. Emmeline's land had a single well, but the water table had suddenly dropped this year.

She wasn't about to give up her fight, though. The one thing that irked him about Emmeline Amity Callahan was the fact that she dared oppose those who wanted to keep the land free from the developers.

It was also one of the things about her that he loved.

Along with the way she narrowed her eyes at him, her hands on her hips, and told him in no uncertain terms what was on her mind.

It didn't matter that he disagreed. His gruff responses only made her cheeks flush prettily and her eyes turn bright with ire. He melted inside when he saw her looking like that. And sometimes he'd bully his way through a conversation about cowboys versus growers, just to see the spitfire in her eyes.

And the spitfire was there more often than not.

He'd formed a cooperative of ranchers who wanted to keep the land from being developed for oranges, lemons, or housing communities. They called themselves Citizens for Keeping California Wild.

Emmeline had immediately formed her own cooperative—Citizens for California's Citrus. When he told her that ten ranchers had joined his cooperative, she boasted a membership of eleven.

She was sitting on the porch in her high-necked lace blouse and dark skirt, watching him walk toward her. Bounding up the stairs, his heart thudded a quick cantering beat when she stood to meet him.

He bent to kiss Gertie's cheek, then grinned at Emmeline as he tossed his hat on a nearby post. "I stopped by to see if you wanted to ride into Riverview with me tonight."

"Are you planning to join us at the three Cs?" Her smile told him she was jesting.

"I wouldn't dare." He sat with his back against the porch railing, reached for a handful of beans and popped one into his mouth. Gertie playfully slapped his hand, so he snapped the rest and dropped them into the pan. "Your friends would likely throw rotten oranges at me."

She glared at him. "My friends wouldn't stoop to such theatrics. Yours, on the other hand…" She reached for another bean.

He grabbed it from her and popped it into his mouth. "You're insinuating mine would?"

"Not oranges," she said. "Perhaps buckeyes or stones. Neanderthals, all of them."

Gertie rolled her eyes heavenward. "Children, children."

He narrowed his eyes at Emmeline. "Neanderthals?"

"Cavemen, if you'd rather." She kept her gaze on the beans she continued to snap. "Against progress of any kind. Irritated by women crowding you out of your land, though it doesn't seem to matter that these same women are improving the economy of California." She named prominent women in the area, those who were making fortunes with orchards, vineyards, and commerce.

"Once it's used, the land can never revert back to the wilderness God intended," he countered. "There's no going back once it's gone."

She stared at him, cheeks flushed, eyes bright. Her smile had faded. "Men like you stand in the way of progress. That's exactly what may lead this country into economic troubles."

He let out a guffaw. "Economic troubles? Where did you come up with that?"

"You forget, my father is a senator."

"Well, Miss Senator's Daughter," he said, his tone laced with sarcasm, "tell me what else this country is headed for"—he gritted his teeth and lowered his voice to a growl—"besides the decay of our wildlands, the killing off of our wildlife, on land and sea." He stared at her bent head. "Besides the loss of what can't ever be retrieved. Losses that will indeed someday affect that same economy."

She didn't look up, but just kept snapping beans hard and fast as if each one were his neck. "Without progress it won't matter if wolves and bears and buffalo roam the country," she said. "Without development children will starve—"

He let out a guffaw. "Children will starve?"

She met his gaze and gave him a decisive nod. "Children."

"Now, that's an argument I haven't heard before."

Two angry bright spots graced her cheeks, and he felt himself melting again. Just as always.

"The economy will die. Fathers will be out of work."

"They should have stayed on their farms," he muttered.

"Not everyone chooses to ranch or farm. Cities are growing. With each building that rises, workers are needed. With each road that is laid, workers are needed. With each—"

He held up his hands. "I get the picture. You don't need to go on."

But she did anyway. "Each job provided means that children won't go hungry."

"I said I understand."

Gertie chuckled, still snapping beans.

Quaid reached for another, popping it into his mouth. He grinned at Emmeline. "I provide work for families too, you know. Every cowhand on my ranch is paid good wages. Even Neanderthals have hearts."

She didn't give up. "I happen to know for a fact that ninety-seven percent of all cowboys in America don't have families."

He let out another guffaw, nearly choking on the snap bean he'd been chewing.

She rushed on without pausing. "It's a proven fact that cowboys prefer living alone. They prefer wide-open spaces to enclosed dwellings. They prefer keeping to themselves, sleeping under the stars, riding the range for weeks at a time without so much as a bath—"

"Where did you hear all this?" he interrupted her tirade.

"My father often oversees studies."

"Studies, you say?" He noticed the fiery flecks of gold in her chestnut eyes.

"On various subjects," she said, meeting his gaze, then swallowing hard. "All sorts of studies are done in Washington. You would be surprised." Her hands were all aflutter now, and when she reached for another snap bean, she dropped it.

He reached to the porch floor to retrieve it at the same time she did. Their hands met and their gazes locked. He handed her the bean. "Thank you," she whispered, taking it from him as though it were some precious jewel.

Gertie cleared her throat. "What were you saying about the three *C*s?"

"I was about to ask Emmeline if she might accompany me to town this afternoon. Of course we'll go to our separate meetings once we're there."

"Then why should we ride in together?" She snapped another bean and dropped it in the pan.

He grinned. "You go with me, and after our meetings, I promise to show you something about California you've never seen before."

"Sounds intriguing," she said nonchalantly. "But I know your tricks. I'm certain it has to do with why wilderness should be preserved."

"Can't shoot me for trying." He noticed how her lashes rested on her cheeks when she looked down. "Actually, you've never experienced summer until you've experienced it in California."

"It's still May," she said. "Won't be summer until next month."

He reached for another bean, crunched it loudly, then dodged another of Gertie's playful slaps. "Summers in California start in May, then disappear until July. June can be our dreariest month. Heavy shrouds of fog and drizzle that seem as if they'll never leave."

Emmeline frowned. "You're teasing me."

The one thing that got her ire up faster than anything else, he'd learned, was the thought that someone might be poking fun at her. Especially if that someone was a man.

"Trust me," he said with another grin.

She didn't smile. "That kind of weather can cause leaf mildew."

He let out a deep breath. "Can you think for a moment about May, instead of worrying about June?"

She glanced up at the clear blue sky and leaned back in her chair. "We made it through the first winter with barely enough rain to keep my plants from dying. We made it through the first windstorm of the season that nearly ripped off all their leaves. Then came the first of the firestorms in the mountains above us." She sighed. "Now you're telling me I've got leaf mildew coming around the corner—and you want me to think of some pretty summer excursion instead of figuring out how to keep my trees from dying yet again?"

He laughed. "Maybe that's why you should consider raising cattle instead of trees."

"Humph" was her only reply as she went back to snapping beans.

He stood, dusted himself off, and kissed Gertie's cheek once again. "I'll be back at six," he said to Emmeline. "You'll need a mount. We'll not be taking the buggy."

"I didn't say I would go."

"I have faith in your curiosity."

She stood to walk with him out to the patch of grass at the front of the adobe where the horse was grazing. He mounted, and she looked up at him with an unreadable expression. "I can see myself into town," she finally said.

Trying not to show his disappointment, he gave her an indifferent shrug. Then he glanced up at Gertie and had an idea. "Gert," he called out, "will you talk some sense into this stubborn young woman?"

Gertie cackled. "Of course. Though if it's your virtue you want me to convince her of—it may be an impossible task."

He let the sorrel dance sideways to the porch, leaving Emmeline standing, hands on hips, in the grass. "That's it exactly," he laughed. "Tell her I'm a fine, upstanding citizen, entirely conscious of Miss Emmeline Callahan's honor and well-being. And that though I'm a member of the loathsome Citizens for Keeping California Wild, I swear I will not hold her hostage until she joins. I will not even mention the dreaded organization if she will consent to come with me tonight."

Behind him, Emmeline was now laughing. "All right," she said, striding toward him. "Six o'clock, you say?" Again she studied him with that unfathomable look, then grinned, her nose wrinkling prettily. "I still say you're trying to convince me that the land should be left for wilderness—not for crops. And especially not for fragrant citrus."

Quaid smiled at her from atop the skittering sorrel. "You will have to wait and see."

Quaid rode up to Emmeline's rancho as the afternoon shadows lengthened. Her horse, an Appaloosa, was saddled and waiting near the porch. Gertie met him at the door and, standing on tiptoes, greeted him with a hug.

"I declare you get taller every time I see you, young man," she said. "Either that or I'm shrinking."

"I don't think you're getting smaller," he countered. "Just ornerier."

She reached up and tweaked his cheek. "You're the only one I'd ever let get away with talkin' to me that way."

"Maybe, then, these will help keep the peace between us." He handed her a stack of dime novels he had picked up in Riverview.

She beamed with delight as she took them from his hands. "I'm ready for some adventure. Things are gettin' too tame around here for my tastes."

He followed her into the kitchen. "Did I ever tell you how disappointed I was that you didn't turn out to be an outlaw?" she tossed over her shoulder.

He chuckled. "At least a half-dozen times. But that doesn't mean I'm going to head into a life of crime just to please you."

He sat opposite Gertie at the ancient farm table. He wondered how many generations it had been in the Dearbourne family. He didn't ask his father much about his childhood here. Mostly it had been unpleasant, he'd gathered. Spence spoke lovingly of his mother, Sara, and his brother, Jamie, but he had little to say about his father, Hugh Dearbourne.

Quaid figured that when the time was right, his father would tell him anything he needed to know.

He glanced around the kitchen and noticed the big room still needed restoration from the earthquake. Emmeline never complained, and in the spring when Gertie had put up her strawberry jam, he thought she had grumbled about the stove not working properly just to needle him.

Now he stood and walked over to have a look. Two of the six round iron plates were askew, jammed out of position, and a wide crack ran straight down from the center of the top shelf, through the entire apparatus. One leg was propped up with adobe bricks. He jiggled it to check its stability, and it moved precariously. Not so dangerous when it was empty and cold. But judging from the banked embers showing beneath the pot of beans on one side and the kettle of water on the other, the women did indeed use it.

"You're fixing to make us some supper?" Emmeline said from behind him.

He turned, frowning. "This is in no shape for use, Emma. It's dangerous. You should have said something."

"The entire house is in need of fixing, Quaid," she said quietly. "I'm doing as much as I can, as quickly as I can."

That she had such disregard for their safety made the hair on the back of his neck stand on end. Didn't she realize this was a fire hazard? If anything happened to these two… He didn't finish the thought. "Surely this stove should have been at the top of the repair list."

She walked over to him. "Are you questioning my sensibilities? Because if you are, you'd better think about it and march yourself right out of here."

They glared at each other, then Gertie started to laugh. "You children are worse than two grizzlies fightin' over a fresh kill." She walked over to the stove and pumped the bellows at the banked embers.

Quaid laughed and the tension was broken. "Sandy and Kerr are down to fetch a milk cow for my grandparents. I'll get them to help get this monstrosity out of here tomorrow morning. Then we'll hitch up the buckboard and ride to Riverview to order you another."

"Order another?" Gertie sputtered. "What are we supposed to do meantime?" She pumped the bellows again to emphasize her point.

"Now that the weather's turned warmer, we can set up a firepit outside the back door." He hesitated. "Or the two of you can join me at La Paloma for dinner each night until the new stove arrives."

Gertie and Emmeline exchanged a look. "You'll be doing the cooking?" Gertie asked with a twinkle in her eye.

"Josefina cooks for me."

"She's older than I am," Gertie said with a chuckle. "I bet she could use some help."

Quaid thought about Josefina's proud ownership of the rancho kitchen. He could only imagine the sparks that would fly if both women tried to cook—Josefina making tortillas and tamales, Gertie making grits and fried okra. He swallowed a smile. "I'm sure she could."

Emmeline was studying him again, and he turned to face her.

"I have it in mind to build a new house," she said. "That's why I'm in no hurry to make the repairs on the hacienda."

He let out a whoosh of air and fell into a seat by the table.

She stood over him, hands on hips. "Don't succumb to apoplexy, Quaid. I'm not starting it tomorrow."

"The day after?"

She sat next to him. "Have you seen the grove houses being built in Riverview?"

"The ones that look like tall wooden castles?"

She rolled her eyes and muttered something that sounded like "Neanderthal."

He felt the color drain from his face. "Don't tell me you're planning to have one built here?"

"I am indeed. Of course, that's after I've made a tidy profit and gotten Sara's approval."

He hit the table a little harder than he intended. "You can't do that!"

She tilted her chin, folded her arms over her chest, and glared at him. "And why not, pray tell?"

"It's—it's unnatural, that's why not."

Gertie laughed. "And you think adobe is more natural than wood?"

"It's just the idea of those castle-looking things. They go up instead of out. They don't fit here. They belong in...in England or someplace. Not in California." He stood up and paced. "You can't do that, Emma." He stopped and faced her. "I've heard some folks are even starting to call them Victorians after the Queen of England! It's—it's unpatriotic or something. You flat-out can't do such a thing on our land."

"First of all, it's not *our* land," she said calmly. "It's my land. And if I decide to build myself and Gertie a new house, a Victorian with turrets that reach clear to heaven, I can and I will."

Gertie stood and crossed her arms. "Do the two of you realize you can't have a pleasant conversation that lasts longer than three minutes?" She peered up at them both. "Now, you're going to be late to your soirees, the California citizens committees for raising Cain, or whatever they're called. You need to skee-daddle before I pump the bellows again and take care of the question about the house once and for all."

Emmeline suddenly laughed and hugged the older woman. "You're a caution, Gertie!"

Just looking at the little woman, with her white bun atop her head and bright piercing eyes, caused Quaid to chuckle along with Emmeline. Gertie walked with them out to the front of the house, then leaning against the railing, waved as they rode off to Riverview.

Emmeline's meeting of the Citizens for California's Citrus was always held in the town hall. She hitched the Appaloosa to a post in front, then nodded good-bye to Quaid. He rounded the corner and disappeared from sight.

Emmeline headed up the walk and into the two-story brick building. A few of her new friends, wives of citrus growers, came over to her immediately, each vying for her attention as she entered the meeting room.

"We have a surprise for you," Easter Southwell said with a wink.

The other two women were nearly bursting with whatever news it was they had to tell.

"What is it?" Emmeline pulled off her jacket and draped it over the back of her chair.

Alvina Thorpe settled into the chair next to Emmeline. "My Henry brought the most interesting man home for dinner tonight."

Emmeline held up her hand. "Don't tell me that he's the perfect man for me! You've done that before, and I've told you how I feel."

Mary Heywood scooted her chair closer. "But this man is different."

"I don't care," Emmeline said. "Please, don't try to play matchmaker."

"He's an expert from Washington, D.C.," Alvina whispered. "Hired by President Harrison himself to help us with planting and shipping methods. He has some revolutionary ideas to tell us about tonight, plans to add refrigeration cars to the trains so we can ship our oranges east."

Now Emmeline was interested. "What's his name?"

"Courtland MacQueen. Though he told me"—Alvina sighed dramatically—"that he prefers to be called Court."

Court MacQueen. Emmeline hadn't heard of him, so she breathed a little easier. Though she seldom thought about her life in Washington, she certainly didn't want her new friends here to know about the scandal or anything else having to do with her life before she arrived in California.

Soon the room filled, and Henry Thorpe stepped forward, the horticulture expert by his side. He held up his hands to gain the attention of those in the room. All conversation ceased.

"It is my special privilege to introduce Courtland MacQueen," Henry said. "He's been sent here as a special envoy to observe California groves up and down the state. He'll be spending a few months in Riverview. Tonight—and on several occasions in the future—he'll give us the latest findings on packing our fruit to minimize spoilage. He'll also be telling us information about when we might expect the refrigeration cars to be in service on the Santa Fe."

Emmeline leaned forward in anticipation. Her first crops wouldn't be ready to ship for three years, but she promised herself that year would be her first year of profit. A big profit to make up for the lean years between now and then.

Court MacQueen, a straw-haired man with a chiseled face, stepped to the dais and gave the small assemblage a friendly nod. "First of all, I want to congratulate you on beginning this cooperative," he said.

Henry Thorpe spoke up. "It was our own Washington transplant who suggested it." He looked around until he spotted Emmeline. "Emmeline Callahan, stand and take your bows. It was your inspiration to get us to work together."

Court gave her a wide smile and a nod.

Emmeline felt her face flush, but she stood and gave a short wave, first to the group, then to Court, who met her gaze with an appreciative look—for her business sense, she had no doubt. Cordial applause followed. She nodded her thanks and was seated.

Court MacQueen held the small audience mesmerized for nearly an hour, speaking about soil peculiarities in the Riverview area as well as the types of citrus and their propensities to certain diseases. He said that he would be joining their meetings weekly and hoped to become personally acquainted with each of the growers, visiting their groves, testing the soils and the fruits and trees for pests, and advising in any way he could.

Heavy applause erupted when he finished. Emmeline stood back as the other growers gathered around him to make appointments for him to visit. Finally he broke free and headed to where she was standing by the door.

He reached for her hand and shook it. "You've done the community an excellent service," he said.

"Thank you. I'm just surprised no one had thought of a cooperative before."

He laughed lightly. "With this fine example, you can be sure other communities will think of it in the future." He paused. "Actually, we're seeing co-ops spring up throughout the state. As the groves are planted, the growers find that banding together helps all involved. Some are building joint packing houses, splitting the costs from A to Z."

"I hadn't mentioned it to the others," Emmeline said, "but the thought of a shared packing plant had crossed my mind." She had even begun designing a building for the operation. It was another way to increase her profit margin even before her first crops were ready to ship. She would provide the land and the collateral, then receive payments from the growers who used the facility. Many had crops ready to pick and ship, but there were too few packing houses.

"It's a good plan." He looked thoughtful. "Tell me about your grove."

She liked nothing better. "I've planted the new Bahia."

His eyes widened appreciatively. "Where did you find them? There are very few in the U.S."

"I went straight to the source. Bahia, Brazil. I traveled up the Rio São Francisco by canoe to get there."

"I've been there!" His expression said he was delighted to find someone else who'd made the same journey. "You must tell me everything about your trip—starting with when you were there."

Emmeline laughed at his exuberance. "Just last year. I left Washington in the dead of winter and landed in the glorious tropics. It was truly a wonderland of fragrance and blossoms and lush greenery."

"Emmeline, we must talk further!" He smiled into her eyes. "May I call on you tomorrow? I will be delighted to see how the Bahias are surviving this climate. I can also help you if you're having problems with the arid soil here."

"Tomorrow will be grand," she said. "Shall we say two o'clock?"

"Yes, yes! Perfect." He touched her arm. "It has been a delight to meet you, Miss Callahan."

"Until tomorrow, then."

"Yes," he said, his gaze warm.

And Emmeline headed out the door.

Twilight was falling when Quaid dismounted in front of the town hall. He waited by the Appaloosa for Emmeline to join him. Several of the other growers exited the building, then the walkway was empty. He waited several minutes. Still no Emmeline.

He reached the door and strained to see through the glass. There, standing no more than ten feet away, was Emmeline.

She was in the midst of an animated and clearly enjoyable conversation with a man. A dapper, handsome, citified man.

Quaid stepped back abruptly, feeling betrayed. Betrayed? The thought surprised him. Why should he feel betrayed? He had no claims on her. She was a beautiful woman. Tall, statuesque, robust. What man wouldn't be attracted to her?

Still, the whole idea of her talking with another man stuck in his craw. He sauntered back to the sorrel and mounted, waiting impatiently for her to appear.

Finally she did, talking and laughing with Mr. Citified as they moved slowly down the walkway. So lost were they in conversation that for a moment Emmeline didn't see Quaid.

"Oh, Quaid!" She looked vexed and brought her hand to her mouth. "Have you been waiting long?"

"Not long," he growled. He couldn't help it.

"Oh, Quaid, I completely forgot about you coming by to fetch me. I am so sorry."

She looked genuinely regretful. That made it worse. He didn't want her pity.

Mr. Citified nodded in Quaid's direction, then headed across the street to the fancy Glenwood Inn.

"Now, where was it you wanted to take me?" Emmeline asked as she mounted. But the dreamy look on her face told him her mind was a thousand miles away.

TWENTY

Emmeline and Quaid rode along in the deepening dusk, heading east through the Big Valley. She wondered what had caused him to fall silent; he had seemed particularly annoyed after they left the town hall.

He was slightly ahead of her on the sorrel, and she nudged her heels into the Appaloosa, urging her horse to catch up with Quaid's. Soon they were riding abreast on the road.

She looked over at him but found it difficult to read his expression in the twilight.

"Who was the man you were with?" He sounded peevish, and he didn't turn to look at her.

She almost laughed. Could it be that Quaid Dearbourne was actually jealous? She swallowed her smile and adopted a nonchalant tone. "Oh, you mean Court MacQueen."

"Court MacQueen?" A loud laugh nearly burst from him. "What kind of a name is that?"

"What's wrong with his name? I think it's lovely."

"Lovely?" He laughed again. "Lovely isn't a word I'd want tied with my name."

"Quaid," she said, her voice heavy with sarcasm. "Quaid. Yes, you're right. Now that's a true man's name."

She saw him cast her a sideways glance. "All right, you win. I don't judge a book by its cover. Neither should I judge a man by his name." There was another stretch of silence. "So tell me about this MacQueen."

"He's a citrus expert sent to California by President Harrison. He'll be working with the growers to improve our chances of turning a profit."

"He's from Washington."

"Yes."

242

Quaid turned to her. "Did you know him—from before, I mean? When you were in Washington?"

She laughed, considering such a fanciful notion. "No. I hadn't met him before tonight."

There was a pause, with only the sounds of their horses' hooves thudding along the dirt road. "Tell me about Washington," Quaid said after a few minutes. "What was your life like there? Was it glamorous, being in the middle of the social whirl?"

Emmeline was yanked suddenly back to the life she had left, and it made her heart catch. For a moment she thought she couldn't breathe. "Life in Washington isn't what you might think," she said finally. "Some choose to live in a whirl of soirees and parties and plays. Others don't."

"Did you?"

It was a natural question, but one she couldn't answer. She couldn't lie to him; neither could she admit the awful truth.

"I would rather not speak of my life in Washington," she said quietly.

He nodded and let it drop.

They rode along in the deepening velvet night. With the advent of warmer, milder weather, sounds of summer created a night music so beautiful it made Emmeline's heart skip beneath her ribs.

Quaid seemed to notice the melody too and glanced over at her with a grin. "Prettier than man-made music could ever be."

"Depends on the man playing it."

"You complaining about my harmonica music?"

He looked worried, and she laughed. "No, actually. I enjoyed it the one night I heard it."

"Want to hear it again?"

She nodded, smiling at him.

"We need to head to the lookout before the moonrise." He tilted his head toward the hills to the east and pulled the harmonica from his pocket.

"Moonrise?" It was a delightful thought.

"Over the San Jacintos. Probably within the hour." He looked down at her Appaloosa. "Is he pretty surefooted?"

"I haven't had him out at night, but he seems to be."

"I'll take the lead, then."

For nearly a half-hour they climbed, Quaid playing the harmonica, haunting and lonely tunes. He drew the sorrel to a halt several times, so that the horses could rest, then urged his mare farther up the hillside, the Appaloosa following just yards behind. Soon the valley floor dropped away, and they had left the scrub sage and cactus for the alpine forests on the heights.

The scent of pine and loamy soil filled Emmeline's senses. She breathed it in slowly, her eyes closed.

A chuckle made her eyes fly open. Quaid had craned in his saddle and was studying her. "Orange blossoms don't hold a candle to this. And the look on your face tells me that you must surely agree."

She shrugged. "My first Bahias will be in bloom next spring. You'll have to decide for yourself."

Laughing, he turned again, moving the sorrel to a quicker pace. Rocks and dirt clods rolled backward from under the clambering hooves.

In the distance, moonglow outlined the craggy mountains in silver, and in front of her, the silhouette of Quaid's shoulders stood out against the brightening sky.

Emmeline had built a fortress of stone around her heart. Without knowing it, Quaid was chiseling away at it. Piece by piece, chip by chip, he was tearing it down. It frightened her to trust him, though she wanted to with all her heart.

It frightened her to see this new image of herself, an image reflected in Quaid's eyes when she caught him watching her. She was afraid that what she saw there, in him, wasn't true. That somewhere, somehow, everything he was to her now would turn out to be false.

She chuckled to herself. *Merciful heavens, Lord! Here I go again, worrying about tomorrow, forgetting how you've worked in my life, how you've brought me from sadness to joy.*

Why can't I enjoy today…enjoy this moment…knowing that you are in it?

Why is it that yesterday's heartaches and tomorrow's frets rob me of the pleasures you've given me today? Will I ever learn contentment in you?

She looked up at the slice of the moon, its light slipping through the pines, and considered the changeless love of her heavenly Father. His love for her wasn't based on whether she fretted or remained content in his care. He loved her even when she stumbled. He loved her when she kept her eyes on the stone that caused her to fall instead of on the Lord who walked beside her.

Teach me about resting in your arms of grace, Father, she breathed as the moon rose higher. She chuckled to herself. *And about staying put, once I realize that's where I've landed.*

"We're nearly there," Quaid tossed over his shoulder.

Yes, Lord, maybe we are!

Grinning, she nudged her horse in the flanks to move him closer to the sorrel. Soon the trail widened as they neared the top of the bald mountain. A scurrying sound in the brush caused her horse to shy, and she calmed him by patting his neck.

She could see, by the rise of boulders ahead, that they were nearing the crest of the mountain. The air was sharp, having lost its soft, balmy feel with each foot they ascended. She pulled her coat close and followed the sorrel along the ridge.

After a few more yards, Quaid dismounted. She drew the Appaloosa to a stop near his horse, then slid from the saddle and dropped to her feet beside him.

By now the large orb of a moon had risen, and its soft light spilled over the mountains, the pines, and the brush- and rock-strewn ridges around them. Emmeline laughed and danced in a circle, her arms out, watching her shadow in the moonlight.

Quaid caught her hand and led her to the farthest point at the edge of the lookout.

"This is what I wanted to show you," he said. "Surely one of the most glorious sights in all of God's creation."

Below them the moonlit valley spread for miles until it disappeared into the starry horizon. Closer in, the soft light spilled across wild lilacs and flowering manzanitas, casting a silvery white look. The fragrance of the blooms mixed with the pine, and Emmeline drew in a deep breath, shivering with delight.

Beside her, Quaid chuckled. "It just occurred to me that you might not be able to make out the stars...the details of the valley. Even the lilacs in the bushes around you."

"Because I'm missing my eyeglasses?"

He nodded, looking concerned.

She laughed. "When I was a child, a doctor recommended that I wear them because I complained of headaches. I soon learned to depend on them. I was afraid I would either go blind or suffer from headaches again. Until I lost them I didn't realize that I can actually see perfectly well without them."

"Did you start having headaches around the time your mother married Jamie?"

She tilted her face downward, feeling suddenly shy, then looked back up at him. "How did you know?"

"Just a guess."

"I might have had a mild one once, enjoyed the attention I got, and promptly had another. Or said I did." She laughed. "I suppose those wire-rimmed glasses became my declaration to the world that I was different." She had never admitted such things to anyone. It warmed her clear down to her toes to do so now.

"Or something to hide behind?"

She wondered how much he had guessed about her ugly, awkward, spinsterish reputation. Pondering the question, she turned to look out at the moonlit valley once more.

He touched her shoulders, one hand on either side. "Emma—" His voice was husky.

She drew in a deep breath, praying that she would not see pity in his expression. She felt as if she might sink right into the ground if she did. She bit her lip and turned to him.

"You are beautiful." There was no pity in his eyes. Only the reflection of the moonrise.

She swallowed hard, then cast her gaze down, hoping he couldn't hear the thudding of her heart. He placed his hands on each side of her face and lifted it gently, tracing the dimple in her chin with the side of his thumb.

Suddenly, though Quaid's face was before her, Derian Cadman's face floated into her mind. His eyes. His smile. The expectancy of his kiss. The raucous laughter that followed. A sharp sting accompanied the tears that filled her eyes. She turned away.

He laughed gently, misunderstanding. "Forgive me for being so bold, Emma."

She blinked the moisture away and continued looking out at the moon-washed horizon. She sighed. "We really should be getting back. Gertie will be worried."

"Yes, of course," he said. She could feel his gaze studying her profile. "But there's something else I must show you before we leave." He grabbed her hand and, with the exuberance of a little boy, pulled her past a copse of blooming manzanita and wild lilac. "Watch for thorns," he said as they barreled through.

A large granite boulder rose up in the middle of a clearing, and Quaid headed toward it. She couldn't stop herself from laughing as they scrambled to the top like children and plopped down square in the middle of the large flat stone.

"Now," he said dramatically. "I want you to close your eyes until I tell you to open them."

Myriad thoughts whirled through her head. They all had to do with trust. She bit her lip and stared at him.

He gave her a puzzled look, as if wondering what caused her reluctance. Then he smiled. "I promise you, this is a sight you'll never forget."

With a deep breath, she let her lids drift closed. From behind, he cradled her head in his hands, then eased her downward until the back of her head rested on another small stone. Gently he released her. She heard him inching backward, away from her.

Again the question of trust darkened her thoughts. What if she was the brunt of another humiliating prank, just as she had been before? Any moment, others would rush out of the trees, laughing and—

Quaid's whisper broke into her thoughts. "Now, Em. Look straight up. Don't look at me or anything around you. Only look into the heavens."

Slowly she opened her eyes. Her focus was drawn into the depths of the star-loaded skies. It was as if nothing around her existed. Not the earth or anything in it. A shooting star dropped to the horizon, followed by another a few seconds later. Her gaze moved back to the canopy of stars, and she stared at the blackness between each pinpoint of light, knowing that beyond those stars she could make out, millions more existed that she couldn't see.

She let out a small cry of joy. "I'm tumbling upward," she whispered. "It's like falling into a well filled with stars, only I'm falling up instead of down."

Behind her, Quaid chuckled, a sound she was learning to cherish, right along with the sight of his crooked smile. "It's my gift to you, Emma. This place. The starry skies."

She blinked, unwilling to let herself be drawn back to earth. Finally she sighed and turned on her stomach to look at him. He was squatting on a stump at the base of the boulder, several feet below her. She rested her chin in her hands, staring at him. For several moments she didn't speak.

"Thank you for showing me," she finally said.

He stood and brushed himself off, then climbed up the rock to sit beside her. "It's not over yet."

She wondered if he might be thinking about kissing her again, but instead he took her hand and nodded toward a clearing on the down slope of the hillside. "Near the cactus, by that rock—do you see it?"

Frowning, she followed his gaze. But she saw nothing.

"Look again," he encouraged, grinning. "Down there, in that spot of moonlight."

She looked, and this time focused on some tiny lights. Red lights. There must have been a dozen or so, not one bigger than the head of a pin.

Beside her, Quaid laughed. "Can you guess what they are?"

"Red stars, but they're in the wrong place," she laughed. "But everything you've shown me tonight is magical, so I wouldn't be surprised."

"Spider eyes."

She choked. "Spider eyes?"

He nodded. "You can only see them when the light of the moon is slanting a certain direction. You can create the same effect with a lantern or a torch, but it's seldom the moon will do it."

She looked back at the tiny lights with amazement until the moonlight drifted away from them and the eyes disappeared. "It's truly magical," she breathed.

"Now we'll need to wait quietly," he said. "Not a word. And don't move."

"I promise," she said, feeling the urge to giggle.

Around them rose the sounds of the night—the sawing of crickets, the musical cadence of frogs. An owl soared by, soundlessly, its wing catching the glint of the moon. Beneath a nearby wild lilac, the skittering of mountain creatures could be heard.

Quaid reached for Emmeline's hand and nodded to the east. The faintest sound carried toward her, and she frowned at Quaid. As it drew closer, it grew louder. Something large was heading their way.

There was a look of delight on his face. "Sit perfectly still," he mouthed.

A few minutes later, a small black bear ambled into the clearing, grunted around, sniffing at the foliage. Then it sat on its haunches, scratching itself, and stood on all fours.

Emmeline was afraid to breathe, both in wonder and in fear. She had never before been this close to something so dangerous and wild.

The bear seemed to suddenly notice it wasn't alone and lazily glanced their direction before turning and ambling off into the woods.

Emmeline let out a pent-up breath. "Merciful heavens!"

"It's magnificent," Quaid said, seeming lost in thought. "All of it."

They sat in silence for a while longer, then Emmeline said, "You've brought me here for a lesson tonight." The thought of it stole some of the night's magic from her heart.

He turned to her. "I suppose that's part of it."

She had anticipated his reply, but it hurt anyway. She stood and brushed herself off. "As I said earlier, I think I should be getting home."

He took her hand to help her climb down the boulder, then released it as they walked to the horses.

"Why didn't the bear bother us—or spook the horses?"

"Bears are plant eaters. They'll attack a human or an animal only if they feel threatened or are hungry. It's not a worry this time of year—there's plenty of food."

When they reached the horses, Emmeline stepped into the stirrup then swung her leg over the saddle. "Back to the lesson..." she said as he mounted. "You're trying to convince me that the wilds can't coexist with development. That what we saw here tonight would be spoiled by such things as orange groves and Victorian houses."

"Couldn't have said it better myself." His shoulders were stiff as they headed back down the trail, Quaid in the lead.

She wondered if she had offended him, but she pressed on, "There's plenty of wilderness to protect, Quaid. It doesn't all have to be saved in its natural state."

He didn't answer, and she urged her horse to catch up with the sorrel.

"Don't you think there's room for people like me in your world?"

Quaid turned to her and studied her face as if puzzled by her words. Then he shook his head, still staring at her with a slightly annoyed look. "Did you know that in the 'wilderness' that used to exist between here and the Pacific Ocean, sixty new towns were plotted out in just the three years between eighty-six and eighty-nine? That the biggest land boom ever to hit the States was here—within miles of the Big Valley?"

"There's room for us all, Quaid," she said. "I agree, that's a lot of new towns, but the growth can't continue forever. Neither can the way of life you'd like to keep. Progress is coming, and right now it appears that it's in the form of oranges."

"Don't you think I can see it?" he growled. "That doesn't mean I have to like it."

They rode without speaking for a few minutes. "You can't stop it," she said.

"Oranges are the hot ticket today. You aren't the only Easterner to buy into the California dream, you know. They're heading here in droves, all planning to be millionaires." He flicked the reins as if for emphasis. "They want to snatch up the land. Tear out the natural plant life, plow it, and ready it for the seedless orange. By the time refrigeration cars on the Santa Fe are common, still more Easterners will come to make their fortune."

He halted the sorrel. "Can't you see, Emma? The land can't support them. Even now we don't have enough water to supply our needs."

"There's the new Eastern Sierra canal project being talked about—"

"That's supposed to solve our problems?" he cut her off. "Borrowing water that isn't ours? Bringing it miles to supply our appetite for growth? I don't think so." He shook his head and chirked to the horse to move forward again. "Besides that, it's a perfect example of big business gobbling up the profits of those it's supposedly helping."

"Wait!" she called up to him.

He halted the sorrel and looked back at her. She moved the Appaloosa closer, then stopped beside him. "What did you just say?"

"About the Eastern Sierra project?"

"Yes." Her horse danced sideways, and she steadied the beast with a gentle touch on his neck. "I've heard about it and thought the Big Valley might benefit from the canal when it's completed."

He laughed bitterly. "The businessmen who pushed it through the system are the biggest beneficiaries. Seems that they secretly bought up every arid, sage-covered foot of land on the west side of Los Angeles. *Before* they let it be known that the canal would bring water there."

"So they'll be rich men when it's completed."

He nodded. "More than just rich, Emma. They'll be multimillionaires. I've heard rumors about the housing developments already being laid out. Hundreds of thousands of matchbox houses that all look the same." He stared at her, his expression humorless.

Her countenance fell. "None of the canals are planned to bring water to the Big Valley?"

"None." He turned the sorrel and headed down the trail in silence.

"You're living in the Stone Age, Quaid," she said, wanting to have the last word. "We've nearly reached the twentieth century. The progress we've made as a nation is astounding. Think of the new inventions that are already bettering our lives. Even New York City has been electrified for almost a decade. Can you imagine such a thing?"

He looked back down over the moonlit valley under its soft canopy of stars. "Tell me, Emma, can it be better than this?"

She followed his gaze, but didn't answer.

"If this valley was as populated as New York City, would it be any better than it is now?"

"That's not the point," she said. "You can't stop progress. And when it's good development such as bringing a new crop into Southern California—it's wrong to try to block our efforts."

"Block your efforts?" He craned in the saddle. "What are you talking about?"

"There's talk, that's all."

He snorted. "About what?"

"About your cooperative actively trying to block our need for water."

"Who told you that?"

"It was discussed at our meeting tonight."

"And you believe it?"

"I didn't until hearing you talk about the encroaching developers just now."

His shoulders were stiff as they rode on.

"Is it true?" she called up to him. "Are you trying to block me from getting water from the county?"

Finally he halted the sorrel and waited until she drew the Appaloosa even with him. "I will do everything in my power to stop development, Emmeline. I thought you knew that by now. I don't care if it's oranges, lemons, or alligator pears—"

"Avocados," she corrected.

"Or electrification of the entire state—I'm against it."

"So it's true, then."

He stared at her, then turned and continued riding down the trail. When they reached the base of the mountain, he headed toward La Paloma.

He didn't say another word to her, not even good-bye. She halted the Appaloosa, and as she watched him ride off, she wanted to call out to him. She wanted to tell him that she loved the music of the night. She loved the way she had tumbled up instead of down into the well of stars. And that she understood the wild beauty of the deer and bear, the crimson spider eyes. She had cherished them all.

But she said nothing.

Quaid let out a pent-up breath as he rode. The woman exasperated him. That's all there was to it. Pure unadulterated exasperation.

Just when he thought he was making progress, she pulled business dealings out of her hat.

He pictured the way she looked in the moonlight, the glint of it on her hair, the way it made her skin look petal soft, like a white rose or a dogwood blossom. The look of starlight in her eyes. The deep, honeyed sound of her voice. The woman had no idea what she did to him.

He looked heavenward as he rode, settling into the rhythm of hooves thudding on the road. The night was one that would stay etched in his memory, he decided, as the sorrel headed through the arched gate at La Paloma. After he dismounted and gave the horse to the stableboy, he headed back toward the house.

Just before he stepped onto the verandah, he lifted his face to the brilliant heavens. As sure as Emmeline said she was falling upward into a well full of stars—just now, picturing her, thinking about her, he felt the same sensation.

He grinned, staring at the sky. "If this is love, Lord, let me tumble upward." Then he threw back his head and laughed out loud for the pure pleasure in it.

TWENTY-ONE

Emmeline's favorite time of day was morning, when the sun cast jewels of light across the dewy fields and birds sang in chorus from her groves. Mockingbirds tossed themselves heavenward like feathered clowns, and purple bees buzzed around the hollyhocks. A breeze rippled the grass and fluttered the leaves of a pepper tree, just as a covey of quail headed from beneath it, scratching at the sandy soil.

At such moments, when the glory of God's creation burst with such grace across her land, she was willing to concede to Quaid his victory. She liked walking among her young trees, slowly and thoughtfully, prayerfully, as the earth awakened. She didn't like to think that such places might someday be replaced with brick and mortar, towns and cities that might forget to leave space for trees and flowers and God's precious creatures.

She walked to a rise behind her groves and, shading her eyes against the slant of the sun, watched the flight of a red-tailed hawk as it circled. This was the place where the grove house would someday be built. She pictured it, sheltered by the drape of the pepper tree, its white walls proud and stately.

She climbed farther up the dirt path to a scrawny morning glory vine she had planted in April. Smiling to herself, she knelt to touch a blossom and pat the soil around it. She would need to come back later with a pail of well water. Someday it would climb the wooden rails on the Victorian's porch. And in years to come, it might tangle up one side of the wide porch and cascade down the other, framing the entrance.

The spindly little vine wasn't much to pin her hopes on, but it was a start. With a sigh she stood to head back to the house where Gertie would have started the coffee on the cracked stove and, more than likely, put a pan of buttermilk biscuits in the oven.

A movement caught her attention in the fields to the north, and she could see an approaching wagon pulled by two mules. She couldn't stop herself from smiling when it drew nearer and she recognized Quaid in the driver's seat.

There was a curious light in his eyes when he swept off his hat to greet her. And judging from the curve of his lips, he was having a hard time not smiling.

Once he had halted the team, he jumped down from the wagon. She walked toward him and thought how natural he looked in the beauty of the morning, with the sparkling dew in the fields behind him, with the breeze rippling his hair, his crooked smile greeting her.

"G'morning," he said, not moving his gaze from hers.

"Good morning." For the slightest heartbeat a silence fell between them, then she said, "I was just thinking that you're right about the beauty and glory of God's wilderness, how it shouldn't be touched."

"I was just thinking that you're probably right about progress—at least, some of it." He laughed. "I don't want to see hillsides covered with houses and factories."

"Neither do I," she said, smiling into his face. "But I think that hillsides covered with orange groves is a bit of both. Wilderness and progress I mean…well, not wilderness, perhaps. But orange trees aren't all that unnatural, you know. They grow wild in…well, I'm not certain exactly where…but…"

Grinning, he touched her lips with his index finger. "I agree," he said, shushing her prattling.

"You do?" She looked into his eyes. There was a tightness in her chest that suggested she might not be able to draw another breath. "You do?"

He nodded. "I do. Furthermore, I would never do anything to block you from getting water for your trees."

"You wouldn't?"

"No."

"I didn't think so."

For a moment they stared at each other, then Quaid cleared his throat. "I was perturbed that you would believe it of me—or my co-op—no matter the rumors being bandied about in your meeting last night."

"I suppose it's a matter of trust," she said.

"Trust. Yes." His gaze still locked on hers. "You're ready, then?"

Her cheeks flamed, and she wondered if he might be ready to kiss her right out there in middle of the dew-covered grassy knoll. Right there in full view of, well, anyone who might happen by. "Ready?" she croaked.

He seemed to be studying her lips. He nodded. "Ready for the ride into Riverview."

She let out a sigh. "Oh, that. Well, yes. Yes, of course. We'll have to tell Gertie. She's in the house…the kitchen. Baking biscuits, I think."

"I've arranged for Sandy and Kerr to stop by later to move the old stove out of the kitchen. We'll need to tell Gertie they're on their way, that she needs to let the oven cool," Quaid said, but neither of them moved. "See if she minds waiting here for them while we head into town. Instead of heading to town with us."

"Yes, we should. Ask, I mean."

A flutter of finches sang from the branch of the pepper tree, and a ground squirrel skittered from behind one rock to another and disappeared. Finally Emmeline gathered her skirt slightly and started to head toward the house.

"Emma—?" He caught up with her. He grabbed for her hand, caught it, and didn't let it go.

She looked up at him, puzzled.

A slow smile spread across his face. He touched her cheek lightly. His fingertips were softer than the quivering wing of a gypsy moth. Before she could protest, he bent nearer and touched his lips to hers.

She gasped and blinked up at him in surprise.

He laughed, kissed her again, and pulled her into his arms. For a moment he held her close. She sighed, leaning against him with her eyes closed. She was close enough to hear the thudding of his heart and feel the warmth of his skin through his shirt.

Then she came to her senses. She drew back and looked up at him with a frown. "You, sir, are taking advantage of me!"

The corner of his mouth twitched as if he might laugh, and his eyes were merry.

"Don't you dare laugh."

"I wouldn't think of it," he said, "except that your indignant retort doesn't match the honey-sweet lips I tasted a moment ago."

Honey-sweet lips? She touched her fingertips to her mouth. *Honey-sweet lips?*

He stepped closer and tilted her face slightly upward with his index finger. "You're beautiful, Emma."

A kaleidoscope of ballroom dancers whirled into her mind, the raucous laughter of Cadman and his friends. *Ugliest girl at the ball,* one had said. *Homeliest you've ever picked,* one of the others hooted. Even in her memory, the words twisted her heart.

Emmeline swallowed hard and backed away from Quaid, her eyes filling. For a moment she couldn't speak. She shivered in the morning sun, though it was the memory of her family's verandah during the Christmas ball that made her bitter cold.

"Don't make sport of me," she said, her voice a whisper. "Please don't ever make sport of me...or deceive me in any way!" Then she gathered her skirts once more and hurried into the house.

"You look like you've see a ghost," Gertie said when Emmeline burst into the kitchen.

"Quaid's here," Emmeline announced in an airy voice. "He's come to take me into town to order our new stove. Also to let you know that Kerr and Sandy will be here later to move the old one out."

Gertie wasn't fooled. She turned from the stove to look Emmeline fully in the face. "You've got more to tell me than business about the stove. What is it, child?"

Before Emmeline answered, Quaid barged into the room. With a quick nod of greeting to Gertie, he headed straight for Emmeline. "You care to tell me what I did wrong? Near as I can tell," he huffed, his hands on her shoulders, "I paid you a compliment when I said you're beautiful."

Speechless, Emmeline gaped at him with her hands on her hips.

He moved closer. "You ought to know by now that I don't throw out compliments easily. In fact, I usually don't throw them out at all. If truth be known, I'm more at ease in my own world." His eyes were warm. They melted her resistance. "The world we were discussing last night, if you remember. I'm more at home in the wilderness with creatures that don't talk back—or get offended."

He moved even closer, and she had to look nearly straight up to meet his eyes. Behind him, Gertie chuckled.

"You're not only the most beautiful woman I've ever come across in all my picked-up-and-put-together, but you're also the most hardheaded." He let out an exasperated sigh.

"In all your picked-up-and-put-together?" She tried to keep from smiling and, especially, to keep from laughing. But she wasn't successful with either.

Behind Quaid, Gertie was cackling now, bent double with laughter. The stench of burning biscuits filled the room. Gertie grabbed for a potholder and headed to the stove.

Emmeline lifted her arms and placed one hand on each side of his face. Standing on tiptoe, she kissed him soundly. It seemed to surprise him as much as it did her.

She laughed at the startled look on his face and kissed him again.

Behind them, Gertie rattled and clanged the iron plates on the stove, opened and shut the oven door, grumbled as she pulled out the smoking biscuits.

Quaid laughed and, pulling Emmeline into his arms, rested his chin on top of her head. "Something tells me it's time to go after that new stove."

Quaid couldn't keep his eyes off Emmeline as they drove into town. She sat on the bench seat next to him, close enough for him to hold her hand. It rested warm and strong in his.

Quaid was happy just to be in her company. The wagon rattled along as she chatted about fashions and hats and whether someone might build an opera house soon in Riverview. Then she settled on the citrus industry and Court MacQueen, and she didn't leave the subject until they pulled into town.

He headed the mules to the mercantile, where he had seen a Marshwell's catalogue on his last visit. Lars Hansen, the proprietor, flipped the pages and showed Emmeline the finest stove made, a Niacara. He discussed its merits before Emmeline finally settled on the style she wanted. "It will take a week for the order to get to Duluth," Lars said as he wrote out the order. "And if the stove is in stock, they'll ship it back within another two weeks."

Emmeline traced the drawing of the stove absently with her finger, then looked up. "And if it isn't in stock?"

Lars shrugged. "They'll have to put the order in with the manufacturer. It could be as long as six months."

She leaned against the counter, looking down at the stove. "Six months?"

"Don't forget my offer," Quaid said, stepping closer.

"Six months is a long time to stay for dinner." Emmeline looked up to give him a shy smile. "In that length of time, we most certainly will have worn out our welcome."

He already knew that she never could. In fact, the longer the stove took getting to California, the better. He studied the catalogue illustration while he imagined what it would be like to sit in a kitchen with Emmeline in front of that stove every morning for the rest of their lives.

She told Lars to place the order, then turned to leave. She had walked a few steps toward the door when she glanced at a display of hats near a stack of gloves.

Apparently the hats were irresistible. She headed for the hat tree and plucked one off. First she tried on a felt hat with feathers at the top. After preening in the mirror for a moment, she put it back. Then she lifted a heart-shaped, wide-brimmed affair onto her head and tied the wide ribbon into a bow beneath her chin. She narrowed her eyes, looking at herself in the mirror, then picked up the next. It was straw, flat as a fritter, with a brim that perfectly framed her dark eyes.

She smiled at her image in the mirror, adjusted the narrow black ribbon, and fluffed the smattering of silk daisies around the brim.

Seeming to sense his scrutiny, she pirouetted gracefully toward him, a wide smile on her face. "What do you think?"

Quaid thought it was lovely. "I'd say it was made for you."

Smiling, she removed it from her head and put it back on the hat tree.

"Aren't you going to buy it?"

She shook her head. "It's not a necessity. Until I can show Sara that we're making a profit, there's no room for frivolity."

"Someone may have purchased it by the time that day comes."

She laughed. "You must not have much faith in my ability."

"You've been very clear about not making your first profit until the trees have been in the ground three years." He swung the door open for them to exit. "That's a long time to wait around for a hat as pretty as that one."

She lifted a pretty brow. "Perhaps I have other ideas in mind."

"Such as?"

"I'm thinking about building a packing house."

The light went out of his day. She'd never mentioned anything about such a venture—he envisioned a large, ugly building ruining the Dearbourne landscape. "A packing house?"

She nodded. "Yes."

"On your property?" He was incredulous.

"Where else?"

"That's like putting a factory in a flower garden," he sputtered, then added, "in full view of your parlor. You just don't place something like a packing house on that beautiful wild land."

"It will help my profit margin," she said, lifting her chin. "I see nothing wrong with the idea."

"There will be workers?"

"Yes."

"How many?"

"Perhaps one or two dozen." She was looking at him with those fiery amber eyes that unnerved him.

"They'll be riding across your land to get to this…factory?"

"I suppose so. Why?"

"Think of the noise and clamor, Emma. The wagons you'll have to bring in to transport the oranges to the train depot. You can't do it."

She halted midstep right there on the boardwalk and faced him, hands on hips. "You have no right to tell me what I can or cannot do, Quaid Dearbourne."

He stared at her, thinking of all the retorts he might use. Before he could pick one, she rushed on. "This might not be important to you, but I must make a profit on my land, or I'll lose it. Water is scarce, so my orange crop may not be abundant enough to make that profit. I have to use my wits—" She narrowed her eyes, glaring at him. "You, on the other hand, have plenty of water. Plenty of cowhands to help you run the rancho. It doesn't matter to you whether you make money or not. All you care about is keeping your precious land wild and free from developer vermin."

"Developer vermin?" He swallowed the laugh that threatened to erupt.

She nodded her head vigorously. "Vermin." The sunlight slanted across her face, and he thought he'd never seen a more beautiful sight.

"I understand," he said quietly.

Her mouth fell open in surprise. "You do?"

"But may I make a suggestion?"

She frowned, considering him with a look of suspicion.

"I admire your head for business, and I admire your plans to make a profit by building a packing house." He paused. "But, Emma, could you please consider building it anywhere but the Big Valley?"

She stared at him. "I don't own any other land."

The determined look on her face said that nothing would deter her, so he tried another ploy. "What if you someday marry and have children?"

Her eyes widened and her mouth fell open. She seemed too stunned to answer.

He grinned, knowing he'd captured her attention. "Would you want your husband and children to wake every morning to the sounds of the electrified machinery chugging and clamoring and clanging?"

Still speechless, she shook her head.

"I thought not." He paused. "Or would you want your little ones running around wagons as they come in to pick up their loads of Bahia oranges? Terrible things happen when little children fall off wagons or, God forbid, in front of a wheel."

She gasped.

"If I were to live in such a place, as your husband, as the father to these little children I've just described—and I'm not saying I would—" He paused again.

Her eyes were even wider now. She swallowed hard.

"I simply would not allow such a thing for my family. I would want to take my family on picnics in fields unhampered by buildings and businesses. I would want my family to know the natural beauty of the land that God created."

He was proud of himself for thinking of such a way to change Emmeline's mind about the land. Until he noticed the two bright spots of anger on her cheeks.

"What you've just done is despicable, Quaid," she said, her voice cold. "You've turned my head with flowery thoughts, just because you wanted your way. You've spoken lies to me about your intentions."

That wasn't what he'd intended at all. "Emma," he said, reaching for her.

She shrugged out of his reach and marched to the wagon. All the way back to the Big Valley, she didn't say a word. She just sat there stiff-spined and pinch-mouthed, facing the road.

The sun was starting its downward arch when he helped her from the wagon and walked her to the door. He listened to Gertie complain about the old stove now being out under the pepper tree where it wouldn't do a soul any good, then he bade the two women good-bye.

Emmeline wouldn't look at him. Nor did she tell him good-bye.

He climbed back onto the wagon bench, wondering how he could possibly make it up to her.

＊

It was nearing evening when Court MacQueen rode onto Emmeline's property. She had been expecting him for hours, and she swallowed her annoyance that he was late. But she figured that a man of his stature must have been in great demand. She wondered how he could be expected to work all the needed visits in with other groves and horti-culturists. So she forgave him. Even though he didn't apologize.

Gertie, who had decided that the stove would still work in its new location, had already boiled water for tea and invited Court to join them in the parlor. She poured the steaming liquid into three teacups, placed the service on a teacart next to Emmeline, then settled onto a set-tee near the window.

Court MacQueen seated himself in the tall horsehair chair across from her and soon was showing them his Washington wit and charm. He skipped from subject to subject, dropping names of dignitaries and politicians and even the titles of books he had most recently read.

Emmeline was surprised that she hadn't noticed his propensity to drop names when they spoke before. She only had to close her eyes to be drawn back into the Georgian mansion of her mother and stepfather. How many young men had practiced their conversational savoir-faire on her sisters or other social butterflies in her hearing! Never once had one used his parlor wit on her. It seemed so superficial, she thought she might not find air enough in her lungs to draw a deep breath as long as Court MacQuaid was within a stone's throw of her.

Court droned on about his trips abroad, and Emmeline hid a yawn behind her fingers. He didn't seem to notice. He spoke of his voyages to China and Australia, looking for the perfect seedless fruit. He told of his trekking through South America, following rumors about phantom trees and hiring Indians to guide him up the Amazon.

She had finished her cup of tea by the time he had taken his first breath. She stood and filled Gertie's cup and her own. Court's hadn't been touched.

"Oh, dear, but I do go on," he said, shaking his head and taking a sip of the now cold tea. He put the cup down, and it rattled in the saucer. "Tell me about Bahia. I am so delighted to find that we were both there. What did you think of the horticulturists you encountered?"

Emmeline warmed to the subject and described how she had come into possession of the Bahia trees. She told how she and Gertie sailed down the east coast of Brazil, then transferred to a skiff, then later into canoes with guides who led them up the Rio São Francisco. She talked about the compound where they stayed, the horticulturists who developed the seedless fruit, and the techniques they learned of splicing and grafting new plants.

"How did you hear about the oranges? I mean, in the beginning?" He leaned forward in interest. "Were you in Washington at the time?"

"Yes. My grandmother—Sara Dearbourne—who's the true owner of this property, wrote me from California about the Bahias. She mentioned that they were from Brazil, and I decided to go there and see them for myself."

He spoke for a few minutes about some of the other varieties of citrus just coming into California, then turned the conversation back to Washington. "Had you lived in Washington long?"

It made her uncomfortable to speak of it, but she decided it might raise more questions later if she wasn't forthcoming. She sipped from her teacup, watching him across the brim. "Nearly all my life, actually," she said, setting down her cup a little harder than she intended.

"And your family's business there?"

Emmeline wanted to bolt from the room. It was obvious this envoy of President Harrison's was entrenched in politics and as well connected in the same social circles as her parents. He was watching her expectantly.

"My stepfather is a U.S. Senator."

He looked puzzled.

"Senator Jamie Dearbourne," she answered his unspoken question.

A light went on in his eyes. "Ah, yes. Of course. Senator Dear-bourne."

"You know of him?"

"I've met him once or twice. Socially." He took another sip of the cold tea. "I haven't had the pleasure of meeting the rest of the family."

Obviously he knew there was a rest of the family. More than likely, he'd heard of the beautiful Glenna Elise and Hazel Leigh. Her heart stuck in her throat.

She stood abruptly, sending the teacart rolling and a spoon clatter-ing to the floor. Flustered, she reached for the spoon, then dropped it again. Laughing nervously, she shrugged off her clumsy behavior and stood again, this time grabbing the cart to hold it stationary. The china and silver rattled.

"I would like to show you the groves before dusk," she said, straightening the tea service as Court stood to join her. His gaze flick-ered with the slightest recognition of her discomfort. He merely nod-ded, a puzzling half-smile in place, and followed her from the room.

When they arrived at the first of her groves, the shadows were long. Now that she was in the fresh air, her earlier feeling of suffocation was gone. She breathed in the sweet fragrance of the early evening and tried to forget Court MacQueen was from Washington.

He bent to get a sample of her soil, scooped up a small handful, and dropped it into a glass vial. He repeated the process several more times, choosing soil from different locations in the grove. He carefully labeled each vial, set it in a wooden case, and made notes in a journal. As he worked he explained the soil conditions and possible problems he was looking for, also the pests and mildews common to the area.

Then he inspected the trees. They had been in the ground just seven months now and were varied in size, some thigh-high, others as tall as Court, who towered over her. She was proud of how well the trees had adapted to the new conditions.

Court agreed. "They are thriving. Whatever you're doing, keep it up. I'll need to do some testing, but from all appearances they've sur-vived quite nicely."

They walked together back toward the house. "I am still in awe of their sturdiness," Emmeline said. "They survived the voyage from Brazil to Charleston, the train ride across the continent, and after transplanting, a spring with little water."

Court stopped and looked down at her. "I hear you're planning to investigate your water rights."

She gazed east to the San Jacintos. "I'm sure you've heard about the dam."

He followed her gaze, shading his eyes. "Yes. It's unfair that your water was cut to a drizzle, when the cattlemen seem to get all they need."

She nodded. "None of the growers plan to give up. We can't depend on rainwater. California's too prone to droughts."

"That's the Byrne rancho just to the north of you, isn't it?" He looked toward Quaid's land.

"Rancho de la Paloma, yes."

"You are aware that the San Jacinto River runs through his property?"

"Yes, but whatever claim I had to it—or rather, Sara Dearbourne had—disappeared when the dam was built. The river forks in the mountains to the east. It was my fork that was dammed."

"Are you certain?"

She started to defend Quaid, then hesitated. "What do you mean?"

"I don't want to cast aspersions, but if I were you, I'd check with the Bureau of Land Development."

"But you are casting them by your insinuations," she blurted. "If you know something that I should know, please tell me."

Kneeling, he gathered his materials, placed them neatly in the small wooden box, and fastened the lid. Then he stood and looked down at her. "You have a lot at stake here, Emmeline. Your orchard has the potential to produce one of the greatest yields of citrus I've seen in my California travels.

"You've laid out your groves in a perfect manner to ensure drainage. You've wound your groves around hillsides, rather than in straight lines, to keep the frost from settling. Even the desert winds from the east are in your favor."

"I lost some of my trees when I put them in last winter," Emmeline said. "I began with three thousand. I lost five hundred of the smaller trees."

"That's natural. In fact, it's less than what some growers experience. And I see you're not coddling your trees." He smiled. "That will pay off in the long run.

"You and the other growers have a built-in labor force," he continued, "the Soboba Indians locally, the Mexicans just beyond the border."

"I paid them well when they put in my trees and dug my irrigation ditches."

"I didn't mean to imply that you didn't."

They walked in silence for a few minutes. He steered her toward his buggy, which he had parked near the carriage house behind the main adobe.

"You didn't answer me," she said as they approached his vehicle, "about your accusations regarding my neighbor."

Court placed the wooden case in the back of the vehicle, then turned to face her. "It's not idle parlor talk when folks speak of becoming millionaires by raising oranges. When I see what you've done here in a half year, I can only imagine the riches that will be yours in another two and a half."

She looked at him with surprise, feeling her mouth go dry. She moistened her lips before she could speak. "Millionaire?" she finally croaked. "Me?"

He stepped a bit closer. "What I am trying to tell you is that you must beware of those who might find it in their interest for you to fail."

She stared up at him. "You're speaking of my neighbor again."

He went on as if she hadn't spoken. "Those who might not openly oppose you but who certainly will not help you." He paused, his face a portrait of concern. "Perhaps they won't tell you that the water they swear is theirs really belongs to you."

She stared at him, uncomprehending. He couldn't be talking about Quaid. She refused to believe such a thing. Quaid knew that she was desperate for water before the dry, relentless heat of summer and fall settled over her groves like a blanket of fire.

"Emmeline—?" a voice said behind her.

She turned to see Quaid striding toward them. A hatbox, bound with a pretty red ribbon, was tucked under his arm.

He met her eyes and smiled, then hesitated as if reluctant to move his gaze before sticking out his hand to shake Court's. She made the introductions.

"You remember what I told you, now, Emmeline," Court said, climbing into the seat of his buggy. He settled back into the seat with a sigh, then popped the whip over the back of his horse and was off.

Emmeline watched the vehicle rattle and creak down the road until it was out of sight.

"I need to apologize," Quaid said to her. "What I said was hurtful and wrong. I thought my reasons were clear…"

Her mind was on water rights and the strange conversation with MacQueen, and for a moment she didn't know what Quaid meant. She frowned. "You want to apologize?"

He was watching her curiously. "Yes, for what I said to you in town about your future husband and children." He placed the hatbox in her hands. "I know nothing I say can make up for it, but…" His voice dropped, and he seemed to search for words.

She stared into his face without smiling.

"Please," he said quietly. "Forgive me?"

"You poked fun at me," she finally said.

"I was merely trying to point out future possibilities."

"I will not be made fun of," she told him.

"I wasn't trying to be lighthearted about such a thing as—"

"Such a thing as what?"

He hesitated. "Marriage. It's truly sacred. Certainly not something to make one uncomfortable. I was merely trying to tell you that it might truly be part of your future."

Emmeline laughed, interrupting him. "Do you think the only way you can get me to forgive you is to sweet-talk me into marrying you?"

His blue-gray eyes widened, and he stammered, "Well, now, I didn't, I mean—"

She giggled again and poked her index finger into his chest. "If it is, mister, let me tell you that if you were the only man left in the Big Valley, I wouldn't marry you."

He'd recovered his tongue. "I *am* the only man in the Big Valley," he pointed out, looking offended.

"So you don't need to worry that you provoked an old maid by mentioning marriage in such a cavalier manner."

"I never thought about you in such a way."

She interrupted him again, still pressing her finger in the center of his chest. "You, dear sir, have many things to learn about me. One of them is that you can talk to me about nearly everything. You can even argue with me and expect a lively argument in return."

He swallowed hard, his Adam's apple bobbing.

"But you can't poke fun at me. Ever."

His eyes were bright with affection when he spoke again. "There's one question you haven't answered."

She waited.

"Can I give you a hat?" He held the box out to her.

Grinning, she opened the lid, then, feeling his gaze, looked up to see a warmth in Quaid's eyes that made her heart dance. He unfolded the tissue paper and lifted the headpiece. She stood perfectly still while he tilted it just so on her head and awkwardly fluffed the daisies at the brim. Then he stood back, admiring her.

A movement in the trees behind Quaid captured her attention. She frowned, and Quaid turned to follow her gaze just as Court MacQueen scrambled into his buggy. He popped his whip above the horse, and moments later the buggy rattled down the road.

"I thought he left several minutes ago," Quaid mused.

"So did I." Even as she spoke, Court's accusations came back to her. She watched the buggy pull into the falling dusk. "So did I."

She glanced up at Quaid's face, wondering if such treachery as MacQueen described could possibly be true.

TWENTY-TWO

That night Emmeline and Gertie joined Quaid for supper, just as he'd promised they could when he arranged for the new stove. Over her bowl of *pozole*, while Gertie and Josefina fussed over the next course in the kitchen, Emmeline chatted amiably, seeming to have forgiven Quaid completely.

She didn't once mention the packing house. Instead she spoke about her plans for the groves. She asked his opinion about bringing more trees from Brazil, perhaps older trees than those she had brought last winter, and asked where he thought she should plant them. She spoke happily about the new stove, wondering how it would fit through the door to the kitchen. And she thanked him several times for the hat, listing the many places she would wear it.

Her voice held the same honeyed timbre he was growing to treasure, and he bent forward to catch every word, every nuance.

He'd taken only two bites of roasted sweet corn, Josefina's prized *maiz tierno,* when he realized what was bothering him. Emmeline had not mentioned one snippet of conversation between herself and Court MacQueen. Instead she seemed bent on avoiding mention of him or their talk.

He narrowed his eyes. By his feet, his dog, Blue, thumped the floor with his tail, and Quaid absently reached down to rub the cartilage behind his ears.

It was true that the expert's visit to Emmeline's groves was none of his business. Nonetheless it was strange that the man's name wasn't once spoken of. Yet MacQueen had spent the afternoon with her. And he had mysteriously reappeared just when Quaid was ready to pull Emmeline into his arms and kiss her thoroughly.

He attempted to set aside the uncomfortable, unusual feelings of jealousy as he took another bite of *maiz tierno*.

MacQueen was from Emmeline's social strata in Washington. He hobnobbed with the president, just as her family did. Now that Quaid thought about it, he wouldn't have been surprised if MacQueen had followed Emmeline to California, hoping to woo her and win her. Perhaps even take her back to Washington.

The idea incensed him. Quaid became so agitated that he stood abruptly, bumping the table and sloshing the rest of his roasted corn from its bowl.

Emmeline set down her fork, looking up at him in surprise. "Is everything all right, Quaid? You seem rather out of sorts tonight."

Feeling foolish, he dropped into his chair. "Yes, yes, of course. I don't know what I was thinking." He reached for Gertie's basket of rolls, took one, buttered it, and crushed half of it with his teeth.

Emmeline dabbed at her lips with her napkin, then folded it back onto her lap. "Do you have a copy of the plat maps for your property?"

He laughed. "Now that's an abrupt change of subject. What makes you ask?"

"I have questions about the river rights."

"We've gone over that before."

"But I've not seen the maps."

"They're a matter of public record."

"I realize that. I can go to the courthouse," she said, "but I thought you might have a copy and save me some steps." She smiled, but he could see that something was nagging at her.

Josefina brought a heaping platter of tamales and placed it in the center of the table. Quaid reached for Emmeline's plate and served her three of the fragrant little bundles of cornhusk-wrapped pork.

"Why the sudden interest?" He scooped a half-dozen onto his own plate.

She let her gaze drift to the tamales. She carefully cut into one, lined it up with her knife and fork, and took a dainty bite. Then she chewed slowly as if buying time.

"Was it something that MacQueen mentioned?" The coincidence was too great. The expert's visit. The questions about the water rights. Quaid frowned as he took another bite. "We've been over this before. When the dam was built, the water to your property was cut off."

"Making it through the summer will be difficult. We've had too little rain. I've had tests done. The water table beneath my land has scarcely enough for drinking and bathing."

He lifted his fork, hesitated, then put it down again. "Emma, I would give you half of mine if I could. But the snowpack is low. That means the San Jacinto won't hold water through the summer either. There's not enough behind the dam. I'll need every drop I can get out just to get the herd through the summer and fall."

She let out a deep sigh. "I understand." Still, there was a flicker of something new in her gaze. Distrust, perhaps?

Disturbed, he went back to stabbing at his plateful of tamales as an uncomfortable silence fell between them.

They might have continued sitting in the stilted quiet if Blue hadn't whined and headed to the door, his tail wagging. Quaid excused himself and followed the dog.

He opened the entrance just as his Aunt Brighid pulled up in a buggy. Songan stepped around to the side and helped her out. The big man touched her face in a tender good-bye, and after a last lingering look, drove the buggy back down the road.

Stepping up to the verandah, she greeted her nephew with a quick embrace. When she drew back, he searched her face and noticed the dark circles beneath her eyes.

She gave him a slow nod. "We discovered Merci's trail," she said softly.

"Did you find her—speak with her?" Even as he asked, the answer became clear from Brighid's expression.

She twined her forearm around his, and they moved back into the house. He told her that Emmeline and Gertie had joined them for dinner and asked if she would like to join them in the dining room or if she would prefer tea in the parlor. The question was a practical one, meant to comfort Brighid as she surely would want to tell what she had learned about Merci.

She smiled and gave him a grateful press to the palm. "Thank you. Tea would be perfect. But the evening is lovely; perhaps we should gather in the courtyard?"

"I'll tell Josefina to serve us there."

"I will join you in a few minutes." She left him at the stairs leading to her suite of rooms on the second floor. She stopped at the landing and looked down. "I'm glad you're here, Quaid. My news isn't easy." She paused. "Your presence is a comfort."

Quaid watched her walk away from him, her shoulders stooped with weariness, then he patted his leg for Blue to follow him to the dining room.

When Emmeline heard that Brighid had returned with news about Merci, she nodded a signal to Gertie that they should head home.

"You'll be speaking of a private concern," she said to Quaid, pushing back her chair and placing her napkin by her plate. "I'm certain that Brighid would prefer it to remain in the family."

Just as Emmeline spoke, Brighid stepped through the door and headed around the table to greet the younger woman with a hug. She grasped both Emmeline's hands in hers, her eyes luminous with tears as she spoke. "I would like for you to know what's happened to my daughter. Merci's is not an easy tale to tell, but when you hear it, I think you'll know better how to pray for her."

"I'll stay, then."

Gertie reached up to greet Brighid by giving her a quick peck on the cheek. "You'll have to excuse me from joining you. I promised Josefina I would show her how to make apple griddle cakes. I declare, I think now's the perfect time." She scurried through the swinging kitchen door.

It was dark by the time Emmeline, Quaid, and Brighid sat down together in the courtyard. Emmeline settled onto the stone bench beneath the big live oak. Blue circled and then rested at her feet, his nose propped on his forepaws. Brighid sat beside Emmeline, and Quaid pulled up a chair opposite them.

Josefina brought a tray of Spanish cakes, placed it on a table between them, then set a pot of tea to one side, pitchers of coffee and warm cream to the other. She placed a candle on the table, encircled it with a fluted glass sleeve, and left them.

Brighid stood to pour the tea. "Song and I left here thinking that we'd find Merci in Santa Isabela." She handed the cup to Emmeline and continued talking as she poured another for Quaid. She told them about the saloon called the Ice House, about their discovery that Merci had been there for a few weeks before moving on.

Emmeline listened with growing dismay. Quaid had once alluded to his cousin's heartache and sorrow but had given Emmeline none of the details. From the sound of it, the Ice House was a despicable place.

"Were the rumors about Merci's…uh, activities…true?" Quaid asked, looking grieved. "You haven't said what she was doing…at the Ice House."

Brighid seemed unable to answer, and she was clearly struggling to keep from weeping.

Emmeline didn't understand what he referred to, but Brighid's sorrowful face spoke volumes. She reached for the older woman's hand. "If there's anything I can do…go after her, talk with her…whatever it is, I'm willing. Just say the word, and I'll leave tomorrow at sunup."

Brighid looked across at Emmeline. "It's an offer I don't take lightly." She stared into Emmeline's face. "But I feel it's time to let my daughter go." She swallowed hard. "It's the most painful choice I've made in my life."

Brighid looked to the rock fountain at the center of the courtyard. Standing thoughtfully, she walked over to the place, trailed her fingers along the bottom tier, then stared into the empty basin. She turned back to face them.

"Quaid knows the details about Merci's reasons for leaving. Please don't be offended if we keep them to ourselves to honor what I think would be my daughter's wishes."

Emmeline nodded. "Please, don't worry about my feelings." She stood, walked across the distance that separated them, and embraced Brighid. "It's Merci who matters most right now. I will pray for her every night until she comes home."

Quaid's seething fury was all-consuming. What he'd done to Merci, what had become of her because of his selfishness, made him want to walk away from Rancho de la Paloma and never turn back. When Emmeline got up to console Brighid, he quietly slipped from their presence. Forcing himself to take long, even breaths, he moved up the stairs to the terrace above the courtyard and, without looking back, continued through the house to the verandah.

Emmeline found him there an hour later, still staring into the darkness. A drift of clouds had obscured the moon and only a smattering of stars blinked between them. But it didn't matter, the beauty of creation was lost to the darkness in his heart.

He heard her approach, but he didn't turn. She put a hand on his shoulder. "Quaid?"

"I'm not very good company right now."

"Would you prefer that I leave you?"

A beat of silence fell between them, then he sighed. "No." He turned. "Please stay."

"You left without saying good-bye to either of us."

He looked over her shoulder, focusing somewhere in the distance. "It was too much for me to bear…hearing what she's gotten herself into. I know Merci. I can't help but believe she was forced to…" He couldn't finish, but stood there, clenching and unclenching his fists. "I thought I might explode if I stayed a minute longer."

She nodded. "I can't imagine what Merci must be going through right now."

He closed his eyes for a moment, then looked at her. "I sent her away that night." He swallowed hard. "I blurted out my news about this house, this property…about our grandparents leaving it to me." He shook his head, remembering the look on Merci's face, the devastation and sorrow.

Emmeline reached for his hand and wrapped both of hers around it. The gesture made him feel sheltered and warm. "You didn't know," she said. "You couldn't have known."

"She might not have left if I hadn't been such a braggart. She needed the love of family, not the announcement of my inheritance."

"You don't know that it would have mattered," she said, stroking his hand. "You must believe that."

She still held his hand, and he covered hers with his free one. He lifted her fingers to his lips and kissed them.

"Emma," he whispered, moving closer, "when you're near me, I can't bear the thought of you leaving. And when I'm away from you, I count the minutes until I see you again." She started to speak, but he touched her lips. "Please, let me finish." She blinked and stared up at him.

"I don't ever want to be away from you. That's why this is so difficult to tell you."

Her eyes suddenly glistened. "You're leaving."

He nodded. "I haven't talked to Brighid yet, and I will seek her blessing before I leave, but I must find Merci."

"Brighid said she felt the need to let Merci go, to let Merci find her own way and discover God's lessons on her own."

He nodded. "God doesn't lead all of us in the same way at the same time." He turned and walked to the end of the verandah to look out at the far hills. "There's a restlessness in me that won't be satisfied, a sorrow that won't be gone, until I find her."

Emmeline leaned against the railing, supporting herself with her hands. "Be sure that you're not doing it to soothe your own conscience, Quaid."

He didn't answer.

"Once I felt God's 'still small voice' urging me to abide in him," Emmeline went on. "I sought his voice and meditated on his Word. I made the scripture in John part of my life: 'If ye abide in me, and my words abide in you, ye shall ask what ye will, and it shall be done unto you.'"

She stared out into the night thoughtfully. "At the time I dwelt more on the asking than the abiding. There were so many things I wanted in my life. I thought if I asked, it would be done." She snapped her fingers. "Just like that."

"Did God answer your prayers?"

For a moment she didn't answer. "I said the words and thought I understood. I mean, that if I abided in God and he in me, if I meditated on his word, then he would give me what I asked for."

"Isn't that the point?"

"I took things into my own hands and made a real bungle of it." A shadow crossed her face.

He touched her cheek. "I can't imagine you bungling anything."

She didn't smile. "Think about it, Quaid. It's not a trade that God is promising—if we do this, he'll do that. Like some sort of magic formula." She shook her head. "He's telling us that if we abide in him, we'll know his heart, we'll know what to ask for within the realm of his will."

Quaid looked at her, his thoughts solemn. "If I want to seek his guidance," he said quietly, "I must abide in him to know his heart."

"I don't have all the answers, Quaid. I've thought about this a lot since leaving Washington. I wonder how things might have turned out if I had waited on God. If I had abided in him—daily, hourly, every minute of my day."

"Was coming to California part of what you were asking God?"

"Yes," she admitted, smiling. "But I made some pretty big mistakes along the way."

"Still, he answered your prayer," he persisted.

She let out a long sigh. "I'm beginning to see that it's his grace that picks me up when I stumble." She looked thoughtful. "And it's proof that he loves me in spite of myself."

That night, long after Emmeline and Gertie rode off in their buggy, Quaid and Brighid sat under the century oak in the courtyard. They spoke of heartache and love and sorrow and pain and God's shining grace. When he told her about wanting to follow Merci's trail, Brighid's eyes were solemn and luminous.

"You would do that?" she whispered. "It wasn't right for me to go. I know that as a certainty—but you?" She looked up at him thoughtfully.

Her expression told him that she knew what it would cost him. Summer was approaching, and his leadership was needed as the cattle were driven into the mountains for grazing. Rustling was likely unless he was there to watch over his property.

They spoke for a while longer about Merci, then Brighid reached for his hand. They stood and walked back into the house.

"I'll give you my decision in the morning," he said as she ascended the stairs to the second floor.

He sat for a long time in the library without turning on a lantern. The moon had dipped from the cloud cover and came through the window in bars of light.

Father, what does it mean to abide in you? It's been a long time since I read your Word and prayed. At least a long time since I uttered a prayer with more substance than blessing the food or telling you good night.

How is abiding different? Or is it?

He stared through the window, thinking how he was much the same as Emmeline had described herself tonight. That stubborn streak that made them seek their own will first, then ask God to bless their efforts second.

He leaned forward, conscious that he was sitting at his grandfather's desk. He'd always imagined God as somehow combining the gentleness of his father and the tough love of his grandfather.

When his grandfather prayed, he seemed to be sitting right in the same room with his Lord, having a conversation, Irishman to an Irishman's heavenly Father. His grandfather's prayers had seemed so big and all-encompassing to him as a child that there was no need to pray for himself.

But now? Quaid frowned as he twisted the lid onto a squat jar of ink, danced it around the ink blotter a bit, then set it upright near the pen holder.

Now?

Lord, I'm not very good at this. But something is calling me. Or maybe it's you calling me. I don't know.

He rubbed his forehead and eyes, squinting into the darkness.

All I know is that I'm tired of trying to find my own way. Tired of being selfish in my pursuits.

Merci's image appeared in his mind, and he felt the threat of tears behind his eyes.

Father, I'm so tired of the greed in my heart. And pride of spirit. Vainglory.

It makes me sick, and I can only imagine what it does to you, Most Holy God! Forgive me for my reprehensible ways.

Merci's image wouldn't leave him, and he felt the need to kneel on her behalf. He stood and walked over to a wing chair and knelt before the Lord, resting his forehead in his hands.

I've harmed her with my greed, Lord.

The full impact of what he had done weighed too heavy for words. Without realizing he was doing so, he wept.

Father, I don't know how to pray for Merci. I'm not even sure where she is or what she is doing.

But I lift her before you right now.

I need help here, Lord. Give me the words, the utterances, to make sense of this.

Her image floated before him again, and with it a sense of great peace. *Sanctify my imagination, Father*, he breathed in wonder.

He pictured Merci in a room above a saloon. Then he imagined Jesus coming to her, reaching out to take her hand. Jesus led her from the filthy room, as he would the most precious of his children. He brought her down some stairs, and before they stepped out into the street, Jesus removed his cloak and covered Merci with it.

For the longest time, Quaid knelt before his grandfather's chair, and he thought of Merci in Christ's arms, sometimes being carried, sometimes being led by the hand. Together they walked in a garden, and

Merci was talking and laughing with her Savior. Then Quaid pictured them walking along a beach, stooping to examine the wonder of a shell or a starfish.

Always, Jesus was with her, helping her if she stumbled, carrying her when she grew tired.

Don't leave her. Father, keep her close.

He had just uttered his first real prayer for someone else.

Sometime after midnight he awoke, a vivid dream still with him.

A shepherd had been searching for a lost lamb, and he turned to Quaid, asking for his help. But the flock of lambs behind the shepherd changed into cattle. Quaid argued with the shepherd that it didn't matter whether they were sheep or cows, all would be lost if he left them.

But the shepherd said the one lamb was more important than the cattle on a thousand hills.

Quaid heard the cry of that lamb.

He knew from the pitch of its bleating that it was injured. He raced to find it, following drops of blood across a rock-strewn landscape. He knelt by its side, lifting it in both arms before carrying it back to the shepherd. The shepherd smiled at him, and Quaid awoke relieved, settled.

He rose before dawn, and by the time Brighid descended the stairs, he was ready to leave. "I've decided," he said simply.

"My prayers will be with you, Quaid." She pressed a small Bible with a cover of tooled leather into his hands. "This is for Merci when you find her."

He turned to leave.

"Godspeed," she called after him. "Godspeed."

TWENTY-THREE

The dappled slant of the early morning sun warmed Emmeline's shoulders as she bent over the stove, now perched on some adobe stones under the pepper tree. The metal plates clanged and rattled as she adjusted them, then worked the bellows on a small pile of fresh embers.

She turned at the sound of hoofbeats on the road and watched Quaid approach. When he reached her, he swept off his hat, then dismounted. The sunlight caught his hair, and she fought the urge to comb an unruly tuft back from his forehead with her fingers.

"I've decided to go," he said without preamble, and she noticed he looked pleased about it, as if he'd settled something in his soul.

"I prayed last night for your decision," she said. "And I can see you're at peace with it."

He smiled and stepped closer. "The only thing I'm not at peace about is leaving you."

When he'd said similar words last night, she thought she might have misunderstood. But here he was, saying he didn't want to leave her. Last night he said that when he was away from her he counted the minutes until he saw her again. She looked up at him in wonder. *Merciful heavens!* Could it truly be that he loved her?

"We have some serious business to discuss when I get back."

She couldn't stop smiling. "We do?"

He nodded and stepped even closer. "I'm not sure how long it will take to find Merci. Or even what I'll do when I find her." A shadow crossed his face. "I'm just taking it one step at a time and plan to do plenty of that abiding you told me about. I'll abide in my Father and see where he leads me."

"I will pray for you—and for Merci—each day while you're gone."

He touched her face. "There won't be a moment that you'll be out of my heart, Emma."

"And you'll be in mine, Quaid." She had never spoken so to a man before, and her cheeks flushed. "I will think of you every day and watch for you to come riding over the hill."

He caught her hand, and they walked the short distance from the house to the edge of the orange groves. Birdsong rose from the small trees, and a breeze off the mountains ruffled the grasses to the north, carrying with it the scent of early summer grass and wildflowers.

Quaid walked over to a Bahia, knelt, and rubbed one of the waxy leaves between his fingers. "How long till these bloom?" He looked back up at her, grinning. The slant of the sun hit his face, and her heart caught.

She tried to guess his purpose in asking. "Two years from now they will be in full bloom. In the winter, we'll have our first crop."

"Where is it you want that Victorian castle built?"

She turned around and pointed beyond the pepper tree. "Over there. It provides a perfect view of the mountains and will catch the breezes when we open the windows."

Then she realized she'd just said "we," and she wasn't referring to her and Gertie. She grinned at him.

"And do you think, in those plans that you have, that our children will have enough room to play? To run around a big yard and make mischief?"

Tears were stinging her eyes, and she could scarcely see him for the shimmer in them. But she nodded. "And I figured we could tie a swing from the biggest branch of the pepper tree."

He pushed himself up and walked back over to where she was rooted to the ground. "I have a plan, Miss Emmeline Amity Callahan," he said. "I can't tell you all the details, but it has to do with marrying you before those Bahias ripen and make you a millionaire. The way I see it, you won't take a second look at the likes of me after that happens."

"The way I see it," she said, thinking she might not ever stop smiling, "the scent of orange blossoms would be perfect for a wedding."

"Perhaps we can decorate the whole house with them."

She laughed. "Garlands of orange blossoms wound around the turrets."

He rolled his eyes. "Now that will be something to see." Around them a hum of bees and grasshoppers rose to join the singing of the birds. He studied her face, his expression solemn. "I don't know how long I'll be away."

"I will wait."

"I may not be here to see the new stove delivered."

"Keep in mind that we'll already know how to use it when you get home. You'll miss all the sacrificial burnt biscuits and flat-as-a-fritter cakes."

He chuckled. "You help me see the good in things."

"Such as orange groves and Victorian houses?"

"Even those." He stepped closer and pulled her into his arms.

"And you help me see God's handiwork in things I'd never noticed before."

"Such as tumbling up into the heavens," he said with a chuckle. "Or finding spider eyes?"

"Such as seeing him in you, Quaid. Seeing him reflected in your eyes."

For a moment they stood perfectly still, their arms wrapped around each other. Emmeline rested her face against his chest and heard the drumming of his heart. She closed her eyes and memorized the sound of it and the feel of her cheek against his warm chest.

His grip tightened. "I love you," he whispered in her hair.

No one had ever uttered those words to her before. She buried her face against his throat, letting the words fill her soul.

"I love you," he repeated and pulled back slightly. Placing his hands on either side of her face, he lifted it gently until their eyes met.

She swallowed hard, almost afraid to breathe because of the caring in his gaze. He bent his head and brushed his lips against hers. She shivered with delight as he kissed her a second time, this time letting his lips linger. Curling against him, she sighed, content to stay in his arms forever. Content to kiss him for the rest of their lives.

"One more thing," he said, looking down at her.

The sun caught his face, and she thought she might weep from the beauty of him.

"Anything," she sighed.

"Anything?" He grinned wickedly.

She nodded.

"Don't you dare build that packing house while I'm away." He kissed her on the tip of the nose, laughed, then kissed her on the forehead.

He was still chuckling when he mounted the sorrel and rode away from her.

<hr />

His first letter arrived three weeks after he left.

Santa Barbara Inn
July 20, 1890

My dearest Emma,

I arrived here this morning, and it is the first opportunity I have had to post a letter to you. For the past week, I have camped under the stars—as your father's Washington studies have shown cowboys are prone to do. I am following the map that Aunt Brighid was given of the King's Highway. It spans nearly the entire length of California, and if necessary I will travel each mile until I find Merci.

How I long to see you and wish that you were here with me. Yesterday I stopped at the Mission Santa Ventura and spoke with the caretaker and his wife. They met Merci right after she left Santa Isabela, and, as you know, welcomed Brighid and Song into their home and hearts a few weeks ago. Someday I hope we can return here together. I know you will love these godly people. They pray for Merci daily.

I visited Mission Santa Barbara this morning, disappointed to find it deserted. It is sad to see the decay in these ancient buildings, though it was better kept than the one in Ventura. There is no way to tell if Merci ever stopped there.

I send you all the love that's in my heart, my darling Emma. Kiss Gertie for me, and give my love to Brighid when you see her. I will write to you again from the next mission north of here, Mission Santa Inez.

Affectionately, Quaid

It was Emmeline's first love letter. She folded it and kept it near her heart, missing him more now, after three weeks, than the first day he left. One week later she received his next letter.

Santa Inez
July 28, 1890

My dearest Emma,
This is by far the most beautiful mission I have visited thus far. It is not because of the structure itself—which is in crumbling disrepair—but because of the beautiful garden someone has planted in the inner courtyard.

I spoke with a few people in town who said a woman once lived there but has been away for some time. Another said a second woman stayed at the mission for a few weeks, then moved on. No one seems to know, or care, if the women are together. If it's Merci they described, she has changed. They called her dirty and unkempt, tired looking. I asked about her hair color, for surely it is a distinguishing feature. The unkempt woman, they told me, had dark, colorless hair. This can't be our Merci they describe!

I visited the mission on two occasions, hoping the

women might have returned, and I plan to stop by once more on my way out of town.

Strangely, the inner courtyard seems as intimate a place as someone's home. The gate leading to it is locked with a chain, allowing only the narrowest view of the courtyard. I have called out Merci's name on several occasions, but there was no answer.

From here, my darling, I plan to head north toward San Francisco. I will camp under the stars again, but will post another letter as soon as I can.

I thought of you many times today and wished so much that you could have been with me to see the magnificent garden of this mission. Nothing I have seen, however, matches the beauty of your face. I long to kiss you this moment!

Affectionately, Quaid

Emmeline read and reread the letter, memorizing the last few lines. *Nothing I have seen matches the beauty of your face. I long to kiss you this moment!*

Merciful heavens! She brought both hands to her cheeks, feeling the heat of a blush move from her chin to her forehead. Closing her eyes, she pictured him with his crooked grin, and she longed to feel his arms around her.

By September, Quaid's letters reflected his discouragement, but he didn't mention giving up or coming home. When his next letter arrived, her heart dropped as she read it.

San Francisco
September 21, 1890

My darling Emma,
I think I have found Merci. I will know for certain tonight. I stopped at the San Francisco Mission this morning and

found that two women stayed here last week. The caretaker looked uncomfortable when he told me about a red-haired woman who slipped away each night after the other woman was asleep.

Though he didn't tell me where he thought she might have headed, I took it upon myself to go into San Francisco's red-light district. I will spare you the details of the abysmal place, my dear one, but suffice it to say, my heart broke for the humanity I saw there. The darkness and depravity in which these women live seems to have come straight from hell itself.

I found a madam who told me about a crimson-haired prostitute who had drifted in to do business for a time before leaving again. This "lady of the night" called herself Little Dove.

Darling, I don't want to believe it, but the prostitute she described has to be Merci. The madam told me about a woman that Little Dove worked with, a woman named Jewel. I plan to find her tonight. Perhaps she will tell me if Merci told her where she was going next.

I had so hoped Merci had found a different life by now. I can only lift her up in prayer. I implore you to do the same, beloved. I don't know when I might write again, because I will be leaving the city to travel *El Camino Real* once more—should that be the path Merci has taken. Many of the missions are in deserted locations, and I have no way to post the letters I write to you.

I cherish your memory, my precious Emma, the trust we have between us, and the love that grows stronger with each day.

May our Lord hold you in his care until we meet again. Kiss Gertie for me, and tell Brighid as much of this as you think is appropriate when you see her.

Affectionately, Quaid

Emmeline wept when she read the letter, her heart aching for Merci, for Quaid, and for Brighid, who'd become her friend in the months Quaid was away. Each breath became a prayer for Merci as she worked in her groves.

Missing Quaid more each week he was gone, she threw herself into the business of running the rancho to dull the ache in her heart. In mid-October she hired a small work force from across the Mexican border and worked side by side with them along the even rows of soil, weeding and checking for parasites. Each day her back and limbs became stronger, and her hair, once a muddy brown, was now streaked with gold from the sun.

Her worry, as always, was about having enough water for her trees, and she constantly checked the level and quality of her well water. It was dwindling, there was no doubt, but her theory about toughening her trees was working. The small yearlings clung to life, even without the freely flowing water she so desperately needed.

Court MacQueen stopped by each time he was in Riverview County. He made a point of driving out to see Emmeline. More often than not he mentioned the water rights that were clearly marked on the La Paloma plat map.

Finally, to put the matter to rest, Emmeline agreed to meet Mac-Queen to see the plat map for herself—and tried to ignore the nagging thought that she was somehow betraying Quaid by even looking.

<hr />

The following morning she watched Court bound up the city hall steps to meet her promptly at nine, just as he had promised.

"I have the grandest surprise for you, Emmeline," he said when he reached her.

She smiled. "My new shipment of orange trees?" She had ordered them three months earlier, but they hadn't yet arrived. She was eager to get them in the ground before the onset of cold weather.

He laughed. "No, something entirely different, I assure you. You'll have to wait until we have a look at the map." He caught her hand. "You must also promise to have lunch with me at the Glenwood Inn."

"I must get back to my groves. But thank you."

He looked crestfallen. "But you've just ruined my surprise."

She shook her head. "Some other time. I'm sorry." She started for the door leading into city hall.

He caught up with her. "Supper, then? Tonight?"

"No, I'm sorry." She took a few steps, and he caught her hand.

"You must come into town anyway for the co-op meeting. Truly, I have the most wonderful surprise for you."

She studied him for a moment. "Has it to do with my groves?"

He raised a brow. "It has to do with you personally, Emmeline."

She laughed. "With me? I can't think of anything more ordinary than that." She walked into the foyer, feeling more than a little annoyed at Court's persistence. She nodded to a door down the hall and said, "I believe that's the office we want," before heading for it.

Court soon matched her stride and caught up with her. "There's someone who wants to meet you," he said, opening the door for her.

She stepped through. "I'm not interested." Then she looked at the clerk. "I would like to see the plat maps for the Byrne property known as Rancho de la Paloma. Also the map for the Hugh Dearbourne rancho."

The clerk disappeared among the stacks of shelves and dusty boxes.

"He says he knows you," Court said.

With that her eyes flew open, and she turned to Court. "Knows me?"

"I've been telling him about our glorious Eastern transplant, Miss Emmeline Callahan." He laughed. "He said the woman I described to him certainly wasn't the Emmeline Callahan he remembered from Washington."

Heat flooded her face as the image of the old Emmeline flooded her memory. If she'd had on her eyeglasses she would have pushed them up on her nose. She stared at Court in disbelief.

"I have no interest in seeing anyone from Washington," she said. The clerk brought the maps—lengths of rolled paper—and unfastened them. She started to unroll the first.

"He insists on seeing you."

"I'm not interested." She continued opening the plat map. Then she stopped and looked over at Court. "I know you have my interests at heart, but I was a different person when I lived in Washington. I don't want to hear about anyone, except perhaps my family."

"Or Derian Cadman," he said.

She dropped the map on the counter and spun. "What did you say?"

"Derian Cadman." He laughed. "The young man said that the mere mention of his name would get a reaction."

She swallowed hard and felt the room start to spin. She touched the counter with her fingertips to steady herself and briefly closed her eyes. When she recovered, she turned to see Court studying her carefully. She might as well get the encounter over with.

"I think we'd better go," she said with a nervous laugh. "To lunch, that is."

"I'll arrange for you to take the maps. These may be copies."

She sank into a chair and attempted to breathe while Court conferred with the clerk. Indeed, the plat maps were cartographer copies, so she could take them as long as she promised to have them back within the week.

"Now," Court said, map rolls tucked under his arm, as he escorted her from the building, "about that lunch…"

They walked through the doors of the Glenwood Inn to the Patio Room, elegantly appointed with its linen tablecloths and formally dressed servers. Court spoke to the maître d', then they followed him to a private table toward the back of the room.

She stopped in midstride when she saw Derian Cadman.

Derian stood, and for a moment neither of them spoke.

Drawing a deep breath and keeping her head high, she crossed the distance between them. She stuck out her hand to shake his, then seated herself across from him.

"You are looking well," he said, his eyes bright with admiration.

Court settled into a chair on her right.

"You look well yourself," she said lightly, "considering you are presumed dead."

He stared at her a moment, then laughed. "Oh, that."

"Yes, that," she said, lifting her water glass to her lips. "That little stunt you pulled had me whispered about for months. The word *murderess* was only one of the terms being bandied about Washington, thanks to you."

He flushed. "I told you I had to get away."

"Did you have to fake your own suicide—or murder—to do it?" She watched him evenly.

"This is fascinating," Court said, leaning forward, his elbows on the table. His tone said he'd known about her and Derian all along.

Emmeline turned to him. "You sound bored with these details, rather than surprised. You're well connected in Washington. Something tells me you and Derian have known each other for years."

"He didn't tell you?" Cadman said, glancing toward Court.

"That you've know each other for years?" She looked from Cadman to MacQueen, then back to the younger man again. Their expressions told her the answer.

MacQueen nodded. "One of the joys of my life has been to see you blossom in the California sun, my dear."

"Are you really a government horticulturist?"

"Oh yes. One of the best."

"Why didn't you tell me?"

He studied her for a moment. "Derian is a friend. I felt it was up to him to tell you what really happened at the Potomac. Besides, I sensed you wanted to begin afresh. Derian told me what you said about following your dream, your heart, to California. I wanted to honor that."

His words sounded decent enough, but looking into his eyes, she wondered how much she could trust him. Either of them. Derian's past friends had betrayed her, humiliated her. Was this friend any different? Already he'd kept the truth from her about knowing Derian. What else might he be hiding?

"I followed your advice," Derian said, interrupting her thoughts. "I was a Harvard dropout, frightened to tell my parents where I'd gone. It might have been cowardly, but I could think of no other way to leave."

"So you pretended to die in the river—and pinned the tragedy on me."

"I'm sorry for any aspersions my act may have cast," Derian said, looking truly sorry.

"Do your parents know you're alive?"

Court broke in. "I wrote to them just weeks after it happened, letting them know their son was alive." He chuckled. "Though I think they'd guessed it themselves when they received Derian's marks from Harvard Law."

It chilled her to think of the callous and cavalier deed the men had carried out. His parents must have agonized over what they thought was his tragic death. She considered the sorrow Brighid endured because of Merci, the agony of not knowing whether her daughter was alive or dead from day to day. The escapade Derian Cadman had pulled made her sick.

Then, as if he were a chum catching up on old times, Derian began talking about his dream of heading to the Alaska gold fields. Emma sat for a few minutes, speechless. This man was utterly selfish, with no regard for anyone but himself. She thought of Quaid out looking for his cousin, leaving his rancho during the busiest time of the year. The two men weren't even from the same universe. Finally she decided she'd had enough of Derian Cadman to last a lifetime.

She stood in midsentence. "I must leave," she said abruptly. "What you've done…to me…to your parents…to others is irresponsible. No, worse than that…it's unconscionable."

"Don't go," Derian said. "Please. I must ask you something important. It's the reason I came here today." She hesitated just long enough for him to rush on. "I need a job," he said. "Court tells me you need a foreman. I'd be willing to do anything. Just say the word."

"I'm sorry," she said and shook her head. "I have no position available for you. Even if I did, I wouldn't hire you." She shrugged and turned to walk to the door.

Court pushed himself up from the table and followed after her. He looked troubled and, taking her elbow, escorted her to the foyer of the inn.

"I know what you must think of young Derian. You're right. What he did was a tragedy for all involved. You must believe me, though, Emmeline, when I say that he's genuinely sorry for what he did to you. He's grown up since leaving Washington. He's been forced to work with his hands for the first time in his life. It's been good for him."

He steered her to a corner away from the other guests. "As for my part in the deception. I felt a loyalty to his family. I didn't want to break a confidence—"

She held up her hand, interrupting him. "Your decisions were yours, Court. Don't apologize or explain. Ours is a professional relationship. What matters is that I can trust you in our business dealings."

He stiffened as though she'd struck him. "I thought it was more," he said, "more than just a professional relationship."

She looked at him evenly. "We may have been friends in the past, Court, but I want to keep it strictly professional from now on."

He inclined his head, studying her for a moment. Suddenly he smiled and broke the tension between them. "I will work to change your mind." He chuckled, the old Court she'd grown to enjoy.

She turned to leave, and he stopped her. "About the foreman's job?"

"I wouldn't let Mr. Cadman work for me for all the oranges in Riverview," she said, "and you may tell him that for me."

That night after Gertie had gone to bed, Emmeline moved the lamp to the kitchen table and unrolled the plat maps. She studied them carefully, comparing them one with the other. At first she didn't see anything unusual about them. Rancho de la Paloma's dated back to when MacQuaid Byrne had to prove his land's boundaries some twenty-five years before. Hugh Dearbourne had recorded the map for his land, though the dates didn't match those recorded for La Paloma.

She squinted and moved the La Paloma map nearer to the lamp. It appeared to have been altered. Frowning, she bent closer.

There it was, the slightest smudge mark, as though someone had lightly scratched off the ink.

She rubbed her head, feeling a dull ache beginning in her temple. Then she studied the map again. At the very place where the river forked, where her land lost the rights to the river, the map had been altered.

She stared at the spot, trying to understand what it meant.

Why would the smudge be on a copied map? The cartographer wouldn't make such a mistake.

If someone wanted to make sure the changes were official, they would substitute the copies for the real thing. There would be only one way to prove her theory, and that was to examine the originals, at least those maps known as the originals, to see if they too had been altered.

⊰⊱

The following day, she headed back to the courthouse. At the desk, she handed the clerk the copies of the maps and asked to see the originals. He stood back, watching her carefully as she unfurled them on the long oak table.

"Something isn't right," she murmured, absently tracing a grain of wood on the tabletop with her finger. "It's just not right."

He stepped closer. "What seems to be the trouble?"

"Here, where the dam is drawn—" She pointed to the place.

He nodded. "Yes, I see."

"Compare that one inch square with the identical square on the copy."

Pulling out a magnifying glass, he bent over the map. "Yes," he said, "you're right."

She straightened, feeling a small triumph. "You agree, then, that they have indeed been altered."

He looked at her in surprise. "Now, little missy, that's quite an accusation."

She put her hands on her hips. "You just agreed with me that they've been changed."

"I agree they've been changed. I don't agree they've been altered. What was done here was likely done on purpose because of a mistake in the original. Perhaps a cartographer's mistake that was later corrected."

"Whoever made the change," she sputtered, "took away my rights to the water flowing out of the San Jacinto." She pointed to the dam. "This was built in the wrong place—don't you see?"

He scratched his head and looked at her as though she were mad. "You're saying that the experts working for the Department of Water put the dam in the wrong place?"

"Not exactly. But because someone drew the wrong line on this plat map—it lies in the wrong place for me."

His mustache twitched, and he coughed as if covering an urge to laugh.

"I want to speak to your supervisor."

"Ah, that would be Charlie, but he's not here right now. He's across the street having a sarsaparilla."

"How do I go about getting something like this changed back to the way it ought to be?"

"You would need to petition Sacramento to have a new map drawn. Hope you're not in a hurry. Disputes like this can take years to investigate. Years more to settle."

She stared at him. "I'll investigate it myself then."

He chuckled as he rolled up the original map. "The cartographer who drew these left for Mexico years ago," he said, rolling up the copy. "He didn't sign either one with a date. I just know that certain plat maps in Riverview County are his work. Both of these are his, believe me."

"Could someone else have forged his work?"

He studied her for a moment. "It would be highly unusual, but I suppose so." He looked at her more sympathetically now. "Instead of going off on a wild-goose chase, if I were you, I'd look hard at the party who might benefit most from such an alteration of your water supply. Then I'd make peace with the culprit and work out a solution between the two parties. You'll get further in your quest for water that way than by going through Sacramento."

She nodded her thanks and left the courthouse.

On her ride home that night, and later as she stared at the ceiling from her bed, unable to sleep, the image of Quaid's gentle face and the memory of his gruff voice filled her senses.

She ached to see him, to touch him, to feel the warm strength of his arms around her.

And she refused to believe that he was the one person who would benefit the most from blocking her water supply.

Twenty-Four

December 1890

Merci rode Sadie's swayback mule to the arranged meeting place, an abandoned lighthouse at the end of a rock-strewn spit of land north of Santa Barbara. Specifically, near Point Conception—an ironic choice. It had been Jewel's idea to meet there at noon on the first of December to talk about the plans they'd made in San Francisco.

Jewel was waiting for her. Leaning against a rock wall in front of the lighthouse, she looked up as Merci rode closer. Beside her was a bottle of brandy, and she nodded to it as Merci dismounted. "Want some?"

Merci shook her head. She'd come to talk of business and wanted to be certain her senses remained keen. No chance of being dull-witted today anyway, she thought, shivering. Not with the frigid wind stinging her face. A bank of dark clouds was building near the horizon, signaling the approach of a winter storm.

Jewel was kindhearted, but life had aged her. She was losing her figure because of the brandy, and her eyes held a hard, lined look above puffy circles. The more she tried to cover her face with paint, the more grotesque she appeared. She'd confided in Merci that her days in an elegant parlor house were going fast. Besides, she'd said, she was tired. Bone tired.

Jewel took a swig from the bottle and wiped her mouth with the back of her hand. "Warms the spirits on a cold day," she said, grinning up at Merci. Then she patted the ground. "Sit yerself down, honey, so we can talk."

Merci slumped against the wall, looking out at the ocean.

"You still want in?" Jewel asked.

"More than ever."

Jewel chuckled and took another long draught from the bottle, then replaced the cap. "We need capital. Lots of it."

Merci nodded. "I have some ideas."

"If you're planning to do tricks for the money—you'll never get enough. I been savin' for years and still have only half what we'll need."

Merci turned from the sea to look at her. "I have a way to get more than we need."

The old prostitute's eyes glittered. "Now that'll make the old gal glad she came all this way." She paused. "You gonna tell Jewel how you intend to 'make' this money, darlin'?"

"The woman I'm staying with showed me something of great value last week. I think we'll find it useful." Her laugh was cold.

"I don't know if I wanna double-trick ol' Sadie Rose." She unscrewed the brandy cap and studied the liquid in the bottle. "She and I go back."

Merci frowned, wondering if she meant her Sadie. "Sadie Rose? And what do you mean, you go back?"

"I saw Sadie Rose with you in San Fran." Jewel took a swallow, forced the liquid into her cheeks, and swished it audibly.

"You didn't tell me."

Jewel swallowed, her eyes closed. "You left before I had a chance to." She laughed, looking at Merci again. "Sadie Rose and me go back, but honey, if you got a way for us to go into business, I say it's our turn. She's had hers. Long as it don't hurt her, I suppose."

"How do you know Sadie?" Merci pressed, though she'd already guessed.

"She don't look nothing like she did then," Jewel said, gazing out at the ocean. "We were both young, just starting out. Later on she got her own place."

"She…worked with you, then…in San Francisco?" She considered the Sadie she knew now, sweet and humble, and tried to imagine the same holy woman with paint on her face and eyes lined with kohl. The image didn't fit.

Jewel turned back to Merci. "When we started out we were about your age. I didn't ask about her past. She didn't ask about mine. Those things are best left alone."

"Yes, they are," Merci said absently, still trying to picture Sadie Rose, San Francisco madam.

"Now, tell me about this fortune you're about to make. And especially, tell if it's gonna be enough to start our own place."

"More than enough."

Jewel let out a long sigh. "At last," she chuckled. "At last I'll be sittin' pretty instead of sittin' and waitin' on my next john." Overhead a sea gull cried and swooped. "When you start waitin' for the next one to knock on yer door, honey, you know you're over the hill. Should be the other way around. Them lined up and waitin' for you."

She turned to Merci again. "We'll be madams soon with a place of our own. Isn't that right, honey?"

"As soon as I take care of a last piece of business at the mission."

"You gonna do it tonight?"

Merci drew in a deep breath. "Yes. Tonight."

"I'll wait for you, and we'll head to San Fran together." Jewel's eyes were glittering again. "I got a place all picked out for us. We can buy it if there's enough, or rent it, if not."

"There will be enough to buy it, if all goes well." Merci stood and brushed herself off. "I'll meet you at daybreak tomorrow."

Jewel stood with her and shoved the bottle into her hand. "You take this, honey. I have a feelin' you're gonna need more courage than what you've got inside. This will help. Always does."

Merci took the bottle from Jewel with a nod of thanks. Lifting it, she took a deep drink. It burned her throat and warmed her. Jewel was right. She'd needed it. And she might need more before the night was through.

She headed to the old mule. Before she could put her foot in the stirrup, Jewel called out to her. Merci turned toward the old prostitute again.

"I nearly forgot to tell you in all my excitement…"

"Tell me what?"

"A man came asking for you, honey."

"Here?"

"In San Fran."

Merci frowned, thinking it must have been one of her johns.

"Called you by your given name 'stead of Little Dove."

Her heart caught. "Who was it?"

"Had a funny name. Started with a Q." She laughed heartily. "I'd been in my cups that night. Can't remember much about the man or what he said." Some gulls called overhead, and one glided down to land beside Jewel. She flicked sand at it with her painted nails. "Now I remember," she said triumphantly. "Quaid, it was. You know someone named Quaid?"

Her heart stopped. "Quaid?" she whispered.

"That's it, honey. You know someone by that name?"

Merci didn't answer her. "Did you tell him where I'd gone…where I am now?" Her heart raced. She didn't want to be found.

Jewel cackled. "Not sure. Could have. Though I'm usually more careful than that. Don't want johns knowin' about our personal lives and all. As I said, though," she shook her head apologetically, "I was in my cups that night. I might've told him anything. Might've made up something—I don't remember."

Merci nodded, glad she would be on the move again in the morning. She mounted and looked down at Jewel. "I'll be here just past sunrise." She tossed Jewel the bottle. "You may need that to keep you warm tonight."

Jewel cackled. "Honey, I'll keep warm. Don't you worry. I'll be plenty warm." She was still laughing as Merci rode down the spit of sand and headed back to Santa Inez.

Merci couldn't bear to ride back to the mission quite yet. Instead she headed down the coast, keeping close to the water. The mule plodded slowly along, and she tried not to be impatient with the beast. It was nearing dusk when she reached a stretch of beach just west of Santa Inez.

The wind off the ocean caught her hair and whipped it around her shoulders as she slid from the mule's back. She drew her thin wrap close and walked to the edge of the water.

Sitting near the surf, she circled her arms around her knees. After a moment she let a handful of sand sift through her fingers and gazed out at the approaching storm. The wind was already churning the gray ocean, kicking spray from the growing waves.

She longed to feel something of the ocean's power or the might of the storm. Instead a sense of despair nearly overwhelmed her. No longer did she feel sorrow or pain. She was empty of anything except decaying hopes.

No regret for what she was about to do to Sadie, no twinge of guilt for stealing the silver chalice that Sadie cherished.

The woman's goodness irritated her. The contrast between Sadie's piety and Merci's evil was too great. It was like having a bright lantern suddenly turned on when her eyes were comfortable in the dark. The light brought pain.

Leaving Sadie, her pretty garden, and the holy feeling of the mission was a way of escaping the light. The woman wouldn't stop trying to help Merci. Even after Knight was stolen, Sadie hitched their dilapidated buggy to the mule and helped Merci search for her beloved horse. She'd been willing to go to the dangerous Adam Cole's ranch when Merci hinted the man might have been behind the theft. After Sadie heard a rumor in town that the horse had been sold to a horse trader in San Francisco, it was she who insisted they go there to look for him. Merci didn't deserve her kindness.

They didn't find the horse, naturally, but Merci's acquaintance with Jewel made up for it.

A wave crested and broke in front of her, pulling her back to the task ahead. She pushed herself up from the sand, brushed her hands off, and stood facing the sea. The wind whipped her hair and stung her face. She felt drawn by its power, its voice that called her, told her that peace would be hers if she would only step into the roiling waters.

She thought about the notion for several minutes, wondering what it would be like to kill herself. To end her pain, her dark despair. Gulls wheeled overhead, their mournful cries echoing her sadness.

Merci tried to act as if nothing was amiss when she arrived back at the mission. She chatted with Sadie companionably over their bowls of rabbit stew, and later in the evening, as they sat in the great room, she caught Sadie studying her. Embarrassed, she turned away to lose herself in a book.

"I sense a restlessness in you," Sadie said after a while. She was sewing together the rows of a braided rug, and she held it to the lamp to check her stitching. "Is everything all right?" Rain pounded the roof and the winds howled against the windows.

Merci nodded quickly. "Of course." She buried herself again in her book.

Sadie stood and walked to the open fireplace, stoked it, then returned to her chair by the lamp. "Have you thought about going home?" It was the first time Sadie had mentioned it.

Merci shrugged. "It's not a consideration." She laughed. "I doubt that my fine, upstanding family wants anything to do with me."

Sadie said no more about it, and for a moment the only sounds were the crackling fire and the drumming rain on the roof. Taking a deep breath, Merci knew she could wait no longer to set her plan into motion. "The chalice you showed me last week…?" She attempted to sound as nonchalant as possible, though her heart pounded with nervousness.

Sadie tied a knot in her thread, bit the end with her teeth, and looked across the room at Merci.

"I noticed how tarnished it is," Merci went on. "Have you ever tried to polish it?"

A wide smile lit Sadie's face. "I haven't."

"I was thinking it might be a nice addition to the chapel, but perhaps we should polish it first."

Sadie didn't hesitate. Standing, she stretched her cramped hand and laid her unfinished rug on the chair. Her face was a wreath of delight. "Do you think soap and water will be strong enough?"

Merci laughed lightly. "It's a good start. There must be centuries of dirt and grime on the thing."

"I'll get it," Sadie said and stepped from the door into the rainy courtyard. Merci sat back, satisfied. The first step in her plan had been accomplished.

Sadie returned a few minutes later, brushed the rain from her shoulders, and held out the chalice. Merci took it in her cupped hands, pretending to hold it reverently. Sadie had told her it was sacred, most likely used for the sacrament of Holy Communion.

The lamplight cast an amber glow on the cup as Merci turned it in her hands.

"His blood is all that can cleanse us," Sadie said quietly, then looked up to meet Merci's gaze. "No matter what we've done, no matter how we feel about the blood that courses through our own veins." She fell quiet for a moment, staring at the chalice. "And it's his life in us that changes us. We can't do it ourselves."

From the weight of it in her hands, Merci thought it must surely be solid silver. It was dull with age, but after a bit of rubbing it might fetch a tidy sum. Perhaps just the sum she needed. Only the market value of the goblet mattered. She didn't want to hear about its symbolism or the lies that went with it.

She turned it again in her hands. Circling its exterior were seven relief portrayals of Christ's life—beginning with his birth, through his ministry, to the crucifixion. One, perhaps because it was covered with less grime, shone brighter than the others, and she held it to the light. Jesus sat on a stone with a group of young children around him. He held a little girl in his arms, his face inclined toward her with an expression of pure love.

Lies. All of it lies. Her heart twisted, and biting her lip she considered hurling the hateful cup into the fireplace. Instead she stared at the image and forced herself to remain calm.

She looked up to meet Sadie's clear gaze. The woman, with her loathsome, pious look, studied Merci as if she knew her every thought.

"I'll get the soap and water," Sadie said softly.

A few minutes later the two women scrubbed the silver over a small pan of sudsy water. They took turns attempting to scrape off the years of accumulation.

After a while, Merci spoke with a forced, light tone. "I think we should let it soak overnight. Maybe a few hours in the water will loosen some of the dirt." She flicked at it with her fingernail and shook her head.

Sadie agreed, and Merci moved the pan to a table in the corner of the room. They went back to sewing and reading until Sadie excused herself for the night. Merci read for a few more minutes, unable to concentrate, her gaze drawn away from the book to the chalice resting in the pan of water.

Finally she turned down the lamp and crossed the courtyard to her own room.

During the night, after she was certain that Sadie was asleep, Merci rose and lit her lamp, keeping it dim. The rain poured steadily, so she covered herself with a thin wrap, clutching it with one hand and the lamp with the other.

She picked her way gingerly along the rain-slicked walkway and across the courtyard to the great room. Once inside, she set the lamp on a table. Shadows shifted against the walls as she moved to the corner where she'd left the chalice.

She lifted the silver cup into her hands and turned it slowly, admiring the workmanship. Even with the layers of grime covering its sides, it spoke of riches and security—a new beginning.

Moving with haste, she removed the wet wrap from her shoulders, wound the heavy silver piece inside it, and tucked it under her arm.

She slipped through the doorway and back to her room. After admiring the chalice once more, she returned to bed. Unable to stop the quick beating of her heart, she turned this way and that, pounded her pillow, and attempted to rest again. A rooster crowed in the distance just as she slipped into a troubled sleep.

A nightmare followed.

She was in the deepest night, lost in a desperate place, alone and afraid. She could see no glimmer of light. Trembling, she tried one road and then another, but all of them led to a dark, dank place whose stench turned her stomach.

Creatures the size of her fist moved about, frightening her with their gaping eyes. They reminded her of the formless lump of an unborn baby she had once scraped from her womb. They told her she belonged with them and promised she would never feel the pain of light again.

"Come to us. Join us," they chanted, clinging to her, beckoning her with their huge, glazed eyes. "Be one with us."

She tried to run, but her legs wouldn't move.

"Your blood is the same as ours," one said, with a knowing look. "You belong with us."

She saw into their translucent bodies, through their flesh and into their veins. They were filled with putrid filth, the same that pumped through her heart and veins.

She fell to her knees, terrified, crying.

A voice, soft and still, broke through the clamor.

MERCI, MY BELOVED…

She looked around, but all she could see was darkness.

MERCI, MY BELOVED, the voice called to her again.

This time she knew the words came from deep inside, and the murky shadows no longer terrified her.

A small flame burned in the distance.

Slowly she stood and moved toward it. The darkness lifted, and she looked up and saw a man standing there, waiting for her. He was clothed in a robe the color of the flame. Its light was made of love too deep to bear.

I AM THE WAY, BELOVED, he said. COME TO ME.

Merci trembled in fear. "I can't. There is vile death inside me, a decay that can't be cleansed." She began to weep.

COME TO ME, BELOVED, he said again, reaching for her. COME TO ME.

The flame blazed brighter now, surrounding him with a light more brilliant and painful than before. She needed to run from it, back to the darkness, back to the creatures twisting in their filth.

Heavy-hearted, she turned from him.

MERCI, MY BELOVED, he called after her.

She woke, crying. The dream, so vivid at first, soon disappeared. Merci was left with only a vague ache in her heart that caused her to wonder at its source.

She dressed and waited for the ashen dawn to light her way. When at last she slipped from her cell of a room, the rain had turned to a drizzle. Across the courtyard, Sadie's window was dark. Carrying the chalice in a bundle on her back, Merci headed through the puddles and mud to the courtyard gate. Once there she hesitated only briefly, looking back at Sadie's garden. Sadie had once said it was a gift, something to give back to God for the abundance of joy he had put in her heart.

What rubbish. What delusions.

Merci stepped through the gate, holding it carefully as it closed to keep it from creaking. The burden of the chalice seemed even heavier than before. Her shoulders ached, and she stopped to rest.

She slogged through the mud, past the chicken coop to the stable. Minutes later she mounted the mule, and without a backward glance she chirked for the animal to head out.

The rising sun was breaking through the clouds at her back, and she glimpsed the thin, bright strip of ocean to the west. The waves crested and broke in a mesmerizing rhythm, calling her closer.

She kicked the mule in the sides, and its quicker pace caused the chalice to thump painfully against her back.

It wasn't San Francisco she wanted, she realized with clarity. It was rest. Utter and sweet and irreversible rest.

The waves surged and foamed pale green and white. She was closer now, and she watched their thundering power, the lace they left behind on the wet sand. Lace that reminded her of her window curtains at the rancho.

She halted the mule and stumbled blindly to the water's edge, letting her legs fold beneath her. The chalice tumbled from the bundle on her back. She touched the figures on it, trailing her fingers over them only briefly before turning to the cresting waves.

They beckoned her, just as they had too often in the past.

Sweet rest. Darkness that will cradle me forever. No more pain. No more sorrow or tears.

No more thinking about the blood coursing through my veins, through my heart, blood putrid with sin.

She stood and took a single step toward the ocean. Then another. And another, until the water lapped at her ankles, ebbed, then covered her feet again.

God, if you are listening, let me die! I beg of you, let me die. I want to end my pain. The suffering I've caused others.

She waded deeper into the water. The waves swelled, whitecaps spraying from their crests. She felt their power moving against her legs, her torso, lifting her from the sand, then setting her down again. One more step, one more wave, and she would be free.

Let me die, she whispered, terrified of the rolling and crashing waves. She moved deeper into the water.

Another wave crested, and as it washed back into the sea, it swept her with it. She swallowed a mouthful of brine, coughed, and spit it out. Another wave swept over her head, and she closed her eyes, feeling it pull her deep under.

Let me die!

She heard a soft voice, still and utterly quiet, yet more powerful than the roiling waters around her.

MERCI, BELOVED.

It was the same voice she'd heard in her dream.

BE STILL, FOR I AM HERE. I AM WITH YOU.

Frantically, she opened her eyes, seeing only the rushing, foamy waters. *Where? Where are you?*

She was still holding her breath, her lungs ready to explode with the pain in her chest. *Let me die!*

NO, BELOVED.

I want to die!

Unable to hold her breath a second longer, she tried to propel herself to the surface. It was too far above her head. Weak, she quit struggling, and felt herself carried with the current as a mouthful of seawater flowed into her lungs.

TWENTY-FIVE

Quaid urged the sorrel to a brisk trot along the road leading from the village. The Santa Inez mission lay across the small valley in front of him, nestled among distant hills.

He'd awakened before sunup this morning, restless, unable to get thoughts of Merci from his mind. The prostitute in San Francisco had been drunk the night he asked her about his cousin. But he'd pieced together enough of her slurred words to figure that Merci was living with an ex-prostitute named Sadie Rose here in Santa Inez. When he asked about Sadie Rose, no one knew of her. Just as he was about to leave town the night before, someone mentioned a woman named Sadie who lived at the mission.

He remembered the garden—how, though no one answered his call at the gate, it seemed to contain an intimacy, as though someone lived there and cared for it. Today he noticed smoke curling from a small chimney in the back of the courtyard. He dismounted and headed to the gate. It was slightly ajar and creaked when he pushed it open to let himself through.

A woman was in the garden, pruning a rosebush when he entered. She looked up in surprise, stood, and walked toward him. The old drunk prostitute must have been wrong. This woman couldn't possibly have been the Sadie Rose she spoke of, a San Francisco madam.

"My name is Quaid Dearbourne," he said. "I'm trying to find my cousin Merci Byrne. I was told she might be here."

"She's spoken of you." She extended her hand to take his. Her grip was strong, and her look was full of inner peace. "My name is Sadie. I'm glad to meet you."

"Then, she's been here—or *is* here?" They walked to a bench in the center of the courtyard.

"She was here until sometime during the night, last night. I'm not certain if she's gone for good or if she's taken the mule for the day."

"Did she have things here? I mean, can you tell if she's planning to be back by what she left behind?"

Sadie let her gaze drift from his for a moment. When she looked back, her eyes were troubled. "I'd like to think otherwise, but Merci took something that makes me think she's gone for good.

"She didn't have much. Just some clothes and personal things," she continued as she moved to a statue of Saint Francis of Assisi and turned toward him again. "She also took a precious artifact belonging to the mission."

He stepped closer. "That doesn't sound like Merci. She's as honest as the day is long."

"She's changed since you saw her last." Sadie seemed to look straight into his heart. "Since you followed her here, you must have an idea of what happened to her."

"I've come to take her home."

Sadie looked thoughtful. "Unless her heart changes, I doubt that she'll go with you."

"That's been my prayer for the weeks I've been searching for her."

"Only God can change her heart—and she's got to want him to do it."

"You know her well."

"Merci didn't tell me much about her childhood or what drove her to this black place inside herself. I only know what God revealed to me of her spirit. There were times I caught glimpses of her darkness and pain. I sensed that she felt abandoned by God, by her mother, her family."

"Merci has borne a great tragedy, something that destroyed all the beauty in her world—the beauty of her own being, created by a loving God. The knowledge that she is worthy of love beyond all measure by him, by her family."

"What caused you to look for her?"

"A sense that I must."

She smiled gently. "The still, small voice."

"Merci's mother traced her path for a time, then felt she must let her daughter go." He let out a sigh. "I felt this urgency to take up where Brighid—her mother—left off."

"Sometimes God works that way. He lets more than one of his children care for his lambs on their journey."

At her mention of lambs, he remembered his dream the night he'd prayed for guidance about leaving. "Yes. Just as you cared for her." He paused. "I'm sorry about how she repaid you—stealing the artifact, I mean."

Sadie looked at him for a moment, then gave him a gentle smile. "I fear the burden of what she's done will weigh heavier than my loss."

"Do you know how long she's been gone?"

"We had a heavy rain last night. I doubt that she started out until the rain stopped just before dawn."

It was too much to hope for, but he asked anyway. "And her direction—do you have any idea?"

"She spoke often of San Francisco after our visit. Her desire to return there."

"San Francisco?"

Sadie nodded. "A prostitute can sell herself for more money there than anywhere else in California."

"She told you that?"

Sadie stared at him for several heartbeats. "I know because I worked there."

So the old prostitute had been right. He again studied Sadie's joy-filled face with wonder. "Then you've understood what Merci was going through."

"More than you can know." She looked thoughtful. "More than Merci could know." She hesitated as if puzzling something in her mind, then continued, "If you plan to follow her there, I can give you the names of madams who might help you."

She left him, then returned after a few minutes with a list of names and addresses. "Another thing—likely Merci wouldn't have wanted to be seen in town this morning. She might have headed to the beach.

There was a special place she rode to watch the waves and think—when she still had Knight."

"She sold him?"

"No. Some thugs overpowered her one time when she was alone. They didn't harm her other than breaking her heart. We searched but couldn't find him. She mentioned once in passing that she suspected a man named Cole was behind it. I believe she said he's from Santa Isabela. I offered to take her there, but she was too terrified of him to go there and find out for herself."

He took Sadie's hand and shook it. "Thank you for taking Merci in. For all the care you gave her."

Sadie inclined her head slightly and gave him a quick nod. "Jesus said, 'Feed my lambs.' I didn't do much by others' standards, but it was for him. And it's into his care we must release our Merci." Her eyes suddenly watered. "When you find her, tell her no matter what she's done or whether she thinks she has offended me, I am her friend. Tell her I love her."

"I will."

Within minutes, he'd mounted and was heading down the road that Sadie had told him about. A growing sense of urgency drove him on.

He urged the horse to a canter. The early morning sun had moved from behind its cloak of clouds and now hit him at a slant. He rode steadily toward the ocean. Soon salt and brine blew toward him on the breeze, the crash of the surf sounding like distant thunder. As he rode, every breath became a prayer.

Father, protect your lamb. Surround her with your mercy and grace. May it fall over her like a cloak.

Uphold her with your righteous right hand. Lift her now from the darkness and despair that threaten to overwhelm her.

Let her see your light. May it shine like a candle in a dark room and grow ever brighter.

I beg you to be with Merci. Hold her close, and let her know she is loved.

Quaid nudged the sorrel to a gallop, and soon the mare's hooves were thundering along the dirt road. They came over a rise, and the ocean showed in the distance.

A mule, its head down, grazed in a patch of weeds. Quaid scanned the beach, the stretch of sand and craggy rock formations, as he drew the sorrel to a halt. There was no sign of Merci.

His heart pounding, he looked out at the surf, the swells and the whitecaps. Surely she wasn't so despondent that she might take her own life. Or was she?

"Oh, God!" he cried aloud. Could that have been why he'd felt led to find her all those weeks ago? "Help me find her! Show me where she is. You've brought me this far—help me!"

The sky had darkened, turning the water a murky gray. His heart pumping, he started down the empty beach, stopping to search the rock formations and the surf, then running again.

He ran for a half-mile or so, then stopped and moved his gaze up and down the strand. Nothing.

He turned back to the clump of sea grass where the mule grazed and checked for footprints.

A spot of color caught between some points of volcanic rock near the surf captured his attention. Frowning, he walked toward the place.

Then his heart caught. Crimson hair streamed out onto the sand. Wet. The color of Merci's. He skirted the mound of stones and came around from the other side.

A woman lay facedown in the wet sand. She lay utterly still, her skin the color of marble.

He knelt beside her and touched her neck to check for a heartbeat, holding his breath and praying as he did.

It was there, as faint as the beat of a butterfly wing. "Oh, God, let her live," he whispered. "She is loved and cherished. Let her live, Father. Let her live!"

Merci saw a man in the distance. He spoke to some children sitting around him, calling them each by name. She heard their laughter bubbling, their childish voices calling out to him. "Abba, Father," they cried, and surrounded him with hugs and kisses as he sat down in their midst.

"Abba, Father," she breathed as she walked closer, wondering what it meant.

As she spoke the words, the man met her gaze and smiled. The children scampered off, laughing and running in the wind.

MERCI, BELOVED CHILD, COME UNTO ME.

She stepped closer, then fell to her knees in front of him. She was afraid to look him in the face and bowed her head in shame.

As she knelt, she felt the warmth of his hands on her bowed head. Her gaze down, she saw that his bare feet were imprinted with deep, ragged scars. She touched them, lightly pressing her fingers over the hardened wounds.

I am unworthy, she whispered, her head still bowed.

Tears filled her eyes and trailed down her cheeks, dripping onto her hands, her fingers. She rubbed the scars with her tears, flowing harder now. Her shoulders shook with the burden of her sin, the filth that filled her. Her hair fell forward, its tendrils mixing with her tears. Gently, she dried his feet with the matted strands, still aware of the warmth of his hands on her head.

I am unworthy, she cried softly. *So unworthy.*

He reached for her hands. At his touch her heart was stilled with a strange peace.

IT WAS FOR YOU I DIED.

Still weeping, she touched the scars on his right palm, then his left. She turned his hand and stroked the scars on the other side, and her tears trailed from her cheeks onto his flesh. She traced the ragged imprint with her wet fingertips. The suffering this One must have endured!

YOUR FACE WAS BEFORE ME WHEN I DIED, MERCI.

I WOULD HAVE DIED FOR YOU HAD YOU BEEN THE ONLY ONE IN THE WORLD.

Who are you? She was terrified.

I AM THE LORD YOUR GOD, THE ONE WHO IS WITH YOU ALWAYS, EVEN UNTO THE ENDS OF THE EARTH.

I am filthy, she cried in despair. She buried her face in her hands once more. *Don't look at me. Even the blood in my veins is filled with sin.*

MY BLOOD CAN MAKE THE VILEST CLEAN.

O God, I've denied you so many times. How can you love me now?

THOUGH YOU DENY ME, I LOVE YOU WITH AN EVERLASTING LOVE.

No! I don't believe in you!

GIVE YOUR HEART TO ME, MERCI. IT WILL NO LONGER BE STONE.

It turned to stone the day I found out about Mama's tragedy, she sobbed. *Why weren't you there? Why didn't you save her?*

I WAS THERE, MERCI. I FELT EVERY SEARING PAIN, EVERY HEARTACHE, EVERY FEAR. I CARRIED MY LAMB. I CARRY YOU NOW.

He lifted her into his arms, holding her on his lap as if she were a child, and she leaned against him. He held her fast, and she felt her tears begin to dry. Then he wrapped her in his robe, and she relaxed against his chest.

It should have been this way always, she thought. *I should have known the warmth of my father's arms around me. I should have known the feel of his heart thudding, the scratchy cloth of his garment against my cheek. I should have known my father's love.*

YOU ASKED THE MEANING OF ABBA, he said.

She nodded, still too overcome to speak.

YOUR HEAVENLY FATHER, he said, holding her close. ABBA, FATHER…DADDY.

She caught her breath in surprise and looked up at the man who held her. *Daddy,* she whispered in awe.

MERCI, MY BELOVED…

This time, as he spoke her name, his voice seemed to be made of rushing winds and the music of the seas and the earth and all their creatures, the stars in the heavens, singing together. His music rushed through her blood, filling her to overflowing. It flooded every part of her being and melted her heart of stone. Music so pure and filled with light and love, it cleansed and healed and washed away her filth. In awe, she looked into his eyes, seeing only love. Love more beautiful than an earthly father's for a child…love that would never end.

Smiling into her eyes, he stood and lifted her as though she were a child. She rested against his shoulder, and he carried her along a seashore that seemed to stretch into eternity.

Merci felt pulled from the velvet darkness that had enveloped her. Someone was standing over her, and at first she thought it might be the same One who had carried her along the seashore, held her with a strength she'd never known before. The One who said his name was Abba.

The One who had cradled her the way a father would a baby.

She wanted to go with him now, to feel the strength of his arms around her through eternity. But he had told her that it wasn't yet time.

Now, with her eyes still closed, she felt the sun on her skin, warming her.

She heard the voice of someone nearby. Perhaps bending over her.

She listened carefully, incredulously. It was Quaid, and he was telling God how much she was loved—by her Lord, by her family.

She didn't think she had the strength to open her eyes, so she reached for his hand. He stopped his prayer in midsentence, and a smile twitched the corner of her mouth. She knew her cousin never could stand a shock.

"Merci," he whispered. "Are you there? I mean, can you hear me?"

She opened her eyes.

He was staring down at her, his face as white as the clouds behind his head. "Merci?" he breathed.

"I'm home," she whispered. "I've come home."

Rejoicing, Quaid gathered her into his arms and put her on the horse in front of him. He wrapped his coat around her, and he tied the mule's reins to the back of the saddle. With Merci leaning against his chest, he chirked to the sorrel to start out.

"Don't expect too much cooperation," Merci murmured, still weak. "That mule is ready for the glue factory. And stubborn."

Quaid chuckled and glanced down at her. Her eyes were closed, but she looked more at peace than he'd ever seen her. "I've missed you, Merci. We all have."

Eyes still closed, she gave him a crooked half-smile. "We have a lot of catching up to do."

"I know…but if you'd rather not, well, say…"

"I won't want to talk about it for a while. I've got a lot of healing to do, a lot to work out in my mind."

"I understand."

"Tell me about my mother." Her voice was low and hoarse.

"She searched for you. She found a Bible in a room you'd used at the mission in Buena Ventura. She said that it made her think that God was directing you to people to help you on your way."

Merci kept her eyes closed, and her face was still deathly pale, a stark contrast to the wild tangle of dark red hair. "I'm so ashamed that I left the way I did. Only now can I think of the hurt she's endured."

"We've all been worried sick." He thought of his own part in her leaving and knew he couldn't wait any longer to ask her forgiveness."

"That day you left…" he began.

She reached for his hand. "I know what you're going to say." She paused as though the strain of talking was too much. They rode in silence for a few minutes before she continued. "What you told me that day had nothing to do with my leaving."

"We both wanted La Paloma. I need to ask your forgiveness, Merci. Please don't tell me it didn't matter to you. I know that it did."

He glanced down at her again and saw that her eyes were open. She nodded and drew in a deep breath. "Yes, I was hurt by it, Quaid. But it paled in comparison to what my mother had just told me." She gave him a soft smile. "And you are forgiven." Then her eyes filled. "But what you did is such a small thing—compared to my list of sins."

"Tell me what happened back there."

"On the beach, you mean." It wasn't a question.

"Yes."

She closed her eyes, and for a moment she didn't answer. "I'm not certain what happened." She fell silent again. "All I know is that the decay inside me became too much to bear."

"But you didn't take your life…" he prompted. "What made you change your mind?"

She opened her eyes and smiled at him, tilting her head up. "I didn't change my mind. When I understand it more fully, I'll tell you about it." She closed her eyes and leaned against him again, as if exhausted. She fell asleep, and the expression on her face was one of utter peace.

⎯⎯◆⎯⎯

"I've decided to stay on here," Merci told Quaid that night after supper. "That is, if you'll have me," she said to Sadie.

Sadie put aside the needlepoint pillow she was stitching and met Merci's gaze. "I think it's the perfect thing to do. You have a home here as long as you'd like."

Quaid had imagined killing the fatted calf and gathering the family for a celebration, and he felt a keen disappointment that Merci wouldn't be returning with him. But he knew his cousin needed time to heal, and Sadie was the only one who knew what she'd been through and what she faced in the future.

Sadie stood to get tea, leaving them alone.

"You will come home someday, though?" Quaid said to Merci.

"A herd of horses wouldn't keep me away. Is my suite of rooms still there? Or have you rented it out to bring in more money?"

He laughed. "It's still there, but I've got other news to tell you."

"You've inherited still another rancho?" She grinned.

"I'm getting married."

Merci nearly dropped her soup spoon. "You're what?"

"Me. If you can imagine such a thing. I'm marrying the most beautiful woman in the world."

Merci threw back her head and laughed. "Who's the unlucky…er, lucky girl?"

"Emmeline."

This time she did drop her spoon. "Emmeline Amity Callahan?" Her mouth fell open and stayed open. "You must tell me what happened."

So he told her every detail.

Merci smiled and leaned back to study him. "You sound like a man in love. Actually, you *look* like a man in love."

"I am!" He felt like shouting for joy again. "And you must promise me you'll be home for the wedding."

"That same herd couldn't keep me away. When is it?"

"We plan to be married in the spring—when the orange trees are in bloom. Some of those she put in first are nearly ready. We won't have the abundance of blossoms that we'll see in years to come, but still, there will be the fragrance—"

Merci choked. "Orange trees? You?"

He nodded. "They're not as hideous as I'd once thought. They grow on you."

She let out another choking laugh. "They *grow* on you?"

"In a manner of speaking." He didn't think he'd ever stop smiling. The joy on Merci's face was contagious. "There's something else I want to ask you, Merci."

She sobered at the serious tone his voice had taken. "What is it?"

"I want to give you the rancho."

Her mouth dropped open, and she stared at him as if uncomprehending.

"The house," he said, "where you grew up. Your home. Will you take it?"

Her eyes glistened with tears. Still, she gaped at him.

"I've made a tidy profit already, which was part of the agreement with our grandfather. So it isn't that I haven't been able to make a go of it."

Her silence was unnerving. He cleared his throat. "I was thinking that I'll take the cattle-grazing land that butts against Emmeline's property, and you can have the acreage north of the house. Even the river will be yours."

She just stared at him, an unfathomable expression in her eyes. And he wondered if she hadn't forgiven him after all. Maybe his gift was too little too late. He felt his face flush, and again he cleared his throat. "Well now, if my offer isn't acceptable, I'll give you the cattle grazing land too. I just didn't think you'd want a bunch of smelly—"

She reached for the needlepoint pillow that Sadie had been sewing and threw it at his head. Her smile spread from ear to ear across her face. "Just be quiet a minute, Quaid, and let me cry."

"Cry?"

"You'd better get used to it. A woman cries when she can think of no other way to adequately express her joy."

In the soft lamplight he could see that, sure enough, Merci's face was filled with a shining glow he found wondrous.

It had been a long time since he'd seen such a beautiful sight.

Merci and Sadie walked to the stables with Quaid at dawn the next morning. He gave Merci a hug and shook Sadie's hand, then mounted the sorrel. Sadie handed him a small parcel of bread and fruit for his journey.

He headed down the road leading from the mission, then craned in the saddle. Merci's thicket of bright red hair stood out against the gray dawn. She smiled and blew kisses to him with both hands.

He thought his heart might burst with joy.

The sorrel moved into a brisk trot, and Quaid headed to the coast, taking the same road as the day before. This time, however, he turned south and headed straight for Santa Isabela, where he planned to find the man named Cole.

TWENTY-SIX

The shadows were long when Quaid rounded the curve leading into Santa Isabela. A low-burning fury filled him when he spotted the Ice House. He dismounted and, without a break in his stride, burst through the swinging doors.

The saloon keeper looked up with a frown. "You in a hurry, mister?"

"I'm looking for Adam Cole," he said, winding his way through a swarm of small wooden tables. He tossed his hat onto one. "I understand he frequents this place."

"Who's asking?" The barkeep's voice wasn't unfriendly, but it was cautious.

Quaid forced himself to give the man a half-smile and a nod. "I heard he's got a horse for sale. It's all the talk just north of here."

"That right?" The man poured a shot of whiskey for someone at the end of the bar and slid the glass toward him. He looked back to Quaid. "I suppose I can give Cole your name. Where're you staying?"

Quaid ignored the question. He planned to get out of Santa Isabela as quickly as possible. "He live around these parts?"

"He might."

"As a rule, I'm long on patience. Right now I'm in a hurry to be on my way. If you don't think he's interested in selling, then so be it." Quaid shrugged, and turned to head to the door.

"Wait a minute," the barkeep called to Quaid. "He's in the back. I'll see if he wants to talk to you."

Quaid gave him a nod and pulled out a chair by the table where he'd left his hat. Within two minutes, a man fitting the description that Merci had given him sauntered into the room.

He stuck out his hand. "Adam Cole," he said with a curt nod and a hard look as he sat down opposite Quaid.

Quaid matched his look with a plastered-on smile. "Dearbourne," he said simply. He leaned back in his chair, balanced it on the back two legs, and laced both hands into a knot behind his head. "I hear you might have a stallion you're looking to sell."

"I raise horses. I have several I'm ready to sell."

"My family's got a spread near the Central Valley. A place called Valley of the Horses. We're always on the lookout for good horseflesh."

There was a flicker of recognition in his eyes. "Are you related to Spence Dearbourne?"

"He's my father."

Cole's face split into a grin. He stood, reached across the table again, and grabbed Quaid's hand. This time he shook it vigorously. "Why didn't you say so?" He sat back down, shaking his head and still smiling. "I've long been an admirer of his way with horses. I've never met him, but I've always wanted to see him work. From what I hear, he can gentle a wild horse just by whispering in its ear."

Quaid's laugh was short. "It's not quite that easy. But you're right. That's part of it."

Cole leaned forward. "Tell me, do you have the gift?"

"The gift?"

He nodded. "Yes. Horse gentling. Did your father pass it on to you?"

"I'm not certain it's a gift. Perhaps it's just a mix of patience and an understanding of animals. Treating them the way you might treat a fellow human being." He met Cole's look with an unblinking gaze. "Provided you treat your fellow human beings in a decent manner."

"Can you do it?" Cole persisted. "Can you gentle horses?"

Quaid studied the man. The conversation was taking a different turn than he'd anticipated, but he was eager to see where it might lead. "My father taught me some of the rudiments, yes." He paused. "That's not why I'm here. My father's always on the lookout for breeding stock. The reputation of a black stallion you recently acquired has spread around the countryside. I'm sure he'd be interested." He gave the man a charming smile. "I just thought I'd stop by and have a look at him. I'll let my father know what I think."

"The horse you speak of is a firebrand. Can't be handled."

"Are you saying you'd like us to take him off your hands?"

Cole laughed. "Not at all. I'm saying I'd like to talk to your father about hiring him to train the horse. Calm him down. Get a saddle on him again."

"He's been ridden before then?"

"Oh yes. Though we hear he's not been ridden with a saddle for some time."

"What happened?"

A shadow crossed Cole's face, and he frowned. "We, ah, bought him from a middleman. We're not certain what happened during transit. But apparently something spooked him. He's been in a rage since he arrived. Bit a stableboy who tried to groom him."

"My father might be willing." Quaid shrugged. "I wouldn't know until I asked him." He laughed lightly. "I can tell you one thing for sure."

"What's that?"

"My father doesn't make house calls."

"I didn't expect he would."

"You would have to bring him to Valley of the Horses yourself."

"Perhaps we won't need to do that." Cole looked at Quaid with greater interest. "I'll take you over to my spread, show you the beast. See what you can do."

Quaid held up his hands, chuckling. "I'm not the man you need. I'll take a look, but if the horse is in that much distress, you need a real trainer."

"I'd appreciate it if you'd come along. Tell me what you think." He stood and nodded toward the street. "I drove my buggy in this morning. You can ride with me. I've got business in town later. I'll bring you back.

Quaid stood and put on his hat. "Let's go." He led his horse to the livery pen for watering, then climbed into the buggy next to Cole.

A half-hour later, just at dusk, they pulled onto a long, winding road at the top of a cliff above the Pacific. A two-story adobe hugged the side of the precipice. Other than the outer white-fenced boundaries, the landscape was broken only by some bald aspen and a couple of barren oaks interspersed with tufts of winter grass. A dozen or more horses grazed in the waning light.

They drove around the house to a large barn at the northernmost edge of Cole's sweep of land. Cole unhitched the team and led Quaid into the barn. All was quiet until they reached the rear of the cavernous room and Cole opened the stall.

A dark stallion in an iron muzzle looked out at the two men, bulge-eyed and wild. It was too dark to know if the gleaming black stallion was Knight.

Cole disappeared for a moment, then returned with a lantern. Quaid was sick with fury when he saw the raw flesh beneath the muzzle and the fear in the horse's eyes.

"Let's get this thing off," he muttered to Cole.

The other man shook his head. "I don't want to be responsible for you losing your hand."

"I'll take my chances. Get it off now." He stepped back to hold the lantern while Cole unfastened the iron monstrosity. The man quickly threw it to the ground and backed out of the stall. The horse reared, his hooves raking the air just inches from Cole's head.

Cole fell, then scrambled backward, crablike, lifting his hands to protect his head.

Quaid didn't think he could keep his own fury at the man from exploding. First because of what he'd done to Merci. Now this. It didn't matter whether it was Knight or some other helpless victim of the maniac's vicious control. For one deranged moment, he considered putting the muzzle on the man's despicable face. Instead he focused on the horse.

The authorities would be notified about Cole and his illegal practices later. For now Quaid just wanted to get this horse to safety.

As he considered the mud-caked beast, with its wild eyes and running wounds, he doubted he could calm it. Saddling it would be out of the question. For his plan to work, he would have to make a run for it bareback.

If this was Knight, perhaps he could be calmed enough to ride. But only one person had ever ridden him without so much as a blanket. That person was Merci.

Cole pushed himself to standing, behind Quaid and at a healthy distance from the horse.

Perfectly still, Quaid stared unblinking at the angry stallion's eyes, then he moved slowly, effortlessly toward the horse.

He waited a few seconds, watching the quivering beast. Puffs of air blew from his nostrils, and he shied backward away from Quaid. His eyes rolled, still wild and angry.

Quaid had watched his father hundreds of times as he calmed horses. It was an art that hadn't captured Quaid's imagination, so he hadn't paid close attention. Merci had, though, at every chance. He closed his eyes, picturing his father teaching Merci how to work with the magnificent horse. He remembered the gentle strength of his father as Spence wordlessly communicated with the stallion, and he remembered his cousin Merci's face, as bright with joy as it was with freckles, as she stroked the beast, patting and rubbing his neck, whispering in his ear.

Quaid opened his eyes to see the horse watching him warily. "It's all right, boy," he said quietly and took another step closer.

The horse backed into the pen, lifted his head and snorted, his nostrils flaring as he exhaled.

"You're safe now, big boy. You're safe."

The stallion's eyes rolled again, and he reared, though halfheartedly. Quaid held his ground and waited. "We'll get you out of here. You'll see. Things are better beyond the door. You'll find safe pasture. I promise." His voice was calm, smooth, low. "It's all right, big boy."

He stepped closer, and again the horse shied away. His sides had stopped heaving, and he exhaled again, this time accompanied by a shudder and a shake of the mane. Quaid looked into the beast's eyes, and the animal reared.

When the horse had settled again, Quaid closed his eyes and pictured his father. Why hadn't he paid more attention? He tried to remember those things his father did—or didn't do—when gentling a horse.

Spence never looked a horse in the eyes, Quaid remembered. He kept his gaze averted, so the horse wouldn't think he was being challenged.

Drawing a deep breath, Quaid moved forward, this time keeping his eyes to one side. He focused on the big stallion's mane and took another step. Soon he was close enough to reach out and rub the beast's neck. Instead of following his first instinct, he remained as still as a statue, crooning and whispering, and at times almost singing.

The horse danced sideways, then calmed again. "I'm here to help you, big boy," Quaid whispered. "But you've got to trust me. Can you do that?" He sidled closer, and holding his breath, touched the stallion's neck. He let his hand rest there only briefly before removing it. The horse stood perfectly still, so Quaid ran his palm down the stallion's side, rubbing gently.

He continued patting, crooning, whispering, as he moved his hands to check the big animal for injuries. There was indeed a cut, and fairly deep it seemed, on one fetlock. But by far, the worst damage had been caused from the iron muzzle. Even in the dim light of the lantern behind them, he could see that the sores would take weeks to heal. Likely they would leave scars. Quaid's heart went out to the beast.

It now seemed that this horse was indeed Knight. Perhaps Quaid hadn't watched the details of his father's work with horses, but he had never seen one gentle as quickly as this big black did. He figured the horse knew his voice. Quaid had never ridden him, but he'd cleaned out his grandfather's stables many times, led this big fellow out to pasture and talked to him—also to Merci or their grandfather—in his presence.

He looked back to Cole. The man looked amazed at the transformation in the stallion. "I ought to hire you, young man."

Quaid gave him an amiable grin. "Make me an offer." He continued patting down Knight's back, stroking and crooning. Then he said to Cole, "I'd like to take him out to the pasture. Maybe try riding him before I leave. Make sure he'll be all right with it."

"You're going to try to saddle him?"

Quaid shook his head. "Might spook him. He's got some nasty sores on his head from the muzzle. He'd never stand for any kind of restraint right now." He chuckled. "We'll have to start over with him."

"Whatever you say." The man was obviously in awe of Quaid's work with the horse.

"All right, big guy," Quaid whispered to the stallion and stepped back from the stall's opening. "You come with me now. Nice and slow. Easy, boy. Easy." And he led the horse down the center of the barn to the outer door.

A moment later they were outside. "All right, boy. You can halt." The horse's nostrils were flaring again, and his sides were heaving in fear. Quaid touched his neck, running his hand down, patting gently. "I'm here, boy. I'm here."

His hand on the horse's back, he continued walking a few steps toward the fence, then back again. He took away his hand and continued walking. The horse followed.

Quaid drew in a deep breath. Knight trusted him. At least he trusted him as a walking companion, Quaid thought wryly. It would be something else to trust Quaid after he'd mounted.

"I believe I'll try riding him a ways," he called over to Cole.

Standing by the barn with the lantern, Cole gave him a salute. "Have at 'er." He laughed. "Don't go too far, now."

"I may take him down the road, just see how he behaves. I don't want him to spook when we try to saddle him. I think that's probably what started all this—am I right?"

"Yes sir. Now that I think about it, you're right. First time we tried to saddle him, he took off like a bull out of a chute."

"That's what I figured. Something tells me this horse may be more at home with a bareback rider than with a saddle."

Quaid tried to calculate how to mount the beast without a stirrup. He'd seen his father do it plenty of times. Also Merci, but for the life of him, he couldn't remember how either accomplished the task. He sized up the fence, then walked with Knight toward it.

"This is going to be harder on me than it is on you." He grunted as he stepped onto the bottom rung. He swung his leg over the stallion's back and settled onto him. The horse sidled a few steps, then moved back again and snorted.

"I'm just as new at this as you are," Quaid whispered, "but your well-being may depend on what you do these next few minutes."

Quaid gave Cole a friendly wave to show off the horse's behavior, then nudged Knight's sides gently with his heels. "Not too fast, boy, or you'll be riderless again. Can't have that, big fella."

The horse moved slowly toward the gate and through. "Good boy." Quaid patted his neck. "Nice and slow, now. Keep going. Good boy."

They moved along the outside of the fence. "I'll just see how he does on the open road," he called over to Cole with another wave. "Take him up that way a piece." He pointed north.

"Go ahead, young man," Cole called. "You earned it!"

A full moon was yet to rise, but the road was visible in the fading twilight as they turned south. "I think we may have done it," he breathed after a few minutes.

Once they were out of Cole's sight, he urged Knight to move to a brisk trot. It was difficult to hold on, even bent over the horse's neck and clinging to the mane, so Quaid slowed him again. He knew Cole would be after them any minute. He just hoped the man would ride north first, before turning back.

They had ridden a half-hour when Santa Isabela loomed before them in the moonlight. Behind them the distant sound of hooves carried on the night air. He headed the stallion to the livery, dismounted, and led his sorrel from the pen.

Quickly he mounted his own horse, then whistled to Knight and headed off the road. Moments later, the surefooted stallion followed the sorrel down a winding trail to the beach below the cliff. Quaid urged the sorrel to a canter, and from time to time, craned to see if Knight was following. The big horse kept pace behind them, mane and tail flying.

The moon had fully risen and cast a silver glow on the breaking waves. Quaid grinned at the sight of the black stallion running across the sand in the moonlight. He wished Merci were here to see it.

He halted the sorrel, and Knight stopped alongside them, sides heaving from the exertion.

As the moon rose higher, Quaid smiled. The sight was the nearest thing to heaven he'd experienced lately. The horses running along the silver-foamed water…the biggest moonrise since the night he'd ridden to the overlook with Emmeline. Heaven itself couldn't have been prettier.

The one person who would make the evening perfect was Emmeline, riding her Appaloosa beside him. Sighing, he pictured her the last time he'd seen her. She'd been standing near her groves, watching him as he rode in to say good-bye. The morning sun touched her in a way that made her hair look like spun gold, her eyes like liquid amber.

It sparked a flame in his heart to think of her, to remember how she felt in his arms…the touch of her lips on his. Honey sweet, they were.

Tomorrow he would be home. Grinning, he decided he would head straight to Emmeline instead of Rancho de la Paloma. Nothing was more important than pulling that handsome woman into his arms again and holding her tight against his chest.

The horses began running along the sand again, and he laughed, considering her surprise to see him. He'd bought her a ruby ring in Carmel-by-the-Sea, and he imagined her beautiful face, the light in her eyes, when he presented it and asked her again to marry him.

He chuckled. This time he'd do it proper. He would kneel, take her hand…and pledge his everlasting love.

As the horses thundered along the beach, wet sand spraying from their hooves, he wondered if Emmeline still loved him as much as he loved her.

TWENTY-SEVEN

"The proof is undeniable," Court MacQueen said, spreading the plat maps on the table. He looked down to study them a moment, then back to Emmeline. Absently he pushed back some strands of hair that had fallen across his forehead. "You can't ignore the truth any longer, Emmeline."

At his request Emmeline had arrived at the town hall before the other members of Citizens for California's Citrus. Sitting across the table from Court, she watched him place stout bottles of India ink at each corner of the maps to keep them unfurled.

Seating himself with a heavy sigh, he looked solemn as he pulled papers from a valise to his side. They bore the seal of the U.S. Department of Agriculture.

"I refuse to believe that Quaid Dearbourne had anything to do with the altering of these maps. I know him." She leaned back in her chair and studied the man in front of her.

Seeming unaware of her scrutiny, he let his gaze flick across the documents he held in his hands. Finally he looked up and met her gaze. "I'm afraid it's out of your hands now. This is a more serious matter than simply a land dispute between two neighbors."

"I assume you've called this meeting because you have new evidence?"

He nodded. "Irrefutable evidence showing that Quaid Dearbourne made the changes." He paused. "I'm sorry." He paused again. "And I'm assuming—as are others whom I've asked to investigate—that his group for keeping California wild is behind it." His voice was laced with sarcasm.

"I'll believe it when I see it." She looked at him evenly.

Court handed her the first document, a letter from the first under secretary of the Agriculture Department. She took it from him and leaned forward to read, frowning. She skimmed the opening paragraph, a word of greeting from someone who was obviously a friend of MacQueen's.

The second paragraph caught her attention.

> Regarding the matter you have asked me to investigate, I have made inquiries into the federal government's role in the original plans for and the subsequent building of the dam on the fork of the San Jacinto River in Riverview County.
>
> At your request we have located the cartographer who conducted the original studies for said dam, its placement, the land directly and indirectly affected by the dam and its subsequent irrigation systems. The cartographer, Quinton Rafael, is now living in Mexico City. I have corresponded with him, and at my request he has generously provided an affidavit swearing to the truth of his statement.
>
> His statement, with notarized signature, is attached to this post.
>
> If I can be of further assistance…

The letter was signed by the under secretary, his official seal affixed on top of his signature. She handed it to Court, who handed her the second document.

She glanced at it quizzically. It was written in Spanish. Shaking her head, she gave it back to him. "I don't read Spanish."

"Here's the translation," Court said, thumbing through the papers in his valise again and placing the text in her hands.

She began to read the cartographer's affidavit.

> Of course I remember my work on the San Jacinto River and the properties that border it. I mapped many sections of land during the years 1859 to 1889. I do not recall every

detail about every plat map, but I do recall the disagreement between the Byrne property owners and the Dearbourne property owners. This is a dispute that goes back to the 1860s.

At various times I have met with members of both families to examine the maps and to reiterate the lawfulness of the property boundaries.

My most recent meeting was with Quaid Dearbourne, heir to the Byrne property, Rancho de la Paloma. As I recall he was made heir to La Paloma in 1889, just before I traveled to Mexico City to make my home here. It was early that same year that we met. I also provided him with copies of the identical maps to both properties.

When he asked to see the plat maps and discuss the quadrants with me, I readily agreed. We sat together in the County Office of Records, and I explained how the lines had been determined in accordance with the wishes of the original rancho owners, Hugh Dearbourne, his paternal grandfather, and MacQuaid Byrne, his maternal grandfather, to bring water to both ranchos.

I also explained that because of unusual canyon topography, the lines were drawn so that the dammed river fork sits on Rancho de la Paloma. The fork of the river running freely belongs to the Dearbourne lands—an exact opposite to what one might expect on a plat map such as this.

This is a complex property-line differentiation. To answer your question in as straightforward a manner as I can, I will say this: *The water flowing from the San Jacinto River belongs to the Dearbourne Rancho, not to Rancho de la Paloma.*

I can return to Riverview and swear to the truth of the above statement, should it be required in a court setting. I can also attest to the authenticity of my documents with witnesses from the years in question, whose positions at the Riverview County Office of Records put them in a position to verify the truth of my statements.

Emmeline's heart thudded in her chest. She stared at the letter, then reread it twice before handing it back to Court.

"It doesn't prove that Quaid made the changes himself." She glared at him, her mind desperate to find a plausible explanation. She couldn't come up with one.

"No, it doesn't," Court agreed, putting the documents into his valise. "It does prove, however, that Quaid Dearbourne knew of the original course of the river. The water now flows through his land—wouldn't you think he'd question such a turnabout in a river?" He paused. "And I ask you again, who else would benefit from keeping silent about such a matter, even if he didn't tamper with the maps?"

She clenched her jaw and didn't answer.

Court pointed to the plat map, tracing his finger along the lines that had been altered. Heartsick, she followed his gaze. "Quaid wouldn't do such a thing. Perhaps one of the more radical members of his cooperative."

"I've taken it upon myself, on behalf of the U.S. Government, to ask Quinton Rafael to travel back to Riverview and testify in court to the authenticity of his original documents—and to declare that the two maps before us are forgeries."

Apprehension flooded through her. She stood and leaned forward. "Why would you do that?"

"For one so concerned about her groves, especially after last summer's drought, my dear, you don't seem too concerned with getting back your water rights."

"Of course, I want those rights—but what kinds of charges are you planning to bring against Quaid Dearbourne?" Her heart caught as she said his name. "You mentioned taking him to court. What are the criminal charges?" She drew herself up to her full height. "I am the injured party, and I am not going to bring a single civil charge against him. As far as I'm concerned, there is no case."

Court raised a brow. "Think about it. He or someone in his group committed several federal crimes that I can think of and probably a host of others that we don't know about." He laughed. "We'll start with forgery, tampering with official U.S. Department of Agriculture documents, the County Office of Records documents, conspiracy…"

"Conspiracy?"

He nodded. "Conspiracy to commit fraud."

She couldn't listen to another word. She turned to leave as members of the Citizens for California's Citrus began drifting through the door, chatting amiably, and taking their seats.

"One more thing, Emmeline," Court said, above the noise of chairs scooting across the tile floor.

She halted and looked at him.

"You might want to stay for this meeting. I've invited Quinton to join us. He'll be speaking to us about water rights."

She stared at him.

"Specifically, I've asked him to tell us what he knows about the Dearbourne and La Paloma boundary lines and water rights. It might prove interesting to you. Please stay." Smiling, he held out his hand to the chair nearest him. "We'll also be joined by two officials from the Riverview County Office of Records."

Instead of sitting, Emmeline stood near the door at the back of the room. The three officials filed in and began to testify to the truth of what Court had already told her. She listened to each of the men speak, then, as the group bent over the plat maps, slipped from the room.

She hurried from the town hall, eager to gulp in huge breaths of fresh air.

A familiar voice behind her caused her to turn around. Court was rushing toward her. "I have some calls to make out your direction this afternoon. I'd like to stop by and see how the new grove is surviving the rains."

She stared at him, her mind anywhere but on her groves. A damp breeze lifted her hair, and she reached for her hat to keep it from blowing away. "They're thriving," she finally said. "They were in desperate need of moisture."

"I can stop by later this afternoon. Will that be convenient for you?"

His job with the Department of Agriculture was to help the growers. He had helped her and others. Countless times. He'd taught them how to use smudge pots to keep the trees from freezing. Gave them illustrations of parasites and pests, and tips on how to handle leaf diseases. But that didn't mean she was required to let him see her groves. She shook her head. "There's no need. Really."

"Lack of drainage and the resulting root rot can damage or even kill young trees. I probably should come out and take a look. I'm examining your neighbors' groves for the same disease. It's no trouble to stop by on my way." He laughed lightly, obviously trying to put her at ease.

He reached for her hand. "I'm terribly sorry to put you through all this. I realize how distasteful it is. Your families go back years, isn't that right?"

She pulled her hand from his grasp. "I'm not related by blood, but yes, the Dearbournes and Byrnes have been close for decades."

"This isn't easy for you—your father being a Dearbourne and all." He was watching her expectantly.

She didn't answer.

"I'll see you this afternoon, then," he said somewhat awkwardly.

"All right." She started to walk away, then looked back. "What time?"

"I'll be there at four o'clock." He beamed and waved heartily. "No hard feelings now, Em, about the investigation, I mean," he called to her. "I'm simply looking out for your best interests. Yours and those of the other growers."

She glared at him until he was out of sight, then she turned to head down the boardwalk to the livery to fetch her buggy.

She blinked. And halted in midstep.

Quaid stood in front of her, muddy boots a few feet apart, duster snapping in the wind. He nodded and touched his hat brim. "Emmeline."

Her mouth went dry. "Quaid," she croaked, then cleared her throat and tried again. "When did you get back?"

"Just now."

He nodded, seeming unable to take his eyes from her. "I see you've been busy while I've been away." His gaze drifted over her shoulder to the place where Court had been standing a moment earlier.

Emmeline didn't know what to say. She just stood there, gazing into his eyes and feeling she might melt away at any minute. "You've been gone a long time," she finally managed.

"Too long, it appears."

She stared at him, taking in everything from the stormy hue of his eyes to the cut of his strong jaw. She bit her lip to keep from hurling herself into Quaid's arms. His glowering expression told her that that was the last thing he wanted.

He gazed at her for a moment longer, then spun on booted heel and strode back across the cobbled street. Silently, she stared after him as he mounted the sorrel, then headed out of town, a riderless black horse behind him.

When he was out of sight, Emmeline's heartache hit her full force. Blinking back the sting that threatened her eyes, she hurried across the street toward the livery. She reached the weatherworn building and hesitated, unwilling to leave town just yet. After a moment's pause, she walked along the river to the small, white church, opened the door, and stepped inside.

The sanctuary was dimly lit, which suited her mood. She slipped down the aisle and entered a pew toward the back. Once seated, she lifted her eyes to the stained-glass window behind the altar.

I need answers, Father.

Can it possibly be that his man I love is capable of deception? Did he really do this thing that Court thinks he's done?

ABIDE IN ME.

Life used to be simple, Father. Now it's more puzzling than ever. When the questions are uncomplicated, it's easy to abide in you. But now...this? She laughed lightly. *Oh, that I could sequester myself from the world. If I could live in a monastery and seek your face…then, perhaps, I would know the answers to my questions.*

My questions plague me, Lord. Did Quaid know about the change in the river rights? Should I warn him about what others are saying? If I do, will he think I don't trust him?

Do I trust him?

ABIDE IN ME, BELOVED.

You've said you'll give me the desires of my heart…if I abide in you. I keep looking at my circumstances instead of you, Father. I abide in them!— in my groves, in my troubles…especially in my questions.

What should I do, Lord?

ABIDE IN ME, PRECIOUS CHILD. ABIDE IN ME.

She sat in the quiet of the church, listening to the falling rain outside the windows.

A door opened in the foyer behind her, then closed with a soft thud seconds later. Approaching footsteps echoed through the sanctuary, slowing when they reached the pew behind her. The bench creaked as someone settled into it. The smell of damp buckskin wafted toward her.

She turned, and Quaid met her gaze, his face solemn. He looked travel-worn, but now, an irresistible warmth flickered in his eyes. His lashes and brows held a sprinkling of raindrops. His boyish look disarmed her. He tossed his hat to a place beside him on the pew.

"I couldn't leave without speaking to you," he said quietly. "I turned back in time to see you come in here. I waited around out front for a few minutes, then couldn't wait a minute longer to see you." He grinned. "Besides, I was getting wet." Rivulets of rain were dripping from the sleeves and collar of his duster.

She nodded. "I'm glad you came back." Then she thought of speaking to him about the plat maps, and a chill traveled up her spine. *Oh, Lord! How can I ask him what I must?*

"I apologize for what I implied out there awhile ago…about MacQueen," Quaid went on.

"There's nothing between Court and me. There couldn't be." The corners of her mouth curved slightly. She couldn't hold back her smile.

He raked his hair with his fingers and slouched back in the pew. It didn't strike her as an irreverent pose—instead, his position spoke of his comfort at being in God's house. She turned sideways to face him, stretched her arm across the wood, and set her chin on her elbow.

"I've missed you," he said, his voice gruff. He touched her forearm lightly, then pulled back his hand. "When I saw MacQueen say he'd see you at four o'clock, I lost my temper."

Merciful heavens, the man was jealous! Her smile deepened.

Quaid frowned. "I have so much to tell you. I was hoping to come by this afternoon—after I see Brighid." He gave her a half-grin. "But as I understand it, MacQueen will be there."

"I'd rather spend time with you, Quaid." She paused, delighting in the way his face lit up with the invitation, then she went on, "Brighid read us your telegram. We rejoiced with her about Merci."

He sat forward, supporting his elbows on his knees and letting his hands hang loose. His face softened as he related how he'd found Merci, and after he finished, they settled back, looking at each other in the soft darkness of the room. A light wind had kicked up outdoors, and the rain sliced against the windows.

He played with her fingers. "I'd like to see you home."

"I would like that too."

They spoke for a few more minutes, then stood to walk down the aisle. They had just stepped outside the door, when another gust of wind caught them by surprise. Emmeline shivered. She'd always hated the wind.

"Just the excuse I needed," Quaid said, circling his arm around her.

Holding his duster over her head, they made their way down the main street of town. She snuggled close to him beneath the protective cover, delighting in his warmth, in the scent of damp buckskin mixed with lye soap, in his tender expression when she tilted her face upward to meet his gaze.

As soon as they reached the livery and he'd paid the groom, he hitched her horse to the buggy and tied his sorrel to the back. He let the black out of a pen by itself, explaining as he did that the stallion belonged to Merci. Laughing, he told her in great detail how he'd deceived Adam Cole so he could free the horse.

"Besides," he said with a wink, helping Emmeline onto the buggy bench, "this horse belongs to Merci. I was just taking back what was hers."

Just as the water rights belonged to her, not Rancho de la Paloma.

She caught her breath and turned away from him. She hadn't meant to consider the terrible thought!

"Emma," he said, looking puzzled, "what's wrong?" Gently, he turned her face toward him.

"You deceived Cole."

His laugh was short, bitter. "You are questioning why I rescued Knight?"

"Not why. Just your methods."

"The man is evil. You don't know what he did to Merci," he growled, looking away from her. "You don't want to know." He rounded the buggy and stepped up to sit beside her.

Soon they headed away from the stables and onto the road. The rain pounded the buggy's bonnet, and Emmeline worried about whether the muddy road home would be passable. Not as much, though, as she worried about the silence that had fallen between them.

"Something is troubling you," he said finally, glancing over at her. "And I don't think it has anything to do with my methods in taking Knight back from a horse thief."

The rain fell softly around them, and Emmeline closed her eyes as the carriage swayed and rumbled along through the mud. How could she tell him? Should she tell him?

"You know how I feel about deception," she said. Only after the words were out of her mouth did she realize she hadn't meant to utter them at all.

He glanced over at her, frowning. "What are you talking about?"

"Please don't ask me to explain." She looked over at him bleakly.

"When two people love each other," he said, "they don't keep from speaking their minds."

She nodded miserably. "I know. That's what makes this so hard." Her hands were trembling. She pulled her gloves from her pocket and drew them on.

Quaid reached over and placed one hand above her two small ones. "You're shaking," he said, studying her with a puzzled expression. "What has happened?"

Oh, Lord, how can I tell him? She looked into his face, desperately wanting to tell him, desperately wanting him to laugh and explain it away. Fear struck her heart and made her bite back her words. The question would cause him to think she doubted him. "This isn't easy, Quaid," she sighed.

He frowned. "Perhaps I guessed right about Court MacQueen after all."

"No," she whispered. "This is something else entirely." Her throat constricted as she tried to swallow. She stared into the gray veil of rain ahead of them, aware that she couldn't bring herself to tell him anything more.

He halted the buggy, right there in the rain in the middle of the muddy road. "We spoke once of love and marriage, yet you're keeping whatever is worrying you to yourself. Don't you think I deserve to know whether it's something so troubling that you're thinking of changing your mind…about marriage, I mean?"

The sting behind her eyes started again, and she blinked, knowing tears were about to spill. She stared into the rain, fearing that once the question left her lips, a chasm would result so wide it couldn't be bridged. Ever.

Because it had to do with trust.

She reached across the buggy seat and touched his face, stroking his jaw with her gloved fingertips. "I can only tell you one thing, Quaid."

He frowned.

"I love you more than I can ever imagine loving anyone."

"Oh, Emma," he murmured, his voice a husky groan.

He pulled her close, and she relaxed in his embrace, feeling only the thud of his heart and the warmth of his arms.

After a moment, he pulled back and looked deep into her eyes as if searching for answers of his own. A heartbeat later, he popped the whip over the horse's back. Emmeline ventured a glance his direction as they turned onto her property. He was staring into the gray mist, apparently lost in thought.

They pulled close to the front door, and he halted the mare. Then he stepped from the buggy, rounded it, and looked up at her.

Giving her a crooked grin that made her heart turn over, he swung her onto the ground. Before he released her, he lifted her face with his hand, and brushed a soft kiss across her forehead. He gathered her into his arms and held her there, rocking gently back and forth. She sighed, wanting to stay there forever.

He pulled back and, after gazing into her eyes, bent to kiss her again. This time she thought her knees might buckle before he was through.

"Merciful heavens!" she whispered when she could breathe.

Closing her eyes, she attempted to push the question of trust from her mind once again.

Twenty-Eight

Quaid was halfway to Rancho de la Paloma when the rain turned to a drizzle. He rode through the rancho gates just as the late afternoon sun was streaming through the clouds, creating bars of light that bore down on the land. The sky seemed alive with an explosion of power, both from the light and from the thunderheads building in the west.

As he rode toward the hacienda, Brighid waved from where she stood waiting on the portico, Quaid's dog, Blue, at her side. He grinned at her and headed around the house to deliver the horses into the care of the stableboy. Brighid was waiting for him when he returned. He gave her a joyous hug, lifting her off the ground.

She threw back her head and laughed as he put her down. "I got my first letter from Merci yesterday! The telegram you sent warmed my heart." She looked as if she would never stop smiling. "But it didn't compare to hearing from her in person!"

He opened the heavy entry door for his aunt, then followed her through, Blue trailing at his heels. He stopped to rub the dog behind his ears, and Blue sat, his tail thumping the floor vigorously. "She's been through a lot of pain." He paused, thinking about all that his cousin had been through. "It wasn't accidental that God led her to someone who could care for her. Someone who's been through the same thing."

They walked down the hall toward the library, and when they reached the door, he opened it to let Brighid enter.

"She told me about Sadie—also about Sadie's patience with her." Brighid laughed lightly. "The woman has got to be a saint."

"Just as you said, God hasn't let Merci out of his care for a moment. It didn't mean that she had an easy time of it. Only that he was there, waiting for her to turn around and look to him."

Cheerful flames crackled in the fireplace. The room smelled faintly of leather-bound books and pine smoke. Brighid sat down in one of the two high-back leather chairs that flanked the hearth. Quaid stoked the fire, then settled into the other chair. Blue curled at his feet, tail still thumping the floor.

"Merci's letter wasn't long," Brighid said. "She didn't go into detail about anything except what happened that day on the beach. She told me that God rescued her, nothing more." She smiled, though her weariness showed around her eyes. Her quiet sorrow over her daughter had taken its toll. "It's the triumph we need to dwell on. Not the other." It was her gentle way of telling him that she didn't want to hear about Merci's dark journey. Not now from him. Perhaps not at all.

"I'm certain Merci would prefer to tell you herself."

Brighid looked relieved. "She didn't say when she's coming to La Paloma again. I hope it's not long."

He reached across the space that divided them and took his aunt's hand. He could see that she was close to tears. "Merci will come home. The change in her is real. Don't doubt the work God has done within her." He smiled, then let go of her hand as he stood to stoke the fire again, stirring a flurry of sparks.

Brighid took out her handkerchief and looked across at him. "Quaid, I haven't thanked you for what you've done. It would have been easier for you to stay at home. It took you months…"

He reassured her with a grin. "The ranch looks fit as a fiddle. With the two of you running it, I wasn't missed."

"Songan enjoyed taking the herd to the high country," she said. "I think he liked the brief exchange of his headmaster's role for that of a cattle baron."

"It's a good way to stay out of the summer heat." He grinned. "For animals and humans." He sat down again and smiled at her. "Speaking of Song, have you set a date?"

She laughed. "We plan to wait for Merci."

"I told her about the other wedding…" he began.

Brighid gave him a conspiratorial smile. "Ah, yes. I heard rumors while you were gone," she said with delight. "I couldn't be happier for you. I've grown to cherish your Emmeline!"

He stared into the fire, studying the flames. "I was certain of our plans until this afternoon." He let out a heavy sigh and turned again to Brighid. "But now I wonder if she isn't having second thoughts. Though she claims to love me, there just seems to be something she's holding back. Maybe I'm imagining things…" He remembered her reaction when he'd told her how he'd rescued Knight—it had been swift. She'd practically accused him of wrongdoing, as if sympathizing with Cole. It puzzled him.

He stood and walked to the fire, warming and rubbing his hands. Then he turned again to Brighid, hands clasped behind his back. "You've spent some time with Gertie and Emmeline while I was gone. Did you notice anything amiss?"

Brighid shook her head. "She often mentioned your letters. She read to us from some of them." She smiled. "At least just a few sentences."

"She couldn't write to me because I was on the move. If she had, maybe I would have detected some cooling of her affections."

The fire popped as some pitch dropped onto the embers.

"I felt a distance between us today," he said. "It had nothing to do with the time I've been away. I sensed she had something to tell me but couldn't get the words out." Quaid stared into the fire again.

Brighid leaned forward in her chair. "Perhaps it has to do with the investigation into water rights in the Big Valley. Some folks, led by Court MacQueen, are disputing an area near the dam. He's begun a full investigation about some discrepancy that Emmeline found. No one would tell me anything more than that. Only that it may involve bringing charges against some of our citizens."

The hair on the back of his neck bristled. "Emmeline found a discrepancy?"

Brighid nodded. "Yes. She examined the plat maps at the Office of Records. I heard that a few weeks ago she took the maps home from the County Courthouse as the first phase of the investigation.

"You're sure?"

"Yes." Brighid frowned. "Why are you so concerned?"

"If it's the river and its forks around the dam she's investigating, it has to do with *our* water rights."

Brighid started to laugh. "That's nonsense—" Then she stopped abruptly. "You surely don't think she's trying to terminate our rights to the river?"

Blue thumped his tail. Absently Quaid reached down to scratch his ears. "I'll certainly find out," he said.

Then Emmeline's words came back to him. *You deceived the man.* Deception could have been on her mind if she suspected Quaid of tampering with the water rights. But would some sort of misplaced accusation cause her to back away from his love?

He shook the thought from his mind. After all, why would she suspect him when he hadn't done anything wrong?

That night he pulled out his copies of the plat maps for both his and Emmeline's properties. He spread them on the long oak table in the dining room, brought a magnifying glass from his grandfather's desk, and moved a lamp near the area in question. Nothing was out of the ordinary.

He moved the lamp closer and studied the representative drawings of the river, the dam, the surrounding areas.

Indeed it was a shame that the fork of the river supplying Emmeline's land had been sacrificed when the dam was built. He stared at the dry riverbed beneath the drawing of the dam, wondering if Emmeline was deluded enough to think that such a thing might have been done on purpose.

He sighed heavily. Emmeline Amity Callahan did nothing on a whim. But she obviously had caught a yellow jacket in her straw bonnet. Its buzz might be driving her to distraction.

He would simply need to set her straight. That was all. He furled the maps and dimmed the light. He would head over to see her first thing in the morning.

Then he thought of how long he'd been away from the ranch. He trudged up the stairs to his room, making a mental list of things to be handled right away. He'd been gone too long to simply ride off like Don Quixote to joust with windmills—or with fair Emmeline, he thought with a grin. She and her crusade—if that was indeed what all this was about—would have to wait until at least eight o'clock.

≪══════≫

The following morning, Emmeline had a headache. She had agonized all night about riding to La Paloma to speak with Quaid. She had awakened in the predawn darkness and paced her bedroom floor. By five o'clock she'd decided she would ride to La Paloma and tell Quaid everything. By five-thirty she'd changed her mind. By five forty-three she'd kissed Gertie good-bye and headed out to saddle the Appaloosa for her ride to Riverview. She planned to give Court MacQueen a piece of her mind.

A gloomy dawn was breaking when she arrived at Glenwood Inn, and the lobby was empty as she strode through it. She gave the bell on the front desk a sharp rap, and the hotel clerk emerged from a back room.

"Would you send someone to fetch Court MacQueen for me, please?"

The clerk stared at her from beneath a green shade that fit onto his forehead. "It's a bit early for callers."

She narrowed her eyes. "I will not go to a gentleman's room myself, and I must speak with Mr. MacQueen about a matter of utmost importance. Please send someone to tell him Miss Emmeline Callahan is waiting to see him."

The man finally turned to an assistant who had followed him to the desk, and after a brief exchange, the assistant trudged up the stairs behind the desk.

A few minutes later, MacQueen descended the stairs, buttoning his shirt and raking a hand through his hair. He frowned at Emmeline, concern written on his face.

"Can we sit a moment in the lobby?" she asked without preamble.

He nodded and followed her to a small sitting area near the fireplace. Without a word he settled into a high-back chair as she did the same across from him.

"I want to talk to you about the plat maps."

His eyes watered with a stifled yawn. "Couldn't it have waited until daybreak?"

She shook her head vigorously. "I can't let your accusations continue a moment longer."

"As I explained yesterday, the matter is out of your hands."

She leaned forward earnestly. "There's got to be another explanation."

He let out an impatient breath. "Such as…?"

"Are you certain the maps had to have been changed since 1889?"

A flicker of uncertainty crossed his face.

She smiled, feeling her first glimmer of hope over the matter in a long time. "It occurs to me that you're too eager to point the finger of blame at Quaid. You began with him as the obvious culprit and have built your case around that premise."

Court raised an eyebrow, looking surprised, but following her reasoning.

She stared at him without speaking for a long moment, gathering her courage. "It occurs to me that you, Mr. MacQueen, might also have had the opportunity to change the maps, you or someone working for you."

His face turned crimson, and he sputtered when he spoke. "How dare you insinuate such a thing?"

"I dare to because you've jumped to insinuations of equal if not worse outrage with Quaid Dearbourne." She paused. "From the beginning, you've told me to look for the person who'd have the most to gain by tampering with the plat maps. I have to wonder if you wanted me to falsely accuse him."

MacQueen sat staring at her, his face full of barely contained anger, his voice measured and cold. "I have investigated this thoroughly for your benefit, Miss Callahan."

"I don't need your help. What I do want is this investigation called off. I want you to stay off my property." When he didn't speak, she rushed on. "I have written to my father to launch an investigation of his own into your work, Mr. MacQueen. As you yourself mentioned, my father is an influential man, well-connected, I believe was the phrase you used of the senator."

He sat back, now white-faced. "How dare you go over my head? I came here to help you, to help the others. Now you're casting aspersions on my work because you can't stand the thought of Quaid Dearbourne deceiving you."

He'd struck a nerve, and she guessed he knew it from her expression. "I dare to because, as I recall, you've played a part in your own deceptions, sir. Case in point, the 'death' of one Derian Cadman."

He pressed his lips together, watching her warily.

She gave him an icy smile. "I gave full disclosure of that little deception to my father and asked him to pass it along to your superiors."

He stood abruptly, glaring down at her.

She stood to stare him down. "You may not have broken any laws by aiding Cadman, but I'm certain your reputation will suffer."

"Have you posted the letter to your father?"

"I plan to before leaving town this morning."

"If I call off the investigation, will you reconsider posting it?" He looked uncertain.

She eyed him evenly, stifling a smile. "I suppose I could."

He gave her a swift nod. "Consider it done."

Now she gave him a wide smile and stuck out her hand to shake his. "I knew you'd see things my way."

She'd turned to walk away from him when he spoke again. "One thing you may have overlooked, Emmeline."

She spun around and quirked a brow. "What is that?"

"You still don't know for certain that Quaid Dearbourne didn't tamper with the maps for his own gain. There really is no one else, you know."

She glared at him for a long moment, then strode across the lobby to the door. Once she was on the Appaloosa, she forgot his words. She had only one goal in mind—she wanted to see Quaid and tell him everything. At last.

He was right. Two people in love needed to speak their hearts to each other.

She smiled and nudged the Appaloosa to move at a faster clip to La Paloma.

Within an hour she had reached the gate leading to the rancho. She reined the horse hard to the left, and she quickened her pace. As soon as they reached the house, Emmeline hurried up the steps leading to the hacienda's entrance.

Josefina had seen her coming and met her at the door. "Señor Quaid is not here," the elderly housekeeper said.

"Is he nearby?"

Josefina frowned. "Señor Quaid rode out to the highlands to check on the herd before daybreak. I heard him tell Señorita Brighid he planned to return early so he could ride to your place. If you want to wait here for him…?" She stood back and held the door open.

"I'll ride out to meet him—if the highlands…that's not far?"

The elderly woman pointed to the northwest. "There, beyond the hills."

A short time later, Emmeline mounted the Appaloosa and headed across the grasslands. Bending over his neck, she pressed her heels into the horse's flanks and let him take his lead. He soared across the smooth landscape, past clumps of sage and thickets of willows.

She rode like the wind, then slowed to a walk when she sensed the horse was tiring. A pale winter sky spread above her, and the whisper of a breeze stirred the shrubs and ruffled the brown grasses of the fields.

A half-hour later, she saw several riders scattered among a small herd of cattle in the distance. Even before she was close enough to make out his features, she recognized Quaid. The way he slouched in the saddle, his hat brim pulled low over his forehead.

One of the riders pointed toward her, and within seconds he wheeled his horse and headed her way.

He frowned, looking worried as he approached. He halted next to her, and his horse sidled a few steps. "Is something wrong?"

She smiled. "No, something's finally very right."

He met her gaze with a warm one of his own. "You've decided to tell me what was on your heart yesterday?" A small clump of granite boulders near a copse of sage lay a short way from them. He nodded toward the place. "Let's ride over there."

He nudged the sorrel to a trot. Emmeline followed and dismounted when he did. Quaid settled onto a boulder and patted the one next to him. He looked at her expectantly.

She drew in a deep breath, praying for courage, for him to understand. "While you were gone, Quaid, I looked into the water rights for both our properties." When he didn't look surprised, she rushed on. "I found that someone had tampered with the plat map. The one drawn for my property."

He was frowning now. "You have suspicions about who might have done such a thing?"

Her cheeks flamed. "There are those who are seeking to bring charges against you, Quaid. But I've defended you." It sounded weak in her own ears.

"You think I'm capable of such an act?"

"No."

He didn't look convinced.

"Do you?" he persisted.

"No," she whispered, trying not to think about the doubt that had plagued her.

He regarded her with eyes that suddenly seemed cold. She shivered. This wasn't how she'd planned the conversation to go. She explained to him about the double maps, how the original had been switched with the copy.

"And what would be my motive?"

"I don't believe you would do such a thing, Quaid." She wanted to believe her own words.

He turned and, with the lightest touch of his callused fingers, lifted her chin so that he could search her eyes. "Something tells me that even your love for me can't erase your doubts."

Her heart twisted, and her eyes filled with tears. "I've taken care of the charges," she said.

He gave her a grim smile. "And just how did you manage to clear my name?"

"MacQueen protected a friend of his in a rather unscrupulous manner—a friend who was part of my past. I found out about it and threatened to reveal the circumstances to my father."

"My champion." His tone was dry. "You didn't think I could defend myself?"

She stared at him.

His voice was soft when he spoke again, "Did you consider that I might want my day in court to prove my innocence?" He stood, his hands jammed into his pockets, squinting into the winter landscape, speaking again without looking at her. "It's all about trust, isn't it, Emma?"

She walked over to stand beside him. She swallowed hard. "Yes," she whispered hoarsely.

He turned toward her again. "It's ironic to think that just six months ago, we were dreaming golden dreams. And now we've lost everything."

"Including us," she whispered.

"Including us," he repeated. "We were the most golden dream of all."

They stood, gazing at each other in the quiet of the winter mesa. She longed to step into his arms, feel his warmth surround her, fill her. Instead, desolation washed over her. It felt as bleak as the winter-barren land stretching before them.

Without another word or even a glance in her direction, he strode to the sorrel. Then he mounted and rode in a swift fluid motion toward the cattle hands, spoke with them, and headed north away from the ranch.

She watched him ride across the barren landscape until he disappeared into the blur of horizon where the pale purple sky faded into the ashen ground.

She knew he wouldn't be back.

TWENTY-NINE

Quaid rode away from La Paloma, wounded as surely as though Emmeline had stuck a knife between his ribs and twisted it into his heart. Even giving away the rancho and its windswept lands paled beside his grief over Emmeline's conclusion about his honor.

He headed northwest toward the Valley of the Horses, taking a back trail. He spent the night in a deserted trapper's cabin he'd once discovered while camping with his father and John Muir. Unable to sleep, he chewed on stale jerky and stared into the fire, trying to keep his mind off Emmeline.

It was impossible. The woman occupied his every thought. He remembered what it felt like to hold her, to delight in her, to lose himself in the tenderness and passion that shone in her eyes. He wondered how long it would be before he stopped thinking about her. Would each day rip open his wounds, bring fresh pain, because he couldn't put her out of his mind, out of his heart?

The next day he headed out before dawn and rode hard all day, winding along the crest of the snow-covered Sierra Madre range, skirting Fort Tejon, then finally heading into the Central Valley. The sun faded as he headed up the narrow, rocky canyon leading to the Valley of the Horses. He was the only one who used the route since his parents had constructed a new entrance at the edge of the towering Tehachapis on the valley's far side.

The sky turned lavender as dusk fell, casting a pink-gray light over the granite cliffs. Below him the river thundered as it rushed along its banks. The low vibration of the waterfall at the end of the box canyon carried toward him. The wild untouched beauty of the place lifted his spirits. He was home.

He once had grand dreams for his grandfather's property, but it was time to put them aside and face the cold reality of his future elsewhere. His inclination was to get as far away from civilization as possible…and stay there, perhaps forever.

Grinning, he considered the notion. Too bad he hadn't been born a century earlier. He was suited to be a mountain man, spend his days trapping, his evenings by a campfire. He thought of old Joe Black, famous for his spirited grizzly encounters. He laughed. Old Joe had nothing on Quaid—he'd never encountered Emmeline Amity Callahan.

It was almost dark when he reached the waterfall at the end of the canyon. He dismounted and led the sorrel up the slick granite trail, across the narrow suspension bridge, and into the cavernous tunnel behind the waterfall.

As he emerged in the fading light, he could still see his parents' low-slung adobe in the distance. Lights glowed in the windows. Horses grazed in the corrals around the spread, their shadowy forms barely visible in the growing twilight. As it grew darker, only the impression of white from a star, pinto spot, or fetlock boot, told him where the beautiful animals were feeding in the tall grass.

He remounted the sorrel and rode around to the stables. His father was just closing the door, and he looked up, puzzled, as Quaid approached.

"Son, what a surprise!" Spence Dearbourne strode over to his son and, after Quaid dismounted, shook his hand and patted him affectionately on the back. "What brings you up our direction?" Spence studied Quaid's face, his concern showing. "Is anything wrong?"

Quaid nodded. "I just stopped in to say good-bye."

"Good-bye?" His father frowned. "Where're you off to now? You just got home, didn't you? We got your telegram about Merci—"

"I was home overnight. Long enough to see that the rancho was still intact."

His mother opened the back door of the adobe as they approached. "I thought I heard voices! Quaid, darling!" Aislin Dearbourne ran to her son and gathered him into her arms. "Child—! What are you doing here?" She pulled back slightly and smiled into his eyes. "Not that I'm sorry you've come home! I'd keep you here forever if I could!"

He grinned. "You may have to, Ma."

Concern immediately shadowed her face. "There is something wrong, isn't there?"

"I'll tell you over supper," he said, "if there's anything left."

"We're just sitting down to eat," she said with a laugh. "Food first. You haven't changed a bit, young man." He followed her into the adobe, his father trailing behind him. "We'll send one of the hands to fetch Sara," she continued as they walked. "She'd love to see you." She smiled. "And she never turns down my cobbler."

They headed through the kitchen to the dining room, and his senses were assaulted with the scents of baking apple cobbler and roasting venison. Coffee boiled on the back plate of the stove, adding to the fragrance.

With its rough-hewn pine table and leather chairs, the dining room was as homey and familiar as a pair of worn boots. A lively fire crackled and popped in a river-rock fireplace at one end of the room. Red-and-white gingham curtains graced the windows, and a bouquet of the last roses of the season spilled from a brass pitcher at the table's center. His mother quickly set another place for him with her treasured blue willow dishes.

Over a stew of roasted venison, potatoes, wild onions, rosemary, and sage, Quaid told them about his search for Merci. He waited until they'd finished eating before telling them about his journey north.

"I've decided to give up the ranch," he said. His mother poured him a mug of coffee. "I want Merci to take over on my behalf."

His parents exchanged a glance, then looked back to him. "How does your grandfather feel about it?" Aislin asked. "It may not sit well with him that you're giving up on his offer."

"My heart's not in it," Quaid said, taking a sip of coffee. "The ranch is running well, though not because I was there to oversee the operations. I made some decisions from a distance, that's all." He shrugged. "After what happened to Merci, I wanted to make it up to her somehow. A homecoming gift, I suppose you could call it."

"What else has happened, Quaid?" Aislin seemed to be looking deeper into his motives. "Sara told us that in one of Emmeline's last letters, she spoke of her growing affection for you. The word marriage was mentioned…"

He took another gulp of coffee, then shrugged. "We thought about it, that's all. Things just didn't work out."

"Is that why you're leaving?" she persisted.

"Indirectly, I suppose." Letting out a deep sigh, he stared into the open fireplace. "And the fact that it's simply time." He looked at his father. "One of the reasons I came is to see if you know John Muir's whereabouts. Has he been by here recently?"

His father nodded. "A couple of months ago. He said he was heading into the Hetch Hetchy Valley. He's trying to get more recognition for the place, try to save it from being dammed."

"He's in the valley now?" Quaid pictured the knee-deep snow.

"You thinking of joining him?"

Quaid smiled. "That's the life I'm cut out for. That's where I'll stay. And I'd like to help his efforts." He chuckled. "I hope no one's thrown away my snowshoes."

They spoke for a few more minutes about Muir and his possible winter campsites, then the door opened and Sara Dearbourne, Quaid's paternal grandmother, walked in. He stood and hugged her.

"What's this talk of John Muir?" she asked, sitting at the table next to him. Aislin poured her mother-in-law a cup of coffee and served the apple cobbler.

"I'm heading to the Hetch Hetchy to find him."

Sara frowned. "You're leaving the rancho—the Big Valley?" She looked troubled, and he noticed her coffee cup rattled when she set it on the saucer.

"It's time," he said simply. He didn't want to worry her about the water rights accusations.

"I thought you and Emmeline…" Her voice drifted off, and she blinked at him as if in confusion.

He reached for her hand. "We love each other, if that's what you're referring to. Some things have come up to give us second thoughts. That's all."

She pushed back her cobbler. "I don't believe I'm hungry after all," she said. She sat in silence for a moment, then stood, looking more troubled than before. "I do believe I'll get back to my cottage," she said.

After giving Quaid a quick hug and a peck on the cheek, she turned to the door.

"I'll go with you, Grandmother," Quaid said, hurrying to open the door for the elderly woman.

"No need." She waved him away.

"I insist."

They walked toward her little cottage at the rear of the property. For several minutes, neither spoke. When they reached her door, she looked up at her grandson. "It's the water, child, isn't it? The water rights that've come between you?"

"How did you know?"

She didn't answer. After looking into his eyes a moment longer, she shrugged wearily and walked through her open door.

"Grandmother? What is it?"

She gave him a gentle smile. "Nothing for you to worry about, Quaid. Nothing at all." She closed the door.

The next morning, Quaid rode away from the Valley of the Horses, heading to Hetch Hetchy. When he reached Sacramento, he posted a letter to MacQuaid and Camila Byrne, giving up all claims to Rancho de la Paloma and letting them know how to reach Merci in Santa Inez.

Three weeks later, he found Muir, deep in the Sierra Nevada high country.

<hr />

Through the winter and early spring, Emmeline tried to keep from thinking about Quaid. It was impossible. Not a day went by that she didn't miss him and think of him dozens of times. She went through the motions of caring for her groves, but her heart wasn't in it. Her trees were thriving in the spring rains, and within a few years her crops would make her a wealthy woman.

A woman of means. She'd done it on her own. It was an empty consideration.

Sometimes as she rode through her property, she considered how her life had changed since leaving Washington a mere two years earlier.

She was highly thought of in the growing community in and around Riverview. She now chaired the committee for building a new opera house and had taken a leadership role in seeing that the city received allocations to build the first library in Riverview County.

Talk of the water rights and plat map alterations had died a natural death after her discussion with Court MacQueen. Now that they'd had some rain, it wasn't the matter of urgency it had seemed months before.

Until a letter summoned her to the county courthouse.

The summons notified her of a meeting, on a Tuesday morning at eleven o'clock, regarding the issue of water rights on her property.

Puzzled, she discussed the letter with Gertie the same day it arrived by special courier.

The older woman pulled fresh biscuits from the oven, served them on two plates with fresh-churned butter and jam, then sat opposite Emmeline at the big oak kitchen table.

"I thought this matter was closed," Emmeline said, buttering her biscuit.

Gertie frowned at her. "Matters like that are never over, child. Far as I'm concerned, you never brought the thing to a close. You and Quaid just left the whole notion hangin' in the air."

Emmeline sighed, knowing her aunt spoke the truth. "I tried to help him out of a criminal investigation. I did what I could to explain." She shrugged, shaking her head. "I don't know what more I could have done."

"You could have gone after him."

"I heard from Sara that he headed into the back country." She laughed. "Can you see me going after him on snowshoes?"

Gertie didn't laugh with her. "If I loved a man as much as you love that one, I'd walk on snowshoes to the ends of the earth if need be to get him back." She spread jam on her biscuit, studying Emmeline.

Emmeline looked down, knowing Gertie spoke the truth. "I broke the trust between us by not believing in him."

"Do you think you're the first to ever make a mistake when dealing with matters of the heart?"

"Doubting someone's honor is more than just a mistake." Emmeline stood and moved to the stove to warm her hands, then turned to Gertie once again. "I've dreamed about following Quaid. Every night before I fall asleep, I imagine going after him…"

"And?"

"The dream ends in the same way each time. I find him, run to him…only to see that awful look of sorrow in his face. The same expression that was there when he saw into my heart—saw that I thought him guilty of a crime against me."

"What about forgiveness, child?" Gertie studied Emmeline's face. "Do you think Quaid has it in himself to forgive you?"

She didn't answer.

"Or are you too proud to ask?"

Emmeline's eyes opened wider. "Too proud to ask?" she croaked, then sputtered, "Of course not. Imagine such a thing. Too proud to ask for forgiveness?"

Gertie looked pleased with her assessment. "In my opinion, your pride—and perhaps his, too—is all that's keeping you apart." She stood to place her dish in the sink. "Also, in my opinion, you need to buy yourself a pair of snowshoes." She chuckled that cackling laugh that Emmeline loved.

Emmeline stepped across the room and gave her a hug. "If I thought there was any hope for reconciliation, I would leave this minute."

Gertie nodded slowly, a small smile playing on her wrinkled face. "Just don't wait too long, child." She patted Emmeline's face. "And when the time comes, don't let your pride get in the way."

Three days later, Emmeline hitched the gray to the buggy and rode into town. She drove to the livery, then walked the length of the town to the courthouse. Once inside, she strode to the door of the Office of Records, following the instructions on the summons.

Opening the door, she frowned in surprise. Seated in the small room were Sara Dearbourne and a man Emmeline had never seen before. Between them was the small table where Emmeline had studied the plat maps many times. The maps, both of them, were unfurled on the table now.

"Sara?" She rushed to the older woman and greeted her with an embrace. "I wasn't expecting you."

Sara gave her a gentle smile. "I realize that, child. I wanted to keep it that way until I could speak with my friend Luis Martine. He's a cartographer and an old friend of mine. He helped me with some difficulties after my Hugh died."

Luis stood and nodded toward Emmeline as she seated herself.

Sara leaned forward. "I have a story to tell you, and I ask your forgiveness for not telling you sooner."

"Of course I forgive you—if there's truly anything to forgive," Emmeline said. "What is it?"

"It concerns the tampering with the maps."

Emmeline frowned. "What would you have to do with them?"

Sara looked at her evenly. "It was I who changed them."

Emmeline almost laughed. Her wrinkled little step-grandmother? Gentle-spirited, soft-spoken, honest-as-the-day-is-long Sara Dearbourne? The woman who'd chosen Emmeline as her heir? It made no sense.

"I see you puzzling with this already," Sara said softly. "I'd puzzle about it too, if I were in your shoes."

"Tell me how you could possibly be involved with this."

Sara glanced at Luis, who smiled and gave her a nod of encouragement. After a long sigh, she began speaking, her voice low and urgent as though it was a story she'd needed to tell for a long time.

"A long time ago my husband, Hugh, did a terrible thing. He betrayed the best friends we had in the world."

"MacQuaid and Camila Byrne," Emmeline mused.

"Yes, the Byrnes." Her eyes held a faraway look as she seemed to step back into the past. "Hugh and MacQuaid were sea captains together. Hugh, though, always worked for MacQuaid, who owned the fleet of ships. It was something he never forgave his friend for—the fact that MacQuaid always seemed to outshine him in everything he did."

"They bought the ranchos at the same time?" Emmeline asked.

Sara nodded. "Yes, within a short time of each other. Our children were born within years of each other and played together. Camila and I were closer than sisters. We all thought Hugh loved MacQuaid like a brother. No one guessed—until much later—that my husband planned to betray us all, even me."

"You?"

Sara's eyes were sad. "I'll save that part of the story for another time."

Emmeline understood and reached for her hand. "Go on."

"Both ranchos were about to be lost because of a financial crisis involving boundaries. With no one else's knowledge, Hugh contacted some government authorities and promised to deliver both properties into their hands for the exchange of money and power.

"When it appeared that Spence and Aislin might save both ranchos because of a scheme they devised—selling wild horses in New Mexico—he even tried to ruin their success. He double-crossed his own son." Her eyes filled. "He never came home again. He died on the trail."

"What does that have to do with the water rights?" Emmeline asked.

Sara looked to Luis. "Would you tell her, please, my friend?"

Luis nodded, then turned back to Emmeline. "I was on the horse drive with Spence and Hugh. I saw firsthand everything that Hugh tried to do to ruin his son's chances of success, chances of saving the properties."

He leaned forward, his expression solemn. "When we returned, Spence shielded his mother from the truth. He didn't want her to know about her husband's betrayal." He glanced at Sara, his expression softening. "I thought she needed to know. She had so many questions…" He frowned as though remembering. "So I told her exactly what Hugh had done.

"I helped her investigate his dealings with the officials who'd promised him the world in exchange for his soul." He paused, settling back in his chair, his gaze steady on Emmeline. "I had just finished my schooling and had become a cartographer for the State of California. That gave me ready access to the property records. I discovered that Hugh had redrawn much of the land in the Big Valley without Mac-Quaid's knowledge.

"He was a greedy man, and little by little he took bites from Rancho de la Paloma in ways he thought wouldn't be noticed. The cronies he was in cahoots with helped him carry it out."

Sara broke in. "No one would have known until it was too late, if Luis hadn't helped me." She looked sad. "MacQuaid and Camila had been through so much with Brighid, I didn't want to burden them with full knowledge of their friend's betrayal. So, with Luis's help, we quietly went about restoring the maps to their original state—including the water rights that originally had belonged to Rancho de la Paloma." She smiled. "We merely switched them back to where they'd been originally."

"No law has been broken after all?" Emmeline asked incredulously.

"Only if you consider what Luis and I did breaking the law. The real lawbreaker was Hugh."

A look of sorrow shadowed Sara's face. "I didn't think anyone would notice. Until Courtland MacQueen rode into town." She shook her head. "He began poking his nose where it didn't belong—and I have my suspicions as to why, young lady—because of you, I daresay. But I digress. None would have been the wiser if he hadn't made you curious about the maps. Made it appear that Quaid changed them."

"It is also clear that he paid the translator of the Quinton Rafael document to falsify the contents, particularly the statement about Quaid's knowledge of the deception," Luis said quietly.

For a moment no one spoke.

"What happens now?" Emmeline finally asked, still trying to absorb all that had been revealed to her.

"That's up to you, child."

"The water rights belong to Rancho de la Paloma after all." Merci was now the owner of La Paloma, and though the maps had been changed illegally, Emmeline would do nothing to change them back. As many others in the region must do, she would pray for rain during years of drought and rejoice in years of abundant moisture. She settled back and gave Sara a gentle smile of reassurance.

Right now, land, water, and future didn't matter. All that mattered was Quaid.

And it was too late for them.

She nodded slowly and stood. "I think it needs to be forgotten. Let's leave everything just as it is—as it should have been all along."

Sara nodded. "Yes, my sentiments exactly."

"Can you come out to the ranch with me?"

"I'd like nothing better," Sara said. "I want to see how those Bahias are doing."

Emmeline wrapped her arm around the older woman's waist, and they walked to the door. Emmeline turned to Luis. "Thank you for your kindness to my grandmother all these years."

He inclined his head to Sara. "She's like an oak that's weathered many storms, only to become stronger and more resilient for it."

As they drove to the ranch, Sara turned to Emmeline. "I want to hear what happened with Quaid."

Emmeline didn't answer. She flicked the whip over the back of the gray.

"He loves you," Sara went on. "I saw it in his face when your name was mentioned."

"Perhaps that's so," she whispered. "But he's turned away from my love as though it never existed."

"He loves you," Sara repeated. "Don't give up on him, child."

She seemed lost in thought, but when the buggy rounded a curve and the overlook lay ahead, Sara asked Emmeline to pull to the side. When they'd halted, the women stepped to the ground and walked to the lookout.

"You've done well," Sara said, looking out at the acreage she'd given Emmeline. "I'm not surprised. When I chose you as my heir, I knew you would make a success of it."

Emmeline nodded, but she couldn't help thinking how empty her success was without Quaid.

"I have no doubt that when the three years close," Sara said, "you will be triumphant in meeting my challenge. The Bahias have certainly changed the look of the place." She sighed, considering the groves that stretched across the valley, nearly reaching the mountains. "Just as I knew they would."

Emmeline remembered the day Quaid first drove her to her property, her dismay at its rocky, windswept land. Now she considered how it had changed, its even rows of trees painting the landscape a verdant green, the first blossoms of spring filling the air with their perfume.

Quaid had been beside her that day. Her heart caught as she remembered the look of him, his eyes taking on a merry glint as he beheld her, the warmth in his gaze even then.

She missed him! Oh, how she missed him! His crooked smile. The way his duster snapped in the wind. The way he pulled his hat brim low and smiled at her from underneath it.

"You could build a house out yonder," Sara mused, pointing to the place where Emmeline had imagined the Victorian grove house. She wondered if Gertie had written Sara about Emmeline's dreams. "You'd still have plenty of room for a passel of children to play outdoors. That big pepper tree branch would hold a lovely swing, don't you think?"

Emmeline didn't answer. She headed to the buggy and climbed in, her tears nearly obscuring the beauty before her. The glorious sweep of groves, a sky so brilliantly blue it nearly hurt her eyes to look, the jagged snowcapped peaks of the San Jacintos.

Sara clambered into the buggy beside her, and Emmeline flicked the whip above the gray. Soon they were on their way.

With each thud of the horse's hooves, Emmeline wondered how long it would take for the ache in her heart to die.

Thirty

May 1891

Merci Byrne stood in front of the run-down boardinghouse in Los Angeles. She took in the old wood-frame structure with eyes that now saw things so differently. Before, she'd thought the condition of the place matched her deplorable circumstances, that the decay matched the blood in her veins. Now it simply seemed love-worn from years of use, the way a beloved stuffed doll might look with its face rubbed smooth from a child's hugs and kisses.

She noticed that since she had been there last, someone had attempted to repair the crooked front shutters, then halted after straightening only one. Instead of looking at it with contempt, she now remembered with compassion the ill health of both elderly proprietors, and she whispered a prayer for their well-being.

She pushed open the gate. It squawked just as it had before. She smiled and continued her walk toward the entrance door.

After she knocked, it took several minutes before the muffled sound of approaching footsteps reached her. Just as before.

The door swung open. Mrs. Johnson stood before her, peering at Merci with a puzzled expression. After a moment, a smile stretched across her wrinkled face.

She held out her arms. "I declare," she said, her eyes wide. "You've come back to us!" Then she called over her shoulder, "Mr. Johnson, come quick! Come see who's here!"

Merci couldn't stop herself from smiling. "I had to see you again."

Mr. Johnson reached the entry. He looked at Merci with delight. "I might forget a face. I might even forget a name. But I don't think I could ever forget that curly carrot-top of yours." He looked into her

365

eyes, perhaps even her soul. Merci wondered if he could see the change in her heart without a word being said.

"Come in, come in, child, and tell us how you've been."

They ushered her into the parlor, and Mrs. Johnson left to fetch them some tea. Merci reached into her pocket and drew out the small leather Bible. She touched it gently with her fingertips before handing it to him. "I wanted to return this."

"It's yours to keep, Merci," he said solemnly. "It was a gift."

"I know that." She studied his kind face for a moment before going on, "I would like to leave it with you for you to give to some other troubled girl God might bring your way."

He nodded slowly, understanding.

"I will never forget your kindness. I was undeserving."

"We're all on a journey of some kind," he said. "And most of us, I daresay all of us, are undeserving."

Mrs. Johnson bustled back into the room and set a tea tray down on the table before them. The room seemed homey and warm. Merci gladly took the teacup and saucer. When she saw the little cakes, she was quite suddenly ravenously hungry. She settled back with a sigh, sipping her tea, glad she had come.

"I'd like to tell you about my journey," she said after a few minutes. "And how your gift of kindness helped changed the direction I was heading."

For the next three hours they talked of what had happened. It was midafternoon when she finished her tale, and the Johnsons' boarders were beginning to arrive for the night.

"I must go," she said finally. "I know you have supper to prepare."

"You're welcome to stay the night," Mrs. Johnson said. "We would be honored to have you as our guest."

"I'm going home," Merci said. "I'm eager to be on my way."

"You'll promise to come back?" Mr. Johnson asked as they walked her to the door.

"I will," she said and gave them each a hug.

Within an hour she had boarded the downtown train for the journey to Riverview. She soon left the hubbub of the city and entered the quiet spring landscape of the Big Valley. It lay before her, bronzed by the late afternoon sun. She settled back to watch the fields of lush grass, blossoming sage, and wild lilacs passing by the train window.

She was coming home. Her thoughts went back to the day she left and all that had ensued. She had changed much since then, but the memory of her pain was still vivid. She supposed it would always be with her.

Surprisingly, it was her mother's pain that she thought of most often now. At sixteen her mother had been little more than a child herself when she was violated. The horror of what Brighid had experienced had broken Merci's heart once she set aside her own bitterness, anger, and dismay.

She was ashamed it had taken her own healing to make her aware of her mother's pain. She had written her nearly a dozen letters, but there were so many things still needing to be said. So many things that she'd waited to say until she could look into her mother's face.

Brighid and Songan were marrying tomorrow. She smiled at the thought. How gracious God was to provide this love after all those years! Even now Merci breathed a prayer of thanksgiving for her mother's life and the love she'd found. And Songan was a godly man; that much she knew from her mother's letters. They planned to serve God together at the mission school.

The train slowed as it neared the Riverview station. Merci bit her lip as the locomotive let out a whistle blast and clacked and screeched and groaned to a halt in a cloud of steam.

Gathering her satchel and cape, she headed down the aisle to the door. As her mother had promised he would do in her last letter, Songan waited for her on the platform. He smiled and waved, then strode toward her.

She waited for him to approach, apprehensive about his reception. This was the first time she had seen him since that dreadful day on the mountain. The day she'd decided she hated him without knowing him, without giving him a chance. The day she learned a truth that changed her life.

She'd had no reason to worry, she soon discovered. His eyes held a special light as he kissed her on each cheek, then showed her the way to the carriage.

"My mother has written to me about you," she finally said. The carriage rumbled along the dirt road to the rancho, its wheels creaking with each turn. "I'm glad for your love for her. I want you to know that."

He looked across at her, and she noticed again the kindness in his face. "Your mother is a fine woman. I'm honored that she'll be my wife." He smiled. "We're both glad you've come home. We hope you're home to stay. We want to be a family."

She stared at a passing clump of cactus and swallowed hard, blinking back her tears.

The carriage swayed as it hit a rut, then righted itself again. In the distance a lavender haze covered the mountains as the sun set behind them. They passed some outlying farms, and the air smelled of sage and wildflowers and newly mown grass. Farther from town acres of blossoming orange groves appeared as if a fragrant white lace blanket had been draped across the rolling green hills.

Merci closed her eyes as a quick, warm gust of wind stung her face and lifted tendrils of hair from her forehead. "I've come home, Lord," she breathed. "Such a long journey it's been."

When she opened her eyes, the hacienda appeared in the distance. It was hers now. During her weeks of healing, she had traveled north to stay with her grandparents at Scotty and Sybil's home in Monterey. It was there that her grandfather presented her with the deed to the land.

She considered it now, the gift of Quaid's heart, the gift of her inheritance, marking her forever as the granddaughter of MacQuaid Byrne, the original ranchero. A desert wind was kicking up, and as they drew nearer, the slant of the setting sun cast a golden glow on the whitewashed adobe walls. The winds had cleared the air, leaving the landscape and the house looking as if etched in purest gold.

In a corral behind the barn, a tall black stallion grazed peacefully. Merci leaned forward in her seat unable to breathe. She blinked and stared again at the horse. Surely it couldn't be Knight. She was almost afraid to hope.

As if sensing her scrutiny, the big horse's ears flicked forward and he raised his head, watching as the carriage rolled by.

Songan smiled, inclining his head toward the corral. "It is Knight," he said simply, his expression confirming that he understood Merci's unspoken joy. "Quaid found him some months back."

"How…?" she began before her throat constricted with raw emotion.

He glanced over at her again, solemnly. "That's a story for Quaid to tell. And word has it he's on his way."

Songan headed the team to the portico, and even before they rounded the corner, Merci saw her mother standing there. The carriage drew to a halt. Merci didn't wait for Songan to help her down. She stepped out and for a moment didn't move.

Her mother looked into her daughter's face, her eyes filled with tears. Then she nodded slowly, as if understanding everything in that heartbeat of time. Understanding Merci's pain. Understanding her shame. Understanding her redemption. And she loved her fully, even with complete understanding of the depths to which Merci had sunk. All of it was reflected in the glow of her mother's beautiful face as she beheld her daughter.

Brighid opened her arms, and with a small cry, Merci ran into them.

Oh yes, she was home at last.

THIRTY-ONE

Early the following morning, Quaid headed his sorrel along the rim-rock trail of the Sierra Madre. He'd been traveling for days after leaving John Muir in the Sierra Nevada back country and was pleased that his calculations had been correct—he would make it to La Paloma in time for Brighid and Songan's wedding.

He had just finished his third trip into Hetch Hetchy with Muir while the conservationist mapped the valley for his report back to other members of the newly formed Sierra Club.

Quaid had been accepted wholeheartedly into the group headed up by the Scotsman-turned-Californian. The club was made up of professors and newspapermen, photographers and writers, all working together toward a common purpose: stewardship of the land. Specifically, to keep as much of the land as possible from the greedy hands of the railroad kings, the timber barons, the real-estate developers.

Quaid had discovered a gift within himself borne of the passions of his beliefs in keeping California untamed. Already in these three months, he'd begun writing about the land and his love for it. He supposed much of this passion had been bottled up inside him after giving up La Paloma, the land he'd dreamed of making his own, keeping wild, and setting aside for wildlife preservation. He'd been published a half-dozen times in one newspaper or another throughout California. His articles about the importance of preserving Yosemite and Hetch Hetchy had been reprinted in eastern papers. His theme was always the same: the repulsiveness of development and greed compared to the beauty of the unspoiled and lyrical land.

He headed the sorrel to an overlook near Old Baldy. The whole of the Los Angeles basin stretched from the Pacific to the snowcapped San

Jacintos. The view never failed to stir him. Especially on a day when the devil winds kicked up and blew the dust and mists out of the valleys below. On days like these he thought he surely could see a thousand miles.

It had been a dry spring, drier than most, which caused him some worry about the possibility of a coming year of drought. A recent spattering of rain had brought the desertlike sweep of land to life. Even from this distance, he could see the wildflowers were in bloom and the grasses grew tall and green. But the moisture in the foliage wouldn't keep long if the winds didn't stop their spirited flow to the Pacific.

They were stronger now, causing his duster to flap. He pulled down his hat and squinted toward the Big Valley.

As always, his thoughts turned to Emmeline. He would see her at the wedding, no doubt. It was a twist of irony that they would meet on such a day, at such a time. They'd once planned to wed during the spring. He remembered the look of her face that glorious morning in her groves when they spoke of it.

Since then, even the lightest scent of orange blossoms filled his heart and mind with the image of her beloved face.

He reined the sorrel away from a pile of sandstone and granite, then headed down the trail leading to the valley floor.

The sorrel sensed that she was close to home and quickened to a trot toward La Paloma. Quaid was glad to let the mare take her lead. His mother had warned him weeks ago about getting there early, reminding him he'd need time to spare for taking on a civilized look again. Her way of telling him it might be a good idea to bathe, shave, and cut his hair before he saw the family.

He grinned. He knew he looked like a French trapper in his heyday, although he hadn't seen a mirror in weeks, only his reflection in a streambed. He'd grown a beard, finding it much easier to manage while on the trail. His hair had grown to below his ears. And his face had taken on a leathery tanned appearance. His clothes were chosen for warmth and comfort, not for fashion. Somehow, it suited him just fine.

Judging from the slant of the sun, it was nearing noon. The wedding was to take place at three. If he hurried, he might have time for a bath. But the family would have to put up with the beard and long hair until he could get into Riverview to a barber. It might bother the womenfolk, but his cousins Sandy, Kerr, and Gregor would simply think he was living up to his image as an outlaw.

Chuckling, he urged the sorrel to a gallop, the warm wind hitting his face. He pulled off his hat and yelped a cry of pure joy as they thundered across the fields.

It was good to be coming home! Suddenly he couldn't wait to see everyone, from his ruffian red-haired cousins to precious Merci, from his grandparents to Jamie, the uncle he'd seen only a few times in his life, and Hallie, Emmeline's mother.

And Emmeline. Always Emmeline.

He slowed the sorrel to give her a rest and looked toward the Big Valley.

Another gust of wind hit him in the face, and he squinted against the dust. That was when he saw the plume of smoke.

Thirty-Two

B ad things happened when the wind blew hard.

A sense of disquiet threatened Emmeline's soul. The desert winds were blowing unusually hard for spring. She tried to put her worries about the wind from her mind. Instead she thought about the wedding.

Brighid and Songan would marry at midafternoon in the family chapel at Rancho de la Paloma. For the first time in years, both families were coming together for a celebration. Her mother and Jamie were arriving by train at ten, her pretty sisters in tow. She and Gertie were planning to take the new carriage to pick them up at the Riverview station on their way to the wedding. Even now Gertie was bustling about the house, readying the bedrooms and seeing to her baking.

Sybil and Scotty, their brood of red-haired sons, and MacQuaid and Camila had also come by train, arriving last night, and settled into the La Paloma adobe. Merci was probably there by now as well.

Emmeline smiled, thinking of the joyous reunion that would take place in just a few hours. So far no one had mentioned Quaid.

And she hadn't asked.

She wondered if he had ever found it in his heart to forgive her. Or if he thought of her at all. As for her, there was never a waking moment when he didn't fill her mind. Even in her sleep, he walked in her dreams. Her heart danced at the prospect of gazing into his eyes once more. And she couldn't help smiling at the thought.

Emmeline turned to go back to the house, but something caught her gaze at the edge of a canyon to the east. Moving away from the cover of the groves, she shielded her eyes with her hand and stared toward the mountains.

A thin column of smoke spiraled upward, bending to the west with the wind. She frowned. It was a distance away, probably ten miles or more, so it wasn't a threat. Only a worry.

It wasn't the first time the winds had brought with them the danger of wildfire. She had seen several across the Southern California valleys since her arrival. Always they came with the winds.

Gertie stepped from the house and waved to her. "Don't you think it's about time to head to the wedding, child?"

"I'll be right there," she called, her voice almost lost in a sudden gust of wind. Her dress whipped around her as she hurried back to the house.

Gertie reached up and patted Emmeline's face. "You're as pretty as a picture, honey." Then she smiled, her wrinkled face looking as merry as the sparkle in her eyes. "I think your Quaid will fall in love with you all over again today. You'll see."

She sighed. "First of all, he's not *my* Quaid. Second of all, we had our chance at love. It simply wasn't to be." She shrugged. "I need to accept it."

"Well, you can, but I don't have to," Gertie said, giving her hand a pat. "Now come inside and see what I've done to your dress."

Gertie had spent weeks sewing a new gown for Emmeline and just this morning had put on the final touches of lace. She brought it out and held it up triumphantly before Emmeline.

Emmeline shook her head slowly. "It looks more like a wedding dress every time you add another of your special touches."

"I planned it that way, child." Gertie touched the lace sleeve and sighed. "I've never been one to stop praying over what I think is right. And I don't believe in sitting back and letting God do it all. I feel inclined to help him out from time to time." She grinned again. "If this doesn't put the sound of wedding bells in Quaid's mind, the boy's more of a dunderhead than I thought."

Gertie meant well, and Emmeline did her best to look grateful. She gave the blessed woman a hug, then stood back and took a fresh look at the gown. It was indeed beautiful, with lace and satin, and ribbon flowers at the neck and sleeves. "It's perfect," Emmeline said and hugged Gertie again.

An hour later they were dressed and ready to head to the Riverview station. The new stableboy brought the carriage around and opened the door for them. The wind whipped their dresses as they stepped from the porch to the carriage. Emmeline held onto her wide, flower-covered hat as she moved inside.

They'd driven only a half-mile up the road when Emmeline turned to look back on the fire. Her heart caught in her throat.

"We must go back!" she said to the driver. "Hurry!"

He let them out at the door.

Emmeline swallowed hard, trying to calm the rapid staccato march of her heart. "Take a horse and head to Riverview. Get as many of the field workers as you can find. Beg, steal, and borrow wagons to bring them here. Tell them to bring buckets and shovels."

The boy nodded.

"And hurry! Please, tell them to hurry!" Her voice came out in a sob as she looked up at the rapidly approaching firestorm and heard the roar of it in the distance.

— ◆ —

By two o'clock, Quaid had cleaned himself up and exchanged hugs, barbs, and greetings with most of the family. As he had figured they would, his cousins teased him unmercifully about his outlaw look. Merci had grinned when she saw him and told him it added years to his stature, also to his appearance. In fact, she'd said, he looked like a grizzled old bear of a mountain man. Something a wildcat dragged in.

By half past two most of the family had gathered in the chapel. The wind was stronger now and howled from the east. Quaid, his father, and his grandfather stepped outside from time to time to check the direction of the fire. For the first few hours, it seemed to be staying in the long canyon southeast of the Big Valley, then it moved up, heading south, away from Emmeline's property.

At two forty-five, when Emmeline, Gertie, Jamie, and his family hadn't yet arrived, Quaid grew worried. He exchanged a look with his father and grandfather, then stepped outside the chapel once more.

The fire had changed its course. His heart dropped to his stomach. It was racing like a wild beast down the hillside.

Emmeline's groves were in its path. The house, the place where she wanted to build the Victorian grove house—all of it—lay in the monster's path.

He ran back inside. "The fire's changed direction!" he shouted. "It's heading straight for Emmeline and Gertie's!" Without awaiting an answer, he sprinted to the stables, saddled the sorrel in record time, and mounted. He leaned low over the sorrel's neck and galloped south.

Emmeline choked with fear as she headed out to the groves. The stable boy had returned as promised but with too few men. She'd pointed them toward the easternmost edge of her property and told them to dig a fire line as quickly as they could. She knew it was likely too late, but it was all she could think of to do. With a hundred or more, a bucket brigade could have helped. But with the dozen brought by the stable-boy, brave as they were, there wasn't much that could be done once the wall of fire reached them.

She'd yanked off the lace dress and pulled on her old clothes, boots and breeches and an old shirt. She'd tried to get Gertie to take the buggy and head for safety, but the woman would have nothing of it. She wanted to stay in the heart of the action and pray, she said.

So she remained in the temporary safety of the house, promising to leave if things got "hot," she'd said with a wry smile. Emmeline headed to the fire line, shovel in hand.

She ran past the place where she'd planned her Victorian. From the corner of her eye, she saw the spindling twist of a morning glory, already wilting from the heat.

Still she ran.

When she arrived where the men were digging, her heart fell. It was too late. The men were bravely hoeing and clearing the brush to stop the fire. But it soared a hundred feet in the air, and its roar was deafening.

She ran to the men. "You must leave," she yelled above the vibrating thunder of the fire. "Leave now! It's not worth risking your life! Go!"

One of them shook his head, followed by another.

"Go!" she screamed. "Now, before it's too late!"

The fire jumped higher, and a finger of flame leapt the break they'd just dug.

"Go!" she screamed again and motioned with her hands. "Please!"

The men turned, glanced at each other, then headed quickly back down the hill. The flames roared still higher. For a moment, Emmeline stared at them, unable to move, unable to stop her tears. At last she turned and followed the men who'd tried to help her. She looked back at the approaching wall of fire, felt the blistering heat, and choked in the smoke.

She had to get Gertie out before the fire took the house. Nothing else mattered. Only their lives.

She rounded the corner at a run, then stopped short.

One of the men was coming back. He had a shovel. Nothing else. "I told you to go!" she yelled at him. "It's not worth risking your life. Get out of here. Now!"

"Help me start a backfire," he shouted at her.

She didn't know what he was talking about.

"Go after the men," he yelled above the roar. "I'll explain. Hurry!"

She did as he bade, catching up with them where they'd left their horses. She motioned for them to follow her up the trail again.

Within minutes the plan was laid out. The backfires were set on the east side of the cleared land. Frantically they worked, digging and setting more fires. Soon two more men joined the group, shoveling and hacking at the brush.

Suddenly it seemed all of Riverview had come to help. She saw members of her citrus cooperative and members of the group that Quaid had formed to keep California wild. She couldn't help grinning as they joined together to change the route of the wildfire.

For hours Emmeline worked alongside the others, barely noticing her fatigue. She noticed only the elation as the fire finally turned southwest, marching slowly back into the mountains.

She stood back, leaning on her shovel handle, staring at the embers and black ashes that edged her property.

"It's yours again, Emmeline," a deep voice said beside her.

She turned with a frown. It was the field worker who'd come up with the backfire plan.

He grinned at her, his smoke-smudged, bewhiskered face looking friendly. There was something about his eyes that captured her attention.

They were the eyes of someone who let his soul shine through. The kind of eyes she'd always thought made a man handsome.

She'd always known that it wasn't necessarily a handsome face that caused her heart to drum beneath her ribs, it was the beauty of a man's soul.

She'd always known that the man she would love for the rest of her life would look at her with eyes that spoke of compassion, sincerity, and intelligence.

That, in her book, comprised the heart of a dashing man. A man she would love forever.

"Hello, Quaid," she said.

She wanted to tell him everything. Tell him how much she had missed him. How, from the moment he left, not a second had passed when he wasn't in her heart. How she longed for his forgiveness. Longed for the warmth of his arms. Longed for the brush of his kisses.

Before she could utter a sound, Quaid pulled her into his arms. His lips pressed against hers then gently covered her mouth. Then he pulled back and gazed into her face.

"You were angry with me," she whispered. "I saw it in your eyes." She wondered if he had forgiven her.

"I had a lot of thinking to do. And praying." His expression was solemn, and he let his gaze drift over her shoulder to the Big Valley below as though what would follow was difficult for him to say. "I concluded that you made no mistake in searching for answers that were rightfully yours. If I'd helped you search, when you first asked me about the maps—none of this would have happened." He looked back into her eyes. "I was a fool, Emma."

"I was the bigger fool for doubting you—"

He touched her lips with one finger, interrupting the apology she'd planned for months. "Let me finish, Emma."

She smiled up at him.

"I decided that if I needed to dig an irrigation ditch from the dam to your groves to get you to forgive me, I'd do it."

"You would?"

He nodded, a slow grin lighting his face.

"There'll be no need," she said.

He looked at her quizzically.

"I've done some thinking and praying as well."

He chuckled, seeming unable to take his eyes off her. "And what conclusions have you come to, Emma?" His voice was low and hoarse.

"I'd gladly leave this place and follow you into your wilderness." Smiling, she let her fingers trail along his beard. "I concluded that home is where you are, not here. It lost all its meaning when you left."

"You would do that for me?"

"Yes." Her voice was barely more than a whisper.

He threw back his head and laughed. "Oh, my darling, darling Emma!" Then, his big hands on her shoulders, he smiled into her eyes. "Tell me how you came to that conclusion."

"The same way I come to them all."

He pulled her into his arms again, letting his cheek rest on her head. "And that is?" he murmured.

"God said to abide in him and he'll give us the desires of our hearts. That means letting go of what we hold dearest and resting in him, his goodness, his direction. I had to let go of you, even let go of the Promised Land he'd given me, to discover it." She leaned back and looked up at him. "If part of that abiding means following you to the ends of the earth—or even Hetch Hetchy—I'll do it."

A low rumbling laugh vibrated from his chest. "You can put away the snowshoes, my darling Emma. I don't ever want to leave the Big Valley again. You can rest in that promise! The Lord and you have brought me home." He held her gaze, his eyes caressing her face. "I love you! And I love every last orange blossom that covers this land! If you'll have me, I want to stay right here for the rest of our lives."

She circled her arms around his neck and nestled against him with a deep sigh of contentment. After a moment she looked up and considered the emotion that had been buried in her heart since the first day she saw him. The day he stood looking like an outlaw on the train station platform, duster blowing in the wind, hat pulled low over his glorious eyes.

"I love you, Quaid Dearbourne," she said, her voice husky. "Oh, how I love you!"

The light of his love for her filled his beautiful smoke-smudged face. She placed a hand on either side of his bearded jaw and drew him close. Gazing into his eyes, she kissed him.

Laughing softly he returned her kiss with one as tender and light as the flutter of a robin's wing. He smiled into her eyes and kissed her again on the tip of her nose, then her eyelids, and finally he covered her mouth and kissed her until her knees grew weak.

He wrapped his arm around her and, holding her tight, led her back down the path toward the old adobe where Gertie and the others waited. Smiling she leaned against him as they made their way through the rows of young orange trees. Past the place where someday a tall Victorian grove house might lift its turrets into the California skies.

Past the spindly morning glory that—miraculously—had survived the intense heat of the fire. Just as it had survived the summer drought and the dry autumn winds.

Strengthened by adversity it would thrive. Just as Merci had. Just as Emmeline had in a completely different way.

She paused midstep, turned to look back to the small plant, then led Quaid over to it. She knelt to examine it, patting the dry soil at its base, touching one of the too few drooping, curled leaves. Quaid watched her with a curious light in his eyes. Laughing, she stood and brushed off her hands.

The winds might blow, and the little plant most likely would tremble when they did, but someday, God willing, it would be a sturdy vine, beautiful and strong.

A gust of hot, dry wind lifted her hair, and Emmeline laughed again, raising her face to meet it.

Merciful heavens, Lord, let the winds blow! Let them blow hard.

Epilogue

Juliet Rose Dearbourne giggled as her daddy pushed her higher in the swing. Up, up, up she soared, almost as high as the eagles. Almost as high as the clouds. Her daddy ducked and pretended she was about to smash into him as she came back down. She laughed again.

"Watch me do it myself, Daddy!" She pumped her legs hard, back and forth, back and forth. Up she soared again. "Watch!" she squealed, feeling the wind lift her hair from her face, then push it backward as the swing again fell toward earth.

Her daddy went back to sitting on the porch with her mama. Her mama and daddy called the land Sunny Mountain Ranch and the house a big Victorian. Juliet didn't care what it was called, she just cared that it always seemed full of love and people laughing.

Like now. Juliet's passel of brothers and sisters played on the big wraparound porch beneath its tumble of morning glories. They squealed and giggled and raised Cain. At least, that's what Great Aunt Gertie called it when they made so much noise. Raising Cain.

Juliet was the eldest of all her brothers and sisters, and if she weren't so busy swinging, she'd be puffed up with pride over the fact. She could do everything better than the others. Like button her shoes by herself. And ride the spotted pony her Grandpa Spence had given her. He'd even showed her how to whisper in its ear and pat it gentle-like to make it do what she wanted without shouting.

Sometimes Juliet got to help Aunt Merci at the La Paloma Indian School over yonder at the old rancho house. None of the little tykes ever got to do that. It was probably because they didn't know how to say their ABCs yet. And they didn't have a McGuffey primer. Not even Jared, who was only four and a half. He cared more about fishin' with their daddy in the river than learning his ABCs. Sully was three, having a hard time getting out of his nappies, so he didn't count; and the twins, Abby and Annie, were just learnin' to walk.

Juliet pumped her legs again to make the swing go high above the pepper tree branches. High enough to see the mountain peaks with their dusting of snow. Dusting. That's what Aunt Gertie called it. They looked like Aunt Gertie's cookies when she sprinkled sugar across the tops at Christmastime.

Everybody was always fussin' about the Big Valley. Juliet didn't know what all the fuss was about. Her daddy kept some of the land wild, he said, for the mountain lions and bears. His land was out toward the far hills, the place in the distance where the sky met the ground and turned purplish. Up close to where she was swinging now, rows of trees—orange, lemon, and grapefruit too—with their oodles of blossoms, tickled her nose with their sweetness. Still and all, it wasn't worth the fussin', she reckoned.

There was a tiny corner of the land, though, just beyond the riverbank, where her mama had built a packing house. Juliet couldn't see it except when driving to town, and it was way off the road so's not to bother anybody's eyes. Her papa had insisted on that part.

Juliet sighed as she pumped her legs to go still higher. If she looked to the mountains, she could see where the big fire had come close years before. Her mama and papa still talked about that day, how the bad wind blew and the fire crackled and smelled somethin' fierce as it marched down the mountain. She heard them whisperin' about a bad man her mama had known once in a place called Washington. Mister Cadman, they called him. They didn't know she was listening when they said he'd set the fire, then run off to Alaska. He'd been 'rested now, though, and put in jail. Juliet didn't know what 'rested meant, but she supposed it was bad if a person had it happen before goin' to jail.

Sometimes it seemed the only thing everybody talked about was the land. The Big Valley. The trees on it. The animals. Especially that's all they talked about when the whole family, her grandparents and aunts and uncles and cousins, came to visit. The land this. The land that.

She let out an impatient sigh, still wondering why they fussed so over something so ordinary as dirt and rocks and trees.

Aunt Merci had taken her into the big city once to see her friends, the Johnsons. They rode a bright yellow trolley and saw ladies in big hats draped with tulle, riding in horseless carriages. Buildings taller than trees lined the streets. People rode bicycles with big wheels in front and little ones in back. All the time they rang bells on the handlebars.

She wanted a bell like that. And a bicycle to go with it.

Sighing, she thought about the city, letting her swing coast to a standstill. For a few minutes she sat there, drifting a few inches this way and that, thinking hard about how much she'd liked the city. The noise, the bustle, the trolleys. She scuffed her toe in the dirt, winding the ropes then letting them unwind, while she thought about what it would be like.

She pictured the people and rumbling carriages, the noises and smells of the city. So different than the silence of the Big Valley where, besides her brothers and sisters, the noisiest thing around was a mockingbird's call when the sun rose or the chorus of frogs when it went down again.

She nibbled at her bottom lip, lost in thought. That was where she'd go when she grew up, she reckoned. The city.

Where she could putt-putt around anywhere she liked in a fancy horseless carriage and drive a bicycle and go as far as she could pedal. Where she could jangle the handlebar bell just because she liked the sound of it.

With a dramatic sigh, she pushed herself upward again, through the lacy branches of the pepper tree and into the sunlight. She closed her eyes, letting it warm her face as she coasted to the ground. The others— her mama and papa, Jared, Sully, Abby, and Annie—could stay in the Big Valley if they liked. Stay put right here at Sunny Mountain Ranch.

Juliet Rose Dearbourne decided, however, on this day in 1900, that as soon as she was big, she would live in the city forever.

Giggling to herself at her secret dream, she called out to her father again. "Daddy, come push me!"

Soon she was soaring upward toward the eagles and clouds.

Beloved friend,

Thank you for traveling to California with me once again. The stories of Quaid, Emmeline, and Merci delighted me, exasperated me, and made me weep as I wrote. This story—and especially these characters—have touched me in a way that few others have. Perhaps it's because their stories reflect how God loves *us* and is merciful to *us*, no matter our flaws, no matter our mistakes.

Often when a writer begins a sequel, it's difficult to imagine the story or characters capturing your heart more than the first story did. Yet, *The Blossom and the Nettle* came to life in just such a way. Merci is one of my favorite characters ever, and her story especially tugged at my heart. Through her eyes, I made some discoveries of my own about God's redemptive power and grace. Quaid, gruff and stubborn, and Emmeline, so unsure of her beauty, will live long in my heart. Did you notice that Merci was physically beautiful yet thought of herself as unlovely inside, and Emmeline, who had a shining inner beauty, thought of herself as physically unattractive? Both of these women were on journeys to discover who they were in God's eyes, precious and beautiful, inside and out!

I am already at work on book 3 of the California Chronicles series—*At Play in the Promised Land.* Juliet Rose Dearbourne, daughter of Emmeline and Quaid, granddaughter of Aislin and Spence, is our heroine. She leaves the family land to seek a new life in the brand-new silent movie industry. Life is exciting and—she thinks—fulfilling. At the peak of her career, she inherits the old family home, and with much grumbling, returns to the Big Valley to make it ready to sell. What she discovers there—about herself—changes her life forever.

I would love to hear from you at either of the addresses that follow. Please stop by my Web site for all the news about upcoming books, reviews, photos, and information about ordering any of my books—even those written under my pen name, Amanda MacLean.

Blessings and love,

Diane

Diane Noble

Photography by *Tilme*

Diane Noble is the award-winning author of ten novels, three novellas, and three nonfiction books. *When the Far Hills Bloom*, the first book in the California Chronicles, is a finalist for the RITA and HOLT (Honoring Outstanding Literary Talent) Gold Medallion awards. Diane is currently working on book 3 of the series, *At Play in the Promised Land*, which will be released in the spring of 2001. Diane lives in the mountains of southern California with her husband, Tom, a history professor and part-time writer. Their nest is mostly empty, except for Kokopelli and Merlin, two fearless felines who rule the roost while Diane writes and Tom experiments with gourmet recipes for an upcoming cookbook.

Diane would love to have you drop by her little corner of the Web at www.dianenoble.com, where you can send her an e-mail. Or you can write to her at the following address:

Diane Noble
P.O. Box 1806
Idyllwild, CA 92549